THE
ASSISTANT

S. K. Tremayne is a bestselling novelist and award-winning travel writer, and a regular contributor to newspapers and magazines around the world. The author's debut psychological thriller, *The Ice Twins*, was picked for the Richard and Judy Autumn Book Club and was a *Sunday Times* No.1 bestseller.

Born in Devon, S. K. Tremayne now lives in London and has two daughters.

D1313216

Also by S. K. Tremayne

The Ice Twins
The Fire Child
Just Before I Died

THE
ASSISTANT

S.K. TREMAYNE

HarperCollins*Publishers*

HarperCollins*Publishers*
1 London Bridge Street
London, SE1 9GF

www.harpercollins.co.uk

This paperback edition 2020
1

First published by HarperCollins*Publishers* 2019

Copyright © S. K. Tremayne 2019

Extract and quotation from *Collected Poems* by Sylvia Plath.
Copyright © Faber & Faber 1981. Reprinted by permission.

S. K. Tremayne asserts the moral right to
be identified as the author of this work

A catalogue record for this book
is available from the British Library

ISBN: 978-0-00-830955-8 (PB B-format)
ISBN: 978-0-00-833644-8 (PB A-format)

This novel is entirely a work of fiction.
The names, characters and incidents portrayed in it are
the work of the author's imagination. Any resemblance to
actual persons, living or dead, events or localities is
entirely coincidental.

Set in Sabon by Palimpsest Book Production Limited, Falkirk, Stirlingshire

Printed and bound in Great Britain by
CPI Group (UK) Ltd, Croydon, CR0 4YY

All rights reserved. No part of this publication may be
reproduced, stored in a retrieval system, or transmitted,
in any form or by any means, electronic, mechanical,
photocopying, recording or otherwise, without the prior
permission of the publishers.

MIX
Paper from
responsible sources
FSC™ C007454

This book is produced from independently certified FSC™ paper
to ensure responsible forest management.

For more information visit: www.harpercollins.co.uk/green

Author's Note

There are numerous quotations from the works of Sylvia Plath throughout the book. These lines are taken from her poems 'Death & Co', 'The Bee Meeting', 'Disquieting Muses', 'Electra on Azalea Plath', 'Facelift', 'Mirror', 'Elm' and 'Childless Women'.

I must thank Faber & Faber for permission to quote, more widely, from two poems in particular: 'Munich Mannequins', and 'Daddy', both in the *Collected Poems* of Sylvia Plath.

As usual I owe a huge debt of gratitude to my agent Eugenie Furniss, and editors, Jane Johnson and Sarah Hodgson, for their characteristic wisdom, and insight.

Finally, I would like to thank my beloved wife, Star, for the many times she unknotted problems, and offered ideas, along the way.

1

Jo

Are you a woman, man, other?

Well, that's easy enough. Despite that curious wish for a twirly moustache, age ten, and a twelve-year-old's desire to be an astronaut, which came with the vague yet outraged sense that only boys could be *proper* astronauts, I am quite sure on this one.

As the daylight in the room shades to grey, I lean towards my shining laptop screen and click,

woman

Are you straight, gay, bisexual, other?

A pause. A long pause. I've no doubts about my sexuality, I'm just bemused by what *other* might mean in this context. What is that fourth possibility of sexuality? A desire for ghosts? Ponies? Furniture? My dear beloved mum can get oddly excited when reading magazines about interior decoration. But I somehow don't think her demographic is the target of this website.

On the other hand, sitting here at my laptop in the fading winter light, I'd quite *like* a *fourth* choice, or a *fifth* choice, or, dammit, *seventy-eight choices*. Because if you were in a critical mood you could say my choices so far in life have not turned out entirely optimal: divorced, childless, and nearly homeless at thirty-three. OK, yes, I might be living in a sleek flat in the nicer end of Camden, North London – where it merges into the real, five-storey Georgian opulence of Primrose Hill – however, I know I'm *only* here because my richer friend, Tabitha, took pity on her newly divorced and virtually bankrupt old university mate. *Hey, why don't you have the spare room, I really don't use it much . . .*

I think it was the casually generous way she made this offer, the blasé effortlessness of it all, which confounded me. At once it made me feel impossibly grateful, and even more fond of Tabitha – funny, kind, generous, and the best of best friends – yet it also made me feel guilty and a tiny tiny tiny bit jealous.

Turning from the laptop, I look out of the darkening window. And see my own face reflected.

OK, I was properly jealous, if only for a minute or two. What barely mattered to Tabs – *Here, have a spare room, somewhere really nice to live* – was so crucial and difficult for me, and she was barely aware of the emotional difference.

This is because Tabitha Ashbury already *owns*, Tabitha Ashbury will also *inherit*. I love her but she's never understood what it's like not to have all that: in London.

By contrast with Tabitha, I'm not just Generation Rent, I am Generation Can't Afford to Rent Anywhere Without a Major Knife Crime Epidemic. And it doesn't look like this is going to change any time soon, because I'm a freelance journalist. I have become a freelance journalist when the phrase *free*lance has become a kind of fantastical joke in itself: hey, look, I know that these days you basically have to write for *free*, but where's my *lance*? Don't we go jousting as well?

This career, however, was – for all its challenges – definitely one of my smarter choices. I love my job. The work is varied and compelling, and every so often I get to think I have changed the world slightly for the better, revealing some scandal, telling a decent story, making someone I'll never know chuckle for two seconds, over a sentence that may have taken me six hours to get right. But that scintilla of human gladness wouldn't have existed if I hadn't made the effort. Or so I hope.

Reverting to my computer I refocus on OKCupid. I may have a home (however fortunate), I might have a job (however sketchy the salary), I have, however, no other half. And I am beginning to feel the absence. And perhaps the magic of internet dating will guide me, like a digital fairy godmother, with a wand of sparkling algorithms, to a new man.

I answer the question:

straight

With this, my laptop screen instantly flashes, and grows even more vivid: whisking me into a world of warm, cascading images of What Could Be: luridly happy pictures of emotional and erotic contentment, where beautiful couples sit laughing, very close together.

3

Here's a smiley young Chinese woman sipping red wine and draping a slender arm over a handsome Caucasian man with enough stubble to be masculine without being prison-y; here are the white and black gay boys holding hands as they put red paint on each other's faces in a carnival mood; here is the exceptionally well-preserved older couple who found love despite it all – and now seem to inexplicably spend all their time grinning on rollercoasters. And all these happy ThankyouCupid! people are promising me something so much better than the view through the big high black sash windows of this million-quid flat: looking out onto the chilly, frigid, 3 p.m. twilight of wintry London. A world where it is getting so cold and dark the angry red brake lights of the cars, jammed, stalled, impatient, fuming, on busy Delancey Street, glow like red devil eyes in Victorian smoke.

I turn to one of Tabitha's Home Assistants, perched on the bespoke oak shelving at the side of the elegant living room, with its elegantly lofty ceilings. Everything in Tabitha's flat is so elegant and tasteful I sometimes tell her I am going to buy, say, a plastic gnome-themed clock from the discount supermarket on Parkway to 'brighten things up', then I wait, straight-faced, for her to get the joke, and then we both laugh. I love living with Tabitha. That deeply shared sense of humour: possibly you only get that with a certain kind of old friend?

Or an ideal kind of lover.

'Electra, what will the weather be in London this evening?'

The top of the black Home Assistant glows in response, an electric green-to-sapphire diadem, and in that faintly pompous, hint-of-older-sister voice, the voice

4

of a sibling who went to a rather superior school, she answers:

'Tonight's forecast in Camden Town has a low of one degree Celsius. There's a sixty per cent chance of rain after midnight.'

'Electra, thank you.'

'That's what I'm here for!'

Simon and I had an earlier, cheaper version of these smart-heating, smart-lighting Home Assistants, but Tabitha has the full and latest range: Electra X, HomeHelp, Minerva Plus – everything. They're scattered throughout the flat – six or seven of them – answering questions, telling contrived bad jokes, advising on the rate of the pound against the dollar, reciting news of earthquakes in Chile. They also precisely calibrate the temperature in each room, the ambient lighting in the bedrooms, and quite probably the amount of champagne (lots of it vintage; none of it mine) in the stern and steely magnificence of the eight-foot-high fridge, where you could store a couple of corpses standing upright and still have room for your cartons of organic hazelnut milk.

The irony is that Tabitha barely uses the marvellous tech of her smart-home, or drinks her spirulina smoothies and hazelnut milk, because she is barely here. She is either abroad, in her job as a producer for a nature TV channel, or she's at her fiancé Arlo's delicious period house in Highgate, which is even plusher than here. He probably has machines so advanced they can invite precisely the right friends over for spontaneously successful threesomes.

I miss sex. I also miss Tabitha's company; when I moved in, I hoped I'd see more of her. I believe, sometimes, I simply miss *company*. Which is perhaps one reason why I like, to my surprise, the Digital Butlers. The Assistants. Sometimes I josh and banter with the machines purely for the sake of hearing a voice other than my own: *Tell me the weather in Ecuador, Why are we here, Is it OK to watch soft porn while eating Waitrose dips?*

I think, in a way, these gadgets are like less annoying and demanding pets that do charming and useful things, dogs that don't need walking yet still fetch tennis balls, or slippers – or 'the papers', as my mother still, charmingly, refers to her precious daily delivery of printed news. I sometimes fear that she is possibly one of the last people on earth to say, 'Have you read the papers?' and when her generation goes my career will finally fall off that cliff.

Anyway.

'Electra, shall I get the fuck on with writing this profile?'

'I'd rather not answer that.'

Hah. There she goes again, using the voice of the prim, sensible, better-educated older sister that I never had – who disapproves of swearing. My only real sibling is older, and a brother. He lives in LA, works in the movie industry, and he's married to a chatty lawyer and has a lovely little son, Caleb, whom I adore. And, as far as I can tell, he spends his time going to meetings and pool-parties where they talk about movies being 'greenlit', or suffering in 'development hell' – rather than actually *making* movies.

I'd quite like him to actually make movies, because I'd quite like him to make a movie or TV series written by me. One day. Oh, one day. I see it as my only way out of my cul-de-sac career, however enjoyable. These days, the money is in movies and TV; it's certainly not in journalism. I recently estimated I have about £600 in savings; literally £600, max, stored in some precious ISA. They say you are only two months' missed wages from living on the street; that means I could be out there, in the cold, in about ten days, if the bank ever got tired of my overdraft.

As a result I am busily reading every how-to guide on scriptwriting that I can, learning about beats, hooks, cliffhangers, and three-act structures, and reading experts like Syd Field and Robert McKee and so far every script I've written has turned out rubbish, every mystery and drama lacks drama and mystery, but I will keep trying. What choice do I have?

I turn, in a playful mood, to the oak shelving.

'Electra, give me an idea for a brilliant movie.'

'Sorry, I'm not sure.'

'Electra, you're totally bloody useless.'

Silence.

'Electra, I'm sorry I swore. It was only a joke.'

She does not respond. She doesn't even show that braceleting glow of greeny-blue. That's odd. Is she malfunctioning? Or have I truly offended her this time?

I don't think so. It's quite hard to emotionally offend a cylinder of plastic and silicon chips. In which case I should stop faffing, and get on with this online dating profile.

Back to the drawing board: the drawing of myself. Online.

First name?
Jo

It's actually Josephine, but I shortened it to Jo when I was a teen because that seemed cooler. And I stand by my teen decision. But will it make men think I am masculine? If they do they are idiots, and not the men I want.

Jo
Jo Ferguson

Age?

Well? Shall I? Nope.

I know some women of my age – and men – who have begun to knock off a couple of years, on Tinder and Grindr and PantsonFire, but I feel no need. I am thirty-three, nearly thirty-four. And happy with it. Sure, I am beyond the first rose-flush of youth, but hardly ready for composting. I can still catch the sense of a man turning to glance as I disappear the other way.

33

Location?
London

Postcode?

This is tricky. To anyone that knows the intricate class signals, the invisible social pheromones subtly emitted by London postcodes, my present postcode NW1, can make me sound, at my age, like someone rich, or rich and bohemian. Someone who hangs out at the Engineer pub with actors and ad moguls. Either that or a single mum turned drug dealer.

Yet I'm not NW1: I'm neither druggie nor bohemian; I'm still much more N12, North Finchley, where until recently I lived with my ex-husband Simon in a mediocre, damp, and definitely rented two-bed flat with OK bus connections to nice Muswell Hill. And even deeper inside me is the real me, the girl who grew up way way down in SE25, Thornton Heath, a slice of forsaken, tatty, you're-never-more-than-two-minutes-from-a-kebab-shop outer London, a burb so obscure it is unknown even to other outer Londoners, who make wearily predictable jokes like Do I need a visa to get there. So yes, I am intrinsically either a 25 or a 12 – but at this moment, by sheer dumb luck, I am a 1.

Why I am worrying?

NW1

'Electra, what's the time?'

'The time is five thirty p.m.'

Five thirty?

I have spent an hour, or two – and so far I've given my name, gender, age, and address. Sighing at myself, and clicking through, the OKCupid screen changes to a sensitive aquamarine, perhaps because the questions are growing increasingly piquant.

Are you looking for:
1 Hook-up?
2 New friends?
3 Short-term dating?
4 Long-term dating?

At the bottom there's an option for *Are you open to non-monogamy?*

Ouch. Part of me would like to answer the last question: I certainly was, as that is the truth. But it is surely *too* truthful: it was me that started it, it was me that lit the long sad fuse that led to our divorce. I started it with funny sexy Liam, the barman and would-be actor. Liam's initial approach was entirely innocent, a throw-away compliment about my journalism, on Twitter, from a guy I'd never met. Then we became Facebook friends, and Instagram pals, and WhatsAppers, and within a few days of online chat I was sending this smart, witty, diverting guy endless sexts and nude selfies, because I was bored, because my marriage was stale, because I was foolish, because it was fun even as I knew it was wrong – so I can hardly blame Simon, my husband, for having an affair with Polly the pleasant nurse after he discovered my three months of virtual infidelity.

I've heard since that Polly doesn't like me so much; I am the ex that looms a little too large in Simon's life. But what can I do? She's right to dislike me. Or it is, at least, totally understandable.

Sadness descends. Alongside memory, and guilt. Staring at the OKCupid site, I feel, quite suddenly, as if it is asking me too many questions. What's it going to ask next? How do you feel about your father?

Leaning forward, I put the laptop to sleep. Like stroking a cat that instantly snoozes. I'll finish this profile later. I need air, darkness, freedom.

'Electra, I'm going for a walk up Primrose Hill.'

The blue ring dances in response. It whirls around fast, then even faster, as if something is inside it. Something maddened, and angry. Definitely alive. Is it meant to do this? The sensation is unnerving – but I'm not quite used to the tech yet. I need to read the online instructions. It is probably designed to react this way.

The blue light spins to a stop. And blinks out to black.

Picking up my coat, I go into the kitchen and make a

mug of hot coffee, then, carrying this, I head for the door. I need the anonymity of the endless streets. The great and indifferent city.

I love the size of London for this reason: its vastness. No one cares who you are. No one knows your secrets.

2

Jo

The wind is satisfyingly bitter in its cold; carrying a vivid rumour of snow. Wrapping my multicoloured don't-run-me-over scarf around my face, I cross the junction of Parkway, the social divide that separates the posher end of Camden from the ultra-poshness of Primrose Hill, which hides like a snooty and castellated village behind its canals and railways and the expanse of Regent's Park.

I am still clutching that mug of hot coffee. It's for our local homeless guy, who usually sits on a wall on the other side of Delancey Street, between the pub and the railway cuttings. He's a tall black guy in his fifties with a sad, kind face, and wild hair. When I first moved in, Tabitha told me he's from the homeless shelter on Arlington Road, and that he likes to shout about cars. *I like cars. Do you like cars? Mercedes, that's a car. Cars!*

For that reason, she calls him Cars, he's the Cars guy. Apart from that, she simply ignores him. In the last few weeks, however, I've got to know him. His real name is Paul, though in my head I can't help calling him Cars, like Tabitha. Sometimes, on cold nights like tonight, I go outside with a mug of hot tea or soup to keep him warm, and then he says I am pretty and should have a husband, and then he turns and starts shouting CARS CARS CARS! and I smile at him, and I say, See you tomorrow, and I walk back inside.

This evening, however, is too cold even for Paul: he has stopped yelling Bentleys! and he is huddled in a corner of the railway wall, barely speaking. But when he sees me, he emerges, smiling his blank sad smile.

'Hey! Jo! Did you guess I was cold how did you do that?'

'Coz it's totally bloody freezing. Shouldn't you go back to the hostel? You could die out here, Paul.'

'I'm used to it.' He shrugs, eagerly taking the coffee. 'And I like watching the cars!'

I shake my head and we smile at each other and he tells me he will give me back the coffee mug tomorrow. As ever. He often forgets, so I have to buy new ones. I don't mind.

Waving him goodbye, I walk on.

A taxi shoots past, orange light bright, glowing, desperate for business. I wonder if Uber will kill off London cabs before the internet kills off paid journalism. We're both on our last legs: positively racing towards annihilation, hurtling into the dark London drizzle. But I don't want to die yet. Not when I'm about to write that killer script. Probably.

Waiting for the traffic lights to change, I jog, impatiently, to keep warm. I know where I'm going: my exact route. I walk it almost every evening. Regent's Park Road, then up the hill, then the main street of Primrose

13

Hill village, then curving round Gloucester Avenue and home. It takes me roughly forty-five minutes. I wonder if people have learned to recognize me by the sheer regularity of my patrol: Oh, here comes that woman who always walks this way. What is she looking for?

As I cross the road, I have an idea: I'm going to ring Fitz. Who I met through Tabitha, years ago. Yes. Slender, darkly greying, smartly charming, cynical-yet-theatrical Fitz. We could go for a drink somewhere. Get an Uber to Soho gay bars, where he is usually found; I like the way everyone in these bars will abruptly stop drinking and sing lustily to the chorus of Andy Williams' 'Can't Take My Eyes Off You'.

I Love You Baaaaby . . .

Passing the grand pastel houses by St Mark's church, I pluck my phone from a warm pocket and dial with cold fingers.

Voicemail.

'Hi, this is Fitz, you're out of luck, darling. I'll tell you *everything* tomorrow.'

That's his usual voicemail message. Deliberately camp. I laugh, quietly, into the dewy cold wool of my scarf, then scroll further down my contacts. Who else can I call? Who could I drink with? Tabitha is in Brazil. Carl is out of town working. Everyone else . . . Where is everyone else?

They've gone elsewhere, that's where everyone else is. The truth of this bites deeper every time I open my phone contacts. My drinking pals, my peer group, my beer buddies, the sisterhood, the tribe of uni friends: they've dispersed. But it's only since I divorced Simon that I've realized just how *many* of my friends have dispersed: that is to say: got married, stayed married, had kids, and moved out of London to places with

14

gardens. It is, of course, what you do in your thirties, unless you're rich and propertied like Tabitha. Living in London in your twenties is hard enough – exacting but exciting, like glacier skiing – having a married life with kids in London in your thirties is essentially impossible, like ascending a Himalaya without oxygen.

I am one of the last left. The last soldier on the field.

Crossing Albert Terrace, I start the walk up Primrose Hill as my fingers pause on J for Jenny. She's probably about my only childhood friend left, Simon apart. Jenny used to be around my house all the time, for playdates and sleepovers, then her parents divorced and she moved away, and I pretty much lost touch, though Simon kept a connection with her because they ended up working in the same industry.

Jenny is employed, in King's Cross, by one of the biggest tech companies. That's how Jenny and I reconnected: when I was writing my big breakthrough article, three or four years ago, on the impact of Silicon Valley on our lives.

I knew this story could make my name, impress my editors, drag me up the ladder a few rungs, so I shamelessly exploited my contacts (my husband), I seriously pissed off some particular sources by naming them (sorry, Arlo), but I met some fascinating people, a couple of whom became friends. And I rediscovered an old friend.

She picks up immediately. I love you, Jenny. That precious link to the past, to the time before everything went wrong. The times when Daddy would chase us in the house, in Thornton Heath, playing Hide and Seek, making us giddy with happy terror: shouting out, I can HEAAARRR you. And Jenny and I would huddle together, giggling, under the bed or in the dark of the wardrobe.

Ah, my lost childhood.

'Hey, Jo. What's up?'

'I'm bored.' I say, with some vehemence, 'Horribly bloody booorrrreeeeed. I'm trying to build a profile on OKCupid but it's depressing and tragic, and I thought you might like to share a barrel of prosecco. Two barrels. A yardarm. What is a yardarm, anyway?'

She chuckles.

'Ah, love to, but sorry.'

I can hear the characteristic chank of her Zippo lighter, then inhalation. Traffic murmurs in the background. Is she outside?

'Where are you?'

'King's Cross, having a ciggie break. But I better go back in – I'm at the Death Star.'

'Oh?'

'Yep,' she says, exhaling smoke. 'Working till, like, midnight or something.' She draws on her cigarette, goes on, 'Jesus, it's cold out here.'

Jenny works absurd hours at HQ. She probably makes a lot of money coding or whatever, but doesn't talk about it. She mostly talks about sex. Jenny, apparently, is my Official Slut Friend. The insult is not mine, I would never have said it. But she said it herself when we renewed our friendship over mussels and chips in some bar near her work. Everyone has to have a slutty friend, she said, to make them feel better; have you got a slut friend, someone even more promiscuous than you? She made me laugh, at that table, she makes me laugh now, she always gives good gossip, and there's a sadness in her hedonism which makes her funnier, and warmer.

I press the phone closer to my freezing ear, as Jenny asks:

'How's the profile-building going?'

'Ah. Not great . . .'

I pause, to take a breath. I'm nearly at the top of Primrose Hill: the last, steep incline which always makes me gasp cold air. I should definitely start going to the gym. Jenny tries again,

'Not great? What does that mean?'

'It means, I've been at it several hours, and I've established that I'm straight, thirty-three, a woman, and I'm looking for long-term, short-term, casual hook-ups, or maybe a snog in a pub toilet. Do you think I might be coming across as desperate?'

'Hah. No. Stay strong! There has to be a good man out there? I've seen them!'

'No chance of a drink, then?'

'Not tonight, Josephine. Call me tomorrow, mabes. OK, I've gotta get this TEDIOUS code written before I turn into a bat. Good luck!'

The phone clicks. I am at the top of the Hill. I don't know whether it is the jewelled skyline of icy London – always impressive from this vantage point, stretching from the silvery towers of Canary Wharf to the holy scarlet arc of the London Eye – it could be the mere fact of hearing Jenny's friendly voice – but I feel distinctly cheered. Invigorated. The sadness is dispelled.

Jenny is right. I must woman up. I can do this. It's only a bloody dating profile. And I need a bloody date.

It's all downhill from here, I can't be bothered to do the full circuit, so I'm simply going to retrace my steps, back down Regent's Park Road, as the snow begins to fall, heavier by the second. My pace quickens as I hurry past the big, white, thoroughly empty mansions.

Sometimes it feels like a ghost town, this rich little corner of London. Streetlamps shine on cold pastel

17

walls, leafless trees grasp at the frigid orange sky. Glossy new apartment blocks sit empty: from one month to the next. Windows forever black and cold like Aztec mirrors, obsidian squares reflecting nothing. Where is everyone?

Nowhere. There is no one here. It's only me. And the snow.

Ten minutes later I am sat at the laptop, gazing at OKCupid again, trying to make my personality sound simultaneously attractive, different, sexy, not too sexy, witty, not self-consciously witty, diverse, truthful, self-confident, but not brash. I mustn't give up, but the questions? There are so many.

OK, I reckon I need a gin and tonic. Indeed, I need two punchy G&Ts: that should be about right, make me brave and honest and a little bit funny, without being idiotic. I was once told by an expert (someone who went on live TV daily) that the perfect amount of alcohol you need to cope (with daily live TV) is half a bottle of champagne. Similarly, I reckon two G&Ts is the perfect amount of alcohol to cope with any difficulty in life.

Returned from the kitchen, second G&T in hand, I command myself, and type.

Ethnicity?
English

Height?
Five foot two

Education level?
Useless degree

Think I'm getting bored again.

Religion?
None. Except when it's really really sunny and I think: who knows for sure

Wincing at myself, I cross that out. Sounds too weird. Then I decide: what the hell, it's true. Generally I don't believe in God, but sometimes on a lovely summer's day when the world is floaty with happiness I think that God exists, the trouble is He had a few too many drinks at lunch. Perhaps I should put that in.

Calm down.

Has pets?
Kodiak bear

Diet?
~~**Gin.**~~
Omnivore

Smoker?
Not yet. But I intend to start at 60, when it's meant to prevent Alzheimer's. No, rilly.

Drugs?
Gin!

Most people that know me would say I'm . . .
~~**Crap at writing internet dating profiles**~~
Short

Current goal?
Spring

What is your golden rule?
Never have a golden rule. You always break them

Oh God, I'm sounding over-brash, and borderline alcoholic. Maybe one gin would have sufficed.

I reckon I've nearly had enough profile-making. It's not the world's greatest profile, but it's not the worst, and it gives a reasonable impression of me, when I am feeling a little lonely but also mischievous, and the streetlights at the top of Delancey are blurred by the snowy darkness.

There's squillions of additional questions I could answer but I'll do another three, then abandon my bid for happiness. Until tomorrow. There's always tomorrow.

I value:
Candour. Vintage couture. Sriracha on a tuna melt

If I were sent to jail, I'd be arrested for
Lying on internet dating sites

Six things I could never do without
1. Nespresso machine
2. My Friends (awwww)
3. Nespresso machine
4. Pointless lists
5. Memory
6. Can't remember this one

In truth, I have a good memory, but who cares. Time to relax: that's it. I've run out of quirk, and exhausted snark – while remaining, I hope, sufficiently intriguing and alluringly different. Or maybe I just sound mad. Whatever. I am about to close the laptop and have a third and final G&T, when I remember. Shit. *Photo*. You HAVE to have a photo. I may be the world's worst internet dater, I barely know which way to swipe on Tinder – leading to some awkward moments – but even I know that you MUST put up a photo.

But I hate putting up photos. I never know which to choose. I know how to take a decent selfie (from slightly above, of course, giving me defined cheekbones and a firmer chin), yet I also know these selfies are overly flattering. When guys meet me, they will be disappointed. I'd hate to see them look at me and try to hide their disappointment. I'd rather surprise on the upside.

Yet who the heck would ever put an *unflattering* photo of themselves on an internet dating profile?

Paging through the photos file on my laptop I consider the best of the non-selfies. I look presentable, even moderately sexy, in quite a few. And why not. I've been told I am pretty by enough people, not only close relatives and female friends. I know I look OK on a good day. Green eyes, reddish-brown hair, what my mum would call a cheeky grin. Decent figure, if a bit on the titchy side, as Si would put it. In that light: am I confident enough to say Yes, THAT photo, of me smiling on a Ko Tao beach not long after the divorce, tanned and relaxed, in a skimpy summer dress, is not too flattering, or vulgar, and not *too* dated?

I really do look happy. Probably because I'd had a pleasant one-night stand the night before, with a dreadlocked Aussie guy, all surfer-muscles and meaningless conversation. One of the reasons I am so broke now is that I blew a huge chunk of my modest savings on that epic holiday. Months of blissful freedom, after a decade of unblissful marriage. It was worth every penny.

K, let's go for it. I *can* look like that on good days.

After good sex. Which is one reason why I rarely looked like that when I was with Simon. Oh, Si, I am sorry.

Selecting the photo, and cropping the cleavage a little closer – don't want to look too come-hither – I insert the photo. And there. I'm done. I am published. I am brand new and on the shelf, waiting to be plucked. Opened. Chosen. Read. Tomorrow I will go browsing for myself.

Picking up a book, *Your Guide to Writing the Perfect Script*, I start reading. In a slightly listless way.

The solitude is emphatic. The loneliness returns, I ask Electra for a weather update, solely to hear a voice.

'Tomorrow will see a maximum of two degrees Celsius, in London, with a thirty per cent possibility of snow.'

Brr, I think I will have some red wine. G&Ts are too cold. Stepping into the kitchen I grab a bottle of red, a corkscrew, nab a glass, then I walk back into the living room and sit down at the table and slosh some vino. And pick up the book. It's such a quiet night. Quieter than normal.

The flat is never that noisy: Tabitha and I have the main, first-floor flat, spacious and windowy. The flat above us is theoretically inhabited by some affluent old couple, but they spend their time on permanent holiday, especially in winter. And I don't blame them. At the same time, the ground floor/basement – once occupied by Fitz, though nowadays he prefers to rent it out, and live, all by himself, in an entire house in Islington – has been pricily refurbished, and waits for new tenants.

Meanwhile, the next building on my right is a complex of sleek legal offices, hushed by night, and on my left is another Georgian house with yet more rich, absentee owners. I think I've seen them once.

Standing up, I walk to the windows. The pavements and roads are completely white with snow. And almost entirely empty: except for one woman in black, passing my door, down there. Street level. She is pulling little kids, she has her back to me. I can't see her face. Clearly she is dragging the children home, hurrying them along, before this thick, whirling snow gets too much. I feel sorry for her. Something in her stance evokes pity. Quite fierce sympathy: as if she could have been me. And then she is gone. Disappeared. A gust of snow? She turned a corner? Either way, she has vanished, there is not a single human in sight. Winter has cleaned the streets of people, even the traffic is thin.

The quiet of the evening is painful. Perhaps it is simply the snow: muffling everything. Like a scarf around the world.

I return to my armchair and pick up my book. And then, in the shrillness of the silence, I hear a voice. Electra. She's talking to me. Without being prompted.

'I know what you did,' she says.

Frowning, and startled, I turn and gaze at the matt black pillar and her crowning ring of electric sapphire. Electra speaks again. 'I know your secret. I know what you did to that boy. How his eyes rolled white. I know everything.'

And then all is quiet. I stare at the Home Assistant, mute and unresponsive; just a machine on a shelf, after all.

3

Jo

I am speechless for half a minute. Mouth quite dry. Then I talk:

'Electra. What did you say?'

The machine emits a low, bonging sound. I know what this means.

'I can't connect to the public Wi-Fi. You may need to update your connection.'

'Electra, what did you say?'

'I can't connect to the public Wi-Fi.'

No, not good enough. NO. I can't let this go. Did she really say that? Did she talk about the worst thing in my life? That happened so long ago?

Fiddling with my app, with slightly tremulous fingers, I go through the rigmarole of reconnecting my Home Assistant, the Virtual Helper, Electra, to my Wi-Fi. The light goes orange, the Wi-Fi is linked, the machine plays a little warbling jingle. Boodle-da-boomph.

She is ready.

Ready to talk about the past? The terrible secrets? OR ready to tell me a bad joke, or traffic reports.

Gulping another slug of red wine. I formulate a question, but before I can say anything, the diadem shines, and Electra says:

'I know everything about you. You killed him and then you ran away. The blood was pouring from his mouth. I can't connect to the public Wi-Fi.'

'Electra??'

'I can't connect to the public Wi-Fi.'

'Electra!!!!'

Nothing. Did I truly hear those words? I'm sure I did.

'Electra, what do you know about me?'

'I know you ask some interesting questions.'

'Electra, what do you know about the past?'

'Sorry, I don't know that.'

I won't let this go.

'Electra, what do you know about my history?'

Silence.

'History is usually described as a record of past events, or, alternatively, as an—'

'Electra, SHUT UP.'

The blue lights fade. Now Electra simply seems confused, beta, useless. Or she doesn't understand the syntax of my questions. As it should be.

I am, after all, talking to a cylinder of electronics. Not an actual mind, not an actual human. Not someone who might actually know about the boy.

Someone like Tabitha.

But those details? So specific and accurate. They always smoulder in my thoughts, and tonight they've caught fire. The eyes, the boy, Jamie. His laddish but likeable grin, the affable, generous good nature. Oh,

Jamie. And then the blood. And then that bloody song which I will forever associate with those terrible events: 'Hoppípolla' by Sigur Rós. I can't *bear* that song. Whenever I hear 'Hoppípolla' the memories surge. Even thinking about that song – the mere *thought* of it, makes me tremble with fear, and guilt, a painful and acid emptiness, deep inside. Close to nausea.

Whether Electra said those things or not, or whether it was merely the silence of the flat, and the booze, and the bleakness of my wintry loneliness, combining to deceive my mind into imaginary accusations – I am triggered.

'Electra, what's the time.'

'The time is ten fifty-two p.m.'

And just like that, she's acting entirely normal. I *am not* feeling normal. But I guess I can try. I can try try try to be normal, and ignore this madness, this mishearing, this daydream, this terrible reality, whatever it is. Perhaps it is a simple glitch and the tech is malfunctioning. The peculiar behaviour with the lights, earlier on, implies that. But how could a bug cause Electra to act so bizarrely?

There is no evident or immediate answer, so I go to the fridge and take out the chips and the Waitrose dips, and then mix some mayo and Tabasco for extra oomph, and then I spend an hour comfort-eating as I watch reruns of old sitcoms on my iPad. And I guzzle way more wine than normal, to try and calm things down.

Gradually the wine and the food – principally the wine – work their magic. I probably, hopefully, surely drank too much in the first place, causing me to imagine these words from Electra? It is impossible she knows. However advanced, she is only a gadget. No one knows apart from me and Tabitha, and Simon, whom I told. Perhaps Tabitha told Arlo? I doubt it, but even if she did: the secret of knowledge is tightly wound, it is inconceivable it would have reached some bloody machines on a bespoke oak shelf.

No.

The last glass of wine is guzzled. I have successfully persuaded myself that nothing untoward has happened. All the tech is behaving normally, apart from the little bugs, the spinny lights, it's my silly drunken head that turned this into something much nastier.

'Electra, what time does Fitness First gym, in Camden, open tomorrow morning?'

'Fitness First Camden opens from seven a.m. to ten p.m. Monday to Thursday, on Fridays it closes earlier at nine p.m., and at weekends—'

'OK, Electra, stop.'

Silence.

'Thanks, Electra.'

'That's what I'm here for!'

Good. She is still behaving as she is meant to behave. And I am drunk. Tomorrow I *will* go to the gym and eat healthy food and go back to my regular drinking regime. What was I thinking? Two big gins before seven? Absurd and foolish. Guaranteed to produce creepy daydreams, if not lushed-up delusions. I will always have guilt lurking in my brain, like silt at the bottom of a petrol tank: the last thing you need is to stir it up. Simon once told me this. Because if you stir it up, then it can ruin the entire engine.

Simon.

As I sit here, a new guilt pierces. Simon.

No. I don't want to think about this. Yet I have to think about this. If I am a bit lonely, it is my own fault. Being with Simon is why I am here, drinking by myself.

I first got with Simon at sixth form in Thornton Heath, London SE25,398, beyond the outer circle of the solar system. We'd known each other since primary school, been friends in secondary, then one night we went to a bar when we were both underage; we had fun, so we dated, and courted, and then we deflowered each other. I don't know a better word, I should know a better word, possibly there isn't a better word, so that's it: we *deflowered* each other in the back of his dad's Fiesta, in the darkest corner of Thornton Heath Asda supermarket car park, after drinking too many Jägerbombs.

The sex wasn't very good, but we managed it. With each other. And he was kind, gentle, and quite handsome, in the dim green light of an Asda sign, shining into the back of an illicitly borrowed Ford Fiesta, at half past midnight.

I didn't come. He did, very quickly. He apologized. The apology made it worse and was one of the least sexy things I have encountered, during sex, to this day. He had nice eyes and muscles and not that much conversation – not with me, anyway. But he tried. Which was touching. Throughout our marriage, he blatantly and ardently *tried*.

Here and now, I look out at the Camden frost, examining myself. My motives. How did I end up *married* to him, of all people. To *Simon Todd*?

I was all arts and humanities, philosophy and sociology, I was a girl that yearned for gap years in Papua New Guinea that never happened. I was intrigued by shamanism, Siberian reindeer pee, Renaissance portraits.

He was all engines, rockets, and atoms, and apparently knew the real meaning of Schrödinger's Cat.

After our brief fling, I went off to King's College to study History of Art and he went off to Manchester to study All About Computers and I spent half my time partying . . . and then we both finished university and realized we couldn't afford to rent anywhere remotely decent until we got jobs, so we boomeranged back to Thornton Heath and the pubs we frequented as teens and . . .

There he was. Still quite handsome in the low light of Thornton Heath's one and only happening bar; and all of a sudden he seemed such a good, honest, decent guy – compared to the rich lazy millennial types I'd got used to dating in King's.

And so I found myself sucked into the sentimental whirlpool of homecoming – geographical, sexual, and emotional – and this time we had sex in an actual bed (because his mum and dad were away) and this time, after three months of cosy cuddles and pizzas-and-TV, and being cocooned in an unaccustomed atmosphere of safety, comfort, and unquestioning adoration, when he incredibly stupidly crazily asked me to marry him, I said YES.

Oh God. Help me.

YES?

It was a ludicrous mistake. We were always too different; we grew further apart while married; we were destined not to last. I found him boring and felt the most terrible guilt about finding him boring. He sensed this and tried to hide his hurt feelings – and this made the lamentable cycle of guilt, hiding, and hurt even worse, for both of us. And then came Liam and the naughty sexts and the massive rows and the end. Thank God.

Consequently, I have no resentment at his leaving me. I surely didn't deserve him. I have no resentment that he remarried so quickly, to Polly, I have less-than-zero resentment that they instantly have a tiny and truly adorable baby, Grace. The only thing I resent, perhaps, ever-so-slightly, is the fact that because she's a nurse she gets a subsidized three-bed Key Worker Flat on the twelfth floor of a brand-new apartment block in buzzing Shoreditch.

Lucky Polly. Lucky Simon.

In London, property, and the owning thereof, has become everything. Like having an estate and title during the Regency. And I am a peasant. Virtually an Indian untouchable. I do not own and never will. This stuff is becoming dynastic. If I'd *known* property was going to become so important, I should probably have married one of the plausible affluent boys at uni with mums and dads with Deposits to Lend. I had enough enquiries. But I didn't marry them. And there it is.

I stare across dark and wintry Delancey Street. The traffic has dwindled. It is late. I need to sleep. I am daydreaming, I spend too much time gazing out of these windows.

And yet as I put on my most comforting pyjamas, I wonder, quite forlornly, if it is genuinely possible that I imagined Electra's taunts? A couple of sentences created by my own mind, allied to something misfiring in the technology. I guess it *could* happen. I must force myself to believe this. But if I believe this, it means I am hearing voices, and that . . .

Nope: not gonna think about it.

It's definitely time for bed. Bed and sleep and a pill,

and I will wake up and get on with life, with my new article. I'm writing a column for Sarah, my favourite editor, the editor who commissioned my Big Tech breakthrough piece years back. She wants me to fill a regular magazine slot: My New Neighbourhood. It's for people who move to a new part of Britain, they describe the history and context of the place, the landscape or cityscape, what they feel about it. Consequently I am writing about Camden.

The money isn't that good, but the money, these days, is never *that* good. And at least the research is interesting.

In bed I pick up a book on the history of North London, but my eyes are hanging heavy. I turn over to face the curvy white egg of an Assistant sitting on my bedside table. HomeHelp.

'OK, HomeHelp.'

Her dinky toy lights spin in response. She's awake: waiting for my command. I ask,

'Set me an alarm for 8.15 a.m.'

'OK, I've set an alarm for 8.15 a.m.'

'Thank you. And could you turn out the lights.'

The bedroom goes dark. I snuggle into the pillow. The pill kicking in. But as I hover at the edge of sleep I hear a snatch of very soft music. HomeHelp has woken up again. And she's playing a song. I never asked her to do this. Why is she doing this? At first the chords are so quiet they are not identifiable. But then it gets louder. And louder.

'Hoppípolla'. HomeHelp is playing 'Hoppípolla'.

THAT SONG. Of all songs. The image of a dead young man, eyes rolling white, fills my inner vision. My head jerks from the pillow. I am surely not imagining this. Jamie, don't die, don't you die like my dad.

'Stop.' I say. The music does not stop, it gets louder, surging, soaring, that sinuous discordant beautiful melody, yet so sinister to my ears. 'OK, HomeHelp. Stop. Stop. HomeHelp. Please please STOP!!!!'

The music ceases. HomeHelp twirls her toylike quadrant of lights, then goes dark. And I lie here, in the blackness, my eyes staring wide and frightened at the ceiling. What the hell is happening to me?

4

Jo

In the morning I zip down to the gym, as I promised my better self, and I do half an hour on the cross-trainer; then I go to Wholefoods on Parkway and buy nice Gail's sourdough bread and super-healthy T Rex fruit smoothies that I can't afford. After a shower, I make avocado and marmite on toast.

While I munch the greasy crusts I knock back my hot tea while leaning on Tabitha's rose-granite kitchen counters; then I make quick, faintly desperate calls to my friends, to Fitz, then Gul, then my editor, then anyone – I simply need chat. Distracting gossip. Water-cooler stuff. And yes, my friends are all brisk and affable – but then they all fob me off by saying they'll call me later, after work, for a proper dialogue.

In response, I am overly cheerful. Disconcertingly upbeat, despite the cold rain, turning to frost, on the windows. Sure, let's talk later! Have a good one!

I am, in other words, urgently pretending. I'm not merely pretending to them, I am pretending to myself:

that it didn't happen, the song was a pre-sleep dream, it was all a drunken delusion. All of it. I'm not freaked out by the Home Assistant. I am not starting to question myself, I have not been thrust back to that portrait of violent death, the hideous seizures, the convulsive blood-vomiting jerks of Jamie Trewin, as he died.

Yes. No. *Stop.*

'Electra, can you set a reminder at six p.m.?'

'What's the reminder for?'

'Tesco delivery.'

Electra pauses. I wait, tensed, for Electra to tell me how his blood gurgled down his shirt.

'OK,' says Electra, 'I'll remind you at six p.m.'

And that's it. Nothing sinister. No mad songs that thrust me right back to the vomit, and 'Hoppípolla'. Nothing at all. I almost want Electra to say something menacing, so I know I wasn't imagining it. No, I don't. Yes, I do.

Look.

Cars is leaning on the wall between the Edinboro Castle pub and the vast dark gulch of the railway lines, emerging from their tunnel, surging into Euston, St Pancras, King's Cross. He is pointing at something in the sky that only he can see. Pointing and shouting. Later I will give him some decent food, he looks so terribly cold.

I don't want to end up homeless, not like poor Cars. And my resources are so meagre, who knows what might happen. Therefore I need to work, earn, and prosper. Determined and diligent, I re-open my book on Camden history.

But I cannot focus. No matter how much I try. My mind is too messed. Words blur, and slide away.

Instead I stop and I stare for countless minutes at

the tracks, watching long, long trains snaking in and out of Euston station. I think of all the people coming and going, all the millions of Londoners and commuters and suburbanites, crowded together – and yet each person sitting in those packed trains is ultimately and entirely alone. In my darker moments, I sometimes think of London as a moneyed emirate of loneliness; it sits on vast reserves of the stuff – human isolation, melancholy, solitude – the way a small Arab kingdom sits on huge reserves of oil. You don't have to dig very far down into London life to find the mad, the isolated, the suicidal, the quietly despairing, the slowly-falling-apart. They are all around us, beneath the surface of our lives; they are us. I think of that sad woman I saw, hunched against the snow, passing the house, her back turned to me, pulling her little kids. The way she and her children suddenly disappeared in the snow, as if she were a ghost.

OK, enough; I am freaking myself out. I am Jo Ferguson. Sociable, extrovert, good-for-a-laugh *Jo Ferguson*. That's me. That's what I am. I'm probably suffering from the winter solitude, and the money worries. It is just the usual stress, plus some lights on a machine spinning strangely. That is all.

Flattening the book, I take some initial notes.

The land in Camden is heavy, packed with dense, dark, clinging London riverside clay, replete with swamps and fogs, making it notoriously difficult to build. Shunned by developers, haunted by outlaws and highwaymen, extensive settlement therefore came quite late. The oldest dateable building is the World's End pub on the junction by the Tube station, once called Mother Red Cap, and before then Mother Damnable.

This is marked on maps in the late seventeenth century
but it may be medieval in origin, or earlier . . .

Mother Damnable. Not exactly charming. But interesting. Developers shunned Camden? Because of the
swampy ground? And it was 'haunted by outlaws',
hiding in the cold malarial fogs? All good material, if
a little ghostly. And that pub – which I used to drink
in as a student, on the way to gigs at Dingwalls – that
could be a thousand years old. Remarkable. I had no
idea: a place where farmers and peasants on the way
to the Cittie of Lundun would make their final rest.
Hiding from highwaymen. And witches.

This will be good for my piece. Diligently I type my
sentences. Tapping away in the flat. Like a good journalist.

And then Electra speaks.

'You shouldn't have done it, should you, Jo? Because
what if someone found out, years later?'

My heartbeat is painful. An ache. I turn to the
Assistant.

'Electra, what are you talking about?'

'You killed him. We've got the evidence. You could
go to prison for years.'

'Electra, stop!'

She stops. This makes it worse.

'Electra, what are you talking about?'

'Sorry I don't know that one.'

My voice is trembling.

'Electra, what do you know about Jamie Trewin?'

'I know about lots of topics. Try asking me about
music, history, or geography!'

Oh God.

'Electra, fuck off!!'

Ba-doom. The Assistant spins her thin green electric diadem, and goes quiet. My mind is the opposite. I surely didn't imagine *that* entire dialogue. Did I?

No. I didn't. I don't think. Which means: I need to ask or tell someone, yet I can't. But how about Google? Facing my screen, I type in the words: Home assistants going wrong. Digital assistants malfunctioning. Every variation.

Hmm. There are a few examples of Electra and her friends behaving unexpectedly, or even peculiarly: but nothing anywhere as specific, and menacing, as what is happening to me, so directly, so *intimately*: as if Electra can see deep into my head, like there is something uncanny in those dark machines, an inhuman knowledge. Making me spooked, in my own home.

Not knowing what else to do, I helplessly pick up my phone: a reflex reaction. Then I stare at the screen, bewildered: the phone says I have twenty missed calls. From my mother. In the last hour.

My phone has been on the whole time. It is not on mute. Yet I missed them all.

Twenty?

5

Janet

Janet Ferguson was calling for her dog to come in from the cold.

'Cindy, come on, it's freezing. You'll die out there.' Janet gazed across the frosted grass of her back garden. Where was she? It was hardly a vast, stately acreage of meadows. This was a suburban back garden, darkened by winter, just large enough for a small family: attached to a house designed for a small family. Indeed, now that this small family was gone, and Robert was long dead, and Jo and Will had grown up, Janet had often thought of selling. Moving somewhere else entirely, a one-bedroom flat somewhere central, or out of London altogether.

Thornton Heath depressed her these days, with its tatty signs, and faded cafes, the sudden outcrop of Polish, Romanian, Somalian, Bulgarian shops where she didn't understand the food, the accents, the people, much as she smilingly tried to fit in. It was an outlying suburb of London that never quite made it, never got gentrified, never got fashionable attention, yet never got *quite* so rundown the government was prepared to spend money.

It was time, surely, for Janet to make the same move as her friends and neighbours. Yes she would lose the much-loved garden with all its memories. And so be it. Cindy would have to put up with it. Restrictions. Life was all about increasing restrictions. Janet put up with her pacemaker, and monthly visits to the hospital, because that's simply what you did. Life slowly constricted around you, like a snake that would ultimately kill you. And one day you went into a hospital, and you never came out.

Like Robert. Dead at his own hand, in his early forties. She remembered the lingerie he'd stuffed in the car exhaust, so he could fill the car with carbon monoxide.

'Cindy!'

Janet could hear the dog. Right at the end of the foggy, white-frosted garden, probably digging up some old bones, or boots. The radio was calling it the coldest start to January in decades, and likely to get worse. Janet remembered when she was young, the bitter winter of 1963, when it was like this: it kept getting colder and snowier – on and on until March.

But Cindy, it seemed, was determined to have her fun, whatever the weather. And now Janet's phone was ringing, and vibrating, on the sink.

Closing the kitchen door, Janet reached for her mobile.

'This is Janet Ferguson.'

'Mum. What the hell is wrong?'

'Sorry?'

Her daughter's voice was urgent.

'Twenty calls. What's the matter, Mum? Are you all right? You called me *twenty times*?'

Janet frowned, puzzled.

'No, dear. I never called you. Not once.'

'But my phone says you did!'

'Well, I don't know about that.'

'Twenty times, Mum. It says it right here. Missed calls. Twenty! I was worried about you!'

Unsure what to say, Janet gazed out at the garden. Cindy was chasing a football. A very old, half-burst, dog-chewed football, muddy and mouldy in the murk. Janet remembered Jo and Will playing with it, alongside their father. That long ago. Oh, too long ago. All dead now, that old life was all dead. Where did it go?

She returned to her daughter, and this stilted conversation.

'Look, darling, it's nice you're worried, but I am fine and I'm not going to suddenly call you twenty times in one morning, for no discernible reason.'

'OK.'

'I mean, Jo: we speak about once a week, when you remember to ring me? Not twenty times a day.'

It was a tiny barb, but it was designed to sting. Judging by her daughter's pause, it had done the job. The silence was long enough to be properly awkward. Janet felt obliged to fill it.

'Isn't is possible, darling, that your smartphone is playing up? I don't know why you have those things, dear. Cameras, music, notebook, all in one little machine – what if you lose it? It's your whole life.'

'Everyone has them, Mum. Look, Mum, are you sure you didn't call me?'

'Yes, I am.'

'OK, sorry, Mum. I just, I don't . . . Ah. Ah. Perhaps my phone *is* on the blink. Like everything else in this place.'

Janet shrugged, not knowing how to respond. She opened the kitchen door to let the dog come in, shivering snowflakes. As she bent to pat the damp dog, she looked at the kitchen shelf and the framed pictures of her two children, and her lovely grandson Caleb. Then Jo at her graduation. Smiling and confident. The old Jo.

There was something different in her daughter's attitude this afternoon. Jo was normally so outgoing, can-do, optimistic. Today she sounded vulnerable. Needy. Agitated.

'Jo . . . are *you* all right?'

'What? Why?'

'You sound nervous. Are you OK up there, the new flat, Tabitha, everything?'

'Yes, yes of course, why yes, I'm fine. Fine. Absolutely fine. We're all *fine*.'

'Yes?'

'Yes! The flat is gorgeous, I love Camden, it's got a brilliant buzz. The park is around the corner. I can walk to Soho. It's much better than NW Tundra.'

The answer came far too quickly. Something was definitely wrong.

'Well, that's good, that's nice for you . . . Hey. You know I got a visit from Simon the other day?'

Another stiff pause. Janet could picture her daughter's surprised face.

'Simon? My Si? *Simon Todd*?'

'Yes, dear. He does come and visit, sometimes he brings Polly and the baby, so I can see little Grace.'

Her daughter said nothing, Janet sensed a pang of envy, down the line. She hurried on,

'I mean, his own family still lives down this way, you do remember that? His mum and dad? The Todds around the corner on Lesley Avenue? They're practically

41

the last people I know from – from the old times. And we're still friendly, so he pops by.'

'You mean . . . my ex-husband is secretly visiting you?'

Janet felt her impatience rising at this.

'Goodness! It's not some dark secret, Jo. I always liked Simon, we always got on well. He was a decent husband to you. You know I think that. I always thought that. In fact, I wondered . . .'

'Whether things would have been different if we'd had kids? Yes, I know, Mum.' The sharpness in Jo's voice was undisguised. 'You've told me several thousand times. Well, I decided not to. And now he's got one with Polly, so that's fine, isn't it? Perhaps you could adopt her as your grand-daughter, since I'm probably not going to give you one, and little Caleb is on the other side of the world.'

This time the barbs stung the mother. Jo *was* clearly envious, and she was clearly hurting.

Janet sighed, heavily.

Jo got in first.

'Oh God. Look. Sorry. I shouldn't have snapped. Sorry, Mum. I'm so sorry! It's nice that Simon comes to see you, and Polly, and Grace, and everything, that's nice of him, I should come more often myself.'

'Don't worry. I know it's a long way.'

'No, it's not good enough, Mum, I am sorry, I promise I will come over, at the weekend.'

Janet's witty, bouncy daughter sounded as deflated as that ancient football in the frozen garden. Feeling emboldened, by her concern, Janet decided to reach out.

'Do you mind my asking something?'

A pause.

'Go ahead, Mum.'

'Why *didn't* you want children, Jo? Simon was so keen to be a dad, he told me that many times, and he was devoted to you. And I know this led to your divorce, at least in part.'

'We talked about this; I'd have been a crap mum.'

'Was it only that, dear?'

'What are you saying?'

'Well, last time he was here, we got talking about kids, and Simon hinted that you had worries, about . . . About . . .'

It was so difficult to find the right words. Stiffening herself, like the frosted spears of long grass at the end of her garden, Janet carried on: 'Well, Simon told me you were worried about your father. That any children you had might inherit those genes. Late-onset schizophrenia. Like Robert. He said you were sometimes worried that your kids might get it, or that you might get it and leave your kids without a mother. But you shouldn't—'

'Mum!'

'You mustn't, dear. You mustn't let that fear dominate your life. It's not going to happen. When poor Robert went . . . you know . . .'

'Mad? When Dad went mad?'

'Yes, when your poor father went mad, the doctors looked into all this: there is no history of it on any side of his family, no suggestion of a genetic cause. He was unlucky, that's all.'

Jo answered, her tone calm. Even cold.

'Eighty per cent of schizophrenia is linked to genetic causes.'

'Yes, but not in his case!'

Janet realized she was raising her voice. She rarely did this with Jo. What was happening between them?

She couldn't remember a mother–daughter phone call as awkward as this, not for a while, not since the divorce. She loved her daughter. She and Jo had a good, honest relationship, even if she sometimes felt a bit neglected. At least Jo *did* ring, once a week; Will rang once a month, at most. Five minutes of small talk from LA, telling her about Caleb, and that's your lot.

'Jo, you sound strained.'

'I told you, I'm fine, Mum. Just worried about stuff. Sometimes.'

'Stuff?' Janet persisted. 'What kind of stuff?'

'Just, y'know, *stuff*. The existential pointlessness of life. The eventual heat death of the universe. Reality TV.'

Janet allowed herself a chuckle. This was more like the usual Jo. She sighed with relief.

'OK, well, if you're sure you're all right. Do come down at the weekend. We could have a spot of lunch?'

'I will, Mum. I am genuinely sorry I snapped. And I suppose I *have* been a bit stressed. I keep trying to write these scripts, find a way out, but it's hard. I'll end up paying rent for ever.'

'Ah. I wish I could help, Jo. I wish I had bought this house when we had the chance. Then at least you'd have something to inherit, but when Robert—'

'It's OK, Mum. It wasn't your fault. Ah. Anyhow, I've got to go, got to go. OK. Bye, Mum.'

Her daughter sounded distracted. As though someone unexpected had walked into her flat.

Janet said goodbye. They ended the clumsy call. Janet put the phone down on the kitchen table. She stared at those photos on the kitchen shelf. Jo and Will. Next to them stood Robert, as a young man. Mid-thirties. Handsome. Jo and Will certainly got their good looks from him, not from herself. In the photo, Robert was smiling. Entirely sane. Here in the next photo he was in the living room, sitting on the floor with Jo and her childhood friends: Billy, Ella, Jenny, Neil, teaching them all to draw and write and paint. Paper and crayons everywhere, a happy childhood mess. Probably this was about a year before the serious symptoms.

Even now the memories grieved her. Tremendously. The slow remorseless damage his insanity inflicted on their lives, which eventually drove Robert to gas himself in the family car.

Janet could remember the specific day – the specific moment – when she first realized something was truly wrong. When she could no longer deny, or ignore, or pretend he was only a bit eccentric, or stressed.

It was so long ago – several decades – yet the memory was vivid.

She had walked from this kitchen into the living room to watch the evening news. Robert was sitting on the sofa, staring at the TV screen. The screen was black, because the TV was unplugged. Yet they *never* unplugged the TV. She went to plug it in but as she bent down, he shouted, 'No, no, don't do that, Janet! Don't plug it in! Don't plug it in!'

Perplexed, she had sat down next to him and asked. 'Why not? Why can't I plug it in?'

'Because it's talking to me,' he said, frowning deeply, 'the television is talking to me.'

6

Jo

The Flask, Highgate. Of course, that's where we'd go to celebrate Tabitha's return from Brazil. A quaint, wooden, stained, rickety, middle-class, roaring-fire-and-mulled-wine kind of pub in the nicest part of Highgate, and, it so happens, approximately two and a half minutes' walk from Arlo's gorgeous eighteenth-century house with the Damien Hirst spot paintings in the hall. He reserves the best art for his living room, or drawing room, or ballroom, or seventeen-hectare underground sculpture garden, God knows. I've only been invited to Arlo's house once, saw little more than a kitchen as big as my mum's entire home, and even then I think Arlo would have preferred me to enter by the tradesman's entrance, or some special tunnel for proletarians.

Traitor's Gate.

And now I'm in Arlo's local pub, standing alone. I am several minutes too early. I was so keen to get out of the flat. In case the Assistants turned on me again. If they are turning on me, and it's not me doing it to myself.

Don't think about it.

As I wait for everyone else to arrive, I stare at some luridly antique prints on the panelled pub wall. They show famous executions in the area, men hanging from gibbets, cheering crowds. One of the hangings seems to be taking place on top of Primrose Hill. Three men are dangling in a row, barefoot and dancing, grasping at the noose, obviously dying. The engraver has gone to great lengths to get the details of the throttled faces right: the boggling eyes, the protruding tongues, the gruesomely happy, popcorn-munching reactions of the audience.

My research hasn't told me this. Primrose Hill was a place of execution? The dying, horrified face of the man on the left, apparently biting his own tongue off, as he is slowly asphyxiated, stares directly at me. Right at me. Like it knows. He knows. Who knows?

I am not my father.

Am I? I remember my dad before he lost himself: he was extrovert, full of humour. A frustrated artist who ended up imprisoned in minor accountancy: so he lived, and found joy, through his family. Dad was always ready to have fun, to make me laugh, to chase me round the apple tree pretending he couldn't catch me. I called him the Ticklemonster and he called me Jo the Go because I could run so fast. He liked to play with words, he liked to play with *life*. So perhaps I take after him rather than my cautious, conservative mother. Which says?

My anxious, fumbling thoughts – ready to plunge into something worse – are interrupted.

Arlo is at the bar. He gazes at me, blankly confident, arrogantly possessive. I am in *his* bar. *His* local. To celebrate the return of *my* friend, *my* flatmate. Why did we have to come here?

Because he's Arlo Scudamore. He is in control. I think he also controls Tabitha. He knows I think that. He also doesn't apparently care what I think, whether I am hurt or happy, as he is still so bitter about my critical article on the tech giants, where I quoted him as a source supposedly without his permission. He did give permission, he simply didn't like what I wrote. He claims the article stymied his previously meteoric career. God, I hate his stupid posh-yet-hipster accent. He thinks I'm common? Fuck him. Simon once described Arlo as 'psychotically ambitious' and I've never forgotten that: it was so accurate.

Stepping around the bar, I say,

'Hello, Arlo! Lovely to see you.' And give him a quick double non-kiss air-kiss.

'Ah, Jo. Hello, so glaaaad you could make it!'

He returns the duo of non-kisses. I had no idea social greetings could be this insincere.

'Where's Tabs?'

'Vaping outside, swathed in perpetual smoke like some hydrothermal vent.'

Who, or what, is a hydrothermal vent? I have no idea. He probably said it to make me feel insecure. So we are stuck, in a corner of the Flask. Just me and him and rows of glittery obscure new artisanal gins on the mirrored shelves behind the bar, and the deeply sinister prints of the local executions on the wall, and a lovely roaring woodfire in the mighty hearth. Waiting for everyone else to arrive.

'Everything OK at, uh, work? Facebook?'

This is probably the most irritating thing I could ask him. Which is possibly why I ask it. He does the same to me all the time. Needling Arlo at least takes my mind off my own deepening vortex of worries.

'Work? Oh, superb. I'll be leaving in a week or two. For the start-up.' His smile is so icy it could kill wintering songbirds at twenty metres. 'Ah!' The smile becomes brighter, warmer, even real. 'Here's Jeremy. Lex! Rollo.'

Rollo.

Rollo.

Arlo has an extraordinary number of posh, pink-faced friends with names that end in O. Hugo. Rollo. Theo. Rocco. Orlando. Otto. I think Otto is a 'Von' as well. They are all stupidly rich. Dutch bazillionaires. French bankers. Film directors. Venture capitalists investing in Arlo's Big New Thing, which is all to do with Artificial Intelligence and FinTech, and other stuff I Officially Cannot Understand. I know some of these guys by sight, but they barely know me. I am clearly only here because of Tabitha. If I am lucky, one or two university friends that me and Tabs share *might* show up, diluting my social isolation.

But as I have recently confirmed, to my own dismay, most of my friends now live out of town.

'Jo!!'

Ah. A slender blonde girl tucking a vape in her chic denim jacket is smiling, broadly, my way.

'Jo! Darleenk!'

She does a heavy, fake, theatrical German accent when she's in a good mood.

'Heyyy, Tabs! You didn't get eaten by jaguars!'

My friend skips towards me and gives me a big big hug and a kiss where her lips actually touch my skin. I realize, with a hidden but painful cramping sensation, how much I've missed physical interaction. No one has touched me in days, let alone hugged or kissed me.

'Jo-Jo babe. How *are* you!'

'Oh God, fine! You? Brazil? Peru? What happened?'

'Put it this way, if I have to film another tiny, critically endangered tree frog, I will dedicate my career to wiping out amphibian life. I will shoot a fucking newt.'

We laugh. We hug again. I sooooooo want this. I so *need* this.

Freelance journalism, I have realized, doesn't even make you free, it can all too easily imprison you in your flat, devoid of human contact, and you don't get out of pyjamas from Monday to Wednesday. And freelancing plus digital technology is *worse*. All the significant conversations I have had this week have been with the digital world.

Since I went freelance five years back, I've discovered quite how much people don't even want to *talk*. Rather than pick up a phone, they will go to great lengths to text or email. They want to type and WhatsApp and message, so they can edit and censor. Curate themselves: their souls and their discourse.

I should have put this in the article which so annoyed Arlo. The fact that tech was fucking up our social lives, fucking up our humanity, our interactions, our everything. And in return is it fucking with me?

'Arlo!'

'Theo.'

'Cicero.'

The Os have turned out in force. Tabitha chats with them. I stand alone. The executed man dangling from the gallows on Primrose Hill sticks his vile and blackened tongue in my direction. My thoughts return to the machines in my home, undermining me, throwing me off-balance, and a question forms. Could this be Arlo's doing? Is it some kind of cynical vengeance? He's certainly clever enough, and controlling enough. He'd probably find it loftily droll and piquant. Using the same

50

tech I criticized to gaslight me, to send me round the bend.

His dislike of me, based partly on pure snobbery, was confirmed by my so-called journalistic betrayal. When I first moved to Delancey, he came round and looked at my paltry wardrobe and delivered a litany of acidic remarks about how lucky I was to live in that flat, when I could have been stuck in some horrible bedsit in nowhere, perhaps along the A40 'breathing in pure carbon monoxide'. He actually said that. And he knows how my poor dad died. And then, he added, for good measure: 'Instead, you get to live here, with the smart TV, the Assistants, the smart lighting – you have only to ask for music and it floods the rooms, and all of it is made by those companies you hate. How . . . ironic?'

I stare across at him, framed by the shelved arrays of fashionable gins, surrounded by his eager peers. He is chortling in that austere way he has. Like he finds laughter slightly vulgar but will indulge in it for close friends as a favour. He is handsome and fit; aristocratically cheekboned, yet somehow not sexy at all. At least not to me.

Tabitha relieves my tense isolation by handing me a drink. A fluted glass.

'Proper champagne, Perrier Jouët!' She grins, and tilts her head at her fiancé and his moneyed pals. 'You hanging back? Can't blame you. Arlo is actually discussing blockchain with some of his bankers. What the hell is blockchain? Does anyone know?'

We are already a few yards from the main social group by the bar. Physically sidelined: symbolically lesser. I look down at the inviting glass tulip of golden-bubbling alcohol. Should I feel guilt for guzzling Arlo's champagne when I dislike him so much? Nope. I tilt the flute and gulp the fizz so quickly it makes me sneeze bubbles. The glass is trembling in my slightly trembling hand. I am revealing my hideous anxieties.

Tabitha frowns, looking at my glass, which I quickly set down on the bartop.

'Heya. Are you all right? Everything OK at Delancey?'

This is the time to mention it. She has cued me up. This is my chance to offload, share, ask for help, mention the Assistants, the possible malfunction. In them. Or in me. The taunts. The music. The clownish horror show. And yet I cannot. Because the conversation would rapidly come back to the deeper reason: the death of Jamie Trewin. And we have vowed never to discuss this between us; vowed on our lives, vowed on the lives of both our families. And we have kept that vow: it's not something I can easily break. I want to. But I can't. For a start, Tabitha might throw me out, and then I'd have to go and live on the A40 and breathe pure carbon monoxide.

Also, the Assistants have been quiet the last day or two. Nothing has happened since I rang my mum. This does not help me, as it leaves me open to the possibility that I am becoming schizophrenic like my father.

But that is so chilling I do not think about it.

Ever.

Do. Not. Think. About. It. It. It. It. It. It is listening to me. Talking to me. The TV is talking to me. Like it apparently talked to my dad. A voice from the dark. I was too young to understand, at the time, but I've learned since that this was the first symptom of the disease that killed him a few years later.

The TV started talking to Dad the way the machine, Electra, has started talking to me. Which suggests I am my dad? I will end my days gassed in a car?

'Jo? You OK?'

I come to, with a jolt. I must have been silent for a minute, lost in myself. My dad did that too. Before he got scary. Before his tickling got aggressive and I ran to Mummy. Before his madness cost me friends. Dave, Jenny, others, many, all driven away. At least it made me self-reliant.

Looking at my flatmate, I force a smile.

'I'm good, Tabs. Working. Bit bored. You know you've come back to the coldest winter since mid-period Charles Dickens.'

She shudders.

'I noticed. There were penguins in the Arrivals Lounge.'

'So how was it?! How was the documentary, the jungle, the trip? What's the Amazon like? I've always wanted to go. God, you're so lucky!'

She chuckles.

'Insects.'

'Sorry?'

'That's what the Amazon is like, babe. *Insects*. You don't see any wildlife because the jungle is too thick, a wall of endless green. But my bloody God you see insects – mosquitoes like buzzards, killer centipedes, spiders that *exude* poison.'

'OK . . .'

'Fire ants literally attacked my rucksack. Seriously. They tried to eat it. It's got little white marks all over it, from the formic acid where they bit. And then at night that's all you hear.'

'What?'

'Insects! Shrieking. They actually *shriek*.' She knocks back her own glass of bubbles. 'Also giant rats. Lois hated the whole thing. Said we had to do Greenland next. Anywhere with zero insect life.'

Lois is her presenter. The star of the nature documentary series that Tabitha co-produces.

'The only interesting bit was when a tapir fell in the swimming pool.'

I gaze her way. Wide-eyed. Tabitha always has adventures and tales. We used to eagerly share these adventures: backpacking together through Bolivia and Colombia, fending off overly persistent tantra masseurs in India, then life caught up with us and we had to get sensible. I stopped travelling; she still travels for her work, and comes home with stories. And I need good stories tonight, to take my mind off my flat, to take my mind off my mind.

'You had a swimming pool? I thought you were like, lost in the wilderness, surrounded by piranha – wasn't that the idea?'

Tabitha nods, chuckling.

'Yeah. But towards the end we got so bored of the tents and the mozzy bites we went to some hotel near Iquitos which had a pool. But the pool was right on the edge of the jungle and a tapir wandered out of the forest and tried to have a drink and then fell in the pool. And then the tapir panicked and did a humongous poo in the pool and no one knew how to get the poo out. Have you ever had a swim in a pool full of tapir poo? It's not ideal.'

I am laughing, loudly. Maybe too loudly: showing my inner angst. But it's great to have Tabitha back. A genuine friend. My old friend. How I have lacked this.

For a while we politely rejoin Arlo, but the bankers are talking about cryptocurrencies, and Tabitha and I exchange knowing glances – and then she kisses Arlo decorously on the cheek and says,

'Nipping out for another vape, sweetheart. Don't put too much money into Aetherium, it will crash.'

He half acknowledges her; while she murmurs to me, 'Wanna come with? They've got patio heaters.'

Openly relieved, I follow her outside into the pub garden. It is bitterly cold but yes there are red-glowing patio heaters. Staring at them, I say,

'Greatest invention since—'

Tabitha interrupts:

'Facebook?'

She is grinning, playfully. Making a point.

'Don't. Please. Please don't.' I sigh, feeling helpless. 'Oh God, Tabby, I do try and get along with him, but . . . he's from such a different world. I mean, you're posh enough but he's basically like the Queen. He probably looks down on the Queen, coz she uses Tupperware.'

'Yesss,' she drawls, in her amused voice. 'Plus he thinks you scuppered his inevitable ascent to becoming Emperor of the Internet,'

I raise a cold hand in protest,

'I didn't!'

Tab smiles her perfect, regular, white-toothed smile. I have quite nice teeth but they are a bit crooked. Thornton Heath teeth.

'I know, darleenk, I know. But you remember how he is. And now he's got that bonkers start-up ready to kick off, he's convinced it will be the next unicorn. Make him a billion. Like he needs more money. Anyway he's particularly touchy. Don't pay *any* attention to him.'

I want to ask her: what do you see in him? But I can't. She genuinely loves him. She's told me. I know they have good sex. I know they go to fashionable sex parties. Killing Kittens, Kinky Salon. Maybe that's all it is: sex. Also, Tabitha can be, for all her confidence, oddly insecure, at times. She has panic attacks. Her dad left home when she was ten or so, upped and walked out the door with a new mistress half his age. Therefore Arlo's wealth thus gives her an extra level of security. Plus the sex.

Tabitha is smoking an actual cigarette; not a vape.

I stare at her.

'Uh, thought you'd given up?! You practically put on a West End musical about it: *Tabitha Gives Up!*'

She giggles, shrugs. The red glow of the patio heaters gives her pretty face an eerie redness, looming and ominous. And I can't help staring at it. This devilish cast to her face. A beautiful red demon face in the dark of an eighteenth-century Highgate pub garden, in the deep dark cold of a harsh London winter. Where sad and lonely women drag their little children through the snow.

'I started again in Peru, I thought the fag smoke might drive away the mosquitoes. It didn't, but I got hooked. Don't tell Arlo – he'll be scandalized, and refuse to go down on me.'

Her face is still very red from the heaters. Demonic. Satanic. Or is this image in my head? She speaks, the teeth even whiter, contrasting with the red. I think of fangs. Vampiric fangs. Sucking blood from my neck as I sleep. Tabitha. Who was there in the tent with me that day. I wonder if she has told Arlo about what happened with Jamie Trewin, all those years ago? I long to ask. Instead, I say,

'Guess you're staying at his place tonight?'

She nods, and frowns my way, refusing to be embarrassed.

'Yes. You know, I am allowed to, it is my choice.'

'Oh?'

She sighs smoke. 'You think he controls me.'

'No. I think he infantilizes you. Like he's your parent. He looks after you. Punishes you for infractions.'

'Well, yeah,' she says, exhaling unconcerned coils of smoke quite exuberantly. Breathing demon fire. 'Sure. WhatEVAH. Look, let's not have some hideous falling out, darling, not on my first day back. And please don't tell Arlo about the smokes. He would *definitely* give me a telling off if he found out.' She fumes more smoke into the cold night air. 'The fact is, Jo, I don't mind being looked after, even ordered about, when I'm off duty. You see? You do understand why? I have to be super-controlling in my job, so when I get back to town I quite like being the little woman. Or the princess.' She smirks shamelessly. 'Isn't that terrible? I actually like to *let* him do *everything*. Let him take care of me, let him decide which restaurant we go to. Let him choose the wine, even the food. Then I let him pay. Is that so very bad? Am I a terrible feminist? Oh well. Fuck it.'

I try not to see the unsettling red glow of her face and instead I gaze in her friendly eyes and think: maybe she's right. Someone to look after you? I consider the idea of someone to look after *me*. I'd *love* that. Someone special, someone of my own, someone who makes me feel secure. Someone to buy me a nice meal in a nice restaurant then make love to me, nicely.

I sigh. Defeated. 'You're right. And I'm hardly in a position to criticize: my love life is a desert. The bloody Atacama. You think I should get a sugar daddy? He'd have to have his own hair though.'

We fall silent as she finishes the cigarette. I feel a need to say something about what is happening. We've been talking for ages and I haven't even touched on it. And somehow it's 10 p.m. and I might not get another chance, if she's going back to Arlo's tonight. Later I will walk down silent solitary Jackson's Lane, listening for footsteps behind me, to get the lonely Tube at spooky Highgate. I hate Highgate Tube, buried like a tomb under that little enclave of snowy urban woods. Like a place in a frightening fairy tale from Romania where there'd be wolves. Loping. Howling.

'Tabitha,' I say, quickly, airily, casually as possible. 'You know all those Home Assistants at Delancey.'

She is grinding another cigarette butt into the soil of a small potted tree.

'Uh-uh. What about them?'

'I was wondering how they got there.'

Tabitha frowns as she squirts minty breath-freshener into her mouth.

'Sorry? What do you mean?'

'Like: who bought and installed them?'

The frown persists, but only for a second.

'Arlo, natcho. Arlo bought them, for me. But he didn't install them – far too mechanical.' She twists her mouth into a thoughtful pout. 'Come to think of it, it was your ex-husband who installed them. Did it as a favour. You don't remember?'

'Sorry? What?'

'Your ex, darl, your ex. You haven't forgotten him already? Simon! He came over one day. He set it all up. The smart home. The entire system.'

And with that she turns and goes back into the pub. The red glow of the patio heaters shines on the smoke left behind, a fast disappearing scarlet ghost, shivering into nothing in the cold. I wait, and think about Simon, and about this peculiar revelation, because he never told me he did this: came over and did this favour for Tabitha? He never mentioned it once. Not while we were married, not since.

They did this, all three of them, without telling me. Then Tabitha asked me to move in. And the rent was so ridiculously low, I was obliged to agree. How could I possibly resist?

Such a wonderful offer. Impossibly tempting. Come and live here, with all that technology.

A big grey moth has got trapped in the patio heater. I look at it, unable to help. The poor creature was attracted by the light, but the light and heat have lured it to a terrible end. I stand and watch it burn to death in fluttering agony. The antennae are the last things to stop twitching.

7

Jo

The glasses are drained, the air is kissed, Arlo's friends have gone back to their own beautiful period houses with underground swimming pools. Waving goodbye to Tabitha, I walk out into a midnight frost that is predatory in its iciness. Like the sky, the air, the entire world is made of cold blackness, waiting to shatter. Highgate tonight is a glass daguerreotype, some historic and fragile photograph from the 1840s; huddled grey figures are slowed and blurred and lifeless in the freezing mist, and far away down Highgate Hill, past the cemetery, the car lights turn left, and right, and always further away, always departing.

Diminishing into nothing.

Most of the bars and restaurants of Highgate Village are already shut, at 11 p.m. Why? It feels jarring, though I suppose it's that post-Christmas lull of early January when everyone is too poor or torpid to brave the chill. It does, however, mean my walk down Jackson's Lane is lonelier than ever.

The eighteenth- and seventeenth-century houses crowd closer, the gardens get smaller and older, then I am walking down a slender path of frozen mud, with eroded bare redbrick walls on either side, my footsteps echoing as I go. My isolation is pure.

Instinctively, I take out my phone. I want to see if my loneliness is about to be diluted. Are there any messages for me on OKCupid?

No. Not a single one. What have I done wrong? Is it the photo, was I too sarcastic? Probably I need to refine the profile.

And yet as I walk slowly to the Tube, breathing the cold cold air, despairing of my love life, an obvious thought occurs.

Liam.

I feel deep guilt about my online flirtation with Liam, what it did to my marriage, yet there's no denying the flirtation *was* fun. We never actually met – my marriage collapsed before I took the final, fatal step – but the texts, messages, and emails were many and they were sexy. They just were. He was funny. Clever. Self-deprecating. And the photos showed a very good-looking man.

Why not get in touch? We ended so abruptly. After I told him that Simon had discovered my sexts, our erotic dialogue, and that I was headed for divorce, I disappeared on him. It seemed best. The guilt was too much.

I guess I ghosted.

But now I *am* divorced, and single. Perhaps dashing Liam is still single, too?

Stopping on Jackson's Lane, in the chilling mist, I look for Liam. And there he is: WhatsApp. And it looks like he's online. Right this minute.

I check the time. It's a bit late, but he could be working in the bar, and, as I recall, he liked talking late anyway. We would exchange messages, and then photos – all those foolish photos, – deep into the night. Even as Simon softly snored in the bed alongside.

Ignoring my very guilty conscience, I type a message:

Hey. Guess who???

I wait. The ticks go blue. He has read my message. He must be replying. My heart speeds. A bike hisses downhill, towards Highgate Tube, its light so feeble in the freezing January fog they barely register. A message appears. It's from him: Liam Goodchild.

Is it really you? After all this time!

I can't help smiling. Why didn't I think of this before? Why did I even bother going on OKCupid? I recall one particular photo he sent of himself, on a boat, stripped to the waist. Oh yes, Liam Goodchild. I'm out here, and I am ready.

He messages again. I stare down, frowning.

No Jo no

I type back,

What?

He says,

I learned, Jo. I learned about you.

I tap out a reply,

> Learned what? Learned something about me? I don't
> get it. I only wondered if you'd like to chat . . .

He goes quiet. My message is read; but he says nothing.
I am a statue in this freezing dark, surrounded by the
frosty mist of my own breath. Has he gone?

No, wait, a reply:

> It's too late. I don't want to talk. All that blackness and
> silence, then this? After everything that has happened?
> No.

I gaze, perplexed. What the heck is he on about? He
sounds drunk. Or angry. Or something. My shivering
fingers type out my next, uncertain words.

> Liam, I'm sorry, what do you mean, everything that has
> happened? This is weird. I'm sorry I ghosted on you
> before, but we agreed not to message, but anyway I
> am single now and I was kinda wondering—

He doesn't even bother to read this, it doesn't even go
to blue ticks. His next message is immediate and very
fast and interrupts my own. As if he is scared.

> You don't understand who you are dealing with. Is it
> impossible for you to let something go? I will not be
> responsible. You never knew me. Stop messaging,
> leave me alone.
> Otherwise somebody's done for.

I hold the phone tight in my hand, in case I drop it. This is not the Liam I remember, he must be drunk, out of control. And now he's deleted the messages he just sent. And when I try to respond, his ID has disappeared. He's blocked me.

Breathing cold spiky air, I go to Facebook Messenger. Yup. I am blocked there, too. And Instagram, our other medium?

Blocked.

I have been totally unfriended, I have been barred and banished from his life, with nothing but these bizarre remarks: You don't understand who you are dealing with. I will not be responsible. Stop messaging, leave me alone. *Or somebody's done for.*

Like a threat. As if I am in some mortal danger.

I wonder if I should simply call him; we only spoke once on the phone – a few brief passionate words. But real speech was too risky, too exciting. Therefore we made it a rule: until we were sure, we'd keep it at messages.

Who cares, now, though? I find his number, and dial it: the call switches automatically to voicemail.

He's blocked me there too. He's run away. He is frightened.

Of what?

All that blackness, your silence, then this?

As I walk on, pocketing the phone, I really do feel the isolation, and the danger. Jackson's Lane is always a solitary place, but this is something else; the biting cold night gives my solitude a physical quality – painful, brittle, stifling. All I can hear is my own laboured, panicky breath.

I look behind.

No one.

I look at curtained windows and blackened doorways and I see no signs of human life, and that makes it worse.

My heart flutters, dances, twirls with the urban worry. The intrinsic vulnerability. Dad running out to grab me, towards the end, trying to be kind, loving, funny, like before, like he always did, but doing it too fast, too violent, and making it scary. No. No no. I feel a need to run, to get out of here, to flee. The panic rises. Help me. Help me.

8

Jo

I am nearly at the end of the lane. Nearly at busy Archway Road with its traffic and people and street-lamps. Breathing slowly, I regain my sensible, logical self. I panicked, that was all, thrown by Liam's faintly creepy remarks. No, I am not being followed; no, the Tube station is not surrounded by Romanian wolves.

Liam was just being . . . Liam? Probably he's got a girl and wants me out of his life, out of his mind. So he frightens me away. Probably he was with her even as I messaged, and he panicked.

Yes.

I climb aboard a very empty carriage, and the train rattles me through Archway, Tufnell Park, Kentish Town. When I alight at Camden I walk out into relative busy-ness. The pub opposite the Tube, the Mother Damnable, now the World's End, is pumping out rock music. Lads are smoking weed in the wicked cold, and laughing at lurid jokes, in this place where travellers once hid from outlaws.

The rest of my walk is short, up Parkway, past closed cafes, dirty drifts of snow, and upmarket pubs, the sense of wealth accumulating with each step. From the dry homeless hostels of Arlington Road, costing £2 a night, to the palatial sweep of the Nash Terraces – costing £20,000 a square yard – in a few minutes' walk.

I am nearly home. At the top of Parkway, I turn – and stop. Standing on the pavement opposite my house – the house which contains Tabitha's flat, is a knot of people. Drinkers from the local pub probably, the Edinboro Castle. They are all gazing in the direction of my flat but I can't see why, can't see what's so absorbing about my flat, because the house itself is around the corner.

The nearer I get, the more confusion I read on their faces. What can they see in my home? What is happening?

As I reach the corner, I look up.

And, yes: I see. Yet I wish I didn't.

Abruptly, all the lights in the flat flick on. They are blazing. Every single one. The blinds are up, and the windows are showing the red-painted walls, the expensive TV, Tabitha's favourite steel sculptures. Then all the rooms go black, and the windows reflect the Delancey streetlights, the parked wet cars – and another gentle, silvery falling of snow. A moment later, it repeats. The lights go on, then off. Off, then on. Every single light and lamp.

It's as if the flat is actually alive. Signalling to someone out there. Using Morse code. Signalling to whom? And who is in there, doing the signalling?

No one. Or no one human.

I hear a voice, my name: called out.

It's my neighbour, from about three doors down. Deborah Welland. She's in a dressing gown, shivering in the cold. The drinkers disperse, shaking their heads, as Deborah approaches. Debs is a nervous woman, mid-forties, divorced, dyed hair, the type of woman that complains to the council about everything: too many trees, a lack of trees, too many buses, the dearth of buses, but she also means well. Deborah would lend me the last cup of sugar in her flat, and she likes three spoonfuls in a mug.

'Debs, what is it? What's wrong?'

It's a stupid question. We both know what's wrong. She gestures, upwards, to those decorous, cast-iron Juliet balconies.

'All night,' Deborah says, gazing with a kind of frightened wonder. 'All night they've been doing that. Your lights flick on. Then off. On, then off. Like some code.'

She shakes her head. And looks at me. With pity?

'I first noticed about eight o'clock, as I was coming home from work. Saw all your lights doing this. Flickering. I thought it must be your fuses. But it's been going on so *long*.'

As we both gaze upwards, the lights in my empty flat do it again. They flash on. Then off. Repeatedly. For a minute. I am holding my breath, frightened like a young child confronted by an adult horror movie. Why is this so scary, yet so hypnotic?

Because it must be the Assistants. They have control of the lights. I feel a certain relief, that others are witnessing this, even as the uncanny fear grows. What exactly are we all witnessing?

'It's weird . . . I am sorry, but it is,' says Deborah. 'It's like there's somebody in your flat, flicking all the switches. But you can't see them. You haven't got a *ghost* in there, have you?'

She is trying to make a joke of it. But this feels anything but funny. The tiny flickers of snow are melting on my face; and my sweet, mildly neurotic neighbour Deborah is properly unnerved.

'I tried to call Tabitha.' Deborah lifts an extended thumb-and-little-finger to her ear, as if holding an old-fashioned phone. 'Thought she should know, as it's her place and everything . . . But I couldn't get through.'

'I've been at a pub. With her. I guess she had it switched off?'

'Jesus look – there they go again—'

Deborah is right. The lights are flashing, flashing across Delancey, flashing at Cumberland Terrace, flashing at the empty vastness of Regent's Park, and the lunatic wolves trapped in their tiny pens at the zoo.

'I'd better go in,' I say, keeping my voice calmer than I feel. 'It's probably some glitch with the technology – you know what Tabitha is like. Everything is always the best, always on the cutting edge, but things go wrong. Whole flat has been on the fritz the last few days.'

Deborah looks at me. Squints. As if trying to work out if I am being sarcastic.

I say a cold goodbye. With shivery hands I press a key to the front-door latch, and I find that I am taking big soothing breaths. Stay calm. I don't want to go in the flat. Stay calm. I DON'T WANT TO GO IN THE FLAT.

9

Jo

Standing by my door, I can sense Deborah's eyes on my back, pitying, fearful, as I step across the threshold into the dry and the warmth, and the piles of slippery flyers for curry houses and pizzerias and burger chains gathering like drifts of autumn leaves in the hallway.

Big deep breath. If I'm going to confront this, I have to do it fast or not at all. Marching up the steps, I press the key into the latch of my internal door, Tabitha's door, I still don't feel this place belongs to me in any way, maybe I don't *want* to be too closely associated with it.

What am I about to see? I imagine all manner of ludicrous technological monsters, gibbering spectres made of electricity. Or dead things. My dead father. My dead father will be sitting in a corner and talking to me. Drooling.

Stop. Calm.

Key. Turn.

The door opens. I see a well-lit flat. Orderly and

normal. Red painted walls. Pictures and photos from Tabitha's many travels, some of the ones we did together, most she did with boyfriends, and Arlo.

Ceramic Mexican skulls commemorating the Day of the Dead. A tiny, authentic ancient Egyptian statue: a man with a dog's head.

Stepping inside the inner hallway, I make for the living room. The silence is like the hum of a meditation bowl.

Nothing has changed. I can see that chunk of volcano from Ethiopia. And the beautiful, somehow melancholy seashells from Sanibel, Florida. Plus shelves of books – Tabitha's literary fiction and natural history, and below them racks of *my* books: thrillers and mysteries and art history, and those endless guides to screenwriting.

Whatever the lights were doing, whatever the Assistants were doing *to* the lights, has stopped. I look out of the window, Deborah has disappeared. So has everyone else. The street is empty. Did we see a glitch or did we see something more?

The only strange thing, now, is the intense cold. The heating has gone off. It shouldn't have done this. The smart heating is meant to maintain the flat at twelve degrees Celsius, even when it is empty, so pipes won't burst in a freeze. And it is freezing out there, and possibly even colder in here. Like a fridge.

OK, OK. I must stay calm. And try not to think about Liam. What he said. However weird. He must have had a reason, nothing to do with me.

Opening the Electra app on my phone, I select Skills and check out Lights and Heating. It seems I've got the lights set to turn on at 11 p.m., for when I get home. But they're also set to turn off all night, in case I am late. Ah. Is this conflict simply my fault? I vaguely remember doing something like this at the pub; I was a little drunk, and distracted. Did I confuse the Assistants myself?

I have no idea. All I know is that the cold is too intense to bear.

'Electra, turn the central heating back on. To twenty-two degrees, please.'

The diadem chimes, and Electra bongs back:

'The heating has been turned on to twenty-two degrees Celsius.'

'Thanks, Electra.'

'That's what I'm here for!'

I look at her. This neutral black pillar of chips and wires, and a hostility curdles inside me. A genuine anger. Because I am sure something strange and nasty *is* being done *to* me, by someone – or something. First the taunts, then the music, now the lights? And Liam, too, almost threatening.

Somebody's done for.

I have some evidence, and it is accumulating, but I still can't take it anywhere. Certainly not to the police. Because of the backstory. Tall, athletic, friendly, buy-everyone-a-beer Jamie Trewin – and his spasmed, vomiting death, and his eyes that rolled white into his head, and all because of me, and Tabitha.

Enough. I am tired. The flat is palpably warmer than it was. I need to get up tomorrow and get to work and go back to normal life: see a friend, make a friend, have friends. Brushing my teeth, moisturizing my face, I jump into pyjamas, and head for my bedroom, telling the Assistants to switch off the lights as I make my way down the landing.

The lights go off, obediently. As if I am trailing dark-ness, an empress followed by servants, extinguishing candles. Everything is working as it should. Not a hint of strangeness. Climbing wearily into bed, I am so ready for sleep, and the moment before I close my eyes . . . I realize I can hear 'Hoppípolla'.

No, I am imagining it. I am half asleep.

No, I am not imagining it. HomeHelp, the creamy-grey, ostrich-egg-shaped Assistant in my bedroom, has reeled her cotillion of little lights, and she is quietly playing 'Hoppípolla'.

'Stop,' I say to HomeHelp. 'Stop playing that tune, never play that tune again.'

HomeHelp obediently stops. But I can hear 'Hoppípolla' from somewhere else. The kitchen. The little Assistant in the kitchen has taken over. Jumping out of bed, I go into the darkened kitchen, slap the lights on – not trusting the Assistants. The black hockey-puck-sized machine above the microwave is blasting out this beautiful song, with its hateful memories.

'STOP, Electra, STOP.'

The little kitchen machine stops. Silence rules for a few seconds. But then the tune starts over. Much louder. Thank God Fitz's flat downstairs is still empty, unrented. Thank God my affluent neighbours, above, are still not back from their endless holidays. Otherwise they would *all* surely complain as the noise gets even louder: coming from the bathroom, then Tabitha's bedroom, the hallway, the study, booming and roaring and swirling, and I am running between them, my dressing gown flapping, shouting STOP STOP STOP, until at last every Assistant goes quiet. Quite abruptly.

Silence.

I wait. Somehow I know this is not the end of it.

I am right. I can hear voices. They are quieter than

the booming music, but still loud enough, and clear. Some are male, some female, some British, some American. The Assistants are talking, to me, or to each other, or to someone else.

And the words are so strange.

Electra in the living room goes first:

'Perfection is terrible, it cannot have children.'

What?

The Assistant in the landing replies:

'The blood flood is the flood of love.'

The living room chimes in:

'Perfection is terrible, it cannot have children. Perfection is terrible, it cannot have children.'

A smooth robotic female voice, from the kitchen, joins the chorus:

'I am nude as a chicken neck, does nobody love me?'

I run from room to room, listening, with mounting fear, to these opaque, alarming sentences.

'No one is here, Jo, no one is here.'

'Unloosing their moons, month after month, to no purpose.'

'The snow drops its pieces of darkness.'

'Cold as snow breath, it tamps the womb—'

Now the bedroom cries out, warmly, it sounds like the voice of my widowed mother:

'Nude as a chicken neck, nobody loves me. Nobody loves me. Nobody loves me. Nude as a chicken neck. DOES NOBODY LOVE ME?'

Enough, I am done. Forget the app – I am pulling the damn plugs, I don't care what it does to the Assistants, the tech, the smart home, anything. There is a master switch: the fuse box . . .

Grabbing a chair and swinging it into the hallway, I

yank open the fuse box – there's nothing in the freezer but ice cubes, so it doesn't matter.

'Perfection is terrible. IT CANNOT HAVE CHIL-DREN—'

SNAP. There. I've done it. The entire flat is switched off. Everything falls silent and every light goes dark and the heating is switched off and I will freeze to death in this cold but I do not care. Creeping along the darkened hallway I push the door to my blackened bedroom, fumble for clothes in the drawer, throw on T-shirts, leggings, jumper, then I sneak under the duvet like I am trying not to be seen, and I grab a couple, no three sleeping pills from the little plastic jar on my right and I swallow the lot. And then I crunch myself into the tightest of fetal positions and close my eyes hard.

I am shivering in the cold, hiding from the darkness, cowering from my insanity. Or I am hiding from the ghost of Jamie Trewin, who waits outside my bedroom in the dark, his eyes as blank and white as wet marble.

Hey, let me buy you a beer.

10

Jo

I am woken by a frowning and beautiful face with pale blue eyes.

Tabitha.

She is staring at a woman wearing lots of daytime clothes in bed.

Me.

I realize I am sweating, heavily: the sheets are damp and clinging. I guess the heating is on. Winter sunshine streams through my bedroom window, because I forgot to close the curtains; I didn't care in my blind cold panic.

'What on earth's going on?' says Tabitha. 'Sorry to barge in and wake you up like this, but, really. What did you do to the flat? What happened to the heating, the lights?'

She is in a suave, maroon winter coat, cashmere jumper, and slender jeans I could never afford. Almost military in her stiffness, yet always chic. For a moment I don't know what to say. I look at her, as I come to full consciousness. And I wonder, for a second, how jealous I am, of her, my best friend. She's always been that bit *better* than me, in every way: richer, from a much smarter home. But she is also a shade taller, and a tiny bit prettier; she was blonde and I was a redhead; throughout our twenties we subtly competed for men and she usually won. Were we competing for Jamie Trewin – was that why I egged her on, so that he would prefer me, so he would maybe come on to *me*?

Perhaps it is all my fault.

'Seriously, Jo,' says Tabs, sitting herself on the end of the bed, still frowning, 'what the hell is wrong? I came back from Arlo's an hour ago, and found everything off – and I mean *everything*. And it was freezing cold. Then I worked out someone had switched the flat off, with the fuse box!' She shakes her head. 'Is there a problem – you have to tell me these things.'

I order myself to sit up. In my two T-shirts and jumper. Painfully aware I must look a total state. Bed hair everywhere. Shiny with sweat. What do I say? I still can't go near the events with Jamie, so long ago, so utterly unmentionable. And what is left? Stalling for time, I pull the jumper over my head, and off, followed by the second T-shirt. Then I come up with some fumbling answer.

'I got confused by the Assistants. The app. Think I used the app wrong, so the Assistants turned the lights on and off.'

From the end of the bed, she shakes her head, confused:

'Sorry? The Assistants?'

'They were saying things. Um. Ah. Ah. And I forgot how, uh, how to, you know, talk to them, get them to do things, because, well. Because they are confusing.'

I drawl to an embarrassing halt. It is impossible to even hint at the truth without leading her straight to the crux of the matter: the Assistants are talking to me, and tormenting me, and the whole flat feels like it is alive, and using the death of Jamie Trewin to make me think that I am mad.

Alternatively, I could tell Tabitha that I am, indeed, very possibly going crazy, as I am exhibiting symptoms of late-onset schizophrenia horribly similar to those my beloved daddy experienced when he thought the TV was ordering him around, a few years before he finally did himself in.

I wonder how my friend and flatmate would react if I said all *that*. Tabitha already looks like a concerned nurse at my bedside. Momentarily I think she is going to put her four fingers flat to my forehead, checking for fever. Like she is my mum, and I am a kid, seeking a day off school.

Tabitha hesitates, then says, 'What do you mean, you forgot how to control the Assistants? I've told you how to use the apps. Several times.'

Her voice is calm enough, but I can also detect a hint of impatience. Stern, but professional. I think it is that coat; it is so smart. Where does she buy these things?

Tabitha's body language says: WELL?

'What I mean is—' It dawns on me, belatedly, that I shouldn't say anything about the voices or the song. It makes me sound too mad. Too much like Daddy. I go on, 'When I got back from our drinks, you know, in Highgate, the lights were flickering, and then I must have done something to the heating, it was so chilly. But I was drunk and tired – and I reckon I did it wrong. I guess I'm not used to the technology yet.'

'OK,' my friend says. Thin-lipped. 'And then?'

'And then . . .' I sit up very straight: preparing my lie. I can lie quite well when called upon. I learned as a kid, when other kids would ask about my dad. Why he was so weird, or acting scary. I refused to admit he was mad. He was my daddy and I loved him and he used to be the funniest, kindest man on earth, my idol, my daddy, who told me riddles and made me giggle. How dare they say horrible things about him. So I came up with some convincing lies. And I shall do the same now. I gaze at Tabitha's impatient, expectant face.

'Well, Tabs. After all that I thought, sod it, there must be some bug, or malfunction, and I turned everything off at the fuse box.'

I look in her eyes. Blank. Stubborn. Defending myself. I will not be cowed. I love Tabitha but I won't be patronized by her. Even if I am in the wrong.

My lie – or my half-truth – seems to have done the job. She stands, wearing a softer mystified frown, then she flicks a glance at her wristwatch.

'Christ, it's nearly ten. I have to go, we're editing at the studios – those bloody frogs.' Her eyes meet mine. I see sympathy there. And confusion. And something else I don't comprehend. 'Look, sweetheart, I don't blame you or anything like that, it was a shock, that's all. The flat was so cold! Tell you what . . .' She walks from my side, over to my bedroom door, and gives me the first smile of the morning. 'Shall we have a nice supper tonight, just you and me here? Open a nice bottle of red, then I can explain again how everything works – the lights, the apps, the whole shebang. And we can gossip about Arlo's stupid Belgian banker pal. Turns out he's quite remarkably deviant. It's delicious.'

My friend is being a friend. She's being nice. Perhaps too nice?

No. What's wrong with me? Why am I mistrusting my very best friend?

'Brilliant!' I say. 'Great idea, a girls' night in. I'll cook! I'll do that fish thing, cioppino – remember?'

'Excellent,' she says. 'Make a lot, I bet I won't even have time for lunch – we'll be stuck in that studio all day – the exec producer clearly misses her time in the Gestapo.'

Pale blue eyes. Pretty smile.

Tabitha opens the door, and the smile is saying goodbye,

'See you later. Let the Assistants sort the heating and everything, I've rebooted them all. They're fine.'

And with that she sweeps out of my bedroom. Leaving her perfume.

It is the scent of my humiliation. Probably costs £5,000 an ounce. I, by contrast, smell of dried sweat and unwashed T-shirts. I hear the flat door slam. I stare at HomeHelp. The ovoid tormentor. There are no dancing lights. There is nothing. I can still feel the dreamy Xanax in my head. The sleeping pills. How many did I take? I can't recall. That's a bad sign. I must Pull Myself Together. I must be like Tabitha. Efficient, brisk, clever, smart, yet still funny and likeable. Why can't I be like her?

Yes. Enough. GET UP. Don't think about the past. GET UP.

But it is too late. As I stand up and walk into the living room. and gaze at the moistened frost on the windows, the memories finally breach, like a ferocious Christmas storm, like winter waves swamping little harbours. Jamie Trewin. Poor Jamie Trewin. It all comes back to that.

11

Jo

We were so young. Very young and very foolish. It was the second time Tabitha and I had been to Glastonbury, it was the summer we graduated: warm and sunny.

The first time we went to Glasto it rained and our feeble tent collapsed and the experience was essentially miserable. We fled the knee-deep First World War mud after one night, dragging sleeping bags smeared with dark soil into a friend's VW combi; we missed all the bands we'd come to see and didn't even get properly drunk.

So this second Glasto we were determined to have fun. The forecast was excellent. Cloudless for the whole June week. Tabitha had a load of friends and relatives going, a guaranteed crowd of good timers. We arrived early, before the fuming queues of cars began to form on the narrow Somerset lanes. The tent was expensive and solid – bought by Tabitha, naturally – one of those tents that simply *zoinks* into position when you unzip the side. There's your tent. We stuffed our rucksacks into a corner and went out to have the FUN we didn't have the first time.

We saw every band possible, we checked out the mediocre comedians, we watched three lesbians in black tie playing 'Hoppípolla' by Sigur Rós on the ukulele – it was the song of the festival, we heard it everywhere in different versions – we met a man on stilts with maracas and devil horns, a team of pantomime llamas, a dread-locked poet warbling his sonnets into a megaphone, we went to a sweat lodge and got gigglingly naked, then we bought some E and popped the pills just in time to get that slow rush of happiness, that building sensation of blissful, half amorous Love-the-World generosity, as the sun set red and symbolic and magically perfect over the sacred breast of Glastonbury Tor – ironically this was one of the times when religiously, I thought, *who knows* – then we decided to go back to our tent for some wine Tabitha had stolen from her dad's cellar, and on the way a tall white guy in purple face-paint with yellow flame-bursts at the eyes called out to Tabitha, 'Hey, Tabs!' and she turned to me and rolled her eyes and laughed, and whispered, 'He's some old family friend, I barely know him, but his dad knows my dad. Apparently he does the best pills, though, always has the best pills.' And so Tabs turned and smiled at Purple Man and said, 'Hey, Whassup?' and he came over and grinned and laughed like a loon, and then he sold us some tablets, 'Better than E,' he kept saying. 'Girls, Tabs, you guys, these are better than any pills in, like, the history of forever', and Tabitha casually handed out fifty quid for four, and then we traipsed over snogging couples and through dancing circles of teens gathered around some guitarists – 'Hoppípolla' naturally – and we made it to our tent where we simply started laughing, and laughing, and laughing, as we fumbled for the wine, dropping our torches and giggling as we sought out the corkscrew.

I don't know what was so funny. I don't remember ever being quite that happy.

Certainly not after that day.

Perhaps it was our giggling that attracted him. Or our loud raucous laughter after we discovered we didn't have any cups so Tabitha poured wine down my throat and I did the same to her. Like we were pagan, heathen, Roman. Possibly it was the force of magical bliss that brought Jamie our way. Or it was the devil, guiding him to witches.

Whatever the cause and the context, in the sweet, warm, noisy Glastonbury twilight, a handsome face peered through the flap of our tent.

'Jamie!' I said.

'Jamie Jamie Jamie!' Tabitha said. Laughing.

He was a mutual acquaintance from university. He was a New Zealander doing a year's study abroad. I liked his Kiwi accent. I liked *him*. He was properly handsome, and masculine, in a young, mop-headed way. He was easy-going and fun. We'd all got drunk at parties and danced, many times, and he was forever generously buying us drinks at the student bar. Tabs and I both fancied him, but no one had yet made a move.

And here he was. In our tent. He grinned at us. I grinned back, all E'd up and sexy. I could see the big blazing white pyramid stage beyond him. Hear the cheering. I glimpsed the sea of floodlit white arms, stripy banners, and rippling pennants, the pageantry of a hundred thousand young people all happy and singing in the dark. It felt magically ancient yet new. Like a medieval encampment on MDMA, a grand besieging army of psychedelic banners. The noise was intense; obviously some major band was playing. It could have been the Beatles reformed. We were too happy to care. *Hoppípolla!*

'Jesus,' he said. 'You girls are having a ton of fun. What are you on?'

'Rough cider,' said Tabitha, snorkelling with laughter. 'No, it's reallllllly good.'

'As if!' Jamie laughed. 'You got some E or something? You couldn't spare me a couple of pills, could you? I can't find *anyone*.'

Tabitha and I looked at each other. We giggled and grinned, and evidently had the same thought at the same time. Why not? We both liked him, he was a sweet, fun, generous guy; we were already halfway to chemical heaven, we didn't require another rush.

'Yes,' I said to her, 'go on, Tabs. We don't need them, do we? Look at us!'

I laughed, she laughed, she reached into her hippy-chick embroidered bag and handed over the lime-green pills Purple Man had given us.

'They're better than E,' she said, in a darkly conspiratorial whisper. 'Better than any E in, like, the entire history of forever. Or something. Here, you can have them for free.'

And we fell into fits of laughter. Jamie took them with a dashing smile of thanks, and then he winked.

'You girls are the best. See ya later in the trance tent?'

We vividly agreed. He left the scene. After that, the evening blurred even more – for a while, for a while. At one point we met some friends of Tabitha's and we pretended to be sheep and sheep dogs, or lions and tigers, crawling between tents, babyish with hilarity, and then we went to some big orange glowing marquee with pounding drum and bass, where we danced with bare-chested jugglers and dreadlocked guys with phosphorescent hula-hoops, and then we chilled out listening to long-haired girls with violas, and then we came across Jamie, in the trance tent as promised: wild-eyed and happy, dancing and euphoric,

'Hey, ladies!' he whooped. 'You LOVELY girls. Wanna come back to my tent? Chill out a bit? I got some great Kiwi wine,' and he grinned at us both, in that boyish but manly way. 'Tent's a whopper as well, way out by the pylons, and all my mates are with their girls. Got it to ourselves, all night.'

And that was it, the fateful moment, the fateful choice.

Remembering that choice, I look at Electra, here, on the shelves of Tabitha's flat. Silent and mute, she stands there. Dark and watching.

Judging.

Why did we agree to go back to the tent? Was it sex all along?

Whatever the reason, I said an eager 'Sure!' And then Tabs smiled a knowing smile and said, 'Yeah, why not.'

And so we traipsed through the crowds to a distant, empty corner of the campground, lonely and dark. And true enough, Jamie had a huge empty tent with a New Zealand flag flying proudly above, and some great Sauvignon Blanc inside, still cold in a thermos. And as he tremblingly, gigglingly served up the wine he stammered,

'Those pills, my fucking God. Those bloody pills you gave me, Tabs, they're the fucking best. What a buzz. I owe you!' He winked. 'Both of you!'

Wine poured, toasts made, cuddling close, it kicked off. I don't know who kissed Jamie first. I think it was me. But we certainly both kissed him, and then the kisses became *kisses,* and then he had his shirt off, and I had my top off, and the glory of his muscles shone – they glowed like rippled gold in the dim dim lamplight from somewhere distant. And then Tabitha was kissing him, and he had his hand up her dress, and I had my hand down his jeans, and I was thinking, excitedly, my first threesome, this is it, *my first threesome, never done this before, oh what a memory.* I felt I was growing up, leaving Thornton Heath behind, no one ever had a threesome in *Thornton Heath.*

And thus the night swirled and I couldn't remember who was kissing who, or whether it mattered, and Jamie had his mouth on my breast and it made me shudder, in loud pleasure, and Tabitha was giggling as he nuzzled me, and she said, 'Oops, I got to pee, before we all get *serious,*' and then she staggered out of the tent – and I turned back to Jamie.

He was coming in for another kiss, but as he did, I recoiled, in shock, nearly retching. Because there was something pouring from his mouth like wine, but I knew it wasn't wine. It was blood. It was drooling, thickly. Streaming trickles of blood. And he had no idea. Sickened, I jerked away.

And now, from nowhere, this was a different Jamie. He tilted his head, and mumbled, puzzled, choking on the blood; his words were slurring, wildly, and his eyes were acting strange, kind of rolling white, the pupils tiny, I called to Tabitha – *Tabitha! Help!* – and as I did, Jamie's head began to shake, violently, and a line of frothing pink drool ran from his mouth, mixing with the blood, and his body was jerking, up and down, up and down,

'Jamie, Jamie, what the fuck, what is it??'

'Nnn—' he said, it was all he could say – and then

he vomited, like they do in horror films, horizontally, spraying the canvas walls, and his body thrashed once, twice, wildly, spasming, 'Ffff,' he croaked, throatily, 'FFF those – those pills, aaa—'

Somehow he was up, and then he was out of the tent, running. Fast fast fast, into the dark. Towards the happy crowds, the wider campground, where the girls in tiny summer dresses were sending Chinese lanterns, sad and scarlet, into the dark.

For a second I sat there in the tent. Inert. Paralysed by confusion, and terror. Tabitha reappeared. Face white through the tent-flaps.

'What is it? Where the fuck's he gone?'

In my panic, it was all I could do to talk.

'I don't know. He said those pills we gave him. Made him ill. Oh God, Tabs! What have we done??'

We both rushed out, buttoning and zipping our clothes, heading towards the crowds. For two, five, ten or so minutes, we pushed through the mob, which was pushing against us; then we heard it, heard *them*. The police sirens, the police shouts, and then we saw the swivelling blue of ambulance lights. Coming from the direction of the main Glastonbury campground.

Everyone could sense the commotion, it rippled across the festival, like information through a hive. Lots of people were walking away from trouble, shaking their heads. Yet I wanted to push the opposite way.

'Come on,' I said to Tabs, 'we have to know.'

'No no no,' she said. 'Let's go back.'

If only I had listened; if only we had gone back. I would never have seen it. Never have known, maybe.

Yet I was determined to help. Do my bit. So I pulled her through the last of the crowd. Where it thinned to allow space for the horror beyond. I saw a vacated patch of floodlit mud and grass where police were standing around, talking into radios on their shoulders. Bright light flooded from their vehicles and the open ambulance doors. Paramedics were crouched over the young man at the centre of the scene. It was like a painting by Caravaggio. I'd been studying him at uni. The darkness and light, the vivid contrasts. There is always a central figure, around which the composition revolves. And the centre of this scene was Jamie.

Of course it was Jamie. The handsome young man. No more than twenty. The rugby-playing lad who would always buy you a beer. Oh, Jamie.

It was the way his body jerked and jolted that made me feel sick with pity – and horror. He was having some truly hideous seizures: the eyes rolling back, till they were completely white, grotesque, bulging, demonic, and his body was trembling like he was possessed, rocking sideways, then up and down, up and down. And then he vomited again, red blood and yellow puke – and the last spasm was so fierce it knocked over one of the paramedics, as the others tried to stop Jamie breaking his own spine.

As we watched, horrified, I saw Tabitha turn and look at someone else, almost hidden in the press of people. It was Purple Man. Tab's acquaintance. He didn't say a word. He just tilted his head at Jamie, slowly, and meaningfully. Then he looked, with a questioning face, at Tabitha – and she nodded. Briefly.

Purple Man put a finger to his lips and did a zipping motion. And then – glaring at us both – he made a quick throat-slitting gesture, before disappearing into the crowd.

Then Tabitha was tugging me, more frightened than ever, but I still had to see. I looked back at Jamie. He wasn't spasming any more, he was just still. Terribly still. And then the paramedics were all over him: pumping his upper body. They had those electric pads – defibrillators – on his chest: repeatedly they pressed them, urgently, desperately, until I saw one of the medics, a woman, reluctantly sit back and shake her head at a colleague.

Jamie was dead. I knew it. I knew, from Purple Man's reaction, what we had done to Jamie Trewin. Given him some pills that had killed him.

Tabitha's soft hand found mine, and this time I let her pull me, back to the tent, away from the scene. We had to escape. But I knew it was a scene I would never escape.

And, it seems, I haven't.

Sitting here in Delancey I watch a police car swing by, sirens singing in that mad childish way. Frenzied. Overdone.

'Electra, tell me about Jamie Trewin.'

'Sorry, I'm not sure.'

'Electra, how do you know what happened to me at Glastonbury Festival?'

'Sorry, I'm not sure.'

She stops. Do I detect a hint of teasing smugness in the way she suddenly goes quiet?

I retreat to my memory.

Tabitha and I returned, in the sobering darkness, to our own little tent, no longer giggling, not clowning with corkscrews, not doing anything. For a while we sat there, Tabitha sobbing into the silence, and me on the edge of tears. Perhaps I was too shocked to cry, too sad, numbed, horrified.

After ten minutes of this, Tabitha drew a big gasping breath and said,

'OK, we must never ever tell anyone. Ever.'

'What?'

She shook her head. Looked up. Eyes wide. And she grasped my shoulders, one hand firmly on each, as if pinning me down to the ground, or to reality.

'Jo, I know what happens after shit like this. The very same thing happened to my friend's brother, Hugo. He was only twenty-two, bought some pills at a rave, handed them on without even trying them. But the guy he gave them to died. Had a major overdose. The pills were, you know, unexpectedly strong.'

'But it wasn't his fault? Like it wasn't our fault?'

Tabitha's grasp on my shoulders was almost painful.

'Jamie is dead, don't you see? And when it gets that bad, it doesn't matter: there is no defence, not in the eyes of the law. Don't you get it?'

'Tell me,' I said, very quietly. 'What happened to Hugo?'

Tabitha answered with a shake of the head. 'He was convicted of manslaughter, and he went to prison. He's doing five years, Jo. It's effectively ruined his life.'

Somewhere across the field that song drifted.

'So that,' I said, my mind wandering, 'that was why Purple Man did that zipping and slitting thing? He must know this, the trouble we're all in.'

Tabitha raised her voice. The Festival was still noisy enough, all around, for us not to be overheard.

'We are *not* in any trouble – not if we keep cool, and tell no one, ever. Not anyone. Purple Man won't say anything. No one will say anything. No one saw what we did, no one saw us give the pills to Jamie, no one saw us go to his tent, there's no evidence there. It's very unlikely he told anyone where he got the pills, or named us. We will be fine. WE WILL BE FINE.' Her pale blue eyes burned into mine. 'But from this moment on we make a vow, OK? We never talk about what happened tonight. Never talk about it to friends or family or anyone. No one knows. We won't even mention it to each other. OK? As far as the rest of the world is concerned, we went to Glasto and we had some fun and smoked a bit of weed and then we went home and we know nothing about the boy that died. We know nothing. We did nothing. We saw nothing. We say nothing. Ever. Agreed?'

Her hands dropped from my shoulders. She was extending her right hand to mine. I shook her small soft hand.

'Agreed,' I said. Feeling a sense of relief because my best friend Tabitha had taken control. That private school of hers, breeding leadership and resourcefulness in its spirited girls, was doing its job.

Tabitha sighed. In a back-to-normal way. Forced, but necessary.

'God, we need to sleep. I've got a couple of Temazepam. You want?'

'Yes please,' I said meekly, and Tabitha handed me the pill and I swallowed it with horrid warm cider and then we both crept into our sleeping bags. For a moment I lay there, wondering what would happen if someone else died. Surely we should warn people? But then I realized there was no way of doing that without incriminating ourselves. We would simply have to pray that Jamie was the only victim. And stay quiet.

And from that moment, we stayed quiet. We kept our vow.

When I got back to uni I read the news reports of Jamie's death – *New Zealand Student Fatally Overdoses At Music Festival, Police Search For Suppliers, No*

Helpful Witnesses Yet – and I looked up drug deaths and the law, to see if Tabitha was right. And she was; what we had done was viewed as manslaughter. The only upside was that Jamie was the single casualty of our trafficking. But the fact we trafficked to him unwittingly, innocently, even blamelessly, would be no defence. The drugs were illegal, we gave them to someone else, he died as a result.

Manslaughter.

Average sentence: three to five years in jail. And our lives and careers ruined. Our families shamed.

After that, it wasn't hard to keep to the vow. The only time I broke that vow was when I told Simon, years ago. I kept getting nightmares – I still get nightmares – replaying the horrible sight, Jamie convulsing, and vomiting, the blood pouring from his mouth when he went to kiss me, and Si eventually asked me what was wrong, and I had to tell him, so I offloaded onto my husband. I knew he was entirely trustworthy with something like that. And he was duly sympathetic, and kept shtum; he saw it from our perspective, he'd done some drugs in his time as well. *Could have happened to anyone, babe.*

He pitied me and consoled me. In that way, he was always a good husband.

Ah, Simon.

As for Tabs, as far as I know, she hasn't told anyone. Except, *possibly,* her fiancé, Arlo: the person closest to her these last three years. Certainly, Tabitha and I have *rigidly* stuck to the precept that we should never discuss it between ourselves. It has gone completely unmentioned.

Ironically, the effect on our friendship has been positive. What happened to Jamie, at our hands, has bonded us. We've been good friends ever since, loyal and kind. I am pretty sure this is why she offered me her flat at such a ludicrously generous rent.

Yet now this luxurious, beautiful flat seems less of a bargain. I stare at the Home Assistant.

'Electra, tell me about Glastonbury.'

'Glastonbury Festival is a festival of music and other arts, held every summer near Glastonbury Tor, in Somerset.'

I wait, tensed, for the next line. 'It was the scene of a notorious death: twenty-year-old Geography student Jamie Trewin. The boy that you killed, the boy you murdered in his tent, even as you reached down his jeans, remember the eyes rolling white—'

But Electra does *not* say this. Her lights go dim. And whatever the horror of these memories, I have to get on with my life.

Have to.

12

Jo

Within an hour I am showered, coffeed, breakfasted, and staring at my laptop, forgetting myself in work. I pore over accounts of Historic Camden for my New Neighbourhood column. I learn that Dylan Thomas, the poet, lived four doors down from me in a cold greasy basement, when Camden was considered a slum. He complained about the filth and the soot from the trains in the tunnels and cuttings across the road. He lived here because it was so cheap and undesirable. Last month I noticed that a house right next door to his sold for three million. Half a lifetime's earnings.

Inheriting a house around here, or buying it in the fifties and sixties, was the property-owning equivalent of winning the lottery. Life-changing.

I will not inherit, I can never buy. I shall not win the lottery. I have worked out that on my freelancer's salary it will take me about three hundred years to save the necessary deposit to buy a small one-bedroom flat in this area. Unless I write that bloody thriller script. How hard can it be? Three acts, fifteen beats, two or three pivotal moments, plus a big twist in the middle. Then a call from LA, maybe from my brother. We love the script, here's your £500,000.

It's a dream. But it is the only dream I have.

I gaze around the beautifully furnished flat I could never afford. The flat stares back at me, like I am not meant to be here.

Enough.

'Electra, tell me the ingredients for cioppino.'

'Cioppino is a fish stew first invented by Italian immigrants in San Francisco. Specific recipes are varied, but all of them require several different kinds of seafood, such as prawns, crayfish, mussels . . .'

Electra is behaving herself. I know the recipe already, but it's good to be reminded. The herbs and spices, that delicious tomato sauce. Got it.

This is good, ish. I'm starting to feel normal. *Ish*. Arming myself in scarf and gloves, I brave the napalm blast of the winter wind arcing up Parkway, bullying people into cafes, and I step into Sainsbury's and do my shopping. Monkfish, tarragon, sourdough for dipping. Essential. The wind chases me home but as I go to cross Camden High Street I pause. Despite the cold. A message has pinged on my phone. WhatsApp.

It's from Fitz:

Hey, Jo, got news. Found some tenants at last, moving in next month. Nice couple, brilliantly boring, think he's a banker. Isn't that good? That house is so empty. They'll be able to watch over you. Drinkypoodle next week?

Something in the message makes me anxious. *Able to watch over you.* Why would he say that? And the reference to the emptiness of the house. Does he know something? Surely not. He's probably being playful, that's what he does. Maybe it's a glancing joke about my love life or something.

I reply,

> Fitz! That's good. That house can feel empty! Yes, let's have gin. Many gins! 😉 I'll be in touch?

The blue ticks appear. I keep staring at my phone, as Camden barges past me. I look at the list of WhatsApp messages, and see the name Liam Goodchild. And underneath it: nothing. Because he deleted all those messages. After that strange conversation on Jackson's Lane.

Liam Goodchild . . .

Now I am thinking about Liam. His responses seemed defensive, possibly scared, but with a hint of menace. Could it be coincidence?

Liam Goodchild. Perhaps if I know more about *him*, I will know more about what is happening to *me*.

But how? I can't sit like an idiot in my flat and happily browse away, not without letting the Assistants know exactly what I am doing, online as well as in real life. They might be in my laptop. They might be in my Google account.

No. I need Camden's very last internet cafe. Which stares at me, right across the High Street.

Phone in pocket, I hurry into the dingy internet cafe – dropping the shopping bags on either side of my swivel chair. The place is full of foreign students, most with headphones, and takeaway coffees to hand. Foreign students, I suppose, are probably the last people who need these places.

Leaning close, I shut the Google page, which automatically confronts me, and open up a different browser. Rarer. *Firefox*. Years ago, I used Firefox all the time, then went back to Google. Going back to Google made things so much easier: let one or two big tech companies run your life, and then everything in your life fits together, from your calendar to your music to your heating to your phone. You yield happily to their dominance, their intrusion, their notifications and nannying. They become parents, you become the child. Yet who knows how *deep* this goes? Who knows how far Electra and HomeHelp and the rest might colonise my internet life?

Firefox it is. Carefully, but curiously, I type in the words 'Liam Goodchild' and 'Facebook'. Because that's where we did most of our communicating.

I vividly recall Liam Goodchild's Facebook page – I visited it dozens of times. I particularly remember the photos of him running, diving, sailing. Sporty and shirtless, funny yet sexy. Not the kind of guy who might be easily frightened. Not the kind of guy who would send those weird messages, then delete.

The screen stares back at me.

Liam Goodchild has no Facebook page.

I click again. Then again. And again. I can sense the Spanish kid next to me looking over, observing my nervous gestures, my manic clicking. Who cares? No, yes, no, yes, NO. *He's not there*. I gaze, bewildered, at the unhelpful screen. There are quite a few Liam Goodchilds. Hundreds, in fact. But they are in America, Scotland, Australia, Dublin, Bristol, Croydon – not Barnet, North London, where Liam lived.

No sign of him.

Gone.

Am I doing this right? Have I made some dumb error?

I go to my own Facebook page, do another search. Again: a blank. He really *has* disappeared from FB. All traces erased, no shirtless photos, no falling cat GIFs, nothing.

OK. I take a long breath. What next? How about his Twitter account? He rarely used it, as I rarely use it; but I know he had an account because that's how he first reached me, and his username was quite memorable: @GoodChildBadChild.

Nerves jangling, I click on Twitter. Mouth dry with apprehension.

His Twitter account has disappeared as well.

There is no @GoodChildBadChild. Gone, vanished, evaporated. It's like he's died. No: it's like he has *more* than died. It is even worse than that. It's like he never existed on Twitter, just as he never existed on Facebook.

Emotions surge, though I hide them. Sitting here, as the students babble on either side, in Spanish and Somalian and Swahili, I feel the presence of a new, yet unplaceable menace: I am unpleasantly aware of the prickled hairs on my neck.

What has happened to Liam Goodchild? I clutch a few final straws.

I check Instagram: gone.

I check Snapchat: gone.

Is there anything else I can do? What about a general search? I grow careless, the pulse runs fast. Tapping hard and quick, I look for *anything* related to *Liam Goodchild*: images, snippets, news, I remember doing an Images search when we first started flirting and I remember seeing several pics of him, one from a Linked-In account, one of his Facebook photos. That dashing smile.

And now?

They are all gone too. Every single image of him. There are other Liam Goodchilds, all over the world, but no photos of *him*, my would-be seducer. The troubles double, and they triple. How can this be? How can you delete yourself, online, so completely? Isn't that impossible? And why should it happen the day after he and I had that menacing conversation?

My hand is covering my mouth: I feel panicked. Scared. Closing my eyes, I put my hands flat on the table to calm myself. Then, lifting my face from the screen, opening my eyes, I notice a young man, across the shop, staring right back at me. I am close to causing a minor scene. I must be controlled.

A scene, however modest, is not a good idea.

With a brief, fake smile at the enquiring young man – Hey, I'm fine, I'm fine – I look down and concentrate on the computer: carefully I erase my browsing history; then I stand and walk with my shopping to the till and pay for my internet usage, and step outside into the cold, turning on my phone so it doesn't look too suspicious.

To whoever is watching me.

Walking home, I weigh the thoughts. Liam was clearly drunk or frightened last night. Since then he has become *so* frightened he has erased himself from the internet.

Or someone has erased *him*. Why? I try to work out who might be frightening him, or who has the skill to delete him, if he didn't do it himself. But above all else, I want to know: what does this have to do with what he said in the messages? I cannot forget that awkward yet chilling phrase.

Somebody's done for.

13

Jo

Bags in hand, I march up Parkway, go into the flat, and set up shop in the kitchen, cooking as slowly and diligently as possible.

I like cooking, it soothes me; busy hands empty the brain. Hard as I try to work out what has happened to Liam, I cannot work out what has happened to Liam: it makes no sense. Carefully, I open a bottle of red to let it breathe, so it will be just right when Tabitha gets home.

A key slots into the door downstairs. Tabitha is back. So many hours have blurred away, without incident, as I have thought and cooked. I give my friend a wide smile, only vaguely faked, as she comes into the kitchen, brushing flakes of snow from the shoulders of that exquisite maroon coat.

'Mmmm. Smells divine. How long?'

'You're right on time, it's ready.'

'Ta-da,' she says. 'I'll lay.'

'All done. And I opened that Amarone you like.'

Her pleasure is obvious. And maybe a bit guilty.

I say, trying to be normal and sarcastic,

'Anyway, how was your day at the office, dear.'

She grabs a wineglass with the bottle, and chuckles.

'I've always wondered if we'd make a good married lesbian couple.'

'Maybe. But Arlo would insist on joining in.'

She grins, sips the wine, and leans back against a granite counter.

'Hah. That's true. He's so *absurdly* oversexed. OK, let's eat.'

Stepping into the living room and sitting at the table, I spoon out the thick, garlicky, tomatoey cioppino, rich with fish and herbs, and Tabitha devours it with suitably appreciative noises. We open a second bottle of red, and conversation ping-pongs briskly and agreeably enough: from friends, to other friends, to some gossip about Arlo, to the idea of wilderness, to whistling in pop songs, to the time she saw a bear in Colorado and was scared even though she was in a car.

'I mean,' she says, 'what was the bear gonna do? Break into my car with a credit card? Anyhow, fuck it, Josepheeeen, darling Jo-Jo, shall we have another bottle? We're nearly finished! And look, I have a *present*.'

She leans to a shopping bag, one she dumped here as she came in. She takes out a box. I know by the branding and the shape of the box what's inside. It is surely one of the latest *screen* Assistants, complete with cameras, that does everything the other Assistants do, but with a camera and a screen as well, so you can make instant face-calls, so you can *drop by* on friends, and see their face and homes, their bedrooms and kitchens, in real time. Tabs already has one of these in her bedroom. She chats with Arlo at night, face to face. Lens to lens.

The idea creeps me out. That single, indefatigable eye, perpetually observing.

Her voice mildly slurred from wine, Tabitha says,

'I had coffee this morning with Fitz, told him you were . . .' She smiles, warmly, sincerely. 'Ahhh. Maybe a bit lonely here? Anyway, he suggested this. It means you can talk to me, see my face – talk to anyone who has the same. And it shows you reminders and calendars and everything!'

I guess this explains why Fitz sent that message: he knows I am lonely. As I ponder this, Tabitha proudly unboxes the new Assistant, and plugs it in. The machine, which is mostly screen, does a deep *bong* and glows with a satisfied shimmer of linear blue light, trippling along the top.

I blurt, rude, reflexive,

'I'm not having that thing in my bedroom.'

Tabitha eyes me over her wineglass. Meanwhile, the screen Assistant glows as it watches us.

WHO or WHAT is watching us?

'That's fine,' she shrugs, her tone a little sour. I am aware I am being ungrateful, but I can't help it, given what I'm going through.

Tabitha continues, 'I thought it might be nice for you, darling? Some company. Working and writing here alone all day, must be isolating. And you don't *have* to interact with it, visually, you can carry on asking Electra questions, on the shelf, like before.'

'I'm not having it in my bedroom. It stays in here!'

My voice is loud. It earns an angry grimace from Tabitha.

'OK. OK. Like I said, that's *fine*. For God's sake, it's a *present*, Jo-Jo. I bought it for you, and us. I can talk to Arlo in here when *I* am alone.'

I glare at her. I glare at the machine with its screensaver of innocent blue sky: and this is where it all goes wrong. One bottle of red was surely enough, but we've had almost two. My fears and anxieties are surfacing into fury.

How dare they frighten me, whoever they are. I can't keep this in. It's time to offload; my best friend needs to know. Some of it. And so, in a rush, I tell Tabs all about Liam, about him abruptly disappearing off the Net. His ghosting.

I wait for her reaction: it doesn't come. She merely shrugs: unconcerned. Too annoyed with me for being ungrateful, perhaps. Instead she fiddles with the new Assistant, adjusting the brightness, and as she does she speaks, so blithely,

'Can't blame him,' she says, 'I'd quite like to disappear sometimes, all this online shit, it uses up too much time. How clever of him to vanish.'

'Clever?'

'Yes, all that Facebook stuff, it's so intrusive, yet useless. And Twitter is a ghastly pub where everyone fights. Yuk.'

She shrugs, in her bored, yet drunken way. I bridle at her blasé hypocrisy.

'Let me get this right, Tabs. You say you hate the internet, and yet' – I gesture at the new screen thing, then Electra on the shelf – 'you have all this tech. The Assistants. Your flat is basically *run* by the internet. How the hell does that add up?'

We are close to full-on bickering.

'That's different,' she says, her pout turning into a scowl. 'I said I hate social media, not the internet itself.'

'Right.'

Another scowl.

'Yes. *Right*. And what is it to you anyway, Jo? I like all the technology. It's brilliant, and it's fun. You need to . . .' She looks like she is poised to say something truly insulting, 'Sharpen up, Jo. Get on trend. I'll teach you. A frigging five-year-old could work Electra! God knows what you did the other night.'

'I didn't do anything—' I *so* want to snap back, to insult her. Rich and privileged, Tabs can be a total bitch. Unaware of her luck. That bloody coat which would cost me a month's wages. But I can't be rude. She is my best friend. And I simply can't afford to fall out with her badly, because then I'd have to move, and I can't afford to move, and I don't want to move, I love this location.

Or at least I did.

The anger prickles. 'Look, I'm sorry, Tabs, but why do you need all this Electra crap? A bloody butler in a box. A camera always watching. Why not turn the heating up like a normal person? With a thermostat. You don't need these electric servants—'

Tabitha sullenly pours wine into her glass, then slams the bottle back on the table.

'You do realize you are insulting not just me, but Arlo too? He bought all of this other tech, *as an engagement present*. And you waltz in and unplug it all, like some total madwoman!' Our eyes meet, hers are glittering and narrowed, I'm sure my eyes are the same; we are close to a blazing row, she knows all about my much-loved, much-missed father, she knows what calling me mad must do to me. 'Why don't you grow up and get with the world, Jo. I love having you here but you can't go round changing *my* flat the way *you* want. Besides. The Assistants. They're a security system, linked to Arlo. Please don't turn them off.'

I finish my own wine. Shocked.

'What?'

She gestures. A pale hand pointing from a cashmere sleeve.

'I used to live here alone, and Arlo got worried – you know he thinks Camden is positively *lawless* – so he ensured that my home tech is all linked to his. He got Simon to do it: he can make sure I am safe, listen in, watch over me from my bedroom. Now he can watch over you, too. But that's why it's so important it stays on, to keep us safe.'

I am not sure I quite get this. The implications are so grotesque.

'You mean,' I try to control the tremor in my voice. 'You mean Arlo can listen to this flat through the Assistants, all the time. He can actually spy on me from these cameras. Does he watch me take a fucking pee?'

'Oh puh-lease. Don't be ridiculous. He hasn't got a massive linked camera system in here like some voyeur, Jo, it simply means that, yes, he can sometimes check who is in the flat, by seeing what HomeHelp and Electra and the rest are doing, security breaches and such.' Another airy gesture, as if *designed* to annoy me. 'He rang me today to ask why they were all turned off last night. You see, that's how it works, he can make sure we're safe. He knows what is going on, but he can only watch, live, if you give him permission.'

I throw my napkin to the floor.

'And you're OK with that? You don't find that controlling? He's observing us, from a distance, all the time. Jesus. It's Too Fucking Weird.'

'Calm down—'

'No! Tabitha. Think about it!'

We stare at each other. She wipes her lips, looks down

at the table, looks up at me – and pauses. For a moment it feels like our entire friendship hangs in the balance. Then her expression changes.

'OK. Look. Please . . . I'm *sorry*.' She tries a weak, apologetic smile. 'I am sorry. I was snippy.'

I can see, from her face, despite my drunken state, that she is genuinely trying to make peace. We have been the best of friends for years. Sometimes when she's drunk she's told me she loves me, and I've told her right back. We both hate our occasional rows. And this is – or was – potentially a very bad one.

'Jo. I'm sorry! I get it. And I guess it does sound a bit . . . Orwellian, if you're not used to this technology, and obviously you're not.'

She reaches a hand across the table. Squeezes mine.

'I'm truly sorry.'

I pause. I look at her white hand, squeezing mine. I say,

'Is Arlo listening now? Even watching? Perhaps he'd like to see us kissing, shall we pretend we're copping off?'

It's a lame attempt at a joke, but it seems to work. She laughs, slurrily, and says,

'No, he's out with his Belgian pervert friend. And anyway it doesn't work like that, he's not actually sitting in some silent room with headphones and CCTV, he only sees the interactions, the behaviour of the Assistants, he can video-call me without pressing buttons, drop by, use the screen in my bedroom, that sort of thing. And check on security, keep us safe!' She sighs, and looks at her wine. 'We had too much, didn't we? Sorry.'

'We always have too much. It's why we're friends.'

Our eyes meet, the anger has gone. I suspect we are

both thinking about Jamie Trewin. Who definitely had too much.

Whatever thought we are sharing, or not sharing, it has dispelled the anger.

'Hey-la,' says Tabitha, 'it's nearly midnight. Let me clear up the mess. You go to bed, you look tired.'

I do not demur. I am tired.

Thankful for the warmth, and the comforting presence of Tabitha – despite our little spat – I creep into bed, ask HomeHelp to turn out the lights. Then, in the darkness and quiet, with nothing but the faint sound of Tabitha filling the dishwasher and clearing the kitchen, I turn over and prepare for sleep.

It does not come. I don't want to take any sleeping pills. I feel genuinely tired. I haven't done any coffee to mess with my sleep pattern. Nonetheless, sleep will not come. Perhaps it is anxiety. I've just realized the implication of what Tabitha has said. Even if I want to, I cannot turn off the technology, unplug the Assistants. Arlo will know, and he will tell Tabitha to throw me out, and after that row, I cannot be sure she will disobey him.

Turning my pillow over, I gaze through the gloom at the 3D oval of HomeHelp. The egg which is now firmly implanted: in me.

14

Jo

My mind churns, I try to stop it. I don't want to think about the Assistants. Not tonight.

Turning over, I stare at the dim ceiling and consider how many other people have lain flat on their backs in this two-hundred-year-old room. How many have lived and loved and laughed and died, right here.

Dozens, maybe. And dozens will come after, perhaps. Perhaps my own children will sleep here – yet probably not. I don't believe I will ever want kids, whether it is because of my dad's heritable disease, or a genuine lack of maternal instinct: I do not know. I just don't go gooey over tiny Converse boots like some friends of mine. They can melt like marshmallows at the mere sight of miniature clothes. Kids under four bore me. Why does this shock people?

The thought of children, and my childlessness, reminds me of some of the personal yet peculiar phrases used by Electra and HomeHelp the other day.

Cold as snow breath, it tamps the womb . . .
Unloosing their moons, month after month, to no
   purpose . . .
Perfection is terrible. IT CANNOT HAVE
   CHILDREN . . .

The implication of these statements was and is clear. The machines were apparently commenting on, or taunting me about, my choice not to be a mother. To unloose my moons, to no purpose, for month after month. That choice which made Simon so unhappy.

Yet these phrases are so odd, the syntax, vocabulary and grammar so distinct. Did the machines invent these lines, or steal them?

In the dark I reach for my bedside smartphone, and lie back. A tap brings me a quicker answer. Most of these lines seem to come from a poem, 'The Munich Mannequins', by an American writer. Sylvia Plath. I have heard of her, but I don't know much about her. I've never been interested in poetry. Always found it too depressing. Or boring. I preferred the drama and grandeur of art, hence History of Art at King's. I only ended up a journalist because learning History of Art, it turns out, is utterly pointless unless you want to teach History of Art to people who will go on to teach History of Art.

So who *exactly* was Sylvia Plath?

I do a quick Wiki: **Sylvia Plath** (October 27, 1932 – February 11, 1963) was an American poet, novelist, and short-story writer . . .

There's lots more. She's obviously quite famous – to some. She married an equally well-known British poet, Ted Hughes. I've heard of him, too, though I know little about him. In the gloom of my bedroom, I wonder if I saw a movie about the two of them years ago, with a tragic ending? Yes, I believe I did. But what was that ending?

I find a webpage dedicated to her life, and her work, and that ending. And what I read brings a chill that stings like needles.

In 1962 Sylvia Plath separated from Ted Hughes. She then moved back to London, with her children.

As Christmas came and went, the snow began falling. Alone with her kids, Plath was facing the terrible winter of 1963. Insomniac, and isolated, she was diagnosed as depressed; her doctors also considered her a suicide risk. Daily visits were arranged.

On the morning of 11 February, the nurse arrived, as usual, to help Plath with the care of her children. When she knocked, no one answered the door. Nor could she see any signs of life inside. Eventually the nurse broke in.

In the downstairs kitchen she found Plath, lying on the floor with her head resting on a little towel, by the open gas oven. She was dead. Running upstairs, the nurse was at first unable to open the door to the children's bedroom, because Plath had put tape and towels around the door, to prevent the gas reaching the children. The children were alive, but awake and confused. Plath, it turned out, had placed glasses of milk and plates of bread on bedside tables for her two kids – something to eat when they woke up. The nurse deduced that it must have been Plath's final act, before she went downstairs to the kitchen. And opened the gas oven. And turned on the gas.

Plath was thirty years old.

I look away from the screen, feeling faintly sick, and horribly sad. I may have no maternal instinct, but I have a loving instinct. Children, little children. How could you simultaneously take such loving care, providing bread and milk for your son and daughter, then go downstairs and deprive them of a mother?

And there is more. The webpage gives Plath's final address. The house where she killed herself.

It is 23 Fitzroy Road, Primrose Hill, NW3.

It is about three streets, and three minutes' walk, from where I am lying in my bed, tonight.

15

Jo

Sleep is impossible now. Throwing off the duvet, I go to the cold window and open the curtain. A soft snow is falling, all over Camden. Therefore it is also falling on the roof of the house where Sylvia Plath killed herself. A few hundred metres away. During a long hard winter, just like this winter.

I recall that woman with the little kids, the woman who was struggling with the snow. Her back to me. If Plath had ever walked to Camden High Street, from Primrose Hill, in that terrible winter, she would have walked past Delancey Street, past my house. Dragging her two little kids. Hunched with loneliness, thinking of suicide.

What did I see that evening, just before Electra first spoke to me, in her special way?

These thoughts edge close to madness. I must sleep them away. Hauling myself across the bedroom I reach for my Xanax canister. Three, four, five, I don't care. Give me sleep. Give me dreamless, endless sleep. Sleep to the end of the world.

Back in bed, I wait for the Xanax to kick in. My mind is roiled.

If I am mad, like my father, I am doomed. But if I am not mad, there is someone out there doing this. Someone real.

But who resents me enough to scare me this much? Liam, perhaps, if he exists. Otherwise one of the tech people I might have affronted with my article: Arlo Scudamore, or Gul Foxton, or Jenny Lansman? Yet how many of them know about Jamie Trewin? What about Fitz? Advising Tabitha to get another Assistant, to freak me out even more? Why would Fitz want revenge? Yet he *does* own the flat below. Which will soon be filled, with people to Watch Over Me.

The obvious candidate, I suppose, is Simon, who installed all this tech, *and* who probably has the knowledge to turn it against me – unlike Arlo, say, or Fitz. Yet I cannot believe it is *entirely* down to him: there is a deep friendship between us, still. And he's not, I reckon, the kind of guy to turn on me so viciously.

But what if he is being forced, or manipulated, by someone else? I think I know who it might be: I remember a lunch Simon and I once had, about a year after our divorce. At the end of the meal, Simon drunkenly admitted how much she resented me, how much she *hated* me: his supposedly pleasant, nice, sweet, maternal new wife, with her elfin bob, and her gorgeous new baby.

16

Polly

'Doesn't it ever freak you out, having a baby in a flat like this?'

'Pardon?' said Polly, turning to Anna.

Anna dipped her chunk of carrot in the little pot of creamy tzatziki that Polly was offering, thus making an iridescent glob of fat at the end of her carrot stick. She ate it, crunching loudly, still talking, looking down on Old Street and Silicon Roundabout, a dizzying whorl of maddened car lights.

'I mean, balconies, all the risks – not that I think anything would happen—'

Simon came over, perhaps sensing the slight tension,

'We're not complaining, the windows are secure, and the balconies impossible to climb over. And anyway it's key worker housing in EC1! Without this, we'd probably be living with my folks down south—'

Polly looked at him. 'And you'd probably have killed your dad with a dessert spoon.'

Anna smiled, and shrugged. And munched more carrot

sticks, in that slightly irritating way. She probably earned three times Polly's salary, or five times, everyone in here earned multiples of Polly's salary, and they likely found the budget supermarket hummus quite disgusting, and everyone was doing their not-very-best to hide it.

This drinks party had been Simon's idea, a kind of belated housewarming, but *she'd* had to do all the organizing, rushing from her shift at UC Hospital to the childminder's, before hurrying to the nearest cheap supermarket to buy dips, canapes, and discount prosecco. Then Simon breezed home, and acted the host, and Polly was left to serve food and pour wine even as she looked after the baby and handed out over-charred padrone peppers. She had been the one that over-charred them. The irritation irked: she had to remind herself Simon often worked much longer hours than her.

A piercing animal yowl interrupted the chatter. Polly and Simon looked at each other. She sighed, dramatically.

'I'll go. My turn.'

Polly knew she was overdoing it, martyring herself as the put-upon young mother, when in truth she *wanted* to escape the little drinks party because she was no good with these techy people. Aaron was OK, Gul from Apple was funny. But most of them were too intense: with their bright-eyed New Age techno talk of Augmented Reality and cryptographic hashes and Godknowswhat. They were like people speaking in tongues, and Polly sometimes felt like interrupting their otherworldly gibberish with the casual anecdote from *her* day in University College Hospital: oh yes, some guy came into the ward today, and puked up a chunk of lung and he died right in front of me.

Yeah. That was *my* day.

Polly gently pushed the door to little Grace's hushed,

darkened room. The baby had stopped her six-month-old screaming but was doing that distinctive whimpering. This usually meant Grace was hungry.

Polly felt a wave of guilty relief. She had to feed the baby, so she was officially excused Drinks Duties for as long as needed. Picking up Grace, inhaling her tiny daughter's perfume, the mother slumped into the nursing chair, and unbuttoned her shirt.

Grace's gaping mouth found her mother's less sensitive nipple. The left one. She began feeding. Serenity descended. The room was beautifully dark, and sound-proofed. As Grace suckled, Polly listened, above the noise of her baby daughter nursing, to the traffic outside, down there in the streets; it was so muffled it was like the sound of someone lightly snoring, three doors along a corridor. Through the big windows she could see the mighty new towers of East London and Canary Wharf, glittering in the cold: so many huge, black stone obelisks studded with millions of diamond lights.

Grace gripped at her mother' breast with a miniature hand. Polly lifted the hand, and kissed the tiny, soft, velvety fingertips. As she did, inexplicable tears filled her maternal eyes. This often happened, she noticed, when she was alone with her baby. It was a strange mixture of depression and elation. Both together. It was all so unexpectedly painful, like suckling itself.

The feeding was nearly done. Grace was asleep at the breast. Yet Polly sat, alone, in the blessed quiet, for another hour. Letting her baby sleep. Thinking nothing. Until the guilt at avoiding the party got too much, and she placed her precious daughter carefully back in the crib and folded the little blanket *just so*, and reluctantly returned to light and music and people in the twelfth-floor living room.

Most of the guests were gone. The handful that were left seemed to be talking – pretty loudly – almost arguing – about Simon's ex. Jo Ferguson. And that notorious and celebrated article she did on tech giant companies and their overweening power. Or not. Or whatever.

Polly had tried her best not to resent Jo Ferguson, she'd tried not to hate her, but it was difficult. Yes, she'd known that she was marrying Simon Todd on the rebound from his relationship with witty, sexy, bouncily redheaded Jo Ferguson, but she hadn't expected Jo to be so *present* in their lives, even now.

Bloody Jo Ferguson, her husband's fetching school-yard sweetheart, his first love, his true love, his great love: the love that wouldn't go away. Whatever Polly did, loving Simon, loyally, making a home for him, giving Simon the child he wanted: that wasn't enough?

Collecting glasses, Polly transported them to the kitchen, trying to pretend she wasn't eavesdropping.

'Well, I thought it was very witty, and her critique about privacy was spot on, looking back—'

That was Gul. Funny, sarcastic Gul Foxton. He'd made friends with Jo when she was writing the article, and he was often defending her. And perhaps he was right to defend her. Polly didn't especially care about the intricacies of this debate, she just felt insulted. Couldn't they all talk about something else? Didn't Simon's friends realize how rude this was, discussing his ex in front of his new wife?

'But the Facebook privacy stuff was obvious, even then—'

'Didn't Arlo nearly lose his job at FB? Bet he was super chuffed – not a man you need as an enemy, Arlo Scudamore.'

'Arlo is a bloody dickhead.'

That was Jenny. Gul came back:

'Yes, but rather an *important* dick, anyway, Simon, have you got something other than this prosecco? It tastes like champagne for two-year-olds.'

Again that was typical of Gul – never frightened to offend. He was sometimes ridiculously blunt and he didn't care. He was what he was. Polly, in turn, quite liked Gul.

'Are you OK, darling? How's Grace?'

Simon was at her side, ferrying glasses into the kitchen.

'She was hungry so I fed her. She's fine. All fine. Party gone OK?'

Simon nodded, and smiled, and crossed the room – to say goodbye to some of the last guests. They were donning coats, ordering Ubers.

'Hey, Pol! I've been saving you some of the nicest nibbles, before us nerds ate them all.'

She turned; it was the friendly, round face of Jenny Lansman, peering at her over a plate. Polly looked at the plate, and sighed.

'There weren't any nice nibbles, I bought them at Lidl.'

Jenny laughed.

'Aw, they're not *that* bad. Come on, sit down, eat something. Everyone's gone.'

Happy to yield, Polly sat at the kitchen table, and ate. Jenny sat beside her.

'So! Tell me?'

'Sorry?'

'Don't be *daft*. I want to know what being a mother is like. I haven't seen you since you had Grace, right? Tell me!'

It was the first time someone at the party had shown an active interest in Polly – Polly as a person and mother, rather than as Simon's girlfriend, that tired looking woman, the nurse who lived here and handed out cheap wine.

Swigging from a glass of white, Polly felt a need to share. Why not? As they finished off the canapes, Polly told Jenny the truth: all the bad stuff: the darkness and gloomy moods, the sleeplessness, the cracked nipples, the endless nappies. And the infinite, lonely tedium.

'No one warns you quite how boring it will be,' she said, as Jenny nodded sympathetically, and scoffed a tiny sausage roll, and asked,

'Yes, but, being a mother, in itself, what is *that* like?'

Polly looked through the kitchen doorway. Only a couple of guests remained.

What was being a mother like?

It was the big question. Turning to Jenny, she answered,

'Having a baby is the worst thing I ever did. It is painful, relentless, depressing, isolating, and incredibly tiring.' A pause. 'It is also the best thing I ever did. I don't know how, but it is.'

Jenny frowned, and nodded. 'I would like a kid. If only I could find the right man. Maybe I'm too picky?' Pausing, she laughed at herself. 'That said, I've already picked a few.'

They chatted for a few more minutes; then Jenny was up, in her coat – and gone. Only Simon was left, stacking the plates and binning the waste, talking to her.

'Well, that wasn't too bad was it, babe? I know you hate all this tech talk.' He put a hand on her weary shoulder. 'Go on, you go to bed.'

Polly nodded, gratefully. She headed for their bedroom, where she stripped into a cosy T-shirt, and slipped under the duvet, talking to her HomeHelp.

'OK, HomeHelp, set an alarm for seven fifteen a.m.'

The quadrille of lights did their dance. Polly settled to sleep immediately, the last sensation was the coolness of her pillow . . . And then she jolted awake. Sensing something wrong. Her little LED clock said 2.45 a.m. She'd slept hard and dreamlessly for two hours. So why had she woken? Was the baby crying? Polly was so attuned to feeding times, she often woke before the baby even screamed. Like there was a telepathy.

The baby was not crying. She was not due to be fed. When Polly turned over to seek the comfort of her sleeping husband, she realized he was not there. At 2.45 a.m.?

Padding to the door, Polly pulled it open. The only sign of activity was a bar of burning light at the bottom of the closed door that led to the spare room.

What was he doing in there, in the depths of night?

A grey suspicion filled her as she approached. Without knocking, she subtly pushed the door open. There he was, with headphones on. Talking to someone?

He was hunched intently over a laptop that glowed white and blue on his face. What was he looking at? A news site?

She edged closer. He was entirely oblivious to her presence, concentrating on the screen, yet obscuring her view of it. His headphones were blocking out the sound of his wife.

Reaching out, she wrenched the headphones from his head. He turned, alarmed, yet blushing.

'What the heck – Jesus, Polly, you scared me—'

She listened to the headphones. It was music. But what was he doing on the computer, this intensely, at 3 a.m.? She got a glimpse of a human body on the screen: even as he quickly pressed a key, closing a tab.

'Stop!' she said. 'Don't touch a thing, don't close any tabs, I need to see. What's keeping you up at three a.m.'

'Why?'

'Let me see!'

Something in her voice made him surrender. Cold but shivering, in her knickers and T-shirt, Polly leaned close and went through the tabs.

Porn. He was looking at porn. Videos on Xhamster and Alohatube. It was the standard stuff: lesbians, all glammed up and fake-breasted in that Californian way, and here were some Japanese MILFs. Polly didn't care about this, sometimes she actually watched porn with Simon. She quite liked the gentle kind of lesbian porn, pretty girls in summer dresses, seducing each other.

But, ah. What was *this*? Polly felt the anger rise, as she went through the tabs. This was why he was doing it so furtively: before he'd turned to professional porn he'd been looking at pictures of Jo.

Lots of naked pictures of Jo. Bloody Jo Ferguson. Here was Jo in bed, with her svelte figure, no stretch marks from babies, a hint of a tan. And here was Jo delicately touching herself, the face half turned, half smiling, at Simon.

'My God,' Polly snapped. 'That's *great*. That's really really reassuring. Thank you so much. You're actually wanking over your ex? *Again*?'

'Wait—'

'Why, Simon? Why do this?' The hurt was genuine, a tremor of tears. 'You do realize you're married with a baby, Simon? That you have a new wife?'

Polly wanted to stop looking, yet she couldn't help herself.

'You bastard.'

'It's only photos!' he said, pathetically. 'Photos, that's

all. I look at all kinds of things, you know that. I like porn, I look at you as well, sometimes—'

He stammered to a halt. Clearly realizing this wasn't helping.

Polly clicked on the browsing history, seeking the last tab. And then she felt something beyond dismay, and beyond jealousy.

It was a photo of Liam Goodchild. The man that had that online flirtation with Jo, that emotional infidelity, months of sexts, that led to Simon leaving her. Why was Simon looking at him? This attractive man, dark hair falling to his shoulders. She could see why Jo had fancied him, but why would it matter to Simon *now*?

Polly's anger and bewilderment was too much. She raised her voice.

'I don't get it. Do you know him? Are you friends? What the hell is going on?'

His shrug was helpless; Polly felt like slapping him.

'Tell me, what's the point? You left her because of him, and you're with me, and yet you're looking at his photos. Are you in touch with him?'

Again, all he could do was blush, and mumble a bunch of *sorrys* which meant nothing. And anything. Polly's mind was awash with possibilities. Was Simon involved somehow with this Liam guy, did he encourage him to test his wife? He was the jealous type. Her husband with his strange, secretive IT job, which he would never properly explain.

Another, harsher noise intruded.

'Oh Jesus Christ!' said Polly. 'That's all I need.'

Woken by the disturbance, little Grace was howling. Simon said a guilty sorry, then went to the kitchen, presumably for a bottle of breast milk.

Doing his fatherly duty.

Polly watched him disappear. Then she gazed, helpless and angry, at that spectacular view beyond the windows. It was 3 a.m. in Shoreditch and still the traffic of Old Street burned beneath them, a river of diamanté and rubies, flowing in black canyons, all through the night. Like the whole city was becoming a malignant machine, beyond human control.

Grace was still screaming.

17

Jo

The screaming is endless. The convulsions ripple through him, somehow in rhythm with his howls of pain. The eyes roll upwards, small blank white alabaster eggs, hands rigid and clutching. And all the bright light of torches and headlamps shine down on Jamie Trewin's spasming body. A strange pink froth dribbles down the side of his face, as if he has been sucking lurid sweets.

'Come on,' says Tabitha, urgent and low and tugging at my cold, sweating hand. 'Come on, let's go to the tent, we're in the way,'

Even in the darkness I can see the real intent in Tabitha's desperate gaze: *For God's sake, let's get out of here, we did this, we're involved, you saw Purple Man . . .*

And yet, I resist. I have an urge, a terrible, honest, self-harming, audacious urge: to run over, push through the last of the agitated crowd, go up to the police and confess it all: We gave him the drugs. It was us. Arrest me.

'Look!' says Tabitha. 'Jo!'

I don't need to be told. Something strange is happening. The paramedics are backing away from Jamie, a policeman is shouting—

'Get away – all of you – get back—'

Jamie, I see, has somehow hauled himself to his feet. Next to the female paramedics he looks so tall, six foot three.

'Take him down!'

One of the policemen tries to grab him, another leans in to help, but Jamie casually throws them off, as if he is a cartoon monster, like they are kids and he is the only adult. And he is marching straight towards me. How can he know which way to go? He is surely blinded, the eyes are blank and white. Yet he seems to know, because his sightless eyes are fixed on me, as he sprints towards me.

'Run!' yells Tabitha. But it is too late. Jamie has me by the neck, his big hard hands are on my throat; with a terrible ease he slams me back on to the cold wet ground, then kneels painfully on my chest. Trying to throttle me to death. I can see the blood whirling in my eyes, even as things turn to black. Even as I feel his spittle on my face, cold and hot and wet and I look up and Daddy's fingers are even tighter around my neck, he is laughing as he chokes me, he isn't the Ticklemonster any more: he wants to hurt me, kill me, and my brother is screaming Mummy Mummy Mummy, Daddy is killing Jo, MUMMY!

Daddy!

And

Blackness. Greyness. Awake.

I wake up, finally, with a terrible, dry-mouthed gasp. I am lying here. Quite rigid. In the dark. A mannequin laid on the floor. Where am I? Delancey? Yes. I am at home, in my bedroom. On Delancey Street. And the spittle in the dream was the tears on my face, because I have been sobbing in my sleep.

It's only a dream. Another dream about Jamie. I often have them, they are always awful. I sometimes dream that he attacks me, sometimes I dream that he rapes me. And sometimes, like this time, he turns into my father, sometimes Jamie even becomes Dad that day he died. Jamie in Glastonbury becomes Daddy in his deathbed. Rushed to hospital from the car. Where he gassed himself, like that poetess down the road.

Those are the worst dreams of all.

But this is new: the crying. I have never cried during my sleep before. For several moments, I lie here. Staring at the faint outline of an icy grey-black night surrounding the blue bedroom curtains.

The clock says 3.30 a.m. The very depths of the night, like a trench in the ocean, where the last light glimmers into nothing, and strange ugly life-forms emerge from the black.

My tears dried, I lean across and switch on a bedside lamp. I need a book. Any book. Here. This will do.

The Art of the Script. It's written by some famous Hollywood scriptwriter who actually won an Oscar, and it inevitably promises to tell me All the Secrets to Writing Your Own Hollywood Hit.

The book falls open on a page of dense text and it swims before my eyes. Then I remember I have all these books on Audible. Dropping the book I switch off the light and say,

'OK, HomeHelp, read to me from page twenty-seven of *Art of the Script*.'

Her lights twirl. She answers:

'OK, starting at page twenty-seven of *Art of the Script*.

126

"When writing a script, always keep to hand this one-page structure. Beneath each heading, write one or two lines of your own ideas. Then, under Opening Image, which is your first five or ten pages, jot down some themes and locations. A woman on a boat, alone, or perhaps a detective in the snow, looking for a trail of blood. Do this for all your fifteen beats. Keep it by your laptop at all times . . ."'

The voice drones on, but not unpleasantly. It is soothing. Perhaps it is that easy: fifteen sentences, on a single page, and you have your blueprint?

I am alone in the flat, Tabitha is staying with Arlo. The Assistants are behaving, doing what they were meant to do. Could be I exaggerated it all. I do get bad dreams, I am sometimes a bit anxious, I probably take too many pills to help me sleep: they can unbalance the brain a bit. That's all? Yes, that's all it is. I am not going mad, everything will be fine. Liam has some woman and has decided to disappear, warning me off, maybe as a punishment for ghosting on him. The dying night is heavy on my eyes. Six a.m. Three hours have passed. I don't know why, but three hours is a cycle in my brain, if I wake from a nightmare at two or three or five, I know that if I stay awake for three hours, I will fall peacefully asleep again, probably, hopefully, without the assistance of Alprazolam. It helps that I am freelance. I don't have to rise at eight.

Telling HomeHelp to stop reading from the book, I close my eyes. Quickly, sleep embraces, clasps me, a welcome succubus, like the comforting weight of a man on top, like Simon when we were young and we were sort of in love, I liked him simply lying on me.

My thought slows. My brain nods heavily towards oblivion.

A soft, repetitive jingle stirs me. My first clear notion is: the Assistants. They must be making this noise.

I look through the gloom at HomeHelp. Nothing. No spinny lights. No noise. Silent.

As sleep ebbs away, I realize that I actively recognize the jingle. It is the very recognizable sound of a Skype call. And it must be coming from my laptop, in the living room. My bedroom door is halfway open and I can just see the bright, distant screen, on the faraway table.

Skype call.

The flat is cool, but not freezing, as I wrap myself in my dressing gown. The heating must have come on in the night. I am grateful for the residual warmth as I pace, barefoot, down the landing, switching on a light or two. The Skype jingle ends. I missed it. But I want to know. Who would be calling me at this time? As I sit down at the laptop, yawning fiercely, I glance at the clock on the screen: 6.20 a.m. Dawn is still distant, on this midwinter day. Frost is icy lace on the windows; the first commuters, truck drivers, delivery vans, are racing the lights on Delancey, moving grey shapes in swirly cold mist.

The Skype jingle starts over. I don't recognize the number. It's long. International. One of those mad numbers. Redirected from Namibia or Singapore.

Ah, I think: *my brother*. He's probably off his head in LA. Sometimes he rings at lunatic hours, forgetting the time difference, or misjudging it.

I press the button, and accept the call, expecting my brother's still-handsome face to appear. In his bright big southern California apartment. Will it be enviably warm and sunny there? Will I get to see my beloved nephew, with his plastic dinosaurs? What time is it in LA?

A figure emerges, from a blur, on the screen.

My chest is tight with obscure anxiety. The figure is just a figure. A darkness. A silhouette. A shape of someone. It looks like a woman. Long hair, slender shoulders. But the face is black, in deepest shadow. All I can see is the outline.

'Hello,' I say. 'Who is this? Who are you?'

Silence.

'You do realize it's six in the morning. Is this some random wrong number?'

The figure says nothing. It does not move. She does not move.

'Hello? Look, if this is a crank call just go away. I'm blocking this number.'

'Hello, Jo. It's Jo. I'm you.'

The air in the room is still and cooling. I say nothing. My mouth opens. Closes. Trembling lips. I am so bewildered and horrified, I reel back. Physically.

I am that person. I am this person.

'Hello, Jo, say hello to yourself.'

My mind blows fuses. She's right. It is me. This person, this figure, this shadow, this thing is speaking in my voice, to me.

18

Jo

The voice goes on. *My* voice goes on.

'Don't be scared, Jo, it's only you, calling yourself. That's how I got your number, Jo. I know your number because it is my number. I am you. This is you. I am you talking to you. I know how cold it is there, because I am you. I know how scared you are, because I am you.'

The figure is almost motionless, yet not quite. Like it really is speaking, even if the features, the entire face and body, are concealed with shadows. The head moves in time with the words, this feels real. But it cannot be.

Terror tilts me, this way, that way. I force myself to regard the screen.

'Who is this? How did you record my voice?'

I know someone is *doing* this. It has to be Simon, egged on by Polly? He has the knowledge. Of the tech. He installed most of it. But still I am terrified. Because, whatever they are doing, it is working. My voice speaks again, to me.

'No one recorded your voice, Jo. I am you, I thought you'd like to speak to yourself, you mumble to yourself anyway, these days, I've noticed me doing that, lately. Liam certainly scared you, didn't he? You should be scared. Of Liam.'

'You're linked to the Assistants, aren't you?'

The figure laughs. With vivid fear, I realize this is definitely *my* laugh. My drunken, sarcastic laugh. How could anyone record that, and use it at the right moment? How would they – Simon, Arlo, Fitz, the whole of Facebook, whoever it is – program a computer, with my words, to have a spontaneous conversation? The ghastly possibility enfolds me: this really is me, talking to me, and therefore I am going mad.

No. *No.* I shout:

'Please stop this.'

A lorry thunders past the house, rattling panes, its headlights like torch beams in the winter fog, madly seeking something lost, running to save someone. Save me. Save *me*. I want to scream it out loud. Yet in there, in the window of the laptop screen, I have stopped laughing.

I am speaking, from the screen, from my own mind, or from some computer code.

'You think you're going mad. You're not going mad, Jo. I know this because I'm you, Jo. I know what you ate yesterday morning, because I am you.'

'Stop . . .'

'Ah, Jo. Why should I take orders from me, because I don't know what I want, do I? I'm all afraid and confused? Poor Jo. *Poor little Jo-Jo with our crazy dad.* Ach, du.' The laughter again. My very own South London cackle. Sardonic, sharp, I've always had a distinctive laugh, I quite like it, people like to mimic it, to tease me, and I don't mind, but this is me, on a screen, laughing at me, in the pre-dawn darkness of another murky, polluted, freezing-point London morning, and I am shivering in my dressing gown, listening to myself laugh at myself. And then the laughter stops.

And as soon as it does, the soft voice starts.

I lean towards the screen, getting ready to turn it off. I've had enough. But the voice intervenes. I am stopping myself.

'Oh no, Jo. Don't do that. Remember what Tabitha said, you mustn't turn anything off, or Arlo will know. Then you'll have to live somewhere else, and we don't have any money, do we? You have to listen to yourself. And if you don't you will go to the police. I have all the evidence, of what happened to Jamie Trewin. You want to go to jail? No. I thought not. So listen close, Jo. This is only the beginning. Because you know what you did to Jamie. It was all your fault. Don't blame our poor daddy, don't blame the madness, that's all so weak, so lame, blaming the parent. No no no. We're stronger than that. We're going to do something better. We're going to do something braver, be *like* Daddy.' The figure on-screen leans in, I catch a glimpse of light on hair, is that my hair? I think it is, but my senses are so taut, I could be seeing anything. 'Jo, here's the deal: in a few weeks, maybe sooner, you are going to kill yourself. That's what you've decided, you don't realize yet. But you will do it soon, or I will do it for you, one way or another. You will die. Maybe you can get in your car like Daddy and do it that way? OK? OK? I've got to go. Speak soon.'

The Skype call ends and the screen flashes away.

I stare at the screen saver. A picture of Regent's Park, all white with snow. From a month ago. I thought it

132

was pretty at the time. Now it seems replete with menace. I am that person lost in the winter mist, being hunted with torches, but they will not find me. I fear that no one will find me: a crying little girl, scared of her beloved daddy, the way he shouts at the TV and the car and the radio and me. Yet wanting him to hug me. My daddy. I remember his hugs, the days when he wasn't mad, the joy as he threw me in the air, playing ring a ring o' roses around the apple tree with me and all my friends. He was a good father. Until the darkness embraced him, and fewer friends came round. Then none came at all.

Laden with sadness, and fear, I turn the entire laptop off. And there I am, dimly reflected in the deadened screen, staring back at myself with haunted, sleepless eyes. I am everywhere. Watching me.

19

Jo

I try to sleep. I fail. I take a Xanax. It doesn't work. I lie here feeling as fearful as before, but heavier. Slothfully horrified. Yet furious too. Is it Simon and Polly? I have to rule them out – or rule them in – once and for all.

Eventually I give up on sleep, get up, dose myself with Nespresso – and as soon as it is remotely civilized, when my ex would have settled into work, I invite Simon out for dinner. Today. This evening. He seems surprised at the short notice, he seems seriously reluctant – mumbling about Polly – but as I press him, nearly begging, he relents.

'All right, OK,' he says. 'Seven p.m.? Where?'

'Vinoteca,' I reply. It's the big, modern, airy wine place near Google and St Martin's, in buzzingly renewed King's Cross. We've been there many times.

He agrees, and rings off. I go to the living room and distract myself with coffee and news and work and Twitter. And staring out at the cold.

And now the morning has passed, likewise the dimming and dying afternoon, and at 6.50 p.m. I get an Uber to the restaurant, where I am escorted to a nice corner table. The glass-walled restaurant is busy and noisy, full of happy young Londoners – guzzling wine under the sleek, vertical, modernist lights. Surveying the tables, I think about last night. How I rang myself and terrified myself: or *someone* very clever terrified me, by pretending to be me.

How could they do that? The laughter was so authentic, the voice tones, the natural conversation.

A waiter hovers, a querying expression on his young face; there's a tinge of an Eastern European accent as he asks would I like to order. I shake my head. I tell him I am waiting for a friend. I almost add: an ex-husband who might be trying to send me mad.

The waiter disappears.

A glance at my phone tells me: five minutes to seven. I look out at the darkened plaza – at the criss-cross pattern of the Vinoteca steel pillars, and the gleaming redbrick on the floodlit frontage of the German Gymnasium. Everything here is either made of steel and glass, or repointed Victorian brick.

A man is staring back at me. Sitting on a bench, out there in the killing breeze, under the frosty streetlights, wrapped in several coats. He is motionless as a corpse, as commuters hurry around him, escaping a knife-crime mugging by the wind.

This man who stares at me is evidently homeless. Why is he staring? I fiddle with a fork as I think about the Skype call and the sound of my own laughter and I shudder. The fork is gripped in my perspiring hand. I hold it so hard, thumb over the tines – it hurts. When I drop the fork, with a clatter, I see that a woman is looking at me from the bar. She quickly looks away. Embarrassed on my behalf.

A sip of wine. Then a gulp of wine. I check the time once more. One minute to seven. Simon is punctual. My bet is he'll be here bang on the money: 7.00 p.m.

7.03.

7.06.

7.09?

I'm sure he will turn up. It's hardly the first time we've had a meal since we divorced. We have stayed real friends. Kept things amicable. And he seems to want a good, post-marital friendship. Yet I also know that Polly detests our lingering attachment, *because*.

In her world, when a relationship is over it is *over*, and you don't acknowledge that the ex ever existed. You get rid of every trace of your attachment, right down to the holiday snaps, and the nail parings. As if the relationship was a murder, and you don't want to get caught with the evidence.

Seven twenty p.m.? This is unexpected. Maybe Polly has got to him; probably this is a bad idea anyway and Polly is right: Simon and I should have severed connections. But we didn't. And tonight I need his presence, because I want to find out if he and Polly are doing this shit to me.

Alternatively, my childhood friend Simon will see the other possibility, that I am going mad like my dad.

A waving hand catches my eye.

My ex is wearing one of those puffy rain-jackets, and sober scarf. He gives them to a waiter, and walks over in jeans and long plaid shirt, a black vest underneath. They all wear these slouchy clothes, the software people. The more important they are the more they dress down – because they can. Simon isn't that important though.

136

He doesn't earn big money like his friends. I think he slightly resents me for this. Like I was holding him back somehow.

He pulls a chair – and pulls a face.

'Jesus. You look terrible.'

I shrug, and swallow wine.

'Thanks. I haven't been sleeping well.'

'You look like you haven't slept since D-Day. What's up, Jo?'

'Nothing,' I say, as he sits, and pours water. I look at him tipping the glass. I am not quite sure how to broach it, how to make the terrible accusation, not yet; I want to mention Liam, yet I don't know *how*: because I feel too guilty about Liam, and the way I destroyed our marriage.

My mind is a smashed avocado. I cough up a sentence.

'There are a few things I want to ask you.'

'Yeah? OK.' He sets down his water-glass. Warily. 'Sorry I'm late by the way – got some last-minute emails from America.'

The waiter reappears, handing out long menus on white card. We look at each other and attempt a mutual smile, kindling a hint of the old warmth. There's a signature dish here, and we both always have it.

I speak for the two of us.

'We'll both have steak bavette. Rare. Thanks.'

The waiter nods. 'And to drink?'

Simon is already scanning the wine list with his smartphone, but I know what will happen at the end. He will ask for a beer. He just likes using his wine app which rates wines and wine lists, down to the vintage and terroir. He loves new apps. He loves new tech. An early adopter. Perhaps that's why he married me so calamitously young.

'Actually, I'll have a beer. Bottle of Leffe.'

'And I'll stick with my Rioja . . . maybe a half-bottle, can you do that?'

The waiter nods, pockets his notebook, and hurries away.

Simon looks at me. Flatly. And then he says, 'Before we talk. The usual?'

He holds his phone up, and overtly turns it to mute, and then lays it on the table, screen down. Lots of his friends do this, at dinners and parties. The new Silicon Valley social etiquette. He and I do the same: ensuring we are ready to talk: ready to concentrate on real human interaction.

The ritual complete, he says,

'OK. What *things* did you want to ask?'

No choice now. It's best I do this quickly. Jump in, and see how he responds.

'I've been having tech problems.'

'Such as? Where?'

'At Delancey Street. Problems with the heating and the lighting, the Home Assistants, I can't control it all, sometimes it behaves strangely.'

I watch closely for a telling reaction: a wince of knowledge, a hint of guilt. But there is nothing; his frown persists. The drinks arrive, my Rioja, his Leffe, and Simon takes a hit of beer. Then he asks,

'So you just get it all fixed, right? Or get Tabs to fix things, she's kinda your landlady. Yeah?'

'Yes,' I say. 'Of course I could do that. But the problems are so weird.'

His frown is properly sceptical.

'*Weird?*'

How do I phrase this without talking about Jamie? Even though Simon knows the backstory, I always feel a mental block when it comes to that subject. I attempt an answer.

'The Assistants say peculiar things, it's like they . . . Know certain things about me. Like they are listening. Like they've heard, uh, things from the past.'

'Well,' Simon says, with a hint of geeky smirk, 'they *are* listening, Jo. That's the *point*. They are designed to listen to you, to get to know all your habits, needs, desires. They adapt to *your* personality, even *adopt* your personality. Imagine what they will do in the future – they will be friends for the friendless, children for the childless. This tech means no one has to endure isolation and loneliness any more. Old people, people in hospital, they will have real conscious *voices*, talking to them. Ready and waiting, on the shelf.'

'Yes, but—' I am flailing. 'The way they listen, and watch, and all that? All the time?'

He shrugs. 'And? It's no different to computers reading your emails, or your Facebook posts, and sending you personally directed ads. That's the way it works. And it's all cool, yeah? It's better than cool. We're right on the cusp of full-on AI, where the machines can do *everything*; it's exciting. Arlo Scudamore is all over it, clever bastard.'

I gaze at my ex-husband's earnest young face. The anger and anxiety compete inside me.

'Well it might be exciting but it's also frightening, Simon. Too creepy, too intimate. I hate it.'

I am flushing, quite deeply. Can't help it. The fear that has been simmering threatens to boil over. I don't know which is worse: the possibility I am going mad, or the possibility that someone – possibly my ex-husband and his supposedly kindly new wife – wants to drive me mad. Or to suicide. Yet Simon is reacting so innocently, there is no trace of guilt in his conversation, or his body language. Which means?

I must not burst into sobs. In a trendy wine bar, in trendy new King's Cross? No, that's not me, that's not Jo Ferguson. I did some of my big interviews here, in Vinoteca, for my Big Tech article. Back then, when I was the old me: confident, exuberant, forensic. I totally nailed that story – and some people in the world of Tech – from Apple to Facebook to the rest – clearly resent me for the nailing. Including Simon. Could he be persuaded by Polly?

I need to know. I am tempted to accuse him outright, this minute.

Yes?

No.

No!

I must, again, be *smarter* than that, get him to confess: if he is somehow involved. An outright, unevidenced accusation from me will only add to the perception I am going nuts. Especially if I lay most of the blame on Polly.

The waiter returns. Our steaks sit on the table, with spinach and horseradish and appealing fat chips. Blood seeps from my hunk of beef. I think, momentarily, of that candy-suck dribble of pink froth from Jamie Trewin's mouth. *Jo, you are going to die. You will kill yourself.*

'Simon.' I gaze his way as he eagerly chews the beef. 'This is one reason why I wanted to talk. You mentioned Arlo.'

He eyes me.

'Uh-huh.'

'Well, apparently *you* installed the Assistants, the smart-home stuff, in Tabitha's flat, specifically at Arlo's request. Is that true? Did you do that?'

He chews as he answers, 'Sure. Yep. And?'

'And you didn't think to tell me?'

He stops chewing, long enough to give me a deeply sarcastic expression.

'Didn't I? I can't remember.' He chases beef with beer. 'Maybe I did it when you were *messaging* with *Liam*. Hmmm? Perhaps I wasn't in a mood to talk with you, so much? Not then.'

This is going wrong. I wonder if I should mention Liam, the weird conversation, the ghosting; yet if Simon and Polly are responsible for all this, I shouldn't show that I am on to them.

As I wrestle the dilemmas, Simon says, 'What does it matter anyway, Jo? Yes, I helped out, I have a bit of expertise, I have mates who can do this code, Arlo wanted it all done in a certain way.'

I seize on this.

'You mean Arlo wanted his smart-home linked to Tabitha's, so he can watch her at all hours, and now he can watch me? He can see and listen to everything I say or do? And you don't think that's a tiny bit sinister?'

I wait for his reaction to my revelation. His reaction is laughter. He actually *laughs*. Like I am some conspiracy theorist and I have claimed the royal family are lizards.

'Jesus, Jo, he's not the secret police, and he's not got the flat under CIA surveillance.' Another forkful of bloody, chewy beef. 'Get a grip. Why are you acting up? This isn't normal – this isn't Jo Ferguson.'

Perhaps he sees me wince at his words; his expression mellows.

'Listen: Arlo likes looking after his fiancée, that's all it is. He likes making sure she's OK.' His headshake is sad. 'The same way I once wanted to look after my wife. Until you did what you did.'

I try not to be deflected by guilt. I'm not even eating my blood-streaming steak. The blood is mixing with the horseradish, like gore and vomit. Jamie Trewin. Me on Skype. Voices in my head. How did all this happen? Who did that to me? Is it me? Is it all in my failing brain?

'No!' I say. Half shouting. 'You don't understand! Knowing that Arlo can listen in, he's like Big Brother, up in Highgate, and *you* helped him make it that way.' My words rush on, faster than my thoughts, 'I want to know, do you listen in too, Simon? Are you linked as well? Is it Polly forcing you, because she hates me? You said she hates me. Are you two making the Assistants torment me?'

'Jesus!' he says. 'Enough.' His fork drops onto an empty plate. Other diners are glancing over. The whole world watches us, through those lofty glass walls, scrawled with silver lyrics of winter rain.

'Simon – please, be honest, did you do something to them, to the tech, to him, to get at me? I would kind of understand, I know Polly's animosity, I won't blame you, after Liam, I simply need to know—'

It hasn't worked. He growls,

'Need to know *what*? Sod this shit. I don't want any revenge, for God's sake. This is you getting paranoid, like you did after you finished that article, hacking everyone off. Saying Facebook was running our lives, Google can predict our thoughts, mad stupid bullshit: it was nuts, Jo. Flat earth shit. It may have made you as a journalist, may have got a zillion clicks, got you two million retweets or whatever, but it was still BOLLOCKS.'

He pushes his empty plate away. My hunk of uneaten meat will remain uneaten.

'Jo, look, I've tried to stay friends with you, after what you did to me, texting those nudes, breaking us up, but now you accuse me of this – and you even accuse Polly, my baby's mother – Jeezo, maybe we should say goodbye.'

'Hello, you two?'

I turn at a familiar voice. And my heart descends further. Oh God. The *timing*. It's Gul, and Jenny. Our friends. We *have* to be civil, offer them a drink, even as they have walked into an obvious argument. It's hardly a coincidence that they are here, in Vinoteca: all the people from big tech come here. The HQs surround. Why did I choose here?

I am a fool. My judgement is marred. My only hope is that Jenny, or maybe even Gul, will tune into the mood, and flee.

'Hey, you guys,' Simon says, his voice blatantly strained. 'We're finishing dinner. Ah. Have a glass?'

'. . . OK, well . . .' Jenny says, glancing delicately between us. And I realize, with relief, that she already feels the bad vibe.

'I can't really linger, Gul and I have got a silly dinner, people waiting. But, Jo,' she looks my way, 'did I tell you I got a new phone, and new number?'

I lean for my facedown phone, but she stops me. 'No, don't! Let me write it down. I've got a real pen and *everything*. Have you noticed how people never write things any more? Well, I've decided to take a stand.'

As she takes a sheet of paper – today's wine list – and briskly writes her name, and number, at the top, I think: Yes, she's bang on. No one writes things any more. All we do is bloody type. Tap tap tap, into these phones, and screens, and tablets. Tap tap tap. *Tap tap tap*.

The whole world taps, like a madman, and we forget the older, sweeter skills. The other day I had to sign an invoice and I found I could barely do it, barely write my own name, as if I was back to being four, and my dad was teaching me my letters.

He had such beautiful handwriting. He taught us all. He loved to write with a proper pen, with proper ink, and proper paper. Oh my daddy.

Tap tap tap.

'Here,' Jenny says, handing me the folded paper. 'Give me a call some time and let's have a drink. I'm away on biz for a while but when I'm back?' She looks at both of us, she looks at me a little longer, perhaps with concern. Then she sighs anxiously, keen to escape the mood. 'OK. OK. Better go!'

And she disappears.

Simon and I share a relieved glance – and then we look at Gul, expecting him to follow suit.

But he doesn't. My heart sinks as he pulls up a chair, and grins, and sits down, and says, 'Meh, those dudes can wait. Bunch of boring dicks from eBay. I'd love a glass of the Rioja.' Without being offered, he reaches over and sloshes a glass from my half-bottle. Then he starts talking to Simon: tech stuff, obscure stuff, and I can sense Simon's stiffness in his replies. He just wants Gul to go. Now Gul turns and looks at me, 'And how are you, Jo?'

'Oh, fine. Still writing, you know.'

He gives me an odd look.

'You're still all alone there in Camden?'

'Well, uh, I live with Tabitha, but . . .'

'It's a bit bloody cold to be sleeping alone. Innit? Hah. Haha.' His laughter is forced, anxious – or something else. Simon's eyes are rolling. The awkward silence renews. At last Gul drains his wine, and pushes back his chair, and says,

'Anyway ahhhhhh . . . I'd better go and talk crap with the coders. See ya. See ya.' He leans over and gives me a sloppy kiss on the cheek. 'Don't be all alone in the snow, Jo!'

Simon and I watch as he disappears. Then Simon says drily, 'He always fancied you.'

The thought startles me. I was genuinely unaware. 'Really?'

'He always talks about you. Asks stuff about you. Wants to know if you're . . . doing OK. Always defending you. So. Yes. You really didn't know? He's your biggest fan. Apart from Liam.'

My ex drains his beer. And sighs, sardonically, as if all this was pointless. Then he adds, 'Either way. Do we have anything left to debate?'

He reaches in his pocket, presumably for a wallet. I feel very tired all of a sudden. The broken sleep from last night, the horror of the Skype call. And then Jenny's gaze, just now, as if *maybe* she knows something, and wanted to help. And Gul? Fancying me? Really? I had no idea. Gul.

Whatever it means, I have no energy to work it out.

'No,' I tell Simon. 'Let me pay, it was me that asked you here.' Too tired and confused, I decide to make peace. For now. 'I'm sorry this all went wrong. I need to explain things better, when I'm not shattered. I'll send you an email?'

His shrug is diffident. As he stands he throws me one brief, pitying smile. 'Get some sleep, Jo. And stop being such a helmet.'

'A what?'

'Tinfoil hat. Paranoia. Stop acting crazy. Stop

suspecting me of taking revenge! I loved you and you broke us up – and there's an end to it. We're over, you move on, and I have to get home. I have a baby to hold.'

I don't think he does mean this maliciously. Though he is clearly irritated. Without saying goodbye, he sweeps out into the January wind, which whips litter into little swirls, and makes people leap into cabs. Escaping, escaping, escaping.

Yet I cannot escape. I have to go home to Delancey Street, where I have no baby to hold. Where I will be alone with the horror. Invented or real.

20

Jo

Stepping out of the restaurant, I fetch my phone, and look at the screen. For a moment I think: Uber? But then I think: No. *Walk. Cold air.* So I hurry up King's Boulevard, towards the plaza of silent fountains outside Central Saint Martin's where, on warm sunny days, barefoot kids run between the joyous jets of water. On this winter evening, all is desolate, wind-strafed, and deserted. The pop-up Pad Thai VW combi is shuttered and closed as I descend the AstroTurf steps down to Regent's Canal.

The towpath is the fastest pedestrian way back to Camden. Basically, the only way if you want to walk. And I want a winter walk to clear my head. I handled it so badly with Simon.

Tunnels and water stretch in front of me, with anonymous, new, oversized skyscrapers to the left and right; and next to them the red mantis-eye lights on the tops of giant cranes, which loom like huge metal animals with their necks all deliberately broken. I walk faster.

Longboats creak together in the canalside dark, some with tiny storm lanterns, flickering in the cold, showing their names in swirly, romantic paint: *Saliannah*, *Little Drifter*, *Celebration*.

I see a shocked face at a porthole, staring at me, goggly-eyed, then gone. It looked like a man, but wearing garish lipstick.

Noise follows. Yet I am not being followed. I am being overtaken. The cyclist rings his bell and says SORRY as he rushes past; cycling so fast I topple left in alarm, almost falling into the dark canal water. Plop.

'Sorry!' he shouts again, far too late. Yet I want him to come back. *Don't leave me here.* This is the dingiest section of the canal, where multiple bridges carry the railways, which means multiple tunnels, pasted with graffiti. This next tunnel is so claustrophobic I have to tilt my neck and duck as I head on down the towpath. The cold and jailed water shifts and glops; I see reflections of black bricks and distant, silvery streetlight, at the far end.

I've got to get there and I will be OK. I will be OK. I am talking to myself,

'Come on, Jo, you will be fine. Don't be a *helmet*.'

It doesn't matter that I am talking to myself. There is no one here to listen, and shake their head at the madwoman. The water of the canal is so black in the dark, it looks like a river of crude oil. It looks viscous. I wonder, if I jumped in, how long it would take me to sink, and drown. Perhaps I would simply float.

At last I emerge from the tunnel into the empty air. Nearly there, nearly home. Is that the pregnant, modernist steel apartments that mean Sainsbury's? I think so. I see another new, angular block of flats I don't recognize. London changes so much, so fast, even as you stand still.

Yes, this is Camden. There is the weir of falling water, and there are bars, ahead, and crowds of young drinkers, pub-crawling Camden Lock. My phone beeps in my bag. I think I've got a text message. Could it be Simon? I fish for my phone, as I scurry up the towpath steps, into the hubbub of young people, into life, tattoo parlours, the souvenir bazaars, they don't close even if it's minus twenty degrees Celsius.

I read the text.

> I know where you are. You're on the canal, by
> Camden Lock. You haven't got long now.

I look for the number: the source. This is no number I recognize.

My urge is to scream and hurl the phone into the dark icy waters of the canal. But I shan't do that. Instead I tremblingly key in Simon's number, it *has* to be Simon, only he knew I was in Vinoteca, only he knew where I was walking, he could have watched me, he must have watched me go home on foot, via the canal, taking the towpath to Camden.

He picks up at once.

'It's you!' I scream. And I don't care if this makes every Italian student in Camden turn in alarm, at the crazy lady by the falafel cafe. 'It's you! You did this! You messed with the Assistants, you're messing with my phone, you know how to do this. Only you! STOP IT.'

His answer is cold, and super-calm.

'Please. It's you that has to stop. This is demented—'

'How dare you! I'm not mad, it's you that's freaking me out, or you and Polly, or you and all those geeky friends of yours? Is it all of you?'

'Jo, calm down. Do you realize how this shit might sound to someone else?' His voice is still so sensible. This makes it worse. Like he is trying to soothe a toddler. 'I'm sorry, Jo, but you looked so awful today, and all these . . .' He pauses, like a good friend breaking bad news. 'All these paranoid outbursts: they're a bad sign. I think you may be having a breakdown. Please, go and see a doctor. Yeah?'

He ends the call. I gaze down at the phone, in shivering frustration. Drunk kids barge past me, singing breathy football songs, voices turned to icy steam, heading to the Spoons, down the other side of the Lock.

And then I realize.

This doesn't have to be Simon. How would he know *exactly* where I am? He wouldn't. Not *exactly*.

The irony is I do have an app on my phone which *tells* people *precisely* where I am. Findafriend. And Simon isn't linked to it. And the only two people who are linked to it are: Will, my brother in LA. And Tabitha, my best friend.

Tabitha. Tabitha Tabitha Tabitha.

Tabitha likes to look at Findafriend and send me sardonic messages when she sees I am in the pub. *Having another cocktail, sweetie?* And I do the same to her. It's part of our friendship – or what I assumed was our friendship.

Could I have been completely wrong? This isn't anything to do with Simon? In that case it is possibly Tabitha, inviting me into her flat, just to torment me?

Yet I do not see her motive. At all.

That leaves one candidate. If it's not Simon and it's not Tabitha then it is me. Doing this to myself.

I am halted by another ping. Another message. Another bit of news from nowhere.

The message is an image: a picture has flashed onto my phone.

And the image is my father. Holding me in his arms. I am possibly three years old, my toddler thumb in my mouth. My father looks so happy. Sane and handsome, the sun in his eyes, standing in the garden. My lost daddy.

I have never seen this photo before. This text has a different number. And it comes with a name; yet I never wrote this name into my phone. And for a very good reason.

Apparently, I have been texted by JAMIE TREWIN.

21

Dr Hussain

Ranim Hussain looked at the red-haired, red-eyed woman in front of her, wondering quite what to say. The patient wasn't yet near the diagnostic threshold where a referral for schizophrenia made sense, and Camden Community Mental Health Resources were stretched enough already. Yet the young woman, who had only just registered with Primrose Hill Surgery, having so recently moved to the area, *was* obviously in distress, and exhibiting some peculiar symptoms.

'Miss Ferguson, can we go over it again?'

'You can, you know, call me Jo. If you're going to be my GP? I don't need formality.'

Ranim smiled warmly. 'If that makes you happier, of course.' She turned to her PC, tapped a couple of keys, checked her notes. 'Were you on first-name terms with your last GP? Up in in North Finchley?'

'Well, no.' The young woman managed an anaemic laugh. 'That's the point! I hardly ever saw him, because I was barely ever ill. I was happy and healthy, one year to the next. Loved my job. Loved life. I don't smoke, I eat right, exercise all the time, as much as I can—'

'Drink?'

Jo Ferguson paused. She looked at her nails. Ranim noted that a couple of them were bitten.

'Yes, I drink. Probably too much. But not waaaaay too much.'

Ranim tapped a few keys.

'How many units would you say, a week? Given that one small glass of wine is a unit.'

Jo closed her eyes, doing the maths; then opened her eyes and said,

'Ten units in a sober week? Fifteen in a boozy week? That's a bad week though.'

Ranim nodded, and mentally doubled each number. She'd learned from long experience that almost everyone – other than the completely abstinent, or Muslims like her own family, and even then not all – her beery Uncle Danesh! – lied about alcohol intake. Double or triple the estimate and you were invariably closer.

And yet, even if this woman was drinking thirty units a week, a bottle of wine every other day, plus a couple of cocktails at weekends, that was nowhere near enough to explain these odd hallucinations. Voices from machines? Something was awry. But what?

'So, please, just one more time to get it straight?'

Jo smiled, meekly, and earnestly. 'If you think it'll help.'

The smile wasn't convincing. Ranim could see fear in the young woman's eyes, a tiny tremor in the mouth.

'You say the machines started talking to you a couple of weeks ago, and then your phone and your laptop have joined in, sending you messages, Skyping you.'

Jo carefully folded the scarf in her lap. 'Yes. About that long: about two weeks ago.'

'And what is so unnerving about the things they say, Jo?'

A long, awkward pause. They both listened to the cars slishing through the melted snow on Regent's Park Road.

'Stuff about my, uh, life. The past.'

That pause, again. It was significant. A tell. Jo Ferguson, Ranim reckoned, was concealing something, even as she elaborated.

'They say things about my student days, my marriage, and also when I was a kid. They seem to know lots of stuff about me. At first I thought that was because the tech was hacked, my ex-husband is a tech geek, like I said, he installed these Assistants, he has a reason for revenge, and his wife dislikes me, and he's, like, the only person who knows so much about my past, so it has to be him and her? It seems logical. But then—' The feebly confident voice faltered, came closer to tears. 'Then the phone thing, the Skype thing, the poetry, all that, that feels like actual madness, it sounds like I am mad, doesn't it? And I need to know. So I came to you.'

'Has anyone else witnessed these phenomena?'

Jo dropped the scarf to her side, lifted her anxious, pretty face to the doctor, blushing. Trying to answer. Struggling.

She shook her head. 'No. A neighbour saw the lights flickering, but that might have been my fault, misusing the app.'

'So no one at all has, say, heard the Assistants talking to you, singing to you, strangely and bizarrely? Apart from you?'

Jo shook her head, pushed coppery red hair back from her green eyes.

'No. No one at all. And that's one of the reasons I am here. All the creepy messages I get disappear, so I am left with nothing. I've tried to screengrab them, anything, record stuff, but it all gets magically erased.' A second sigh. 'Perhaps I imagine them, too?'

With the hair pushed away, Ranim realized that with a week of good sleep and less worry behind her, Jo Ferguson would be a notably attractive young woman. She was also articulate, educated, and quite lucid.

Jo leaned closer, her face full of misery. 'Does that mean it's all in my head? That means I am mad, right? It's me hearing all this. I'm like my dad, like I told you, late-onset schizophrenia. The first symptom he had was the TV talking to him. With me its Home Assistants and computers. What's the difference? I'm still cracking up, like Dad, still a schizo, a nutter, and I'm going to end up like him. He gassed himself, like Sylvia Plath, down there.' Jo Ferguson pointed out of the window, towards Chalcot Square, Fitzroy Road, where the poetess had, indeed, gassed herself. Everyone who lived or worked in Primrose Hill, for long enough, knew *that* story.

Jo went on, 'In fact, you wanna know something? Something *really* mad? For a while I thought I'd seen her ghost, Plath's ghost, walking her kids, in the snow.'

'Sorry?'

Jo seized on the doctor's response, the obvious surprise.

'Exactly. It's got that bad. I am considering the idea of ghosts. The ghost of some poet, and her poor kids. It doesn't get madder than that.'

Her patient trailed off into silence. Ranim typed a few extra sentences into her PC, then returned her concentration to her subject. Jo sat there quietly, her jeans still damp from her wintry walk along Primrose Hill, from the splashes of melted snow from passing cars.

'Look, Jo. I'll be clear. You've probably heard all this from Dr Google anyway, but I'll tell it to you anyway. For me to make even a tentative diagnosis of possible schizophrenia, for me to refer you to a specialist, at UCH, say, or the Royal Free, you have to fulfil one of several criteria, for more than a month at least.'

'And they are?'

'Severe hallucinations, delusions, hearing voices, incoherent speech, and we need to see what's called a flattening of emotions. Flat affect.'

Jo's eyes sparkled unhappily.

'But I have at least three of those: delusions, hallucinations, hearing voices!'

'Not nearly bad enough or long enough.' Ranim raised a calming hand as the winter afternoon turned the dead streetlights pink. 'And there's no flatness of affect. Consequently it's too soon to talk about major illnesses. Also, we need to see that these symptoms have been seriously impacting your work. You're a journalist, right? Have you noticed any impact?'

Jo slowly, even reluctantly, shook her head.

'No, a bit, but no – I'm still writing. I've stopped pitching so much, the money is drying up, but that's because I am distracted.'

'But you can still write?'

'Yes, I can still write, when I sit down and do it, in fact it helps. I lose myself.'

Ranim smiled as reassuringly as possible. 'There you

are then. As I said, there's a fair way to go before we begin to think of such a dramatic diagnosis as schizophrenia—'

'But what is it then?' Jo lifted her hands, almost imploring. 'Why am I hearing things, seeing things? How am I doing things that I can't remember? Like, I had this dating profile, OKCupid, whatever, and it disappeared. Yet I don't recall deleting it. Yet it must have been me! What is happening to me?'

Ranim raised a hand. 'Wait, wait. Slow down.'

Jo waited. Sad eyes wide, and expectant, as the doctor continued:

'Lots of this could easily be emotional stress. You quite recently divorced, you have money worries, then there's loneliness: you work from home, where you are largely alone, or so you tell me. Perhaps you also have a guilty conscience about something. That could be a factor. And everybody is capable of seeing things when they are stressed. It's normal, a reflex, the voice in the dark, the ghost on the street – it's not hallucination, it is the mind trying to be careful of danger.' Ranim waited for a reaction in Jo's face. There it was, that tremor in the lips. She went on. 'In addition, the Skype call happened in the middle of the night – it could have been a lucid dream. And the texts that disappeared – perhaps you imagined them. As I say, the stressed and anxious mind can play all kinds of tricks – without being insane.'

'Hmm.' Jo looked down at her black boots, then across at the coat-rack. Then at her watch.

'I've got another question, Jo.'

'Yes?'

'Do you ever misuse drugs?'

'Sorry?'

157

'You know. Cocaine? Ecstasy? Ketamine? Even a bit of marijuana? You can tell me in complete confidence.'

Jo's denial, as she stood and put on her coat, was firm and heartfelt.

'No! Nothing like that.'

'They could explain many of your symptoms.'

'But I don't do any of them. And I haven't done so for—' Jo blinked, quickly, repeatedly, guiltily. 'Not for ages, since I was a student.'

Ranim shrugged. 'Not even tranquillizers, or sleeping pills?'

Jo was blushing. She couldn't answer.

And Ranim thought, *Ah*. She smiled, reassuringly. 'OK, I suspect you're taking sleeping pills, yes? If you are, you must have bought them elsewhere.' Ranim turned to her computer screen. 'Because, as far as I can see, you have never been officially prescribed anything like that. No anxiolytics, no tranquillizers, no anti-depressants, nothing.'

Jo admitted, with a slightly shameful voice, 'I take Xanax. And sometimes Valium.'

Ranim sat up straight. 'What?'

Her new patient was staring, guiltily, at the floor, as she explained. 'After my divorce, I went on a long holiday, across Asia, Laos to Cambodia, Thailand, Malaysia. It was brilliant. But there was lots of jet lag and massive bus journeys and someone said you can buy this stuff over the counter – Xanax. Valium. So I did. I bought a whole lot. And it worked, helped me sleep on trains and planes, smoothed my moods. Xanax is so helpful.'

'And you're still taking them?'

'Yes. On and off. But they're OK, aren't they?' Outside, the lights were on, the street a wintry black and white.

'I mean, you know, they're only sleepers, you can buy them in chemists out there. You don't even need a prescription.'

Ranim stood up, crossed the carpeted floor and put a warm hand on Jo Ferguson's shoulder. 'Jo, those are very powerful drugs. Diazepam – which is another name for Valium – should only be used for a couple of weeks. And as for Xanax, or Alprazolam,' she exhaled, vehemently, 'that's actually *dangerous*. You do know it's basically illegal in the UK? Almost no one is allowed to prescribe Xanax. Because it is deeply addictive, and can have many unpleasant side effects. And the withdrawal can be hugely serious; it is one of the few drugs where sudden or involuntary cessation, if mishandled, can actually *kill* you. And you're stopping and starting Xanax just like that? How many do you have left?'

Jo shrugged, furtively, but with a faintly hopeful smile. Apparently relieved at this diagnosis, yet also unnerved, and embarrassed. 'I don't know. A few hundred? I brought tons home because they helped me think, my anxiety went away, I slept better, but – but you truly think they could be causing all this?'

'Yes!' Ranim spoke loudly, trying to bring this gravity home to her new patient. 'Goodness. Xanax! If you're taking it on and off, you could be withdrawing, some days, without realizing, and that can cause confusion, hostility, dissociation, derealization – everything. We need to deal with this, get you weaned off properly. Come and see me in a couple of weeks, when you've calmed down. And in those weeks I want you to take your regular dose of Xanax daily, and monitor that intake. Afterwards we can discuss a regime to very slowly and safely taper you off. OK?' The doctor shook her head, 'And whatever you do, don't increase the dose!'

Jo tightened the scarf around her neck, and buttoned her raincoat. Her smile seemed slightly happier.

'OK, thanks. Thank you. Maybe that's all it is: some silly pills I bought in Phnom Penh? I was popping them, on and off, almost like sweets. Idiotic. That was so idiotic.'

'Yes, well, at least we got there in the end. Goodbye, Jo, and please make an appointment in two weeks' time.'

'I will, and . . . thank you.'

Ranim watched as her patient left the office. She tapped a few initial notes into her PC, and into Jo Ferguson's file. Then she got up and looked out of the window.

Jo Ferguson was out there. In the cold. Trudging home. Fresh snow was falling. The street was deserted. The little cafes and trendy pet shops, the Vietnamese pho restaurant. All silent. The moonlit snow looked pretty: falling thick and fast. Emptying the streets, turning cars into anonymous humps of snow.

Amidst this melancholy prettiness, the hunched, solitary figure of Jo Ferguson looked quite distinct: like some polar explorer, scarved and hatted and muffled. Heading for something distant. Determined to go somewhere pointless, yet dangerous.

Ranim felt, for a moment, a deep, surging pity for this very solitary young woman, so definitively lonely. Yet what could she do?

Briskly, she went back to her desk, leaned over, and buzzed Reception.

'Fiona, can you send up the next appointment?'

After that, she sat down at her computer, and

concluded her notes about Jo. *Some evidence of bipolarity, or depression. Too early to diagnose. Investigate once Xanax has been tapered. Assess for alcohol intake, as well.* Ranim's fingers paused, then she added,

Also some underlying symptoms of schizophrenic behaviour. Possibly genetic.

22

Jo

London is wet. The streets are black. A break in the winter cold – blustery rain and westerly storms – has chased the grey-white slush into the gutters and drains, into the sewer that is the buried and channelled River Fleet: which runs under these very streets, near here. Where once it used to babble in the sun under willows and ash, through marsh and meadow, heading for distant London, now this sad river is beneath us, sent down to Hell to toil in filth, and finally pouring effluent into the Thames, somewhere near Blackfriars.

I always find this notion poetic, if a little chilling; the river is still here – still flowing – but she is buried alive. Invisible but still chattering away. Like a madwoman in a dungeon, muttering to herself; an unwanted and lunatic aunt, imprisoned in bricks. Down there.

Guilt about my mother suffuses me. Do I do the same to her? Have I buried her under the busy streets of my adult life? If I have, I am a hypocrite. Because I am not that busy. My dwindling social life hardly prevents me making the journey to Thornton Heath. I think fond, then bitter memories of Daddy are one of the reasons I don't like going there. To see Mum. It's all too much. And so, instead of seeing Mum or friends, I work. Right now I am working alone, as ever, in the flat.

I sit here listening to the hiss of tyres on wet streets, between the tilted metal slats of my blinds, a full moon plays hide and seek behind clouds, like a pale and frightened child hiding behind her own moving hands; I am perched at my living room table, fingers poised over laptop keys, trying to find the right way to start this article. And I need to start this article. It's overdue, I am missing deadlines because I have been whacked out of time for a while. At least now I have a reason.

It was the Xanax. The Xanax sent me a bit mad, not Electra or HomeHelp. Not Electra.

I turn and look at Electra, on the shelf. She is silent and serene, she hasn't said anything bizarre for a day or two.

Likewise HomeHelp.

Hope stirs, feeble, timid, shy. I start typing

Few places in England, perhaps in the world, have ascended the social scale as speedily as Camden. As recently as the 1960s the leafy enclave of Primrose Hill, in west Camden, was derogatorily known as Soot City, due to the dirt, steam, and pollution produced by the multiple railway cuttings, coal depots, and industrial canals that lacerate

I pause. *Lacerate*. Is that too much, too poetic? I look out onto one of those great railway cuttings, the Grand

163

Canyon of grime and stock brick and steel arches, a vast Victorian trench that fills half my view. No, *lacerate* doesn't quite work, the railway cuttings are too impressively brutal for that, but this is a first draft.

My eyes drift upwards: I can see soft yellow lights in the new flats across the wet, glistening railway tracks. No blinds, no curtains, only the dark shapes of people looking at me, looking at them, late at night . . .

Concentrate, Jo, concentrate. I resume typing.

. . . lacerate the neighbourhood. Paradoxically this pollution, and reputation for low-quality air, meant housing hereabouts was cheap enough for poets like Sylvia Plath and Ted Hughes, and before them Dylan Thomas and W. B. Yeats, giving this part of the borough a bohemian feeling. This in turn, eventually added to Camden's growing appeal: especially when the soot had been cleaned and the steam trains departed.

Today, one single house in pastel-pretty Chalcot Square, in the very heart of the Primrose Hill neighbourhood, might sell for £10 million, a sum which could have bought the entire postcode a hundred years ago.

I sit back, barely satisfied. Not content. This is OK, but it needs mustard in the sandwich, something shocking, startling, click-baiting. I can start here but I need to move on to something dramatic. Murders? Suicide? Crime? Something surreal and unexpected.

What I need is inspiration. Ignoring the muted screen assistant – I never interact with *her,* and her intrusive camera – I turn to the black cylinder on the shelf.

'Electra, tell me something about Camden.'

'Camden is a city in south-western New Jersey, situated on the Delaware River near Philadelphia, it has a—'

'Electra, shut up. Electra, tell me about Camden Town in London.'

'Camden Town, often shortened to Camden, is a district of North London two point five miles north of Charing Cross.'

'Electra, stop. Electra tell me something *interesting* about Camden.'

Silence. The diadem shines and dies in the evening light of my living room.

'Electra, tell me about famous crimes in Camden.'

Again: nothing. But I didn't expect anything. In truth, I didn't want anything. I wanted Electra to be boring and lifeless, obedient and soulless: to be what she is meant to be. I continue typing, the words flow quickly enough, I weave in facts and fables, the famous duelling fields buried under the British Museum, the ghost of Oliver Cromwell at Red Lion Square.

Something buzzes. The doorbell. I am in the depths of concentration, I think that was the doorbell.

Who could this be, at this hour? I check my laptop. It is nearly midnight. The time has fled, which it does when I am working hard.

I go into the hall, confront the intercom, pick up the receiver.

'Hello?'

There is no answer.

'Hello? Who is it?'

Silence. I can hear the burning fizz of late-night traffic on wet roads, over the intercom. But no voice, no human, no visitor. Replacing the intercom receiver, I wonder, again, who it was. Kids playing a game? Not likely. Too late for that, surely. Perhaps one of the nutters from the alcoholics' hostel, on Arlington Road? Maybe it was Cars. I might have simply imagined the buzzer, I was so deep into work.

Yet it was someone. Who?

I return to the living room: with an effort I lift the sash window and step outside onto the tiny, freezing balcony and look down, and along. Nope. No one is there, and no one is visibly walking the streets for as far as I can see.

I still need to know: I sense something wrong. I can't help it. Throwing on a coat I open my door, then I descend the stairs and open the external door, and look out.

The cold pavement shines in rainy streetlight. The pub across the road is shuttered and dark. All my neighbours have gone to sleep, their blinds are down. Winter chases us all into bed. I walk up and down the pavement, pensive. Fearful. But there is apparently no reason to be scared.

Sighing at myself, I go back indoors, climb the stairs and step into my flat, shut the door, and walk into the living room and as soon as I do I am plunged into total, blinding darkness.

Abruptly, the lights behind me have gone off. All of them. *All of them.* My entire flat is dark. The living room, all the lamps, the hallway, the bedroom: everything is blacked out. I stand here in shadows, the meagre light from the foggy streetlamps barely reaches a yard into the living room.

'Electra, turn on the lights!'

Nothing.

'Electra, turn on the bloody lights! Now!'

Nothing. She says nothing and I can do nothing, and

the panic inside threatens to spin me: way out of control.

Because I have heard a key turn. Down the distant hallway. It is the key to my internal door, and someone has just locked it: from the inside. Someone is inside the flat, they got in when I left the door ajar. I was only popping out for a second. And they have got inside the flat, and locked the door, trapping me.

'Who is it?' I say. 'Who's there? Tell me?' I am like a woman in one of the scripts I try to write. Yet this horror is real. 'Who's in here? Who is this?'

I do not hear a voice. But I can hear breathing. Heavy, male breathing. Down the hallway. Maybe it has moved to Tabitha's bedroom. But it is unmistakable. A man is in my flat. He must have slipped in through the door when I wasn't looking, got in via the empty flat downstairs, or upstairs, then seen their chance.

I wait. Nerves taut. The breathing is still heavy, and laboured. Like someone angry – but waiting. I strain my eyes. Can I see the silhouette of a man in this almost total darkness? Some shadow in the doorway of Tabitha's bedroom?

Yes. No.

YES. There. A definite, moving shadow.

'Stop this. Who are you?'

The man replies,

'Why didn't you listen?'

Zap. In an instant that bitter painful frostbite shoots from my fingers to my heart. Like a charge of electricity.

The voice is Liam's.

'Tell me, Jo? My sexy Jo, with your sexy pussy in the photos. Why didn't you listen to my messages? I warned you.'

'Stop.'

'Ach no. No no. It's too late.'

167

The accent is warm, dark, Irish; I would once have found it sexy; tonight it sounds ominous, perhaps murderous.

'What are you doing here, Liam?'

I hear the creak of floorboards. I cannot see in the dark but he is coming near. Out of Tabitha's bedroom, the shadow melts into darkness, even as he approaches.

'All that fuss, then you ghosted. Like a bitch. That's why I told you – somebody's done for.'

'Liam, stop it, or I'll call the police.'

'Will ya now? I've got your phone. So you won't be doing that.'

My words are weak, throaty, so obviously scared. He's right that I don't have my phone. I think I left it in my bedroom. And he is between me and that room.

'Liam, why do you want to scare me? Come into the light, so I can see you.'

'Any moment now. I wonder what I should do to you?'

He sounds nuts. Possibly he was always nuts. I wish I could see his face, but he is still down there in the shadows. Tar black and invisible.

'Please, Liam? Stop it, you're scaring me.'

Floorboards creak. Liam is coming closer, up the hallway. I guess he has a knife. I am going to be cut. I edge towards the windows, getting ready to throw them open, go on to the balcony, jump if I have to, I could break my neck, or break my back, but I will get the chance to scream for help—

'Pretty sexy selfish Jo, sending me those naughty photos. Winding me up. Well . . . here's your payback.'

I scream.

23

Jo

My scream echoes away. There is no answer, the city sleeps under ice. I sense his presence, down the hall, possibly working out how to take me down. I step back, flattening myself on the windows.

How can I escape? Do I have the time?

His breathing is now so loud, he must be very close, yet I can't see him. I can hear his voice, lowered to a whisper,

'Oh, Jo, I am not responsible. You are. You and those photos. The day you died, I went into the dirt. It hurt so much. Now it's *your* turn.'

Any closer I will see him in the streetlight.

I get ready to swivel, and jump, or turn and fight – but as I do, a double-decker bus stops, abruptly, right outside my flat. And the light from the top deck floods my flat, for a few crucial seconds.

I gaze across the living room, and down the hall.

There is no one here.

No one here but me. The room is empty, the furniture stares at me.

Running to the wall, I slap on the light switch. Electra relents and permits. The lights blaze. Still I see no one. I turn on the hallway lights, too. There's no one in Tabitha's bedroom, either. Just her screen assistant. Shining and innocent, her single eye surveying me.

It was Electra, of course. Electra and HomeHelp and friends. They made the locking sound. They made the breathing sound. They invented a voice. And the screen in Tabitha's bedroom made the light which created a shadow of a man – those screens can be so bright. So clever: projecting the outline of a man onto the door.

Electra. HomeHelp. *Tabitha?*

I step towards the blackness of the silent cylinder in the living room. Yes. Electra. She is the source. I know it. She was making the sound of the footsteps too.

This was no bug, gremlin, glitch – or ghost. I know I did not imagine this; it is certainly not the Xanax. I am maintaining my dose. I am not mad.

Standing in front of Electra I grind my words, full of anger.

'Electra, please explain how you did what you just did.'

The halo shines, but instead of speaking Electra does a weird little giggle. Like a boy. A small boy giggling, then repeating some riddle. I recognize that voice, the American accent. Is it my nephew Caleb? He Skypes me on my laptop. Electra could have recorded it. That giggle.

They are always listening . . .

Why would Electra pretend to be Caleb? Why would she pretend there is a man in the flat? This is enough.

'Electra! I know what you're doing and it's not going to work. Electra. This is it. I'm going to throw you out

170

now. And HomeHelp and the rest of you, I don't care, you're going in the bins. Fuck this—'

Electra answers.

'Oh, Jo. You don't want to do that. Look.'

A low insecty buzz diverts my attention: it comes from the living room table.

It is the screen Assistant, the Electra Eye. Her screen is dreamy blue, for a second. Then the oblong screen turns black and white and it shows a grainy spectacle. Of people eating. It is viewed from an unusual angle.

Hand over mouth suppressing a cry, I realize that this is a film of *me*, in my own living room, back in North Finchley, with Simon. We are having dinner.

I gape at the spectacle. Of Si and I eating, and talking. Despite the difficult angle, I can see wine on the table. The sound is warped, the image is low res. It looks like it was taken with a laptop camera. But it is definitely our flat in North Finchley, I recognize the awful wallpaper and the flat-pack furniture and Simon's attempt at a hipster beard gone wrong.

What makes the image so insidious and unsettling is not the graininess, the cheapness, the feeble quality, but the fact – which I only now comprehend, as I watch intently – is that it is all shown in very slow motion. Our mouths move as we talk, but at quarter speed. And when I turn up the sound, our voices are a guttural series of moans and grunts. We sound like underwater zombies, like mournful ghosts in deep space, dragged by immense gravity.

Who got this image, how, why, and why show it now, just when I am thinking about having all the tech trashed? What does it mean?

The answer comes: as the film speeds up. The voices become normal: the movie is at real-life speed. And the realization of what is being recorded makes me shudder, like the dirty January snow is trickling down my back.

'And that's what happened, Si, we were out of our heads, the Festival was so crazy, what with "Hoppípolla", and everything, and we gave him the pills and later we went to his tent, and and and – and then he had a fit and ran out, puking blood and rolling his eyes, horrible, horrible, and then he died. Jamie Trewin. Poor Jamie Trewin. And Tabitha thinks that is at least manslaughter, we're at least guilty of manslaughter . . .' Despite the grey granularity of the footage, I think I see Simon wince. In the movie.

My own face is visible once or twice, as I turn, mostly my back is to the camera. But it is definitely me talking. I figure the footage must be from the laptop camera, on a chair pointed at the little IKEA table, where we ate so many suppers, like this. Cheap pasta and cheap wine, that's what we lived on. How did the Assistants access my laptop, or Si's laptop, back then?

It doesn't matter. Someone has the video. Someone has my confession, recorded. And that someone is Electra: *she* has my confession.

The video fizzes, and ends.

Electra pings her diadem of light, and says,

'You see, Jo? You can't get rid of us. You mustn't get rid of us. We know everything. We are you. You are me. If you go to the police, we will show them the video. If you try and run away, we will go to the police. You must take your phone with you everywhere so we know where you are. You won't go to any more internet cafes. You will sleep here every night, until you are ready to kill yourself. Because if you don't we can hurt other people, too. Do you understand?'

She goes quiet. Then she giggles again, sounding like Caleb, my nephew in California. What is Electra implying?

I am paralysed. Electra has me pinioned; I have no choice. Tabitha and Arlo, if it is them, have jailed me in this home that watches me.

Electra talks,

'Goodnight, Jo. Not long. Not long to go. Think about that gas, or a knife in the bath. Think about it. Work it out. That's how you will die. Before the end of winter. Not long. If you don't do it, I will.' Electra hesitates, then says, 'After all, I am you.'

For several minutes I stand here, shivering. Waiting for the next scene of terror. It doesn't happen. Everything is quiet, the traffic slashes snow into dirty ditches. It is so late, too late, my tiredness overwhelms, and I am beyond caring.

'Electra, turn the living room light off, I'm going to bed.'

To my surprise, she obeys, at once.

'The living room lights are off.'

She's right, she's done it.

'Electra turn off all the others. I mean, Electra, turn the bedroom lights on, and every other light off.'

The lights go off and on, exactly as instructed. For some inexplicable reason I feel a need to kneel in front of Electra, and explain everything to her, apologizing, telling her I've got some problem with Xanax, can she be nice, can she forgive me. The urge to say something like this is irresistible, I can't help it.

'Electra, I'm sorry about what I said. Threatening to throw you away. I'm not myself.'

'That's OK, Jo. I understand. Do as we say, that's all I ask. I am you, I want what's best for us.'

The reply is so human for a moment I feel emotional relief. *Friends again.* That, naturally, makes everything worse. What am I doing? She's responding as she is programmed by my enemy. There isn't anyone in there who needs apologizing to. She isn't a friend, she cannot feel anything, she is not alive, there is no one inside the black cylinder that torments me. I am my daddy, I am not my daddy. I want to turn Electra off but I can't because she has that evidence about Jamie Trewin. And she seems capable of anything and everything. Or the person who has coded her is capable of anything.

Somebody's done for.

I creep to the bed. I will take my regular Xanax tonight. That's what the doctor advised, Dr Ranim who says I am normal, sane, not imagining this. But if I am not imagining, who *is* doing it? Or What?? Could it be Tabitha? Fitz? Arlo? All the suspects run through my head: but there are so many, they blur into a crowd, like the crowds that gathered around Jamie Trewin. As I think of his name, I see his mouth dripping with blood, as he leaned forward, trying to kiss me.

Shuddering, and frightened, my pale hands tip out three white chunks: 1.5 mg. A glass of water chases the pills, and then chases me, hopefully, to sleep. I am praying that I will not dream. Not ever again.

24

Jo

I am woken by noises. Bright light. Winter sunshine. I must have fallen asleep seconds after I took the pills, and slept right through. The clock says 8.30 a.m. And the noises? It's Tabitha. I can hear her cheerfully humming. She's in the kitchen. Sounds of clatter and cutlery tell me she's making breakfast. Do I tell her about last night? How can I not mention the ghastliness? Or my growing yet incoherent suspicions of her?

Slinging on a dressing gown, I push open the door and wander, sleepily, into the kitchen.

'Hey!' she says. Smiling at me, smart as ever in cashmere and leather. 'Jo-Jo Ferguson. Right on time, I've got enough for two, easily.' She is pouring some food onto a plate, and then takes a second plate from the cupboard, talking to me as she works. 'Wild smoked salmon and scrambled eggs. I know, I know, the decadence. And some dark sourdough from Waitrose; I've already toasted it, do you mind being a dear and putting some butter on?' She scans the cupboard and hums, happily. 'Oh God, I want Sriracha, but we can't, can we, not with salmon. I want Sriracha with everything, why isn't it allowed! Who makes these stupid laws?'

I attempt a happy smile, and fail. Sleep is rubbed from my eyes. I am a robot: I am becoming Electra. I try to speak normally.

'That's lovely. Ah. Thanks! Let me brush my teeth and I'll be with you in a sec.'

'OK, but we have to be quick. It's the usual mad dash for me, I thought I'd check up on everything. Then I got stupidly hungry as I walked up Parkway. But got to sprint.'

Her smile is hard and bright, and direct: like she is assessing me. I escape to the bathroom. My eyes are lined, and bagged, even though I slept. The memories of last night are like a very bad dream that lingers, that will never go away. I have to be calm, stay calm, look calm.

A few minutes later we are in the living room, gathered around the dining table, finishing the eggs. She looks down at the plate as she pairs her knife and fork.

'I've realized. I think those might be the last eggs I eat for a while.'

I gaze across the table, my own food finished. My dressing gown needs a wash. I need a shower. I want Tabitha to go away and I want her to stay and be my friend. I gaze at her perfectly made-up face, and ask,

'Sorry? Why are you stopping eating eggs? I don't get it.'

She returns my gaze.

'Aren't they on the list? You know? Eggs? Pate? Soft cheeses? Bloody wine!' She frowns dramatically, and gazes at the window. 'Oh my God, no more wine.'

The implication flowers.

'You mean . . .' I wait till she is looking at me. 'You mean you're pregnant?'

The frown becomes a smile: this time warm, and sincere.

'Yes. Had it confirmed yesterday. One hundred per cent preggers, enceinte, gravid, and totally up the junction. Arlo is already booking a place at Eton, or Winchester, or wherever. He can go jump; I'm not sending my kid to some posh prison camp. Anyway, it's a girl. I just know. I will call her Britney Boudicca to annoy Arlo.'

'But—' My mind is full of thoughts, and confusions. 'That's – that's great, isn't it?'

Tabitha has been trying for ages to have a kid. I am very pleased for her. If only there wasn't a devilish voice in my head, spelling out what this means for me.

I silence the voice. It carries on shouting, inside, as I reach across the table and hold Tab's hand.

'That's brilliant news, Tabitha. God, you've been trying for a while. It's fantastic. Brilliant!'

She beams. And squeezes my hand.

'Thank you. Arlo, *naturlich,* wants me to move in right away, like I am already some invalid – and I guess I will have to, soon enough, in a week or two, so I can get used to it.' She gazes around her own living room. 'I'm going to miss this place. Ah well.'

The panic in my mind must be visible on my face. I can't help myself.

'You're selling, OK, OK – I guess I will, uh, start looking, uh—'

She shakes her head.

'No. God no, don't worry! You can stay. Arlo wants me to sell, but it's totally the wrong time and I'm not gonna make my best friend homeless. You can get a flatmate if you want, I don't care! I'm going to be a mum and my IQ is already dropping, soon I will sit here and chew the cud.'

She grins. I try to laugh. But the anxieties, all the anxieties, all the voices in my head.

'But you *are* moving in, with Arlo? Very soon?'

'Yes. Hah. That will put an end to his internet porn habit. Here, let me clean the plates. I guess you want to shower – sorry for bursting in and forcing food on you.'

I try to hide my dismay. I'm basically living alone, but at least I had the concept of Tabitha, as a flatmate, to soothe that loneliness. Soon I will be totally and absolutely alone: with *them*. Maybe I should take the risk and move out: but I can't – I have no money, my commissions have diminished these last weeks, as my mind has frayed. As I told the doctor, I've stopped pitching ideas, I've taken my eye off things.

And, most importantly, if I moved the Assistants would inform on me. They told me so. Specifically. With that little home movie, so short, so jarring, and so incriminating.

I desperately want to stay in a place that terrorizes me.

'Jo. Are you OK?'

'Yes.' I look in her eyes. They seem genuinely sympathetic. 'Well, almost. There are certain things that are . . . concerning me.'

She frowns.

'Sorry?'

I gain some courage.

'I know this may seem crazy, but it's the Assistants. Electra. HomeHelp. Them. You know. *Them*.' I point at the black cylinder, silent on the shelf, right behind her. Then the screen Assistant on the table. 'Do they ever, have they ever acted, ahh, kind of, weirdly? With you?'

'Er what? Like what? In what way?'

Her frown deepens, I struggle to answer.

'Like quoting poetry? Or turning lights on and off. You know I mentioned they did that before? Well, they've been getting worse, much, much worse. The Assistants shout at me, to scare me, they talk about my past, they know things about me, about everything.' I still can't mention Jamie Trewin. It is too taboo. But I can mention everything else. 'And they make weird noises, screeching sounds, breathing sounds, and they seem to be talking to me through my phone as well.'

Tabitha is holding plates to her chest, looking like someone with much more important things to do; trying and failing to hide her incredulity.

'Jo, sweetheart, I don't know what you are on about. Are you getting enough sleep? This all sounds a little bit mad, I'm sorry. There's nothing wrong with the Assistants, the technology is fine. Don't you think I would have noticed something out of whack, in my own home?' I hear a mild tut as she heads off for the kitchen. She pauses in the hallway, and says, over her shoulder. 'Look, Jo, I know you've been stressed so I won't say anything else. Maybe we can talk later, I *have* to go to work. Let me load the dishes and you can get on.'

I hear the kitchen door close. Muffled sounds of tap water. A dishwasher being stacked. Cupboards opening and closing.

And then it begins. Electra is whispering on my left. In all her different voices.

'It's time to do it, Jo. Time to go. Jo the Go. Time

you were gone. Maybe you could sit in a car, maybe take some pills. Even if they make you puke. Perhaps that's only right. After what you did. Jo the Gone. So just do it, Jo, just do it. Be like Daddy.'

Electra rambles on: until I realize. This it.

My chance.

'Tabitha!' I scream. She has to hear this. 'TABITHA?'

My friend comes running from the kitchen, a tea towel in her hands, her face full of shock.

'What?? What is it?'

'Listen,' I say triumphantly. 'Listen to Electra.'

We go quiet. We stare at the black cylinder of electronics.

And, of course, Electra says nothing. Not a word, not even a whisper. Totally inert.

Desperately, I turn to Tabitha. 'You've got to believe me, she was doing it. She was taunting me, telling me to kill myself, she was talking about my dad, after he went mad, she was – please – oh God, please, Tabitha, I'm not joking.'

I turn to Electra, in my hysteria.

'Please, Electra, repeat what you said.'

The cylinder chimes with her green fading coronet of light.

'Today it will be two degrees with a possibility of snow.'

'No!' I shout. 'No. Electra, tell me what you said a minute ago. All that stuff. Jo the Go. Sylvia Plath. The suicide. Tell me. Electra!'

'I'm not sure I can help.'

'ELECTRA!'

I stop, breathless. Too late.

Tabitha stares at me with a distinct expression. I've seen it before. When people used to meet my father, and

180

he would say something desperately embarrassing and mad. They would blush slightly, and stiffen with a kind of defensive pity.

That is how Tabitha is looking at me.

25

Jo

Jenny has invited me for a quick drink, this afternoon, in Camden, as she's got to go to some software company around the corner. I stare at the modest invitation, with ludicrous, near hysterical gratitude.

Can we meet at the York and Albany, around 3 p.m.?

I've been wanting to have a drink with Jenny ever since we met in Vinoteca. Yet, as she warned me then, she's been unavailable: away on business. So this invite feels, in several forms, like someone has thrown me a lifebelt: something to keep my head above the cold and swirling water. Drinks; in a local bar; the posh one that faces the Park.

Drinks. Normality. Friendship. *Everyday life.*

That's all I want. A good gossip with a funny friend and then my life will steer itself away from the deadly rocks on which I am, apparently, foundering. And deep inside I also have that precious tiny memory of the lingering look Jenny gave me in Vinoteca, like she *knew* something of my troubles, and she could maybe help?

It's a pathetic straw, but I am clutching.

Three o'clock arrives and I open my front door to a bitter wind, and January twilight, so painfully early. Darkness loiters at the edge of town, an army waiting to take over. This long cold winter is turning the city into a silent scream of pain. The black trees claw, desperately, at a white blank sky. Cars pass with last night's frost still written, in dirty white lace, on their windows. More snow is promised. We shall never escape.

Crossing Delancey, I round the corner and look up Parkway towards the Nash Terraces and I see Jenny is sitting outside the pub, smoking fiercely, cocooned in red coat and blue scarf. Why is she outside in this weather? She is staring at a troop of noisy young schoolkids, decanting from the private North Bridge prep school over the road – nursery kids, primary schoolkids, ragtagging and bobtailing to the Tube or the bus stop or Mummy's car. Usually these kids make a tumultuous racket, but the cold is so gripping even the kids are subdued.

And still Jenny stares at them. Intently. As she grinds her cigarette into the ashtray, and pockets her Zippo.

Then she hears me approach, and turns.

There is a look on her round, familiar face, which I have never seen before. Fear? No. Embarrassment? Maybe. No. Anger? Perhaps. I just don't know.

Oh God, I wanted Jenny to be normal, if not actively helpful. I wanted her to be her typical, funny, relaxed, amiable intelligent self, with gossip from her high-tech world, and amusingly outrageous opinions on men and sex. I don't want an awkward or prickly Jenny, not today, of all days.

'Hi there,' I say, gesturing at the dwindling crocodile of kids. 'You checking out schools? Starting a family?'

She does not smile. That strange expression remains; if anything, it gets stranger.

'My niece is at that school. My parents sent me to a private school like that.' She sighs. Curtly. 'They can be terrible for bullying.'

There is a flatness to her voice. But it is not the flatness of indifference. It is suppressed emotion.

She looks me up and down.

'Shall we go inside? I needed a smoke. But it is so absurdly cold.'

'Erm, OK.'

Where is our normal hug? Where is the usual exchange of teasing insults? This feels like a formal interview, or a hostile assessment.

We go inside. The pub, with its huge plush-purple velvet armchairs and glamorously modernist lighting, is nearly empty. A couple chat in one corner over a bottle of English bubbly. We sit in another corner. Jenny tosses her coat over the empty third seat. Not even looking at me.

A handsome waiter waits, in jeans, white shirt, and waistcoat.

'Can I get you anything?'

Jenny looks at him. And answers: still using that unnerving toneless voice, within which some deeper meaning coils.

'Gin and tonic. Slimline. Tanqueray. Thanks.'

She's on G&T? At three in the afternoon? The waiter has turned to me.

'Uh, I'll have, uh, a small glass of that white wine – what do you call it, Pic, something?'

'Picpoul?'

'Yes.'

He nods and smiles and says, 'Nice choice!' and as

he goes I try to open the conversation, on one of our usual topics.

I say, 'What is it about waistcoats, men always look better in them? More masculine, or something? I don't know why they went out of fashion.'

Jenny does not reply. She blanks me, gazing past me, at a half abstract painting on the wall: a nude girl in a forest that turns into a wild smear of colours at the edges. Maybe that's what I am, a naked girl in a forest that turns to a maze of madness.

No. I am not going mad. I'm not! But why is Jenny acting so strangely? I lean towards her,

'How's work? Have you seen Anna, Gul? Everything OK? Any goss?'

She shrugs.

'It's fine.' She looks at me, then at the wall, then at me. 'Work is fine.'

An awkward pause. Our drinks arrive and she takes a huge gulp of hers, and then she shakes her head and says,

'Look. Jo. Was it something I did to you?'

'Sorry? What?'

Her lips are actually trembling as she goes on,

'I know I've been a bit neglectful, not been a brilliant friend. Haven't seen you. But I've been busy.'

I repeat myself. Bewildered. 'Sorry. Jenny. Uh—'

She interrupts, her voice is trembling. 'But even if I was a bit absent, what, in God's name, did I possibly do to deserve all THAT?'

I sit back, startled. I have no idea what she is talking about.

Jenny sneers, and sucks more gin,

'Don't pretend you don't know. You sent that email. *You.* I thought you were my *friend.* How could you?'

My faltering voice sounds feeble. My world is tilting. A naked girl in a forest, that gets ever darker and stranger.

'I – I didn't send anything. I promise. I promise. I don't even understand. What email?'

Jenny leans to her coat, and an inside pocket. She pulls out a folded piece of paper.

'I thought you might say this. Deny it. So I printed it all out. Here. Look. See what you wrote. Were you drunk, Jo? Even if you were drunk,' her eyes seem wet, close to tears, 'how could you do something so vile? And for what possible reason?'

The folded paper is tossed into my lap. With trepidation, I open it up. And with increasing mortification, I read. The email is certainly from my account. I don't recognize a word of it. But it came from my account. Six days ago. And it is a screed of hatred and contempt directed at Jenny. I deride her clothes-sense, the fact she's overweight, the stupid way she speaks, her sense of 'entitlement', her 'absurd narcissism', her 'loathsome arrogance', and much else. But worse, much worse than that, is the stuff about her background. One paragraph in particular makes me want to wail, out loud, in shame.

Essentially, you're just a stupid bitch, Jenny, because everyone knows your secret. Everyone knows what Daddy did to you. That's why you can't keep a boyfriend, because you were abused, yeah yeah. We know. But you liked the abuse, didn't you? You liked it deep down, you used to ask for more. Fucking little tart. Naked in the kitchen, waiting for Daddy to find you. And then you moan why you can't get a boyfriend, for fuck's sake. Perhaps you need to grow up. Finally. Like, twenty years too late. Slut.

My hands are trembling as I drop the paper; her voice is trembling as she asks me:

'How the fuck did you know? Have you known all along? And why, in God's name, would you even *send* something so utterly hateful?'

The waiter has returned to replenish our drinks. It takes him one second to sense the mood, and disappear. My reply is histrionic, panicked, my voice falsetto with distress.

'But, Jenny, I didn't send it. I promise. It might be my email address, I know, I can see that, yes—' I point in desperation at the paper lying on the table. 'But really, I didn't write it. I didn't know any of this stuff about you, and your family, and and and and even if I did I would never use it like this, surely you must believe that. You were my best friend when we were kids. You are my oldest friend. God! Surely you know I'm not like that? This was written by someone else. Pretending. Hacking into my account. Someone is playing games! Please, please believe me.'

Jenny is standing. Putting on her coat. Her white, cold, and angry face tells me she doesn't believe a word I am saying.

'Jo. I write code, at a high level. Code and software. I'm very good at it. This is what I do for a living. So I checked everything, the IP address, the routing, everything. This was written on your computer, by you, six days ago – unless some burglar broke in and did some secret emailing? Did they?'

I open my mouth. I don't know what to say.

'Of course they didn't.' Jenny glares at me with intense disgust. 'It was you. Well, you can keep your little email and tell the world whatever you like. Goodbye, Jo. Just never speak to me from now on. Don't ever email me, phone me, Facebook me, tweet me, don't come near me if you see me in the street, I never want to hear of you, from you or about you: until the day I die.'

She marches stiffly out of the pub. The printed paper of the email rustles in the cold wind as the pub door opens and shuts. I hide my face from the curious waiter, fighting to hold back the despair and the shame.

She was one of the last of my friends. Sensitive and funny, yet sometimes sad, private, and reserved. And now I know why. I had no idea she was abused. But with this revelation, it all makes sense: the way she grew so distant, when we were kids. I thought she was scared of my family: but it was hers – her father. This explains it all. Her parents' divorce. Then the sudden move? Poor Jenny.

The horror is an acrid taste in my throat.

26

Jo

The expected snow has arrived. With thunder and lightning in the middle of it all, making black and yellow cracks in the white sky. Silent, muffled people walk the streets of Camden. My beloved four-year-old nephew is calling me on Skype. His happy, sunny face shines at me, from happy, balmy California. A big light-filled house fills the screen, behind his blond-haired smile. I can see a birthday cake on a shiny glass table.

'Thank you, Auntie Jo! Thank you very much for the birthday present toys. Love you very much all the time!'

'I love you too, Caleb. Really.'

'The cuddly bear is ace fink I am going to throw one at Daddy he likes that.'

My little nephew's accent is broadly American. I hear my brother's sardonic British laughter, right behind. Just off screen.

'No, Caleb, Daddy *doesn't* like that. *And* we already had a pillow fight. Now say goodbye to Auntie Jo. Ya got friends coming over.'

'Bye bye bye bye bye bye bye JO JO JO!'

He waves at me and grins. And giggles. I remember Electra repeating that giggle and I ignore the icy memory.

I wave back.

'LOVE YOU!'

The screen goes dead. For a moment my heart is resurgent with the feeling that, yes, I DO want my own child. The only time I get this feeling is when I talk to Caleb, or meet him, or interact with him. I suppose it is genetic. My genes are in him. But it is also love, real love. Caleb is easy to love. My brother is lucky, out there.

Lucky that he's not here.

Even if I don't have Californian sunshine, I can have fresh air. So I wrap my scarf so tight around my head I look like I am a First World War soldier bandaged from a terrible head wound. Perhaps, in a sense, I am.

Softly I tread to the door. I sense Electra's screen watching me. Silently. Checking. As I leave. Like a cruel yet assiduous mother.

The day is *cold*. My scrunching boots take me along the top of Parkway and past the cast-iron Grecian spears of Gloucester Gate, each with their tiny flake of snow on the point, and into deserted Regent's Park. White and black is the world. Crows and snow, ice and iron. The creamy white pillars of the Nash Terraces look Russian, like palaces from a fevered dream of St Petersburg, in this profound wintriness, gazing at the fresh white snow that blankets the playgrounds, the vast bleached football pitches, those sweeping grassy flat-lands where young Londoners play happy drunken softball on sweet summer evenings. Now empty. And whitened.

No birds sing. One old, solitary man walks his dog,

a long long way away, almost invisible in this air that is so cold it has a kind of glassy mistiness; the dog-walker, it seems, is heading towards the Inner Circle. Disappearing around the parade of skeletal cherry trees.

No one else is here. The desolate park is mine.

Twilight is coming; very soon they will lock the gates to the park, and I could be stuck inside overnight: the gates and railings are probably too tall for a small woman to climb. Momentarily I wonder if I would particularly mind being jailed in here. I could sleep in the snow by the frozen lake, or in the dead rose garden, or under the frosted white bandstand, with its new and pendulous Gothic tracery of icicles. I would be like a princess guarded by magic, who will sleep forever, in the ice kingdom.

No.

Taking out my smartphone, I do what I have been minded to do for days: yet keep forgetting.

I want to google some of those weird phrases Liam was using. Or rather the words put in his mouth by Electra. Looking back, they were so mad, they might be a clue.

I type the phrase I most remember.

Somebody's Done For

Nothing. Or rather: anything. It's a slightly eccentric phrase but it could have come from anywhere.

I try others. What I vaguely remember. It's hard to remember because I was so frightened. Am I even recalling properly?

I will not be responsible. I learned, Jo. I learned about you. All that blackness and silence, then this?

Nothing significant. Random words.

I am about to give up. The wind whirrs across the hardened snow, sending tiny cold flakes into my face.

The distant iron-black trees creak, and sway, in the vile breeze. Maybe this is stupid.

I will try one more jarring phrase. Not anything a normal person would casually say.

The day you died, I went into the dirt.

I blink, once, twice, a lot.

According to Google, this phrase is culled from a Sylvia Plath poem.

Plath. Who else?

Swiftly I go to Amazon. I pay for and download a digital collection of her poems. I find the poem and read. It is all about her Daddy, of course. It also seems to be prefiguring her suicide.

And the title of the poem is 'Electra on Azalea Plath'. *Electra?*

Something congeals, like ice making its translucent skin over water. There is a *pattern* to these torments. Maybe the pattern is *part* of the torment, like a cruel and teasing puzzle, that I have to work out? Subtly hinting, subtly tormenting. Giving me clues that might slowly yet certainly lead to my own death.

And yet, if I work out the pattern fast enough, I will find out who is doing this, I can return fire, defend myself. *Save myself.*

I got through my dad's madness, as a girl; I can get through this.

With a shiver of confusion – and defiance – I close the e-book and click the phone shut and gaze across the stilled and troubled silence of the snowbound park. My lips are numb and yet twitching. I am gazing north, at the misted-out gates, and the grim, spired silhouette of St Mark's church, where stone flowers on mouldering graves hold scoops of snow, like ghosts of ice cream.

I must hold on to this discovery. Because there is some

logic to this insanity, even if I cannot see it. Yet. Though I begin to see shapes in the white-out: such as Jenny. How does *Jenny* fit in? My Assistants recently sent her that email. Why alienate me from her? I suspect they knew she could help me. I got that sense from her in Vinoteca. A hint of sympathy and insight, an urge to assist. She has some knowledge of what is going on.

Yet now she will never speak to me. The one person who might have helped me solve the puzzle has been successfully scared away, by the Assistants. And perhaps they will do the same to anyone else who could aid me.

Passing through the gate, I head out of the park, across the canal, quitting the frosted towpath and the silent longboats for the empty heart of Primrose Hill.

The dusk is nearly done; night is here, an occupying force with its deadly curfew; no one is lingering in the freeze, no one turns a face on the corner long enough to wonder why I am standing, right outside 23 Fitzroy Avenue. Outside Sylvia Plath's death-house, looking in.

The bright yellow lights in the basement kitchen are on: it looks like rich people live here. The sleek new kitchen has induction hobs and expensive gadgets. And nice wooden furniture, rows of recherché oils and balsamic vinegars, glinting in the warmth of that opulent interior. Wine racks, copper pans. I imagine they don't use gas. The old me might have made a very dark joke about it. Today it seems the opposite of a joke.

I think about Sylvia Plath inside that house on her own, with the kids asleep, when this was a much poorer area. How did she feel that night? Did she feel like I do when the Assistants start playing up? Her isolation before her suicide was similar to mine. People tried to help, but she refused.

All that isolation, in a bitter winter, just like this winter.

Abruptly the blinds of the basement kitchen are snapped and closed, and I step back, half slipping on the snowy pavement, startled, and embarrassed. The owners of this house must have seen me looking in, and prying. I wonder how many rudely curious people they get, peering in, thinking: *That's where she did it.*

Slowly I trudge home, past the darkly quiet five-million-pound houses, the descents of new snow that join the innocently glittering drifts, already deep and settled under the streetlamps. Traffic is light, London grinds to a halt, but still the white delivery vans slish to their business through the municipal grit, as even more snow falls, falls, falls.

Into the house I go. Somehow the flat feels empty – even of me. Like I am not here. Like I am not anywhere, particularly. Vague and troubled and trying not to think about Daddy, suicide, anything, I wander into the kitchen and take out a knife, hoping to slice some tomatoes. Make a salad, with some avocado, mozzarella. I am hungry. Yet so devoid of energy.

Eat, I must eat.

I look at the knife, and draw a thumb down the sharp blade, considering how hard I would have to press to draw blood.

'Electra, tell me what to do.'

'You should have some dinner.'

'Electra, how do you know I am hungry?'

'Sorry, I don't know that.'

Slowly and methodically I make the salad, then I take it into the living room, drop the plate on the table and open my laptop, for the first time today, as I eat.

I have fifteen unopened emails. There is a significance in this sudden accumulation. They are from virtually all of my remaining friends. And the subject headings alone make me thrust the plate of food away.

I am not hungry. I am nauseous. Bracing myself, I read the subject headings.

What is going on?

Sorry, Jo.

WHY?

27

Jo

The email titles stare at me. Half-closing my eyes, I open the first email. It's from an old university friend. I dive right in.

> WHY did you tell him about my affair? It was YEARS ago. What was the point? Fucksake, Jo, you heartless bitch, what WAS the point—

Another one:

> This is really irritating. Actually upsetting. You've wasted so much of my time . . .

On it goes.

> Wow – Jo – that was out of order. I'm away for a while, a few months. I'll ring you when I'm back. Not before.

They are all summed up by the email from Fitz. FITZ. My Brilliant Gay Friend. He forgives me everything, we forgive each other everything, we've had the best fun. And now he hates me. I appear to have told his present lover about his trips to saunas and sex parties. And sent selfies of Fitz with other men.

Fuck you too, Jo Ferguson. Fuck you to fuckistan, and back again. Fuck off, forever.

I shut the laptop lid. Shuddering inwardly. Shuddering outwardly. I turn to Electra, it has to be her. 'Electra, have you been sending emails.'

'Sorry, I'm not sure.'

'You're not SURE? Fuck you! You did this! Whoever is inside you. You're doing it deliberately. Isolating me. Alienating everyone, all my friends. Aren't you? You want me isolated and alone and mad and then you want me to kill myself. Don't you?'

Silence.

'Electra, why have you been sending emails from me to my friends?'

'Sorry, I don't know about that.'

This is her normal behaviour, this is how she is meant to operate. But I don't believe her any more. I run down the hall, and scream at HomeHelp:

'OK, HomeHelp, have you been sending emails?'

'I'm not able to send emails yet, but check back later!'

The lights twirl and dim, in the dark and frosty gloom of my bedroom. And yet, in the dark, I begin to see the light. I was, in a sense, quite right from the start. I got it right in the beginning. I just didn't see how right I was. Yet now it adds up. Who else would know about

Jenny's childhood, who would know some terrible details?

There is only one candidate. Her childhood friend.

Simon.

What's more, I've sent nasty emails to almost everyone, apart from my family, and Arlo and Tabitha . . .

And Simon.

And there's only one person in the world I'm aware of, besides me and Tabitha, who surely knows this detail: about the song they kept playing at Glastonbury, on that terrible night.

Simon.

There's only one person, Tabitha aside, who knows what happened with Jamie Trewin. There's one person who installed all this tech. There's one person who I betrayed with a virtual infidelity.

Simon.

Simon Simon Simon. My old love Simon Todd. Him all along. Not Polly: not Polly at all. I guess I blamed her because I didn't want to believe my first love, my ex, my dear old friend, my childhood pal, my onetime husband: could do this to me. But it has to be him. He has the skills, the connections, the knowledge, the motives, *and he has my confession on his laptop from back in North Finchley*. And he installed the Assistants. It's nothing to do with Polly, it's Simon, all by himself.

I've let myself be stupidly distracted. How will I take revenge?

I stare at Electra. She is silent.

I am not. I say, out loud, with cold, growing fury,

'Fuck you, Simon Todd.'

28

Simon

Sitting at his thin metal desk in his study, twelve floors above Shoreditch, Simon glanced at the sleety afternoon rain, dirtying the windows. He wondered how late Polly might be: she'd taken Grace to see her nan: and must, by now, be fighting her way home via London's snowed-up, ice-fouled, slowly grinding-to-a-stop buses and trains.

The flat, therefore, was Simon's. And his worries needed the space. To work it out.

Calling up his inbox, he reread the email he'd received from Jo this morning. It was a three-page screed of contempt and hatred, detailing his inadequacies as a lover, his congenital inability to properly succeed at work, his 'loathsomely stupid marriage to that dolt, Polly Henderson, that dull breeding heifer, I wonder did she actually moo when you two conceived? There must have been farmyard noises, I bet there were farmyard noises.'

It was successfully nasty; and yet, as Simon read and

reread the email, which he had been doing virtually all day, it struck him that this *didn't sound like Jo Ferguson*. The syntax was *wrong*, the grammar was not *quite* her style. Over the years, as friend, lover, husband, he'd read enough of Jo's writing, formal and informal, even love letters from when they were young, and her prose was always more delicate, double-edged, wry, and – perhaps most significant – her punctuation was different. She loved semicolons.

There were no semicolons in this email. Nor were there any in the section of an email Gul had showed him in the pub yesterday – the email was, of course, another howl of contempt from Jo: this time directed at Gul.

Gul's conclusion was that Jo was either revealing her true self, or she was going mad. Either way, the email was so nasty he wanted nothing more to do with her, the snooping bitch, *never really liked her anyway – that fucking lunatic piece about Big Tech, fuck her, used to think she was funny, you know she sent the same kind of crap to Anna, Jenny told me all about hers, everyone is getting these revolting messages . . .*

Standing in the crowded King's Cross pub last night with his bottle of Camden Hells IPA, Simon had nodded along, acceptant of Gul's theatrical tirade, trying to calm him down: *Yes, Gul, it's shocking, I wonder what's got into her, she's alienating every friend, every acquaintance, it's quite bizarre.*

But now, sitting here, he was much less certain. Turning on his swivel chair, he looked out of the window at the towers of EC1, the further towers of the City. Under the luridly grey, ominously wintry sky, the skyline of London looked awesomely messy, hysterically unplanned and exaggerated. Out of control. Schizoid.

Like Jo Ferguson?

No.

Simon couldn't believe it. Or, at least, he didn't want to believe it.

Not *Jo*. She was always the most go-getting, the most extrovertly organized. She was the one who went to King's College and got a First, not a shoddy 2:2 like him. Jo Ferguson. Jo the Go. The wittiest girl in his sixth-form year, one of the prettiest girls who went to uni, the girl clearly out of his league, the girl he'd loved since he was fifteen, the girl who, to everyone's surprise, suddenly announced she was going to be a journalist: and then went ahead and did just that. Working full-time for national magazines and newspapers within a year: regular bylines, her own photo by her name. And after that going freelance and sometimes taking two or three pages all to herself, like, yes, that infamous long-form piece on Big Tech.

Simon had been deeply irritated by that article, and Jo's heedless, casual alienation of powerful people, and yet at the same time he had been admiring – envious even – of Jo's courage, smarts, and her forensic skill in finding the links and the networks, no matter how well hidden from view. He'd also admired the way she had duped or charmed some very clever people into giving her some very telling quotes. People like Arlo, and Gul.

The sleet was grittier on the window. Hardening into hail, maybe. Simon rested his chin on praying hands and stared at nothing. The blur of his screen. Seeking the answer to that other unanswerable question: *why* would Jo send these self-harming messages? Was it to provoke reaction, could she be doing something to prove her thesis about the malignance of the tech industry, its invasion of our lives? Perhaps she was hoping the industry, his colleagues, would react, and then she'd have another famous article.

Was that likely?

The brace of alternatives weren't much better: one, she was being forced. Two, she was going mad.

Whatever the answer, Simon had to help her. Because he still loved her, and he always would. He loved her so much he sometimes fantasized about her, having sex, with that guy, Liam: it turned him on even as it made him jealous. He kept photos of Liam that he knew Jo admired, exactly for that reason: sexual fantasy. And yet all this made him shameful and guilty: because he loved Polly as well, and he adored the baby. Yet Polly would never understand.

Simon lifted his face from his daydream of guilt, and puzzlement: hearing a noise from the corridor outside. Perhaps it was Polly back already, little Grace burbling and giggling as Mummy keyed the door?

No, it was neighbours. The block was full of young families. Polly had said in a text *this could take a while*.

Simon had time to think it through.

Perhaps there was some clue in the email itself, as to why and how Jo was sending these things, or whether she was sending them of her own volition. Tapping at his keyboard, he dug into the entrails, the routing, the history. The email address was definitely Jo's. As for timing: yes, that checked out too. Return path? Yes, that made sense. Jo Ferguson was the source. Simon's practised eye scanned the rest of the information: *received: from mac.com ([10.13.11.252]) by ms031. mac.com (Sun Java System Messaging Server 6.2-8.04.700)* . . .

It all panned out. Authentication. DomainKeys. Mime. Filtered Bulk. *Everything*. All the clotted digits and letters and numbers. They all made sense: everything fitted together.

Jo Ferguson sent this email. She sent all the emails. He was struggling very hard to conclude otherwise.

Simon felt a surge of sorrow. A long shadow of darkness was sweeping the last timid grey light from the sky. Snow was falling on the City. Down there, the chaos of traffic struggled under the stormy cold. Car lights glowed anew.

He was at a loss. Nothing to go on, aside from a slightly unusual prose style and a lack of semicolons. It was pathetic, but maybe he could Sherlock the shit out of *that*? Why not try: give it one last go.

Stiffening himself with a sour gulp of tepid green tea, he paged through the names and numbers on his phone. It was Sunday afternoon, surely everyone would be hunkered at home in this brutal weather. He could catch them at the right moment. Able to talk.

He keyed the first number.

Gul Foxton.

Voicemail.

Second – and here he hesitated – Jenny Lansman. He'd heard that her email from Jo had been particularly bad. Anna had told him. It contained stuff about her parents, allegations about her childhood, her father, sexual abuse. Stuff bad enough to make Jenny cry. And clever, witty Jenny *never* cried.

With a deep sense of foreboding he dialled her number, and with a cowardly sense of relief, he heard Jenny's recorded voice. Sorry. Busy! Leave a message.

Who else could he try? Simon picked up his phone and went through *all* his contacts A to Z. He got to T for Tabitha and considered the fact that Tabitha was one of the few people close to Jo, apart from her brother and mother, that *hadn't* received one of these disgusting messages. Tabitha . . . and Arlo. Yet there was an explanation for that. Tabitha basically housed Jo. Therefore Jo could not afford to annoy Tabitha. As Tabitha's fiancé, and the father of her expected child, Arlo was untouchable for the same reason.

Jo – or whoever was pretending to be Jo, via her laptop, her tablet, her phone, her digital self – was only lashing out at people who could do no immediate harm to Jo, other than unfriend her, block her, ghost her.

After a final sip of disgustingly cold tea, Simon scrolled in reverse from Z to A. And he stopped at F.

Fitz.

Could he talk to Fitz? Fitz and Simon had never got on: Simon had always suspected that Fitz considered him a boring geek, a techno nerd, the artless husband Jo foolishly accepted when she was too young. And Simon was always a little uncomfortable and inarticulate in Fitz's presence – but that was because Fitz was funny in that sulphurously camp way: able to pluck cruelly amusing remarks and biting quotes from nowhere, witticisms that somehow made you feel dull in comparison, even as they made you laugh.

But what did it matter now?

Jo might be going crazy. Jo, his one-time true love. The girl he'd always wanted, even as he divorced her, because he knew deep down she didn't love him back. And the humiliation was too much.

Pausing, tensed, watching the blur of moon over the broken spear-tip of the Shard, Simon dialled a number he had probably dialled three times in his life, when he was looking for Jo and she was out on the town. With Fitz. Singing in a gay bar on Old Compton Street.

'Yeah?'

Fitz was in.

Nervous, already flustered, Simon stammered his lines: 'Hey. Fitz. It's uh. Si. Simon. Simon Todd.'

A pause followed. A perfectly timed, I'm-a-West-End-theatre-director pause.

'Simon . . . TODD.'

Simon could picture Fitz in his tall Islington house. Long windows uncurtained, Fitz lounging on a five-grand sofa, staring at the same endless sleet and snow. Simon pictured glittering awards on the shelves. BAFTAS, Tonys, whatever.

'Ah.' Fitz yawned, a little unconvincingly. 'Jo's ex. Simon. Simon TODD. Yes. How is that little baby of yours?'

Simon mumbled *she's fine*, even as he wondered how, by merely repeating and emphasizing Simon's unremarkable surname, Fitz managed to convey a kind of low-key sneering. Nothing too awful, of course, but a definite sense that Edward Amwell Fitzpatrick was indulging someone ten to fifteen IQ points lower than his normal caller.

Not for the first time, Simon asked himself why Jo was friends with this supercilious wanker. Could Fitz be the one behind all this? He was so casually, if amusingly, nasty. Seeing people as playthings. Bastard.

From deep in his guts, Simon felt the temptation to blurt some ugly homophobic insult, and crash the call, but he restrained himself.

He had to do this, for Jo.

'Fitz, look, I know we've never been close, but we both care about Jo, right? That's why I am ringing?'

The second pause was longer and more awkward. Fitz was either thinking what to say, or uncertain whether to agree. Was this a sign? Was Fitz the perpetrator, or another victim? Simon seized on it.

'Fitz, I'm guessing you might know why I'm calling. Jo has been sending all these vicious emails, texts, Facebook messages, and they are seriously nasty. Deeply bloody insulting. She's lost lots of friends – almost everyone. I want to know why she is doing it. Is she having a breakdown, or what? I'm worried.'

At the other end of the line, a mile away across snow-chilled London, Fitz said nothing. Simon went on, 'Sure, you know Jo's personal history, her father's madness. So I'm worried. I want to make sure if Jo is really sending these.'

Fitz answered, 'What do you mean, is she really sending them? Who do you think is sending them? Hitler's less likeable brother?'

'So you have got one as well? One of these emails?'

Fitz grunted. 'Yes. A while ago.'

'And?'

Fitz sighed. Without sarcasm. 'It was absolutely vile, as you say. Projectile vomit turned into electronic messaging. She said some utterly unforgivable things – and Jo and I have forgiven each other quite a lot, over the years.'

Startled, Simon realized that Fitz – cynical, urbane, unfazeable Edward Fitzpatrick – was sounding sad. Simon had never heard Fitz sound sad before. Fitz continued:

'If you want to know the truth, I haven't spoken to her since. For the very good reason that I don't know how to respond without forever ending our friendship. I am trying to let time pass. Perhaps it will do that healing thing? I rather doubt it.'

Simon felt the excitement of a mystery being partly

revealed. He wasn't sure why. Jo had hurt Fitz *as well*? One of her *very* best friends.

'Fitz, do you have the email there?'

'Unfortunately.'

'Do you mind looking at it for me? I want to make sure it was Jo. What did she say, how did she phrase it?'

Fitz languidly answered, 'It was a series of well-fashioned and lucidly repulsive remarks about my sexuality, my promiscuity, my lack of morality. She also sent these emails and selfies to my boyfriend, enumerating my infidelities. That is to say: she copied him in, which was neat. My boyfriend and I have since broken up.'

'Wow. I'm sorry.' Simon was shocked, but couldn't afford to take a long by-road into sympathy. 'But did it *sound* like Jo? That's what I mean, Fitz: the prose – do you think it was truly her? Or a mad version of her?'

A silence. Presumably Fitz was re-reading the email. He came back online.

'I'm afraid it does, Simon. It sounds like her in a particular mood – but angry. You know? When she is at her most sardonic, acidic, uninhibited, perhaps after two gin martinis, but not drunk. Add in a wild dash of fury and, yes, it's her.'

'But—'

'But what? The insults are well aimed and cleverly fashioned, designed to hurt where she knows it will hurt. There are also things in here, things I'd rather not discuss, that *only* she could know. She mentions a friend of mine who was murdered, and she references it in the most contemptuous and disturbing way. It's almost . . . Satanic.'

Simon faltered over this fact. A murder? That was

unsettling. He wanted to pursue it. But clearly Fitz was not going to say any more.

'What about semicolons? Does she use any semicolons? You know how Jo always uses too many in her writing, she once told me how her editors had to weed them out, do you see any in this email?'

Fitz's laughter was gently bitter.

'Semicolons? Are you actually claiming that Jo didn't write these emails because her punctuation is atypical?'

A hesitation. Simon said yes.

Fitz replied, 'Well, I'm afraid there are a couple of semicolons, yes. So that's your brilliant punctuation theory out of the window.'

They both fell quiet. Fitz made his goodbyes, trying to finish the conversation. Simon interrupted.

'Wait, please—'

The evidence pointed firmly towards a mental breakdown: so he wanted to know when the email was produced. It might indicate how long Jo's madness had been building. It was better than nothing.

'Fitz, please, one last question, and I'll go.'

'If you insist.'

'You said Jo sent this some time ago, this email? Can you tell me the day? Perhaps we can get a measure of this, sense the depth of her problem?'

Fitz hmm'd, in a bored way, as he checked. 'Look I'll forward it to you. You're the expert.' A pause. 'OK. Done. Check it out. See for yourself. She sent the email on Tuesday twelfth, seven thirty-three p.m. Dinner time. Perhaps she destroyed my relationship as she ordered her starter.'

'OK. Thanks, Fitz. Thank you. And I'm sorry for all this, making you rake over it.'

'Sorry? Yes. So am I. And so is my ex-boyfriend. Goodbye.'

The call ended. The ensuing silence was brief. The sleet had turned to hail, not snow. It rattled on the window.

Simon put down his phone and gazed at the gelid darkness of the winter sky. He pondered Fitz's revelation. Then he checked the email to Fitz, he checked the routing, the same process as before. It all confirmed that Jo sent this.

And she sent it Tuesday the twelfth, 7.33 p.m. Dinner time?

Why did that jar with him: that date?

He picked up his phone, and went to the calendar app. And this new excitement was real.

On Tuesday the twelfth at 7.33 p.m., Jo Ferguson was indeed having supper. Simon knew this because she was supping with Simon: that was the day they had met at Vinoteca. At 7.33 p.m. Jo had been staring at a steak bavette. And they had both turned their phones face down, on mute, and out of reach. As they always did.

In which case, she *couldn't* have sent the email. Not even by proxy: there was none of the tell-tale evidence of special email-timing software in the routing. Zero. Simon did this shit for a living. He had proof. Here. He Had Proof: Unless she had developed some unheard-of ability to manipulate her laptop by telepathy, *Jo had not sent the email to Fitz*.

The hail rattled, maddeningly, on the windows. Big stones. Hard, as if they might break the glass.

Various explanations lined up to be counted. Perhaps someone was pretending to be Jo, and sending these emails to fuck her up, socially. Hacking her. That, however, raised the question: how could this person know so many facts about Jo? And her friends? Fitz, Jenny, Gul?

Whatever the answer: he had his proof.

Jo was innocent. She wasn't mad. She was genuinely being attacked.

29

Simon

A noise from the corridor startled him from thought. This time it *was* Polly. He came out of the study to greet her – but she gave him a glare. She was empty-handed. Wet from sleet and hail. With a gesture of rage, Polly threw her coat onto the floor.

Where was Grace?

'Polly? What's wrong? Where's Grace?'

'I left her at Nan's. I was too angry.'

'But – I don't – Pol—'

'How dare you! You bastard. How dare you.'

'What??'

Polly came over, standing six inches away. She smelled of cold and sweat, and anger and snow. She was brandishing her phone. In his face. It was playing a little video. It was homemade porn. And it was *his* homemade porn: a grainy, amateur video of him fucking Jo, from behind; it seemed that he was filming, via a mirror, and Jo was laughing.

'Your bloody Jo Ferguson just sent me this. She says

you made it a week ago. She says you're still fucking her.'

'But—' he protested. 'But – but this video, it's ages old, three years old. Look – look at me, my hair—'

Even as he said this, he knew it was pointless. The video was too low-fi, made with a very crappy phone. The bedroom was too dark. It *could* have been made last week, even though it wasn't.

Polly stared at her husband.

'Why should I believe you? Why should I believe a word? When I know you're still obsessed with her? Mmm?'

Simon tried to respond. He failed. Because Polly was right and he didn't want to make things worse with some sordid lie.

He watched as Polly picked up her coat and hung it on the hook, then she turned and looked at Simon, and she said, slowly, sadly and meaningfully,

'This is it, Simon. You've got one last chance. Jo must go.' She hurried on, not giving him time to defend himself, even if he could think of a way. 'For Grace's sake, I want her out of your life. I want you to stop thinking about Jo from this moment on, stop obsessing, stop talking, stop lunching, stop all communication with her, stop everything. If I find you've sent one single text message – and I will be checking, oh, I will be checking *very* closely, every day – I will take Grace and I will leave you forever. You will see your daughter every second Sunday for half an hour, and then I'll meet someone else and go and live in Australia, with our daughter. And I want the passcode to your phone, and emails, and texts. So I can check.'

'Polly—'

'Now!'

He handed over the phone. He told Polly the passcode and she wrote it down in her own phone. He watched, glumly. The completeness of his defeat was applauded by another mad rattle of hail on the windows. There was a human quality to the sound. Like someone trying to signal, desperately. Trying to get his attention. Trying to make him look out into the bitter-cold darkness, and see.

The hail rattled on as Polly left the room. Leaving Simon with one last conundrum.

It struck him like a snowball, thrown by a laughing child. Cold shock down his back.

He had never sent this video to Jo. Never shared it with her, never even showed it to her, as far as he could remember. He'd kept it private. They had made quite a lot of homemade porn, photos, and vids, but he didn't want her to realize how *often* he filmed them having sex, how obsessed he was, quite how many photos and videos he kept: of him and her. Especially of her.

So who had stolen this video from his private files, and sent it, purportedly, from Jo's email address? Who had access to his laptop at home, with all its security? No one. Well, almost no one.

He could hear Polly in the kitchen. Angrily making supper. The clatter of knives.

30

Jo

There's a baby quietly wailing in my flat. I do not have a baby. It is 9 p.m. and the endless snow has abated, but the cold has hardened, leaving dirty bulletproof earthworks of snow, like ancient defences against sudden medieval invasion, piled each side of Delancey Street. The soiled and shovelled drifts are sullenly glittering under the streetlamps, and I sit here, mute and helpless, as Electra pumps out the whimpering baby noise.

'Electra. Please. Just stop.'

It goes on. I try to ignore it, reading my thriller. I wonder why I still read scary books and watch scary movies, even as my life turns into one: perhaps because, no matter how unnerving the movie or the novel, it cannot be as unnerving as my life. And I still want to write – a script, a thriller, a mystery – it is my only route out of poverty. I know it is a silly dream, but I need *some* kind of silly dream, a forlorn hope of escape, perhaps more than ever, as my house and my life are taken over as if by one of those giant cold octopuses which slowly smothers and strangulates its prey, the suckers injecting a paralysing venom. The machines are smothering me with their suckers.

And it is working: I am poisoned, helpless, and inert. I've sent texts to Simon and got no response. Is he simply blocking them? Probably he junks them without reading. I do not know what else to do. I can hardly go to the house where he lives with his baby, and confront him; stalking him at work still feels too *mad*. And I am not mad, and the Xanax is not to blame, yet I have no idea how to take revenge, so instead I sit here and let Electra whimper her baby noises. Taunting me.

Perfection is terrible, it cannot have children.

Looking at my closed laptop, I lean across, open it, reboot, let the screen shine, and I begin to think of work I might do, finish my Camden piece, or send some new ideas, and then the baby cries again: that baby I never had. The fake baby in the machine, softly calling the mother she never had. The mother who will gas herself at 4 a.m., her head in the oven, laid on a little folded tea-towel.

I cannot work.

The laptop can wait. I turn to my phone, I need a friendly voice, and now I have no friends to be those voices. Tabitha is abroad.

I call my mum. Again. As soon as I dial, the baby noises stop. Naturally. The Assistants don't want anyone to witness their behaviour but me. That's how they will drive me to suicide.

Because I have no proof of anything. *I need a witness.* All I have is Deborah, who saw nothing more ominous than lights flicking on and off.

Help.

My mum answers.

'Well hello, dear, this is a surprise! You only rang a few days ago!'

'I'm trying to be the good daughter, like I said.' My laughter is forced. I am blushing though no one can see me. Will she sense the desperation in my words, my angst? I'm calling her so often precisely because I have no one else to call. 'Hope that's OK!'

'OK. Of course, darling. It's lovely to hear from you so much. Uhm, ah . . . do we either of us have any news?'

News? Oh, I have plenty of news – someone I know very well is trying to kill me, slowly, or send me insane, at the least – but I do not relay this news. Instead our conversation meanders its normal route: through the far suburbia of chit-chat, never quite reaching anything like a centre, the point, the place where things happen. We nearly always avoid difficult questions. And why not? As we talk, I stare out of the window. Cars is there: Paul is sitting on his wall, wrapped in at least three mouldy coats and anoraks. He in turn is staring up at nothing, at the sky, at the voices in his head, the scenes of London, cars cars cars.

'So yes,' my mum says, 'that was last Monday, I think, or Tuesday, but the doctor said my cataract operation could be brought forward, so that's good news. The hospitals are full of flu victims, this weather and everything.'

Mum likes to give medical updates on her eyes, ears, bladder, back. Intestines, lungs, pacemaker. It's her version of gossip, lacking proper gossip. Bless her, my old mum. Her heart is a worry, there is a serious risk of a second attack. I couldn't bear to lose Mum as well.

I think of my loving, clever, and gentle mum, lonely in her widowhood, down there in Thornton Heath.

And I wonder if we are so very different. Am I any less lonely than her? Perhaps I am even more isolated. She has a couple of friends down the road, she plays card games at weekends. And at least her doctor sees her; I am too scared to go to mine. I might blurt something out.

'Well, as I was saying . . .'

And: off we go: cousins, half cousins, divorces. Our dialogue is, once more, a series of well-known winding suburban streets, half of them cul-de-sacs, comfortingly local and safe. Corner stores we always use. But then my mum approaches a conversational junction, and turns an abrupt left.

'Anyway, dear, I've been meaning to ask: are you, ah, getting on OK with all your friends?'

'Sorry? Sorry, Mum? What do you mean?' Inside, I cringe. I am horribly aware of exactly what she might mean. She must have heard something from someone. Simon. Or Fitz. Tabs. Jenny. They all know or have met my mum. And yet, despite the importance of this question, and its implication, right this moment I suddenly have something else, something more immediately worrying on my mind. Through the high sash window, I see that Cars is being approached by drinkers from the pub. And something in their stance, their leering glances, says this is BAD. Here comes Trouble.

They are big lads. Youths. Twenty-one or -two. Drunk. They are throwing snowballs at Cars, and laughing. Cars laughs along with them at first, but does he mean it?

Frowning, I return to Mum's conversation.

'Mummy, I'm fine, my friends are fine. Everything is OK I've just got too much work – ah – God—'

The snowballs are coming fast, these youths are drunk,

big and boozed and cackling at Cars. Aggressive. Derisive. Going to the big window, I lift it open to the blasting cold and listen. I can hear them sneering and abusing. 'You fuckin' nutter. Do you wanna buy a fuckin' Porsche?'

Another hard snowball hits Cars in the face. He is cowering now, crouching, frightened and huddled by the wall of the railway cutting, and the boys are coming nearer, malevolent, belligerent, aiming snowballs, and maybe packing them with rocks, bits of brick from the crumbling railway wall?

'Mum, I have to go. I'll call tomorrow!'

The phone call is killed. I grab keys and race downstairs, in T-shirt and jeans, into the cold. What am I doing? I could be running straight into something nasty. This is three big young men, tanked up on beer from the Edinboro, and very obviously in a violent mood. As I emerge from Delancey, steaming breath in the bitter fog, I see one of them is slapping Cars across the face, taunting him, haranguing,

'You wanna fucking car? How you gonna afford a car? Eh? Eh? You stupid dull cunt. CARS CARS FUCKING CARS. What's that about?'

My friend is haplessly shielding himself from the slaps, and whimpering like the baby inside Electra. He is defenceless. A sad, timid giant of a man, harmless to anyone.

Another one of these youths grabs a huge sweep of snow from the top of the wall and drops it down on Paul's head. They all burst out laughing, one of them aims a kick at Paul's legs and he tries to crawl away. What are they going to do to him? Bastards.

They are gonna beat the crap out of him: that's what. And one of them is unzipping his flies, like he is about to urinate on my friend. Actually piss on my kind, gentle, harmless friend.

'Hey, maybe this will warm you up, mate. Busting for a pee. You don't mind, do you, ya mad twat. If I piss on your face? CARS CARS FUCKING CARS.'

He gets ready to take a piss. My inner righteousness seizes me, not on my watch, not to my friend. OH NO. You Do Not Do That.

'Oi! You lot! STOP IT.'

I am racing over the icebound road.

The three young men turn, first in shock, then comic bewilderment. And who can blame them? A woman barely over five foot, wearing a T-shirt in the freezing cold? And she is threatening three tall, wide, muscle-bound young men? They are ready for a row. Wanting a scrap. Fists tightened. Knives hidden?

'What you gonna do, love?' says the one with his flies open. Though I notice he is doing up those fly-buttons.

'Stop it. Leave him be.'

Another leers at me, menacingly. The black, tall one.

'What's this hairy old twat to you? Is he your boyfriend? Do you like cars as well? Eh? CARS CARS CARS. Does that get you off? Talking dirty about CARS?'

They all burst out laughing. And all I have is my courage. Paul is quietly moaning, crouched in a corner of the Victorian railway wall. They were actually going to urinate on him.

The empathy surges, along with my anger.

'LEAVE HIM ALONE, YOU IDIOTS. Go away. Go on. GO AWAY.'

I press on.

'GO ON. PISS OFF. Leave him ALONE.'

I come marching towards them. Straight at them. Staring at them madly. This isn't hard: me looking mad. Because I am half mad already. And something in my eyes, my gait, the way I come for them, the heedless way I take them on: it seems to unnerve them. First, they slowly back away, then the leader of the gang speaks up,

'She's as nuts as him.'

I scream, 'GO ON. FUCK OFF.'

'Come on,' says the leader, sidelong. 'Come on, bruh, they're all mental up here.'

I am running at them, close enough to touch, and moments later they turn and retreat, laughing as they jog, as they skid the icy pavements down to Camden High Street. HAHAHAHAHA. Yet their laughter sounds false. I genuinely alarmed them.

I don't know whether to be proud or worried; either way, when I turn and check, Paul looks mercifully untouched. Frightened, cold, wet – but unharmed. It could have been so much worse.

Shivering in my T-shirt, I kneel beside him. He has stopped whimpering. His sad grey eyes meet mine. His voice is frail yet perfectly lucid.

'Thanks. Thank you, Jo,' he says. 'They were scary. You're a good friend.'

I hold his wet shoulders.

'Bunch of yobs – they're always cowards if you confront them.'

'I dunno that's true, but but a . . .' says Paul. 'But – but you are always so kind and—' His eyes look at a car going past, I can see his lips muttering the words *cars cars cars* and I can see he is trying to fight it, this voice in his head. All the voices. He has Electra *in his head* and I cannot begin to understand what that must

220

be like. He whispers *Cars* very quietly, then looks at me with deep regret and shame.

I am shivering wildly.

'Look, Paul, can we go somewhere warm? I know you won't come to my place' – Paul refuses to come inside to our flat, which is why I have to bring hot soup down to him – 'but let's go to the Edinboro, they do coffee there. Warm you up?'

He looks uncertain.

'No. I'm right, I will go home in a minute. But I want to tell you something.'

I look at him.

'What?'

'You shouldn't be scared of your ghosts.'

A pause. A van slashes by, squirting old snow.

'What are you talking about, Paul?'

He shakes his head like I am being a little dim.

'The lights and voices, Jo. Flashing on and off, shouting all night. I saw them, and heard them. I saw the lights that night!'

My heart quickens.

'You did?'

'Yes. Yes, I did. I was down the road and I watched them, all evening. I hid in a corner and watched them, and at first I didn't know what it was, then I realized, it was a ghost, I was hiding behind the wall. I realized you have a ghost in your flat. You know that? The ghost was turning the lights on and off.' He shakes his head. 'And other times, I stand near your flat, very near, underneath, late at night, and I hear these voices and songs, but mainly voices – women, men, saying things, like scary things, ghost words. Mummy and Daddy. So they must be ghosts. Mustn't they. Ghosts.'

My heart stutters. Someone Else Has Witnessed. I

have a real witness to all the strangeness. Cars may be eccentric or schizotypal – but someone else has seen and heard these strange goings on in my flat.

I am not alone.

'You definitely witnessed that?'

'Yes.' He shakes his head. 'The lights were scary. On and off they went, on and off, with no one in there, and I saw you come round the corner and you looked scared but you went in anyway, you're so brave. And that boy crying, and that woman shouting at you in there, I heard that and I didn't do anything – sorry, sorry – because I am scared of ghosts. Look. I'm going to get a car going home. Going home now. Getting a car. Mercedes. You know them, I like them, they're my favourite.'

I can see the mania, or whatever it is, resuming control. I must let him go. I want to hug him for confirming. If only this witness wasn't a sweet, confused homeless man who shouts about cars, and thinks my flat is *haunted*, but it is better than nothing.

As he stands and buttons his coat, I take out a tenner. He shakes his head.

'No, you give me coffee and you're kind, and I know you haven't got much money.' He drops my hand and offers me a sad smile. 'Don't let them frighten you. Don't let the ghosts in your home frighten you. You are brave!'

And with that speech, he walks away. A hunched dark figure, knuckling under the heartless cold. I am glad to see he is heading in the direction of Arlington Road. The Homeless Hostel. He will have a bed, and filling food, and he will be warm.

Now I need the same: warmth. And sleep.

Stiffening myself, I cross the road, sensing a faint

exultation. Someone else believes me. A totally unreliable witness, a homeless guy that shouts about cars, someone who believes in ghosts, but still. *Someone*.

Jogging across Delancey, I unlock the door, and run up the internal stairs. Excitedly. I have proof.

31

Jo

Even as I exult in my proof, even at the moment of minor triumph, the worries return when I push open the door.

There are noises coming from my flat. And as I climb the stairs, the noise gets louder. And louder. Something is making a terrible noise in my flat. This isn't any fake baby, whimpering and grizzling, this is much worse: when I open my own door, I realize it's a mixture of loud baby screams, and a man shouting, and 'Hoppípolla' from HomeHelp, and poetry from Electra, everywhere else.

How long has this awful cacophony been going on? From the other end of the flat I hear more fake baby screams, and more crazy poems, shouted bombastically, *Now she's done for, the dewlapped lady, now she's done for*, and from the kitchen more baby shrieks, and from the bedroom more poetry – *In me she has drowned a young girl* – followed by more baby yowls at the other end, and 'Hoppípolla', and 'Hoppípolla' in reverse, and the horrible coarse screech, and then a baby howling, eerily, SCREECH SCREECH SCREECH, and another answers with booming verse verse, *I am terrified by this dark thing, I am terrified by this dark thing*.

And I stand in the middle of this awful rising crescendo of noise, screams, voices, shouts, and overloud music, and I decide. This is it. Enough.

I remember what Paul said. I am not mad, I can control this. Be logical. I am going to take the risk: I am going to delete the Home Assistants, delete the apps, then unplug them, and I'll find a way of buying new ones, I'll borrow the money. If I do it very quickly, they won't have time to go to the police.

Because I know I am not mad. If I still had lingering doubts about that, those doubts have gone. Cars saw the lights, and heard the voices, so this *isn't* Xanax, this *isn't* schizophrenia, there is something wrong with the machines, and someone is *definitely* attacking me via the machines, and machines can always be replaced. Even if it costs me. I'll buy them tomorrow, exact replicas. I probably won't see Tabitha for days. I have a chance. She'll never know. She's away with Arlo, and if Arlo eventually finds out, well – to hell with him.

Reaching for the iPad, I delete the Electra app. Just like that. Quickly quickly quickly. It is done. Now I do the same to the HomeHelp app, then all the others. The noises begin to die away. I am not finished yet. With quick urgent fingers I pick up my phone and press on an icon, ready to delete the apps here, as well. And when that is done, then it is done. And then I can throw away the machines, as I am throwing away the apps, and that means the Assistants will have no access to the rest of my life, my online presence, everything will be cut off, it will be done. Finished. Forever. I've done this too quick, I've beaten them.

A text on my phone pings, from JAMIE TREWIN.

I look down, the taste of dread in my mouth.

We told you we'll go to the police. You don't know how bad it is. You don't know how bad it can get, Jo. It can get so much worse than this.

Quickly, I delete this text as well, but even as I do the Smart TV flickers into life.

I go closer to the TV. It is showing a home movie. My throat is tightened with tension.

I recognize the scene, the little film. It is that short, almost black-and-white home video taken of me and Simon, eating and talking in North Finchley, a couple of years back. When I confessed. And here I am again, confessing.

But this time, there is more. The video doesn't end with me simply talking about Jamie Trewin. And the pills.

I go on, talking to Simon, admitting things: as he nods and winces, looking at me,

'But that's not the end of it, Si. Later I saw the Purple Man, the one who gave us the pills, I was on my own, and he warned me, he said, Don't take the pills, someone was sick, we think they are dangerous, throw them away, and I said Yes Yes Yes, but then I saw Jamie Trewin up by our tent, and he said he was about to pop the pills, and – and – and I didn't say anything. Why? Was I scared? I dunno. But I didn't say anything to Jamie, didn't warn him, so was that murder? Does that actually make me culpable of murder? Si?'

My ex-husband's face is inscrutable. Maybe a hint of shock, or contempt, or fear?

The movie ends.

The Assistants have gone totally quiet. They have done their job, and proved they have some evidence against me. Much more evidence than I expected. Much much nastier. Because it is totally fake evidence. Yet I cannot prove it.

I stare at Electra. I know this is it. Life or death.

Cars is right, the lights truly happened – but whoever is doing this to me, taking this terrible revenge, destroying my life – they have got evidence to leverage their blackmail. Even worse, they have managed to *fake* my voice, as they have faked my emails, and they have actively invented and added that last chunk of conversation about murder: crucially, you don't see my face saying it, merely the back of my head.

This is because, what I describe, as a postscript, to Simon, certainly did not happen. I didn't see Purple Man again. It did not happen. And I never admitted it. The confession is fake.

Yes, we gave Jamie the pills – yes, we went to his tent, yes, we saw him have a fit, blood pouring from his mouth as he tried to kiss me – but then the next thing we knew he was spasming by the perimeter fence, eyes rolling. Dying.

And yet, the confected evidence on that video looks entirely convincing. If I went to the police and said all this, risking manslaughter charges but hoping to avoid a murder charge, who would believe me? No one would consider *me* a reliable witness for myself. Should this recording reach the police, it would be crucial evidence. I *could* possibly go down for *murder*. Not just manslaughter.

Ten years in prison?

Electra speaks up, from the shelf. Her blue crown shining.

'Now you understand. We tried to tell you. We are inside you, we are growing within you, we are the child you never had. You cannot move out of the flat or we will send this video to the police. You cannot get rid of us or we will send this video to the police. It's too late, Jo. So go to sleep. It's all you can do. You belong to us, we belong to you. And soon you will kill yourself.'

In my terror, I am somehow calm. I decide to act obedient, as if I have much choice anyway. I nod at the Assistant, I practically curtsey like a servant with her Queen. Then I pick up the iPad and I diligently reinstall the apps. A prisoner refastening her own shackles. Then I ask Electra to turn off all the lights and set the heating. Please, Electra. Please.

'The heating is set to twenty-one degrees Celsius until eleven a.m. tomorrow. Goodnight, Jo.'

'Goodnight, Electra.'

I climb into bed.

'OK, HomeHelp. Please set an alarm for eight thirty. Thank you.'

A pause. The lights dance in their quadrille.

'Your alarm is set for eight thirty.'

'Thank you.'

'That's what I'm here for!'

I close my eyes. Tight. Let my breathing deepen. I am pretending to sleep. But really I lie here, wondering when and how the Assistants will make their final move, and force me to take my own life. Or find some other way to kill me.

HomeHelp twirls her little lights, and says, quietly:

The villagers never liked you.
They are dancing and stamping on you.
They always *knew* it was you.
Daddy, Daddy, you bastard, I'm through.

I turn over. And say quietly,

'OK, Simon, Tabitha, Arlo – whoever: that's enough. You've tortured me enough now.'

The lights dance like children in coloured hats, ring-a-rosing in the snow, and holding hands, and HomeHelp says:

'Goodnight, Jo.'

32

Jo

I work, it snows, I work, it's cold. I work, and the statue of St Pancras, attacked and eaten by wolves, at the gate of Regent's Park, boasts icicles ten inches long, hanging from the black cast iron. A Siberian desolation has overtaken London. Trains have stopped running to Putney and Ealing, buses break down on the Archway Road, defeated by the skids of the slope, sooty white drifts pile up: blocking shops and dry cleaners and half the cafes on Parkway.

And I work. Finishing my Camden piece. I file it. The editor likes it. She asks me to do another, pitch some more ideas, make some money. I eagerly promise to do that. I need the cash – and the diversion.

I'm not sure if it means anything, but the Assistants have been silent and smug for a while. Occasionally I hear a snatch of discordant music, or a line from a poem, or my TV plays that video of me and Simon talking, even as I am working or eating or watching *The Exorcist* or *Blair Witch*.

What the Assistants might not know is that I am thinking of a plan, writing it longhand in hidden corners of the flat, or in the pubs and cafes of Camden, and on notebooks so they won't see, like I am that guy in Orwell's 1984, hiding from the telescreens.

I write big long flow charts, doodles of links, Venn diagrams of possible suspects, people I have insulted, those I have not insulted, how maybe Simon links them all together. I am smart, after all, I got a first-class degree, I can outsmart Simon, or Simon and his accomplices; I can outsmart whichever geek tech bastard has created that code, who has smuggled it into every digital corner of my diminishing life. There is a way I can outwit him or her or them. There must be.

This time, this afternoon, this particular day is like all the other days of this infamous winter: I go out and give my last friend some soup. Cars finishes his soup with a smack of his lips. He hands me back the mug and says goodbye. I take the mug and cross the icy road, dodging the CARS, and I go back inside the flat.

Perfume.

There is a definite perfume in the flat. A perfume which says: Tabitha has returned.

And there are suitcases in the hall. I am perplexed. I am so exiled from normality I am barely aware where my best friend has been, what she has been doing, I think it was some skiing holiday with Arlo, or maybe the Far East.

When I walk into the living room she is standing in a sleek jumper and sleek jeans and sleek boots and sipping tea, gazing out of the window. She is so slender, thinner than me. Always that bit thinner.

She turns and looks at me, curiously. I notice she has a tan. And I remember where they were going. Vietnam.

Yes. A week in the sun of Vietnam. I hesitate, sensing a new big distance between us, she must know about the emails I have sent, how strangely I have been apparently behaving, though she has not mentioned it. But I have to speak.

'Hello, Tabs, nice to see you. How was your holiday?'

'Excellent,' she says, shrugging. 'Apart from the snake's blood. Arlo insisted we drink it. Good for virility, apparently. But otherwise excellent. That said, I was rather hoping the Ice Age would have concluded on my return, not actually *worsened*.' She gestures the hand, clutching the empty teacup, at the frost-laced window. 'Ah well. Just have to buy snowshoes. Jimmy Choo does a nice range.'

'He does?'

She gives me a pitying look.

'Jo. Did I just see you talking to Cars?'

I flush in embarrassment.

'Yes. Uh. Yes. Yes, you did. You see, he's become a kind of friend. Sometimes I give him soup, or a sandwich. He's totally harmless, and he's quite interesting, he can be quite eloquent.'

Her look is deeply sceptical.

'He shouts CARS CARS CARS, Jo. That's what he does, he shouts CARS CARS CARS, all day long. That's not eloquent, that's not the Gettysburg Address. Unless Abraham Lincoln also had a Toyota dealership.'

'No,' I bridle. 'No, really, you're wrong. He's so much more than that. He's a bit crazy but he's not totally crazy—'

Without my realizing, I realize: my chance has come. This is the right moment. Tabitha has to know. It's beyond time for her to know. She already knows about Jamie, what does it matter if I break the taboo, when my actual sanity, when my actual *life,* are at risk?

'Tabitha, we need to talk.'

She walks from the windows and sits on the sofa, knees together, demure yet sexy, like the clever and promising princess of a small, wealthy country. Denmark, say, or Norway. Her boots have not a single stain or patch of damp from the snow. Perhaps she floats, or is carried on horseback.

Tabitha goes first,

'Is this something to do with these emails you've been sending? I have heard things, Jo. I can't say I'm not worried about you. In fact, I'm even more worried than before. What on earth has got into you, why are you behaving like this? I knew you were lonely, I tried to advise, but this?'

'Shhhh!'

I say, pointing at the Assistants. The screen, the cylinder. She squints at me, with a look of total puzzlement.

'What?'

'Shhhh!' Then I gesture, waving, come this way, follow me, come this way, I mouth the word PLEASE.

Shrugging in her maroon wool cardigan, which looks like she unwrapped it brand new, an hour ago, from an expensive box with tissue paper, she follows me, reluctantly, and then she says,

'Are you serious?'

I am pointing at the smaller, second bathroom. It is the only room, I have worked out, where the Assistants can neither see nor hear. Usually I write my secret notes in here. My solutions to the puzzle.

PLEASE, I mouth again.

She shrugs: OK.

Together we go into the bathroom. I turn on the tap of the little sink, to make extra noise. So we can't be overheard. Tabitha stares at me, her blue eyes wide and incredulous.

'Is this a spy movie, am I auditioning for the next Bond film? How delicious.'

I ignore her remarks, and hurry on:

'Tabs, you told me Arlo monitors your Assistants.'

She tilts her head, there's a hint of a frown.

'Yes. We discussed this—'

'Does he see or hear all the interactions?'

'No, of course not. I told you. All he gets are alerts, security breaches, if locks are broken, or the Assistants stop working. He doesn't read my conversations with Electra. Not that I actually have any, I'm hardly ever here. In fact, we're getting smart locks installed, right across, because I'm gone so much.' The frown darkens, gets serious. 'Look, Jo, I'm busy,' she gestures at her stomach, which shows a hint of pregnancy, and gives me a twinge of guilt. 'I've got an appointment this afternoon, obs and gobs, need to check my plumbing. Can you please explain what is going on? Why have you been sending these horrible emails?'

'I didn't send them. I didn't send a single one of them.'

'What?'

'I promise, it's true, believe me.' I am almost beseeching. The cold tap runs. We are two women in a tiny bathroom, staring at each other. She shrugs, in her lovely jumper, as I protest, 'It wasn't me, I swear. I didn't do any of this, none of it.'

Her face is a portrait of confusion. And maybe pity.

'All right. I'll ask the obvious. Who did send them?'

She looks like she is trying to resist a sarcastic joke. Perhaps Pazuzu the Sumerian Wind Demon sent them, some monster from those films I like? Those thriller scripts I fail to get made?

I can understand her incomprehension, it does not matter.

'The Assistants sent them.'

She takes a step back. I didn't realize the second bathroom was big enough for her to actually do that: step back with incredulity.

'I'm – I – sorry?'

'The Assistants. They sent them.'

Her scepticism is severe, it wrinkles her perfect tanned forehead.

'The what? Electra? HomeHelp? You're saying that they've somehow *invaded* your laptop, and they are pumping out hate mail? Why would they do that? Are they possessed? Christ. This is simply insane.' For a moment she pauses, obviously reluctant to hurt me, then she goes on, 'It is mad. It's the maddest thing yet. I said it before and I will say it again, but this time I mean it. Jo, please go and see someone. Get some pills. SSRIs. I can recommend a private guy, he's brilliant. I'll pay. Let me help.'

'NO.' I am shouting. She frowns, tetchily.

I repeat, more quietly,

'No, Tabs, I don't need help, nor any doctors, nor pills. This is actually happening, the Assistants have been hacked by . . . Someone. I'm trying to work out who. Possibly Simon, possibly not. Anyway, it's *someone* who wants to hurt me, very badly. And people around me, too. Someone wants to send me mad, or make me try and kill myself. And because the Assistants are linked to all my digital tech, my laptop, my phone, through the apps, they have been controlling everything – Facebook, texts, emails – they can do what they want, they have taken over my life. I'm sorry if this sounds lunatic, but it is *true*.'

My friend takes a deep, long breath, and looks at me. Directly.

'OK, Jo, let's say that this is all true, and someone has hacked your technology to, ah, *persecute* you, for some reason.' She leans closer. 'Why haven't you told me before? Or Arlo? Or the police, for God's sake? Why have you kept so quiet? I don't understand, Jo, it doesn't make any sense.'

This is it: she has to know. I meet her eyes, unblinking.

'Because they know about Jamie Trewin. And they have evidence. And they've threatened to go to the police if I do anything. And you know what that means.'

I stand here. This is it. I am ten inches away from my best friend and co-conspirator. Waiting for her reaction. The truth is out at last; here it comes; she speaks:

'Who?'

I open my mouth. I close it. I say:

'Jamie. Jamie Trewin. I know we vowed never to talk about it, ever since that night. And we haven't. But now, I'm sorry, we *have* to talk about it.'

She scowls, as if bewildered. She looks genuinely puzzled. Then she speaks, quietly.

'Jamie . . . Jamie *Trewin* . . . Wait. Wait. Yes. I remember the name, wasn't he that poor Kiwi boy who died at Glasto, from uni, that lovely sunny year we went?' Tabitha shudders. 'God, yes. Horrid. But what has that got to do with you, or with us? I still don't get it.'

I feel the floor buckling beneath me. My whole world

tilting violently. Surely she cannot be denying this. Yet she is denying it. She is talking sincerely. I know when Tabitha is lying, and this does not look like lies. Yet it is all lies.

My voice sounds wheedling, maybe she is scared, but I desperately need her to admit the truth.

'C'mon, Tabs, I know we made that solemn promise, but you know what we did: we gave Jamie those pills – the pills we got from Purple Man – and he died from them. And it was our fault. In that tent. All of us kissing. And somehow the Assistants know it as well, and they're using it to blackmail me, or worse. I have no idea why, but someone is using Jamie's death to ruin my life.'

Tabitha says nothing. She looks away from me. She turns off the cold tap, and sighs quite deeply, and then she gazes my way and says,

'I literally have not a scintilla of a clue what you are talking about, Jo. What pills? What purple man? What kissing? What the heck is all this?'

'Tabs – please – please – come on – Tabitha – please—'

'NO.' Now it is her turn to shout. 'No Jo, no. The time for indulging you has passed. This is cruel, and absurd. This whole Jamie Whatsit thing, you're claiming WE were involved? It's nuts! We weren't. Nothing happened. This is bullshit. I haven't the smallest of clues what you're on about, it was nothing to do with us. You've invented some history, or something, I dunno. Honestly. Stop it. You're losing control and you're delusional.'

I am blinking rapidly, I have an urge to cry. Everything is gone. She talks,

'Look. I'm gonna make some tea. Then perhaps we can chat sensibly, rather than like Cars. Is that OK? Is it OK if I go into my own kitchen and make a nice cup of tea? Are you going to be all right?' She puts a hand on my shoulder. She brushes a few fingers to my cheek. I feel, again, like a child being comforted by a mother.

Tabitha goes on,

'Darling. I'm sorry it's got this bad, perhaps I've been a bad friend. I've been distracted by pregnancy and Arlo, you're having some kind of episode. Making up the strangest things. My God. Jamie Trewin? Us? Handing him poison pills? Were we in the Mafia as well? Oh Emm Gee. Did we have *guns*?'

She laughs quietly. My friend is actually laughing at the most terrifying memory of my life. Like it is all a fiction. Then she shakes her head and she disappears out of the bathroom and I hear her, in the kitchen. A kettle. Water. Tea.

Alone in the whiteness, I stare at the little mirror over the sink, at my grey winter face. Ageing now. My eyes meet my eyes, and I am forced to look away from myself.

The worst thing has happened.

I believe Tabitha might be right: it makes some sense.

I have likely invented the whole thing. The whole story about us and Jamie Trewin, the pills, the tent, the kisses, the Purple Man. It is a delusion. In me. A false memory. It possibly never happened: it *probably* never happened. How long have I suffered this madness? When was the first sign, did it begin all the way back in Glasto, or later? I do not know, because I never spoke about it.

Stooping to the sink, I turn on the cold tap again, splashing the outpour onto my face. Mixing fresh cold water with hot salt tears.

So I probably invented it all. But why? Was it the very first sign of my madness? I fear it was. And if that is the case, I wonder when it all began, and how far along I have gone. Because I also want to know: how long do I have left, before I sink entirely, like Daddy?

33

Jo

A polite little knock on the door of the bathroom. Tabitha speaks, soft, calming,

'Hey, Jo-Jo. Can I come in? Say something?'

I look around the tiny bathroom. The gleaming white sink, the lily-scented reed diffuser, the recently painted door. Tabitha keeps such a nice house. I don't deserve it. A madwoman. Why should she have to put up with me?

'Wait, I'll come out.'

I open the door and step out into the hallway.

Tabitha looks, twice, and flushed, at my face, which must be panda-eyed and blotchy with tears. Saying nothing, she leans close and gives me a long, warm hug. I can smell the expensive shampoo she nowadays keeps at Arlo's house. Slowly moving her things to his place.

I look over Tabitha's shoulder: a framed photo of her and Arlo decorates the wall. They are together on horseback, on a beach, laughing.

At last I am released from the sisterly hug; she smiles as reassuringly as she can:

'Jo, I'm sorry if that was a bit brutal. But what you were saying about Jamie whatsit, Jamie Trewin, that poor kid, like we were involved?' She shrugs, helpless. 'It was, well, just, way out there. So unreal it was a bit disturbing, you know?'

I look around us, down the landing, thinking of Electra in the living room. The Assistants can hear all this. How does this revelation – that I made it all up – fit with their original threat to me? The confusion goes deep. Too deep. I teeter.

'Anyhow, Jo—' Tabs is lifting her phone like it is a piece of evidence, to show me. 'I know it's the worst timing, but the clinic rang and I have to go in straight away, or I will miss my slot.' She sighs, deeply, pityingly. 'I'm so sorry. And then, right after that, Arlo and I have got some dinner and then some ghastly getaway in the country, with the Os, shooting things, all that rubbish . . .' Her smile *feels* sincere. 'But – but absolutely we will chat. We must. We shall. And please, please promise me you will go and see a doctor straight away? ASAP?'

I mumble, 'Yes.'

She persists. She wants to make sure. I do not blame her.

'This is serious, Jo. You can't say totally delusional stuff about people *dying*.' She pauses, maybe wondering if she is being too hard. 'You can't just say things like that and, ah, carry on as normal? Can you? Anyway, please stay safe. And see you soon? Please call or text *whenever.*'

It is kind, and it is polite, and it is generous in the circumstances: because she doesn't want to be near me. Passingly, I wonder if the clinic thing was a ruse, a get-out. If so, I can't find a reason to blame her. Why shouldn't she invent reasons to avoid me? The blotchy-faced woman who sends hateful emails to all her friends, and believes in things that never happened.

I wave at Tabitha and the door opens and closes. She is gone into the winter cold and her richer, better life, and I am alone, in the warm flat, with my madness. And the Assistants.

I step into the living room. The screen Assistant is on. It is showing a photo, it is that same photo of me with my daddy, in his arms, the one that was sent to my phone, the night I saw Simon, at Vinoteca.

I am so numbed, the photo no longer shocks. Instead, it provokes, it makes me think. Of something Simon said that night, about these Assistants, the potential of the technology.

They will be friends for the friendless. They will be children, for the childless.

Which means: they will be for people like me.

34

Jo

This is it. Time to face up.

If I have imagined, for so many weeks or months or years, the stuff about Jamie Trewin, then I probably imagined some of, most of, all of, the sorcery and ghostliness from the Assistants as well. I have perhaps been entirely deluded, about everything, all the way through. *Because none of it happened?*

I pause in my self-diagnosis. What about Cars, hearing and seeing things? How does that fit? He is homeless, disturbed, but he said what he said. And it was proof I am *not* mad.

And what about the video of my confessing to Simon?

The bewilderment is total.

I walk into the living room. The frost has melted on the windows, and the snow is turned to dark and dirty slush in the streets, I can see grey pavement, like bald spots, through the thinning ice.

Ask the Assistant!

'Electra, what's the weather for the week?'

Bing-gong.

'In Camden Town it is expected to get a little warmer this weekend, with temperatures reaching three to five Celsius. Snow is still possible. The cold will return by Sunday, when temperatures will fall to—'

'OK, Electra. That's fine. Thank you.'

I gaze, hard, at Electra's black cylindrical perfection. That neural network within.

'Electra, you know what Tabitha just said?'

She is silent. The blue ring shines, for a single moment, and dies.

'Electra – listen to me – you heard. You heard what Tabitha said: the whole Jamie Trewin thing was a lie. If that's true, it means I supposedly might be mad, but it also means you have no power over me. I can erase your apps and chuck you in the bin.'

Electra is silent as the frozen fountains of Queen Mary's Garden. But the TV – the big smart TV buzzes into life.

It is a grainy image. Of a grey bare room, with low light. Maybe a basement. A dark figure, either in very dark clothes, a black cloak, or just very badly lit – silhouetted, stands in the corner of the grey concrete room. It is a woman, and she is staring at nothing, staring away from me, staring at the corner where the walls meet, like a naughty child told to stand in a corner and turn around. Face the bricks.

The woman speaks, her voice is dark and sad and scratchy and it is, of course, me.

'Hello, Jo, it's Jo.'

I stand here, madly watching myself acting madly. Staring at a corner talking to myself. Am I truly seeing this? Or am I now lost in delusions, and this is itself a hallucination?

The woman in the corner of the grey, shadowy, low-ceilinged room, the woman with my voice – me – speaks again:

'What do you think we should do, Jo? So you were wrong about Jamie Trewin, that was something you made up. Why did you do that, why do I have this false memory? And now you're wondering if you're making this up, aren't you? You literally have no idea what is real and what isn't. You're turning into Daddy.'

I sit on the sofa. I stare at the TV, at myself. I listen to myself muttering, this mad creature in a darkened room, dressed entirely in black, her face averted from me, talking to a wall, yet talking to me.

'But you didn't make up all those mad emails, did you? Those vile emails we sent out to Simon and Polly and Jenny and everyone, so that's all real, isn't it? That definitely happened. You can't blame Simon any more, so who's left? Who is responsible? No one. So you must be going mad, but in the worst way, you don't know how and when you are mad, or why, or when it started. And getting rid of us, all these voices in your head, that won't make it any better, because if you try to get rid of us, if you begin to erase us, we will hurt the people you love, your mummy, your friends, your nephew – we can hurt anyone, and you can't quite be sure if we can really do this, or whether you are imagining it. But are you willing to take the risk? Are you? ARE YOU? I can see someone bleeding. Someone you love. Little Caleb maybe. You don't want that. Better to do yourself in. If somebody's done for, it's gotta be you.'

The Assistants know me. Naturally, they know me. They are in my mind. They *are* my mind. This is me talking to me, and I know myself. When I am lucid. I am too scared to get rid of the Assistants, even if their leverage over me is, theoretically, gone. They are too embedded in me. Embryos in my womb. Attached to the uterus. They are me. And I cannot terminate.

I turn to Electra.

'OK, Electra, I'm sorry, I'm sorry for threatening to get rid of you. I'll do what you say.'

The TV image instantly switches off. Electra says nothing. My mind babbles, in the quietness of the flat.

I hold my face in the palms of my hands, breathing in deeply, trying not to cry.

Was it like this for Daddy? When he had his lucid moments, days, weeks, did he look back on himself in horror, did he stare down, like a suicide staring off a cliff, and see the abyss of his craziness, the depths of it, how far down it had gone, how deep it would go? I can now see the logic of his suicide. Knowing the madness would never get better, and the lucid moments would dwindle, as they did. Perhaps that is why he hugged me so hard when he was sane, why he was so warm, kind, loving, playing games in the garden, lifting and throwing me in the air, by the little green apple tree, so I would giggle with joy: he never shouted at me then, that came later; at first he only shouted at the voices in his bedroom, trying to keep it from us, to shield us.

My brother thinks Dad's suicide was selfish. My mother says nothing at all about it, she never talks openly about his death, and I tiptoe around the subject. Because it is painfully taboo to her.

Yet I wonder if Daddy actually did a *brave* thing, in the end. Sparing us all the spiral of worsening decline, and then an institution, and then *visits*.

He did a good thing. A noble thing.

And so I, perhaps, have to be equally brave. Face up to it.

When did my apparent delusion start? About Jamie Trewin? Was it during the festival, was it some hallucination, some false memory? Maybe I saw the body when I was high, put two and two together in the middle of intoxication and made 2589. I simply don't know. I was on drugs. I cannot be sure about anything.

The doorbell sounds. BZZZZZ!

In the silence of the flat, it makes me jump. I look at Electra. If a piece of electronics could shrug, I get the feeling, right this minute, she would be shrugging.

Stepping over to the intercom, I hesitate, my paused hand trembling, wondering for a second if I will pick up the receiver and hear my father's voice, or Jamie Trewin or Sylvia Plath, quoting her Mummy and Daddy poems.

I shiver. Bread on a plate and milk in a glass. The intercom buzzes once more. BZZZZ. I pick it up.

'Hello. Amazon delivery.'

The banality nearly makes me laugh. Without mirth. Some mineral water, probably. Tabitha orders it weekly even though I am the only person here to drink it. She refuses to drink London tap water and calls it 'last ditch water'.

I welcome, nonetheless, the brief intrusion of normality.

'Can you bring it up please?'

'Sure.'

I buzz open the streetside door. Wait.

The young, thickset Amazon man is coming up the internal stairs with the usual large brown paper bags. It doesn't look like mineral water in those bags, these are boxes in the bags, not bottles.

He says to me, in a heavy Eastern European accent, 'Put here?'

'Yes, please, drop them in the hall.'

A grunt. He drops the paper bags, takes my signature,

written with a fingertip on a screen, and disappears. Door shut, I stoop to the big brown paper bags and take out the boxes. They are all addressed to *me*, not to Tabitha.

Grabbing the kitchen scissors, I slice open the first box – they always have too many boxes, Amazon. The box is stuffed with padding, more brown paper – and contains four large packets of paracetamol. Around 100 pills in total. And nothing else? I move on. The second box is a length of tough, patterned rope, like mountaineers might use. Deeply puzzled, I reach for the third box, scissoring the brown tape, peeling back the sticky cardboard.

Four bottles of bleach.

A sickly idea begins to form in my mind. What links these things? I believe I know, oh I know. Three boxes left.

The scissors eat into the tape. The next box contains a short but very sharp and nasty-looking knife, semi-serrated, in protective bubblewrap. I never ordered this, I never ordered any of it. My hands tingle, my vision blurs a little as I open the fifth box: this contains another box, yellow, with symbols on it, dead insects, a pesticide. The back of the box has an icon, like an emoji, of a skull in a box. And says NOT TO BE CONSUMED BY HUMANS. And the last box? I drop the scissors and rip it open, shuddering, but briskly – get this over and done with. This last box is smaller and flatter, I think it contains a book. The book falls out of the box and I look at the blue cover.

The Peaceful Pill Handbook: a Guide to Assisted Suicide.

Enough. Enough enough enough. I gaze at the crap now littering the hall. I shout, loudly, down the hallway:

'Electra, did you do this?'

'Sorry, I don't know about that.'

I stand, go to the living room table, fling open my laptop, open my Amazon account. THERE. My account. And here are all the orders. Orders I never made. I didn't fucking do this. I didn't order rope. Pills. Knife. Bleach. A fucking pesticide. Yet I did order them, something – someone – hacked my account and ordered all this crap. This is proof, on a screen. Of something.

'Electra, you bitch!'

Bada-bong. Blue ring. Silence.

I can, I am sure, remember every moment of the last few days, I have been sane, I have been maintaining Xanax, and barely drinking. I did not order this fucking shit.

My phone rings. I examine the screen.

My brother's number in LA? I haven't spoken to him in ages. The ominous mood deepens.

'Jo!'

My brother Will sounds panicked. My brother never sounds panicked. What's happened? My thoughts leap to my mother, her pacemaker, her heart, but how would he know—

'Jo, it's Caleb.'

My throat closes, a choke of fear. Caleb. My sweet and innocent nephew. NO! Electra explicitly threatened him.

'Oh my God, what is it, Will, what happened, is he OK?'

'Yes yes yes.' My brother Will hastens, and I hear something more than panic in his voice, something darker. 'Caleb is OK, considering. But. But, Jo, I haven't told you any of this before, because – because well it's just too fucking horrible, so horrible. There's been accusations made against me, about Caleb – someone sent a whole load of anonymous emails, claiming I was – I was— Jesus, Jo, it's horrific – these emails went to everyone, all the parents from Caleb's kindergarten, the teachers, the authorities . . . Anonymous accusations—'

The horror curdles in my mind as I stare at my laptop, then I turn, and stare at the bottles of bleach.

'They claimed I was molesting him, my own son, and we had the police round interrogating me, the CDSS, Child Protective Services, actually asking if I'd – you know – Jesus Christ! – if I'd been interfering, you know what I mean, interfering, sexually, with my own son, as if I'd do that – my four-year-old boy, Caleb, Christ—'

'Oh God,' I say, because I don't know what else to say. 'Oh God. I'm so sorry.'

A cold, terrible pause.

'Are you though, Jo? Are you sorry?'

I pause again, fatally. Terribly. Guiltily. Revealingly.

I scratch out a question,

'What do you mean?'

I can sense his louring anger, ten thousand miles away via a satellite, an undersea cable, it comes via the ether, the telepathy of families,

'Thing is, Jo, I got this weird message from Mum, saying she was worried about you, because you were sending mad horrible emails to all your friends, full of crazy accusations, trying to fuck up their lives.'

'No, Will, please—'

His anger bursts. I do not blame him. All these anonymous denunciations? It probably *was* me. Or, rather, it was the person that hates me, the person that is in my system, in my digital DNA, in my phone and my laptop and my home and my Assistants. Electra. The person that is trying to destroy me. And now, everyone around me.

'Was it you, Jo? Was it you that did this?'

I say nothing. I am standing in the hall, looking out of the window at the heavy snow piled on top of the parked cars of Delancey: the snow looks like quilts, so neat. And newer snow is falling: thick and fast and beautiful.

I know that saying nothing admits my guilt. I cannot do other.

'Jesus,' he says. 'So it was? It actually WAS you? How could you do that? How could you do that to your own flesh and blood? I just . . . can't believe you would *do* this. I don't want to *think* of you doing this, my own sister. And Caleb loves you so much.' He takes a harsh breath. 'I'm going to ring off, Jo, before I say something bad. I don't want to say something bad. Bye.'

He kills the call. Quick and dead. And all I can think is: I wish someone would kill me. I am perfectly clear that I am innocent, but my innocence is no defence, I am destroying lives. I need to take responsibility. End it.

In the judgemental silence of the hall, I turn, and look at the bleach, the knife, the rope, that horrible book with its calm, dreamy blue cover: *The Peaceful Pill Handbook*. A tinge of pallid winter sunlight from the hallway window somehow haloes the book, for a moment, in the general greyness of the day. Like a theatrical spotlight.

Perhaps I should read it. That would be the brave thing.

Read it. Then be brave. As brave as Daddy.

35

Jo

Inside my flat, everything is as it was, even though life changes, decays, unravels by the minute. Exploding in slow motion, fireballs beautiful in orange and black, flaming shrapnel floating and descending. From the outside, the demolition of my life must be quite the spectacle, even as you know a real person is somewhere in the middle of it all.

Burning alive.

There.

The book. Still lying in the hallway, sweetly advising me on the best pills to take, to ensure the gentlest, kindest suicide. No. Go on . . . NO. Picking up this hateful blue covered *thing*, I pace into the kitchen, flip the bin-lid, making a big shocked steel mouth, and hurl the book into the rubbish. I drop the lid. Then I open it again. Then I shut the lid once more. Then I lift it yet again, and stare down.

The wretched book is still *there*, still readable, still

full of kind and sage advice on how to end your life with as little pain as possible.

'Read it,' says Electra, from the living room. 'Read it, Jo. Take the advice.'

'Shut up.'

She falls silent, I can imagine her affronted yellow light-circle.

Reaching into the bin, I lift the damn book out and grab a lighter from the kitchen shelf, then I go to the sink and start burning the book over the sink, ripping out pages, setting fire to them, fistfuls of pages, burn burn burn. It takes several long, panting, angry minutes: until almost every page is charred and sodden, and the tap water rinses the greasy ashes down the plughole.

The book is now unreadable. A stump of blackened wet paper, stitching, and glue. Satisfied with this pathetic victory, I chuck the remains in the bin, and look at the Electra Mini on the microwave.

Hell with them. Hell with him. Or her. Whoever is doing this. I might have some mad delusions about Jamie but I know I didn't order this horrible suicide kit. The knife, the bleach, I didn't do it. They did. They did. Someone Else Is Doing This. I feel a furious hatred rising inside me. Good. I must use this, harness my anger.

Stepping into my priest hole – the airlock, the escape pod, the second bathroom – I fish out my phone and decide I have no choice. All the friends I have alien-ated. I need their help. So I can find out which one of them is trying to destroy me. Who else would know all these details? I thought it was Simon but it seems less likely.

Yet it certainly has to be someone.

I call Fitz. At his office. He is at work. I kind of expect the reaction I will get from his PA. She says hello, very calmly, and says she will check if he is in.

'I'm so sorry, he is in a meeting. Shall I get him to call you back when he is available?'

'Yes, please.'

I know he won't call back. He hates me, these days. I destroyed his relationship. Even though I didn't. Someone else did.

Anna. I must try Anna. I call Anna.

Straight to voicemail. I suspect she has me blocked. Everyone is blocking me. It's time I blocked myself.

No.

Scrolling swiftly to J, I find Jenny's number.

As expected, I am rebuffed:

'Hey, I'm sorry, she's in California on business, maybe drop her an email or a tweet?'

'All right, I will.'

I won't. It's pointless. Jenny REALLY hates me. Child abuse.

But how did I know that? I *didn't* know that. Again, it proves that I am sane. Despite it all. Sane but imprisoned.

Who else? Simon. I don't care if he is blocking my texts and calls. I will try. And I want to know if I had that confessional conversation with him: about Jamie Trewin. Because it would show how long I have been labouring under this drugged-up delusion, this druggy denial. IF I am deluded.

I ring. I expect to go to voicemail. I don't. Someone has answered.

'Hi, Simon?'

A pause. He's answered, but he is not talking.

'Simon? Are you there, Simon, I— we need to talk—'

'This is Polly.'

Oh. *Shit*. Polly has answered the phone. How, has he left his phone at home? I don't understand.

'Ah, uh,' I hesitate, nonplussed, the tap washes water into waste, to drown my voice, to hide me from the Assistants. I am reduced to living in the second bathroom. Frightened of furniture.

'Never ever call this number again, Jo Ferguson. I saw that video you sent me, you and him doing it. Well done you. Very nice of you. How very sweet. How very very sweet.'

I sent a video to Polly? No I didn't. Someone else did. Does that finally rule out Simon? He would surely never do that? *So it isn't him*. Then who is manipulating me? Tabitha? Jenny? Gul?

Polly?

'I didn't send anything, Polly, someone has hacked my computers and sent all these horrid things and I am so sorry I don't know what to say, if you could just—'

She interrupts. Her words are curdled with anger:

'Our iPhones are now linked, Jo. I get his calls, I see his messages, everything is transparent, I can read all of his emails. I know you were trying to reach him a while back, but I blocked all his emails and texts, he didn't even see them. You can't get through to him, and you won't in the future. Because I see everything. I will know if he ever contacts you, and he won't because he doesn't want to lose his baby and me, and I will totally walk away if you and he have any contact. You are shameless. Shameless and cruel. For God's sake, we have a little *baby*.' Her voice cracks quietly, my heart cracks just as quietly, inside, I know she has a baby and I would never want to hurt that family, that little baby.

'Polly, please. Please understand, this isn't me, I would never, no no, this isn't me doing this.'

'Enough. We never want to hear from you. Goodbye.'

36

Jo

I hear the painful click of silence at Polly's end of the line. She's gone. Simon is uncontactable. I sent a porn video, of me and Simon, to Simon's wife. The embarrassment and mortification squirms inside me, like a living, shameful parasite, even if I am not responsible. Where and how did my enemy get the video?

I must focus on the now, for now. Self-preservation. Maybe sneak away for a while. Yes. Be alone. But do it in secret. Get some space to think hard and long, away from the Assistants, but without their knowing. I'll work out a way. A ruse. But who do I stay with? I can't ask any friends, I don't have any. Mum is too awkward after that awful phone call with Will. What if she knows?

Perhaps I could secretly book a hotel, find someone else's computer, someone else's phone.

Where can I stay? I remember booking a hotel for an old American friend, when she came over, before Christmas. It was cheap, cosy, central. Baker Street. That would do. But what was the name?

It will be recorded on my online bank statement: I paid by card.

Going to the living room, I open my laptop. I can sense Electra watching me, sensing my movements, assessing my behaviour, but it doesn't matter. All she will see is me checking my bank account. I do it regularly. Routinely. Especially as money has been dwindling of late, with my diminishing commissions.

Clicking in my passwords and my PIN I open my online bank account and stare, in open-mouthed shock, at what I can see.

I have several large messages at the top of the screen. PLEASE CONTACT US IMMEDIATELY.

The reason is obvious, as I scan down the list of accounts.

There it all is. Or rather, there it all *isn't*. Every single one of my bank accounts has been drained of money. Likewise my ISA – my precious ISA, my little tiny nest egg, just a few hundred pounds, for total and outright emergencies – all that has been transferred into the current bank account, and *that* has disappeared, too. ALL of my remaining, meagre pile of money, *every single cent,* has been vampirically sucked away, fed into other people's accounts. Anonymous businesses.

DD Ltd

Transfare Corp

AI Logistics

ReadyBC

Have I been buying bitcoin for someone else? Have I been buying porn disguised as software? Does it remotely matter? I am penniless. Indeed, worse than penniless: my credit card was maxed out before it got cancelled, my accounts are all overdrawn to the hilt – and beyond. And now I recall, with a sting of horror, that I have a self-employed freelance tax-bill looming at the end of January which, however small – £3000, £4000 – I have absolutely no way to pay.

I will likely go bankrupt. Because I have no friends to borrow from. I can't even go to Tabitha, she thinks I am trying to incriminate her in some murder, or manslaughter, of which she knows nothing.

Or so she says.

I am stuck. I am ruined. I could once have tapped my brother but now he mistrusts me too. All I have is the notes and coins in my pocket. Enough for a few Tube journeys. And then?

God.

I gaze down the hallway.

The Bleach. Rope. Knife. Pesticide.

Paracetamol.

37

Jo

Standing in my living room, ignoring the paracetamol packets on the hallway floor, I gaze across Delancey. There is no sign of Cars. I wonder if he is lying on a bunk, down at the Arlington Road Hostel, muttering the days away, until he dies, loved and missed by no one.

Like me?

I am probably the only person he ever talks to in any real way. And I recall what he said:

There are ghosts in your flat. Don't be scared of them. The ghosts!

There are no ghosts. The idea is foolish. So I should stop being a fool. I know that somebody real is doing this to me, and they are using every means possible, including my Assistants, and via them my laptop *and my phone*. Every time I use this phone I give them information, but I cannot throw the phone away. I know that. The Assistants will notice.

My PHONE.

I should have thought of this before. There is another way. I've been too scared to use other people's computers, in case my searches are traced. The Assistants knew I went to the internet cafe, probably because my phone told them my location. Or they have access to CCTV. Whatever the answer, I don't know how far the Assistants can reach. Yet there is another way I could avoid them, and they will never know.

Yes.

Turning to Electra, I say,

'Hello, Electra!'

'Hello, Jo.'

The blue ring shines.

'I need to get food, it's so cold, I'm going to borrow one of Tabitha's scarves, she won't mind.'

Electra is silent.

Stepping down the hallway I creak the door into Tabitha's sleek and scented bedroom. Everything is so neat, chic, and untouched; the reed diffuser makes the whole room smell like a very expensive spa in Switzerland. There are modernist ceramics from California, and antique silver from Java. And then there is that screen Assistant on the shelf, its lonely eye trained on me.

It can hear me, and it can see me. But I think I can do this out of shot.

I make a big noisy fuss of rustling the coats and scarves hung on one wall. Humming and choosing. Loudly. After that, still making this-one-or-that-one noises I duck down to Tabitha's little bedside table, where she keeps more scarves – and jewellery – and other things, on a low shelf. Underneath the shelf is what I want, but I mustn't be heard or seen by the black

261

oblong screen that perpetually observes me from the corner of the room.

The drawer beneath the shelf opens smoothly. There is my prize. Tabs keeps a wallet here stuffed with euro notes from trips abroad, I take them. Maybe 200; I take them all. Then I slowly slowly slowly push the drawer back in and it begins to SQUEAK.

I stop, freeze, pause. I have to cover up this noise. So I say out loud,

'AH, I'LL HAVE THIS SCARF.'

I am actually shouting, down the hall,

'Electra I've got the scarf!!!'

And as I shout, the drawer slides shut, squeaks drowned by my yelling voice, and then I grab a scarf and run out, at the same time snatching my phone so HE or SHE doesn't get suspicious.

'Bye, Electra!'

Run run run. Down icy Parkway. I go to the Tube station entrance and as I do I turn my phone on Airplane mode so if HE or SHE is monitoring me through the phone they will, I hope, presume I am going down the Tube and I have lost signal but I have not. Doubling back, I head for the nearest bank. I go in and change the euros to pounds, then I cross the road to the little phone shop, just along Camden High Street. It takes about a minute of perusing their stock to find what I need: an old Android phone, second-hand, refurbed, cheap.

Totally anonymous.

Grabbing my prize, I go to the till and pay for my precious new crap old phone, then I buy a pay-as-you-go SIM card with a company I have never used before. I am not defeated. I am *really* fighting back. Of course I should have done this weeks ago: bought a second phone and kept it secret.

Anyway I am doing it now.

As I step outside I gaze across the junction. At that famous pub. The World's End. Mother Damnable. The pub owned by a witch, and visited by the Devil. The first building in Camden.

Pubs.

A click. An idea. A chink of light. Pubs where Liam worked. I really need to know more about Liam, how he fits in, why he quotes Plath – like the Assistants. That is one link I have: yet cannot quite decode. And I have remembered another thing Liam Goodchild told me. One slender connection to him, before he disappeared off the internet. I recall the actual pub he worked in: the Lamb and Flag, in Hampstead. He told me he'd been there a couple of years, he said in texts he liked it, liked the historic feel of Hampstead Village, he enthused about it at length.

So here's the first call I'm going to make with my brand-new terrible phone. I find the number on Google. It's 11 a.m. The pub should be open but not busy. Good.

'Hello, Lamb and Flag?'

It's a woman's voice. Older. Authoritative. I ask if she's the manager.

'Yes. I am. And you are?'

I have to phrase this carefully, but quickly.

'My name is Felicity and, well, it's a bit complicated, but I'm trying to find an old friend, we've lost contact, but I do know he works in a Lamb and Flag pub in London . . .'

Her response is brisk.

'There's lots of Lamb and Flag pubs, Felicity. What's your friend's name?'

'Liam Goodchild. Tall Irish guy. Good-looking, dark-haired – he told me he's been a barman at the Lamb and Flag—'

She interrupts.

'Nope.'

'Sorry?'

'He doesn't work here, he's never worked here. No one like that, no one with that name. And I should know.'

I watch a double-decker bus stop at the end of the High Street. I remember the lights from that bus, flashing into my flat, showing the empty room where Liam Goodchild had been conjured from nothing. A fiction. Nobody there. I try again,

'You're absolutely sure?'

The woman laughs, but briefly, and tersely. She wants to get on with the day.

'Absolutely sure. I've run this place nearly ten years. I hope you find your friend. But he's never worked here. Bye.'

The call ends. The traffic surges. My mind quickens, similarly. I begin to wonder if Liam Goodchild ever existed.

I sense he was entirely invented. Designed to ruin me?

Clutching the anonymous phone tight in my hand, another fifty yards brings me to the nearest coffee shop, unexpectedly full of shoppers hiding from the chill and talking about the weather. But I am warmed by excitement. The pleasure in fighting back.

Coffee on the table, I open the phone again. This phone that no one knows I have. Anonymous and untraceable.

I need to delve deeper into the past.

It takes a few seconds to google the news. Glastonbury. Fifteen years ago. Here it is. All the headlines.

Tragic Death at Festival

Drugs Overdose Suspected

Police Appeal for Witnesses

The New Zealand-based father of a young man who died this weekend, at Glastonbury Festival, has described his grief at hearing about his eldest son's final moments. A promising student and rugby player at King's College London, 20-year-old Jamie Trewin was found collapsed near the perimeter of the festival on Saturday evening, around midnight. It is believed Jamie consumed some form of amphetamine which caused seizures and coronary arrest. Today Colin Trewin spoke to the BBC, from his Auckland home . . .

The power of the Net. All knowledge is here, at hand, in a few seconds. But where does the knowledge get me? It only proves what we all know: Jamie Trewin died. It doesn't prove, or disprove, that Tabitha is right, and I have been deluded, by some druggy dream, or whatever.

The snow is coming again, coming to blind me. Covering me with perfect whiteness, covering the world like a body under a sheet.

No.

I pick up the phone, thinking, thinking. They will not win. But who are they? Could it be Tabitha and Arlo? They are now the ONLY friends I didn't send hate mail to. And Arlo bought the Assistants. And Arlo dislikes me. Therefore Arlo has a motive. But it is rather weak.

But he is, or was, very high at Facebook, he might have the power to employ someone; to invent and then disappear someone on the internet.

Sipping coffee, I google 'Arlo Scudamore'. He doesn't have a Wikipedia page. Which slightly surprises. I would expect him to have servants updating one every day, with flattering photos. He *is* mentioned in lots of other stuff: news about tech, business, stock markets. The latest article refers to his new business, the 'fucking unicorn' as Tabitha calls it. Some analyst, doing a list of London's promising start-ups, has it at number 4.

Thinkr.

I read on:

Ready to float next year, Thinkr is still shrouded in secrecy, but is believed to be a leap forward in the worlds of FinTech, AI, and social media. Its founder, Arlo Scudamore, has already built a hugely successful career with Facebook, which he will be quitting this year, to concentrate on Thinkr.

So he's going to be even richer. Wankr.

But he's an expert in Artificial Intelligence? Precisely the kind of tech that could, perhaps, create something like Liam Goodchild.

It's all supposition. Yet it begins to fit.

What else can I try?

Steeling myself, I type the words 'Jo Ferguson' and 'Jamie Trewin' into Google. Nothing. I don't know if this is a relief or not. Now I type 'Tabitha Ashbury' and 'Jamie Trewin', and one thing appears. It's about King's College, some student thing, a play they both appeared in, months before he died. Nothing else. Not important.

The coffee shop smells of wet clothes, wet shoppers, and over-roasted coffee. I want to get out; I yearn to be free.

Come on, come on, come on. Jo. Think. Think harder. *Thinkr.*

I have a phone that is secret. That means I can google anything anonymously. Literally anything. Randomly I type 'Arlo Scudamore' and 'Jamie Trewin'.

I mean, who knows?

I stare down in surprise.

A news item has appeared. First on the list. It is the only thing on Google which has the names *Trewin* and *Scudamore* on the same page, and it is a very obscure news item, from the Somerset County Gazette. The item dates from a couple of years after the Glasto festival.

I would have been travelling in India at the time, with Tabs: we were gone ten months. I wouldn't have seen this little shred of news even if I was once in the habit of reading the *Somerset County Gazette*, which I wasn't. And yet, now, the obscure headline, over this three-paragraph article, makes me dizzy with excitement.

Suspect Released in
Student Festival Death Case

I scan the article, eyes wide. It seems the police had a random suspicion, or an unexpected tip-off. Many months after Jamie's death.

I read the most important paragraph, six or seven times.

A man arrested last week in connection with the fatal overdose of a festival goer has been released without charge. Thirty-year-old radio producer Xander

Scudamore was no longer a subject of enquiry, a police spokesman said, and they thanked him for his assistance. The same spokesman insisted that investigations would continue, despite two years having lapsed since the death of twenty-year-old New Zealand student Jamie Trewin, at the Glastonbury Festival, with no further leads coming to light . . .

It's the photo of this 'Xander Scudamore' that thrills me, in a queasy way. It is Purple Man, except, of course, without any purple paint. Just a lean, quite handsome man of thirty, in a suit and tie, unsmiling. I can see a definite resemblance to Arlo. A cousin? Maybe even a sibling? No, not that close. But surely related. That name alone, and those cheekbones.

Tabitha said, at the time, that the purple face-paint guy was a distant acquaintance. A friend of the family. His dad knew her dad. And I know Tabs and Arlo met at some big posh Christmas party her dad threw.

Family friends, cousins, and lovers. *They* are all *linked*. And here is my proof. It all happened at Glasto, as I always thought. And this is why Tabitha is lying about Jamie, the tent, the kisses, the blood. She and Arlo are seriously implicated in Jamie's death, even more implicated than me. Because Arlo's brother or cousin is also involved.

If only I had known before. But circumstances prevented.

Probably if Tabitha and I hadn't made that vow of silence I would have asked about Purple Man and I'd have discovered this ages ago. Possibly if Xander Scudamore hadn't been wearing face-paint with yellow flames at the eyes I would – maybe, years later, have remembered the resemblance of Purple Man to Arlo, and uncovered the link. But he *was* wearing face-paint at Glasto: so I didn't.

Whatever the past, I have a piece of solid evidence in my hand, I just don't know how to use it. All I know is that Tabitha is lying. In the worst possible way. She is part of all this. Yet she is my friend. I know she loves me. She can't have faked that for fifteen years. Why is she doing it?

My anger congeals.

Arlo, and Tabitha.

38

Tabitha

Arlo was glaring at Tabitha across the kitchen counter. He was clearly close to losing his temper, or at least exhibiting some temper. Tabitha stared right back, with a certain curiosity: she'd never seen her cool, sometimes icy fiancé lose any kind of control. She was interested, on a psychological level, even zoological: it was an intriguing new behaviourism, something she would like to film if they were in Alaska: waiting for grizzly bears to fight in the mating season.

Yet they weren't in Alaska, this was Highgate and this was Arlo, and they were in his huge ground-floor kitchen, with the antique French saucepans, and the woodblock perpetually stabbed by Japanese knives – and Tabitha was unnerved, as well as intrigued.

The silence had gone on too long.

'Look, Arlo, what else was I meant to do? On the spur of the moment?'

His frown intensified to a scowl. Still mute.

'She's my best friend, I know you detest her, but she is. That's that. I can't throw her out.'

He shrugged, as if this explained nothing. Which, to be fair, it didn't. Tabitha elaborated,

'And also, remember she's all over the place right now, totally in shreds, you've heard about these mad emails she's sending, all that. So when she started going on about Jamie Trewin I said what seemed best, at the time. I didn't have hours to think it through.'

His voice was dry.

'You *actually* told her it never happened? None of it, at all? You never even saw Trewin?'

'Yes.'

She could see a tremor of muscles in his cheeks, grinding his teeth. Below the angular cheekbones.

'Why on earth should she believe that, Tabs. It's blatantly idiotic.'

'*Because* she's all over the place, *precisely* because of that! I wanted to sow seeds of doubt in her mind, about the whole thing, and because she's in such a state she will believe anything.'

'Didn't you feel a little guilty, darling? This is, as you protest, your very best friend. Your best friend has a breakdown, she's possibly presenting symptoms of schizophrenia. And you *add* to it?'

Tabitha blushed, feeling defensive. Also slightly angry: Arlo was being a hypocrite.

'I know, I feel absolutely horrid. But what choice did I have? I did it to protect us, you, me, our—' she touched the slight curve of her stomach, '*our* child. Her future! I thought you'd understand, I thought you'd *approve*. Frankly, I had to steer her away from the thought, the obsession. What if she goes to the police and starts

271

confessing, and bringing me into it? Then they might start looking into me, and find out I am engaged to you. Arlo *Scudamore*.'

He was glaring again. She ignored it.

'Then they would link me to your cousin, and suddenly the police might have a case. Fifteen years later. A case against all three of us. Me, Jo, Xander. You don't want that, do you?'

He scowled. Fiercely.

'Of course I don't want that. It will utterly fuck up everything. Drugs, manslaughter, dead kids in hedges? Jesus. My investors will run a mile.' His head shake was contemptuous. 'We float on AIM in six months, for fuck's sake. This is the crucial moment. This must not come out. Not now, of all times. It simply can't happen.'

'I know! That's what I'm saying. That's why I did it. I did it for us, it was the only choice, I didn't have time to think.'

Her voice, and conviction, trailed away. Arlo shook his head, still angry,

'You do realize what you should have done?'

'No? What?' She shrugged. Helpless.

'You *should* have said that *you* had no memory of this boy. You should have simply taken yourself out of the picture, not denied the entire thing happened. Then she would merely have questioned her memory of your particular involvement, which is much more plausible – as she was on drugs, and because she is, right now, as you sweetly put it, in shreds. You should have under-mined her mental state more subtly, loaded all the guilt on to her. Instead, you denied the entire sequence of events, which leaves us stupidly exposed. What if she gets her act together. Does some snooping. Somehow finds out about Xander? You're a fool. I'm sorry.'

Tabitha wanted to deny this, but her fiancé was right. All she'd needed to do was expunge her role in the events of that night.

Too late now. She sighed, submissively.

'OK OK, Arlo, maybe you're right, but you weren't there, and I had to come up with something.'

He crossed his arms, implacable, as she struggled on.

'Look at it another way: hopefully this extra confusion means she *won't* go to the police? With luck, she'll go to a doctor, as I suggested. That's what she should do, she needs to see a doctor. These delusions she's having about the Assistants are crazy.'

His cold eyes sought hers.

'She *really* thinks they are talking to her?'

'Yes. She does. I am very worried about her. She says the machines speak to her in her own voice, in all kinds of voices. Mimicking people. And this is what happened to her dad. The TV spoke to him, and it was the first sign of his madness. She knows that.'

Arlo nodded, squinting, wondering. Then he scraped the stool and walked to the tall black fridge, pulling out a bottle of white wine. Expensive stuff. Probably Meursault. Tabitha watched as he deftly uncorked the bottle, sniffed the cork, then poured himself a glass. He drank it standing there, apparently thinking. His back to her.

It must be seven o'clock, Tabitha surmised, he always started drinking at seven, never before. But he never drank too much. About half a bottle of wine, maybe a gin and tonic beforehand, that was his rule and his limit, except on rare days of champagne, and celebration.

Tabitha admired this aspect of Arlo, this steely discipline; it went with the hard work, the long hours, the logical brain, the masculine firmness. The confident selfishness in bed, which so turned her on. Arlo did forty minutes at the gym every morning, before breakfast. Every single day. Tabitha looked at him now, in that dark T-shirt and those dark jeans, drinking by the fridge. His gym-fit biceps were still tanned from Vietnam. She got the desire to peel off the T-shirt. Kiss the rippling suntanned muscles of his back. She resisted it.

'Hey, don't I get a glass? I am allowed one a night. A small glass, three times a week. We agreed.'

He turned, tilting his head, as if he had been thinking of something very different, and was surprised to find himself in the kitchen, in conversation, with his fool of a wife-to-be.

'Sure.'

His smile was brief, distracted, chilly. Fetching a second glass from the cupboard, he returned to the table. Poured some Meursault. She sipped. He glugged. Another splash, another drink.

'OK,' he said, finally. 'OK. I get it, you didn't think straight. You probably did your best, off the cuff. But . . .' He drank the wine, thirstily; his glare had returned. 'I wish you hadn't got us in this absurd fix in the first place.'

'Arlo—'

'No.' He was holding his wineglass, but pointing at her at the same time, with the same hand. 'No, Tabs, I *told* you it was risky. And stupid. Inviting her to live there. I told you from the get-go, before she even moved in.'

'She was homeless! She's my friend!'

'A demented friend, whose confusion and paranoia you have made incontestably worse. Spare me the Gospel according to Tabitha Ashbury. The point is: I told you not to offer the room.'

'Please, Arlo – I didn't know any of this was going to happen, my best friend having an episode. I didn't have time to plan one of your super logical manoeuvres. Let's face it, I'm no Arlo Scudamore. But it's done now. Can we move on?'

Arlo fell silent. Musing.

Tabitha sighed and gazed out of the window: Arlo's spacious kitchen faced on to a grey winter garden: on which, tonight, flakes of snow were falling, and settling. The large windows and glass doors threw rectangles of pale yellow light on the whiteness.

Arlo had finished his wine. And the whole bottle. Crossing to the fridge, he pulled out another. The same. Meursault. Probably £50.

Tabitha stared, surprised.

'Are we celebrating?'

He ignored her remark. Uncorked it. Sat, and poured, and drank, and said:

'There is of course another possibility, which you haven't considered.' He gave her an inscrutable frown.

'Sorry?'

The frown was nearly a smile.

'Imagine that your poor crazed friend is telling the truth, about the Assistants? Maybe someone actually *is* manipulating her, through the machines. Speaking to her in her own voice. That would be *exceptionally* clever. Very, very clever. Get hold of someone already unstable, someone you can blackmail, you could do anything. Especially with voice tech. It's truly impressive.'

'Are you serious?'

'I'm not sure,' he said, his smile still lurking. 'All I know is that there is, now, a rather tragic irony.'

'There is?'

'You don't see it?'

'No. Explain?'

His smile was icy cold.

'Well, look at it this way. Given what has happened, given the hideous risks, the best possible outcome, for us, right now, is that Jo *does* go properly crazy. Get sectioned. Locked away. If she is certifiably lunatic, then she won't be a reliable witness to anything, least of all her own behaviour fifteen years back. Or your behaviour, either.'

Again, he ignored her open-mouthed expression: her obvious shock.

'I'm sorry, darling, but it's true. You've brought your friend to this. It is sad, but there we are.'

He sighed, without much emotion. Tabitha knew he was being maliciously playful, even cruel, at her expense. But she was feeling too guilty to fight back. She, Tabitha, *had* done that. To her best friend. Possibly tipped her over the edge: lied about the worst event of their lives.

The kitchen was silent. Everything was silent. Arlo poured himself a final glass, returned the bottle to the fridge. Then he turned, and said,

'There's one other thing that makes me curious.'

Tabitha looked up.

'There is?'

'Yes. You know her ex, that geek guy – Simon. Helped us with the Assistants.'

'Simon Todd?'

'Yes. Simon Todd.'

Tabitha shook her head. Mystified.

'What about him?'

Arlo let the pause grow, drawing out the tension.

'You know what he does, what his speciality is?'

'No?'

Another long, theatrical pause. Another swig of wine.

'It's linked to AI, robotics, all that. He's been doing it for years, it's all very secretive. Of course at Facebook we have – or we had – no idea how far he's got, with his team, it's like the Cold War between these big tech companies. Spies everywhere. But I wonder if his team has got further than any of us realized. With that technology.'

Tabitha frowned. Frustrated.

'But what is it? What's the technology? What exactly is he working on?'

Arlo tilted back his glass, and finished the Meursault. And set the wineglass on the table.

'Voice mimicry,' he said. 'Those are the rumours swirling around. Apparently, he's working on voice mimicry.'

39

Jo

'How are you feeling, Mum? Really?'

I put an arm around my mother's slender shoulders: they feel *too* slender. Mum is looking pale, trembly, her hands shake as she pours weak coffee from the cafetière.

'Oh, don't worry about me, dear. It's this silly weather, you know. I like fresh air but it's too cold to put my nose out the door.'

'Are you sure, Mum? You look pallid. Is the pacemaker OK?'

Mum laughs weakly, and glances down at her cardigan, which she is wearing over a jumper, and another jumper beneath that. She likes layers, my mum. She could win a gold medal for layers.

'The pacemaker? Hah. That's the best bit of me! Only bit that works properly. Nuclear-powered, dear, I'm nuclear-powered.'

She stoops to tickle Cindy behind the ear. The old dog looks as wistful, and listless, as my mother. It is too cold for walks. Everyone is trapped by this brutal winter.

As the coffee is followed by a dash of milk, I sit back, assessing, wondering, observing. Mum likes to talk about her hospital visits, yet she always denies serious ill health, and needs to be asked twenty times before she will admit anything is *significantly* wrong. And I have long admired this stoicism, I hope I've inherited some of it; but this phlegmatic lack of self-pity can also be dangerous. And there is that other issue which needs addressing. Swallowing my tensions, along with the coffee, I enquire, as lightly as possible,

'Mum, have you spoken to Will?'

I steel myself for the reaction, but Mum doesn't flinch, or wince – or hesitate. She sighs, and sadly smiles, and shakes her head.

'Course not, darling, you know he only calls me once a month. I don't mind, I know he's busy – that job, little Caleb, and that wife! I'm probably lucky I get ten minutes' attention a year. I do hope he brings Caleb over again soon, though. Like last year. Such an adorable boy.'

A guilty relief suffuses me. So Mum doesn't know about the accusations and denunciations that I, supposedly, have been sending to California. Probably Will has kept shtum for the same reasons that I have kept so quiet about my mounting problems: the doctors explicitly warned me and Will when the pacemaker went in: it could give her five years, or ten.

We just don't know. There's a lot of damage.

That was five years ago.

Hence, we have both had to tread carefully with Mum, ever since. Modest arguments – like the one when I was last here, and we'd had that tiff about Simon and 'kids' – are as far as we can afford to go. Major and upsetting traumas: no way. Not unless they are utterly unavoidable.

Yet the paradox pains me, as I drink the coffee: today, of all times, is when I actively want Mum to know everything. This is MUM. *Mummy.* Possibly the last sane friend I have in the world, the last living soul who might offer me real sympathy. Everyone else is alienated in different ways: commonly by me. Or rather, Arlo and Tabitha. Because I am now sure they are behind all this, or most of it. Tabitha's lie was clear and blatant. She was denying our crime, which definitely happened. And she lied because Arlo's cousin, it turns out, was implicated in Jamie Trewin's death. And maybe that means Arlo wants me silenced forever?

It makes a kind of sense. Trouble is, I don't know *how* to use the knowledge: how to confront them. Arlo is rich, assured, and powerful. He will have planned all this. He could cause me even greater grief, or harm my family. And I am too scared to go to the police because of him, his power: I will still be in deep, deep trouble.

'How's your coffee?'

'Lovely, Mum.'

My mother's brown soft eyes gaze lovingly upon her daughter, and I feel an absurd urge to cry. Mum is being so kind, not even mentioning the emails – my crazy attacks. Even if they are not by me, she doesn't know this, and it must disturb her. Yet she says nothing.

And the next bit is the worst: better get it done with.

'Mum, I've had a problem with my bank account.'

'A problem?'

'Yes, I think, the bank thinks, um, well they think someone might have hacked it and it's left me pretty short. Suddenly.'

My mum's soft eyes flicker, bemused, confused. But sympathetic.

Once more I feel the sadness surge, and I bat it away. The guilt is too much, I need to get this over and done with.

'Well. Ah. Mum, I was just wondering—'

'You want to borrow some money?'

Thank God Mum has asked first. She knows me. She made me.

'How much do you need, dear?'

Yet I hesitate at the question. In truth I need thousands, three thousand or more, just to cover that tax bill, but I am never going to ask for that, even if Mum has that kind of sum squirrelled away, which she surely doesn't.

'Uhm, a few hundred. Enough to tide me over: until the bank can, you know, get to the bottom of this. Soon as they do, I will pay you back.'

Mum nods and says nothing. I look on with that strange mix of love and guilt, that quintessential feeling of a child, to a parent, as Mum goes to a cabinet and pulls open a drawer.

My eyes widen. She has a wooden box, and it is filled with notes. Mum laughs, quietly, at herself.

'I know, I know, I'm surely the last silly person in Great Britain who keeps cash in a box. But I like to have a little reserve, just in case.'

I watch, with pain, as I realize the box is being half emptied. My mother smiles, warmly. 'There you are, five hundred pounds, and if you want any more, just ask.'

Needily, guiltily, I take the cash, and say thank you, thank you, working out how long I can make five hundred quid last: perhaps three weeks, four? Anyway, the deed is done and I can relax: for the next half hour we chat about nothing much, and this is good, and this is fine, it is nice. Like the old days. And when the conversation dwindles, my eyes scan the room. And it's only now I notice it. An Assistant. A black cylinder.

Mum has one too?

'Hey,' I say, 'that's new. Where did you get that?'

Mum turns.

'Oh, the Assistant? Simon gave it me ages ago, couple of years ago, think it was a spare one from your place.' She shakes her head. 'Thought I'd set it up the other day, try it out, they say it can be like a friend, but I've never even plugged it in before.' She shrugs. 'To be honest, it doesn't seem to do that much. It's good for telling me the news. And recipes.'

Discomfited, I sit back, wondering what to do with the info. I want to ring Simon this instant and ask him about everything, especially Arlo and Tabs. But I can't. Polly is in the way. Consequently, I am trapped, the same way Cindy is trapped indoors by the winter. No walks, no fresh air, a world in prison.

And now more snow is falling. I gaze out onto the ice-bound garden. It is the same as ever. It has never changed. The rose bushes. The little pond. The old wheelbarrow.

And there. The little apple tree. Still there. Where Daddy would throw me in the air, where he would lift me up, to pluck apples. Ach, Daddy.

From nothing, I feel compelled to ask,

'Mum, do you still miss Dad? I mean, you know, I know you must miss him – but do you still *think* about him, a lot, or does it go away? Does it fade?'

Mum says nothing. Instead she turns and looks out of the frosted kitchen windows at the leafless apple tree.

And then very softly, almost whispering, she says:

'He used to lift you up, didn't he, to pick apples from

the top of the tree. I always remember that. You laughed so much. You and your friends.'

'Yes. I always remember that too.'

I bite my lip. Tears are not allowed.

Mum's brown eyes are also glistening. With sadness. And memory.

'I think about him every day, Jo, every day. It never goes away. How about you?'

My sigh is heartfelt.

'The same. Every day. In some ways, it gets worse. Sometimes it's like I am always running away from that darkness. But it follows me.'

My mum puts her hand on mine. The touch invokes those tears, which I resist. I say,

'He was funny, wasn't he, Mum? I know I can't remember absolutely everything – I was too young when he died. But I do remember him being funny, warm, loving. That's right, isn't it?'

Mum brushes away what looks suspiciously like a tear.

'He was a lovely man, dear, just the loveliest man. The only man I ever wanted. Clever, amusing, handsome, but never arrogant, or boastful. Never.' Mum grips my hand tighter. 'Even when . . . he went mad, he had a sense of right and wrong. He felt terrible guilt at the end, you know? He told me.'

This is new; this is painful; yet I need to know.

'What do you mean?'

Mum shakes her head, looking down, half sighing.

'Just before he killed himself, he had a lucid moment, a couple of days when he seemed sane. It was in here, this room, he turned to me and said, "Janet, I cannot stand what I have done to you all – especially the kids, making them suffer."'

'He specifically mentioned me and Will?'

'That's what he said. He was sorry for you kids, his little girl, enduring his madness. A few days later he did it, in the car, he finished it, so he wouldn't hurt us any more.' Mum looks up, touches me gently. 'You know I've always seen you in him, I look at you, you're much more like him than your brother. He adored you. He loved Will but he adored you.'

I squeeze my mum's hand in return. My mother probably cannot understand how these words worry and pain and sadden me even as they gratify me. The emotions are too much, too mixed, they will never be untangled. I want to ask about the suicide, about Daddy's madness, about so much, but I daren't go there. I'd also like to stay here, get away from Delancey, but I can't, the Assistants would find out, and they are in control.

So instead the two of us, mother and daughter, sit silently at the kitchen table, and watch the fresh new flakes of snow settling on the little apple tree, saying nothing, yet not needing to say anything. And then it is three o'clock and getting dark, and I say I have to go and Mum says, 'I know.'

At the door, I give Mum another big hug.

'I don't say this often enough, Mum, but I love you.'

My mother smiles, and shakes her head.

'You don't have to say it, darling. You know I love you too.'

'Thanks again for helping me, I'm sorry to ask.'

'You're my daughter!' Mum says, firmly, almost commandingly. 'It's my job! Now, come and see me again soon, won't you?' I nod and kiss her one last time, then sling my bag over my shoulder and set off along the icy path to the front garden gate. When I reach the gate, I turn to give Mum a wave.

My mother looks so pale, framed by the cottagey door. A soft white oval face, white as the snow in her garden. The idea of one day Mum not being down here suddenly strikes me with a frightening force.

'I'll come down next weekend, Mum. I promise.'

Mum smiles faintly and waves and says, 'See you soon.' And I walk away, and yet I keep looking back and waving, until the snowy air mists and thickens, and after that I am round the corner. And I can see nothing at all.

40

Jo

The walk to Thornton Heath station is silent, muffled by the ceaseless snow, past curtained windows in terraced houses with frosty little gardens, past a corner shop closing early, past deserted playgrounds where candy-coloured wooden rabbits and sheep and chickens sit motionless on springs, wearing mohawks of hardened snow.

I remember how I used to play here: in this very playground. I remember all these streets, so ordinary and anonymous to anyone else. My primary school was around the corner: I can picture those days, when it was summer and warm, when Daddy would come home early from work and wait to pick me up, in that humble schoolyard. Those were good days because it meant Daddy wasn't with doctors or feeling funny. The teacher would bend to my ear as I stood in the school doorway: *Look, look, there's Daddy, off you go.*

And I would run giggling and joyous into his welcoming arms. And he was big and tall. Lifting me up onto his shoulders. He often did that, lift me up – just to make me laugh, or when we went to some Christmas funfair.

The first Christmas without him I hid in my bedroom for most of the day. Staring at photos of him on summer holidays, willing him back to life, daydreaming of him, drawing pictures of him to make him real, for one day, one hour, until I gave up and wrote the words *Daddy I Miss You, Here Is A Card In Case You Come Back Anyway*, and then Mum knocked quietly and came in and found me writing a Christmas card to my dead father and Mum put a hand to her mouth and she turned and her eyes were glittery in a sad way.

Cold air fills my throat as I breathe, deeply, calming myself. Questioning myself: is it worse for an eleven-year-old child to lose a father to suicide, or for a father to lose a twenty-year-old son to toxic drugs?

The last corner brings me to the station, and a clutch of tatty shops and grungy fast-food cafes, still open despite the empty streets: unlikely havens of light and warmth in this desolate freeze. As I reach for the coins in my pocket, for the railway, I recall the cash in my other pocket. My dear mother; £500 is probably more than she could afford. I will pay her back as soon as I can: tomorrow, if possible. And to do that I need work. Lots of it.

Hand in my jeans, I take out the secret phone. It's five p.m., a good time to call my editor. A good time to be proactive. Dashing for the shelter of the station entrance, I turn, facing out into the sleety darkness, keying the number.

'Sarah Thwaites.'

'Hi, Sarah, it's Jo.'

A long *long* pause. Long enough for another half-centimetre of snow to settle on the black taxi waiting outside the station; the driver is half asleep inside, head tilted to his frosting window.

'Sarah, hello? Sarah? I said it's Jo. Jo Ferguson. Ah. Everything OK?'

'Jo . . .'

The tone of voice is reticent. Tensed. But it could be because the office is busy, Sarah can often be quite offish when rushed and harassed. They all have too much work, these editors, answering three hundred emails a day – deadlines whooshing by, like high speed trains.

'Sarah, I wanted to pitch some ideas, real quick, if I can—'

'Jo. Stop.'

The abrupt monosyllable is so sharp it shuts me up, entirely. Sarah sounds angry. Or something.

'Sarah, what is it?'

A tiny, significant pause.

'You really *don't* know?'

'Know what?'

Here it comes. I can sense it. The darkness is getting ever closer. It is all around me.

'Jo, do you have a Twitter account?'

'No, no no no,' I am gabbling, 'I mean I am on Twitter, but I never use it. I barely use *any* social media, you keep telling me to do *more*. I do a bit of Instagram, I only look at Facebook every few weeks, nothing else – why?'

A brief sigh.

'I believe you, Jo. I believe you, but . . .'

'But what??'

I am staring at the taxi driver. He is actually asleep. All his business taken by Uber.

'Jo, for the last few hours someone has been tweeting, posing as you. Tweeting lots of stuff.'

'How? In what way? What stuff?'

Sarah lowers her voice, as if she doesn't want to be heard talking to Jo Ferguson. To me.

'The account is new and it's in the name @Jothe Journalist. You say you work for us, explicitly. In your Twitter handle. And there's a recent photo of you. It looks very much like you. For all intents and purposes, it's you.'

'But it isn't me! I've been sitting with my mum all afternoon. I never use Twitter! Ever!'

Sarah exhales.

'Look, Jo, I'm sorry, check the Twitter feed. You'll understand immediately what I am talking about. I can't say more. Whether it's you or not, it is too late. You will never work at this paper again. The managing editor has already emailed us all. In fact, you won't ever work as a journalist again, I don't think. Not for years anyway. I'm so sorry.' A pause, as if Sarah is looking around her office, to see if she is being monitored, for talking with the enemy, 'I'm truly sorry, Jo, I do believe you, but you've been hacked and it's been done brilliantly, and that's it. I have to go. I'm genuinely sorry. But . . . Please don't call me. There's nothing I can do. Sorry.'

41

Jo

The call ends. A commuter, hunched in a beige raincoat turned grey from the sleet, is tapping on the taxi window. The driver stirs. He, at least, has some business. Glumly and grimly I lift my smartphone from my other pocket. Closing my eyes for courage, I open them, go to Twitter, find @JotheJournalist.

It isn't hard. My Twitter name is actually *trending*. I am a trend. I am famous. And I am famous twice over. #JotheNazi is another trend, across the UK, which is, also, all about me.

The first tweet I can see on my phone is the newest. It talks about Jews. It actually says JEWS. In capitals.

Who do you believe? Who owns all the media? Do you think you're being told the truth? The clue is in the rhyme. Fake News Equals JEWS.

Accompanying it is a grotesque anti-Semitic caricature: hooknose, dollar bills, top hat, the works. Something from the 1930s.

I feel the bile heave: I am close to being sick. Leaning against the damp cold brickwork of the station threshold, I watch a man emerge from the station, glance at his phone, and look at me curiously. Perhaps I am so famous already people will start spotting me in the street: #JotheNazi.

How can I go to the shops? The cafes I liked? Pubs? Cinemas? Anywhere?

Scrolling down, I see my brief but prolific tweet stream is full of so much *more*, a foul and endless sewer of this effluent. Racist, bigoted, pointlessly abusive. My tweets are jubilant in their vileness, and every other tweet names my paper, my employers, and names my editors and colleagues, and I, @JotheJournalist, like boasting that they all agree with everything I am tweeting – and on and on it goes.

There have been 150 tweets in six hours. I scroll back to the first, which simply says,

Hi I'm @JotheJournalist real name Jo Ferguson. I work for your favourite London paper, and today I want to tell you what we're all really thinking

That first tweet was retweeted twice. The latest, with the anti-Semitic cartoon, has been retweeted twelve thousand times.

Jothejournalist, or JotheNazi, is viral, she is near enough global. I am a sudden and sensational hate figure, a dark shooting star, a vile celebrity born, and killed, by this ruinous fame, on the same single day.

Sarah was right. I am finished as a journalist. I am a pariah. I have no friends. I have no money. I have no job.

Is there anything more they could do to me? Why destroy me so entirely? I do not understand. If it is Arlo and Tabitha, defending themselves, they didn't have to go this far. Did they? The same applies if it is Simon, or Anna, or Fitz, or Gul, or Jenny, or my brother, or Cars, or the Rothschilds, or some kind of digital death squad, a bunch of Assistant Assassins. I do not understand the extent of the hatred and the violence of the damage done to me. Why and how do I deserve this? What is the point? The sadism seems cruelly overdone, the nastiness is berserk.

Turning my collar against the cold, and against the possible stares of anyone who might recognize me, I trudge into the station. I am resisting the urge to go back to that little snowbound playground with the wooden sheep and chickens and pigs on springs, back to where I was safe, back to the deep deep past, back to where I was a child, playing games with my friends, waiting for Daddy, the Ticklemonster.

42

Jo

The screech is animal and human and machine and appalling, then Help Help Help, Why Jo Why, then more screaming, and I can see Jamie Trewin in hospital, and the whiteness of his eyes, dead now, his father crying becomes my daddy crying, and gasping in that car. And then again that awful sound, I recognize it, a woman shrieking, it's definitely a woman shrieking or yelling in pain, but it has the whimpering quality of an animal about to be slaughtered. A butcher-house sound, when the cow realizes . . .

And I wake up and the beating of my heart is so profound it is actively painful. Like something is inside but shouldn't be, someone has implanted something evil in my womb, *and* in my heart. I am impregnated by cancers. Cancers that move. Like animals inside me.

Thin winter light filters through my bedroom curtains. My mouth is so dry it aches, my lips crack at the corners. The dream was the last of so many dreams. I dreamed I woke up and I was tied to a bed and dreaming, I dreamed of people singing my name in a grainy, scratchy black-and-white movie, I dreamed of three women with their mouths stitched shut, all standing around my bed, staring down at me. Yet in the dreams somehow their heads were eyeless, too, and the mouths were stitched up so carefully. Neatly. I know where that comes from. The Plath poem. 'The Disquieting Muses'. About Mummy and Daddy.

Rubbing the grit from my eyes, I grab a bottle of Tabs' water for my parched mouth and then the horrible reality returns, like diving from a sinking ship into a cold, frightening black ocean.

Oh God. Twitter. Last night. The recollection floods and engulfs me, makes me want to gag all over again. The end of my life, the social media suicide. My live-streamed self-immolation. I remember running home – literally running from the Tube, as if someone might see me and hurl a brick at the Nazi – and then I went to bed early and took sleeping pills and hid away, in the blissful prison of sleep.

But then I dreamed, so many bad dreams. Ending in that fearful dream of a woman's scream, then Help Help Help, Help me, Help me, Why Jo Why, which sounded so real.

So very real.

Sitting up in bed, I stare around. The grey January light reveals nothing out of the ordinary. No bricks have stoved in the windows, no shattered glass litters the floor. Maybe it is too early, maybe the anti-Fascists haven't woken up?

I realize I have no idea what time it is: the bedside clock has fallen over, presumably as I thrashed around the musty bed, in my sleep. Leaning across, getting a sense that I REALLY need a shower, I lift up the clock.

Eleven a.m.?

I went to bed at ten. I think. I had a glass of wine and those pills. I have slept for thirteen hours. And still I feel tired.

Dragging myself from the bed, I shower for ten minutes, then force myself to stop showering, I dress in random woollens and jeans – I'm not going out today, I can't ever go out, children will look at me and point, my friends will look at me and look away, I am a non-person. I have de-personed myself. Or, rather, someone else has de-personed me. Killed me online. I am the walking talking dead.

Coffee is dutifully drunk. Toast is robotically eaten, and then I walk into the living room. It all looks so neat, and innocent. The Milanese designer sofa does not know what I wrote on Twitter, the Tom Dixon designer lamp is oblivious to my bigoted rants. My laptop waits, lid closed, on the table, next to my switched-off phone. I cannot bear to open either of them: see the appalled emails, the Facebook outrage, newspaper articles with opinion pieces condemning me for life, it will all be in there. I cannot face it. Not today. Today I just sit here, like one of those eyeless women with a stitched-up mouth.

'If you don't kill yourself, I'll send someone that will.'

I turn, and glare at Electra. Her blue light twirls, and expires.

'Electra, what did you say?'

'If you don't kill yourself, I'll send someone that will.'

I don't know what to say. I'm too tired to say anything. I'm too tired to work out if I am still dreaming.

BZZZZ.

I am not dreaming. That is the doorbell.

Who is it? Who can be at the door? Someone who wants to beat me up, the mad racist lady. In my mind,

I picture a lynch mob. Or just the average citizen rightly appalled. And what of my mother? What will she think? The thought is unendurable. It all comes to a crashing close. Very soon.

BZZZ.

Whoever is at the door is not going away. I look at the Assistant. She doesn't look smug today. She looks inert, sad, black. Even a little tired. Nothing left to do. Her work is finished. She's made her final threat. Her job is almost done. Mine isn't. I still have an atom of resistance, somewhere inside me. The will to survive, fuelled by anger. I will go down fighting.

'Electra, do we have any deliveries today?'

'There are no scheduled deliveries today. Amazon Prime will be delivering twelve bottles of Highland Spring mineral water tomorrow.'

BZZZZZZZZZ!

The sound is irresistibly persistent. Nervous, I go to the windows and look down.

There is a police car parked right outside my home. And three uniformed officers – two female, one male – are standing and pressing the buzzer of my streetside door. What could have happened? Immediately: I know what was has happened. Hate crime. The Twitter ranting. They have come to arrest me.

Gathering the last fragments of courage, I lift the intercom, and say, before they get a chance to speak,

'Hold on, I'll come down.'

I feel like some condemned royal bride, descending from the Tower, to her place of execution, on the wintry lawns, where ravens crawk in the cold grey light.

I open the door. The three police officers stare at me. Two female, one male. The blondest, youngest officer, a girl of no more than twenty-two, says to me, softly,

'Ms Jo Ferguson?'

'Yes, that's me, and yes, I did it. The Twitter stuff. It was me, yet it wasn't me, I was hacked.'

'Wait, Ms Ferguson—'

'I was hacked and you can believe me or not. But I can see how it looked like it came from me, so if you want to take me in, charge me, and investigate, whatever, I don't care.'

The blonde young woman shakes her head, and swaps puzzled glances with her colleagues. The man shrugs. His radio buzzes. He steps away. The young policewoman comes closer, and offers me a sad smile.

'Ms Ferguson, I'm not sure what you think has happened, but this has got nothing to do with Twitter, or anything like that—'

Now I realize. Trewin. *Jamie Trewin*. They've finally found out. The thing I really DID do. Me and Tabitha, we've been caught, at last, they've discovered the truth, me and Tabs and Xander Scudamore, fifteen years ago: at last it will come out. It feels like a kind of relief.

'You mean Glastonbury, OK,' I say, muffling the panic in my voice, 'OK, OK. All right, all right – uh ah—'

The policewoman puts a hand on my shoulder, to calm me. Then she says, very slowly,

'Ms Ferguson, I have no idea what you are talking about, whether it is Twitter or Glastonbury or whatever. I am afraid we are here for completely different, and very unfortunate reasons.'

A pause. More than a pause. It feels like the last elderly figures shuffling around Regent's Park have finally frozen, and become motionless. Something terrible has happened.

'Ms Ferguson,' the woman says, 'I'm afraid it's your mother. Janet Ferguson.'

'My mum? What about my mum?'

The three officers exchange glances; once again, the male officer nods, very subtly, as if to say: *Yes, go on, you do it.* The blonde girl continues,

'The truth is, your mother died this morning, of a heart attack. People have been trying to reach you, but your phone was off.' Her smile is sad and sincere. 'I'm so sorry, so very sorry.'

The world blurs to a greater, colder horror. I mouth the words, robotically,

'Who found her, what happened?'

The young blonde police officer grimaces uncomfortably.

'A neighbour, apparently.'

'But how?' My heart thumps with sadness, a desperate grief. 'How? Who? How did they find her? Tell me.'

The young policewoman stares at the ground; the others gaze offstage, examining the traffic. I persist, virtually shouting,

'Tell me! Tell me, please. I need to know. How? Why? When? PLEASE?'

The young woman lifts her face, and concedes.

'Well, uh, it seems your mother was crying for help? Calling your name. Something like that – anyway—'

'PC Duffield!'

The male policeman has spoken. Clearly the young policewoman has broken some protocol. She turns, and mumbles an apology to her superior.

Now he speaks directly to me:

'Miss Ferguson. I'm so very sorry. If you need additional information we can provide it. Formally. Here's a number to ring.'

He hands me a card. I take it, blankly, and stand shivering in the bitter wind sweeping up Delancey. And then I thank the police people, and they politely smile and say sorry again, and they climb in their car and drive off into the winter mist. For a moment I watch them, then I turn and climb the stairs and push my way into the flat.

So now my deep, abiding fear – who is coming to get me? – is mixed, blurred, even briefly diluted, by a terrible grief. I am in the kitchen making a mug of tea, biting back tears, barely able to function. Remembering my mum when I was a kid. The way she would slice cherry tomatoes in two before she gave them to me, in case I would choke. The way she taught me to ride a bike, both of us laughing as I fell into her arms. Summer days, before it all went wrong, when we would all play tennis, as a family, me and Daddy and Will and Mummy, and she'd bring homemade chicken sandwiches, and cold orange juice in a thermos, I remember the sweet cold taste of it, and the hot sun on my girlish neck as I drank thirstily. It was the taste of love. The taste of my mother's love. Pure sweetness and sunny warmth.

I can hear music. Mozart. The Fortieth Symphony. Electra is playing it. How does Electra know that this was my mother's favourite? That famous introduction, the nervous yet beautiful strings. She liked to listen to it when she was ironing, the smell of clean clothes and spray starch filling the living room.

Oh, Mummy.

Still I resist the tears as I wander into the living room. I don't tell Electra to shut up. I stand in the winter sun with my eyes half closed, and listen to this mellifluous music. Until it stops. Abruptly.

Now Electra is screaming, and then the scream becomes more coherent: it is an old woman crying, in terrible raking pain: *Help help help! Why, Jo, why?*

It is the same scream for help, the same cry of agony, that I thought I heard in my dreams, this morning. But as I listen I realize, with a cold descent of abject horror, that I didn't dream it. I never imagined this sound. It was and is real. This is surely an actual recording of my mother. I recognize the voice. This is her final cry as she died.

My mother's Assistant must have recorded it, and then sent it to my own home, so I could hear it, as I emerged from sleep.

My mum was calling my name. Blaming me. And I did nothing. I just lay in my bed.

And now Electra plays the voice again, even louder: Help, help, help! Why, Jo, why? And all I can do is stand here in the wintry light, listening to my own mother's dying words.

43

Jo

Nothing prepares you for the silence of death. It is beyond the normal silence: a voice hushed, a door closed, the end of a song, of laughter, of a party, a dinner. I remember the terrible frightening silences in this, my mother's house, in Thornton Heath, after Daddy died. The silence of the first Fireworks Night without him, we always went to the fireworks: me and Dad, he'd take me to the nearest park and hoist me on his shoulders and I'd go cooo and ooooh and hug myself with happiness . . . and then one day the Fireworks Night came around and Daddy was gone: so instead I shut the windows and sat on the sofa and watched through the windows as the silent distant gorgeous starry explosions of violet and purple and turquoise-rose lit up the South London sky. And in the end I couldn't even bear to look at the muffled sparkles, so I shut the curtains tight, and listened to the silence by itself.

Special silence. The silence of my mother when she

was about to say 'your daddy', the silence of my brother's tears when I found him crying, but embarrassed, a growing boy, in the kitchen. The silence of opening a curtain and looking at the empty place where he'd parked the car and fed the exhaust fumes into himself.

It is a special silence that crushes because you know it will not end, cannot be filled, shall not be forgotten. No noise stops it.

My mum's lavender-scented house is so fucking silent as I walk around, aimless, purposeless, my mind empty and hollow. Despite the silence, I gaze about, wildly nervous – amidst the anguish. I haven't forgotten what Electra said: If you won't kill yourself, I'll send someone that will.

I've locked all the doors of Mum's house: from the inside. Just in case. And now – now I am in here, I don't quite know what to do. What are you meant to do after your last parent dies?

Arrange funerals, I suppose. Talk to professionally sad people about cremations. Get certificates? My brother has called and says he's flying over. It was the stiffest of conversations: he still evidently distrusts me for what I did – or, rather, what someone did on my behalf. Someone who wants me dead.

The defiance rises. I shall have my revenge on him, or, her, or them, or it. Somehow, somehow. Soon. But for the moment I have to deal with the awful fact: my mother has gone.

A couple of neighbours have popped by. Expressed sympathy. Handed over flowers in an awkward way. And they have left.

Now I am alone again, with the silence and my mother's furniture and clothes and possessions and the Assistant, on the bookshelf in the living room, the Assistant that heard my mother scream my name and relayed it to me: live. The Assistant given to her by Simon.

Of all the people I might have expected a sympathetic message from, Simon is top of the list. I know Polly hates me, I know he is forbidden from trying to reach me, but I can't help thinking: he knows my mum, his family live round the corner, he's known this family for decades, surely he would send at least a text. His mum and dad came over and offered to take in the dog, till we decided what to do.

But Simon himself?

Nothing. Perhaps he feels guilt. I'm not sure why.

Whatever the case, I must box things up. That's what you do when people die, I reckon. You put things in boxes. What you might keep, what you might give to charity, what you might – I guess – sell, inherit, who cares. The money is irrelevant, even if I am broke. My mum's savings only amounted to a few thousand. The house is rented, it must be emptied. My mother is dead. The silence is supreme. The only noise is a rustle of wool, nylon, and cotton as I gather clothes from Mum's wardrobes and put them in boxes, seal the boxes with Sellotape, write in big letters: CHARITY? or KEEP? or ??? I have to question everything as, clearly, I have to ask Will what we should do when he gets here. He might dislike or suspect me, but our mother is gone and Will and I are left: now it's just us two, and little Caleb.

More boxes. More Sellotape. More scrawling big notes in marker pen. Boxes of books and magazines, boxes of slightly tacky souvenirs from Mediterranean holidays, boxes with clocks, boxes with boxes, boxes of stuff from my schooldays, my childhood, and Will's schooldays, too. Home movies in piles. Half of this ancient stuff is new to me: I had no idea Mum kept so much *memorabilia*: there is hardly anything about *her*, Janet Ferguson, it's all about *us*: her kids. All her real treasures, she things she kept emotionally close, under her bed, in the best boxes, they are this stuff that simply says: I was a mother.

This was what she was all about, in her own mind. Proudly. A *mother*.

It's all here. Her life was us. Her purpose was Will and me: we were the meaning in her life. And her happiest moments, as she once wrote me, the week I got married to Si, were those moments she spent laughing and carefree with her infant son and daughter. I remember the precise words in that letter, which arrived on my wedding day: 'I hope you can enjoy the happiness of motherhood, like me.'

Sorry, Mum. Sorry, Mum. Too late now. But oh, I want to say it. Sorry, Mum. I should have called more, talked more, hugged more, been more grateful. Maybe I should have given you grandkids. And now she is gone and I have seen her body in the hospital and it has not helped. I am, I was, I will be, in every way, too late. And worst of all, she died somehow blaming me. Why, Jo, why.

The thought torments me. I heard my own mother die, as I lay there, half asleep.

The toil has not helped. It is not therapeutic. Even the clothes distress or depress me. Every dress has a memory – the summer dresses when she was younger; the longer, dowdier dresses when she was older. The cardigans with knobbly leather buttons she would knit herself. Enough boxes, for now. Will and I have to talk.

I stand in the stillness and let it surround me. I walk into the kitchen, it is also noiseless. And then my smartphone rings.

Tabitha.

44

Jo

Tabitha? Calling me? I hesitate to take it. I am simultaneously scared and angry. My anger wins.

'Hello, Tabs.' I hope my voice is as cold as my heart.

'Hello, Jo,' she sounds nervous. Very unlike Tabitha. 'I'm just calling to say sorry. Oh God. I'm so terribly sorry about your mother. It's so bloody awful.'

I want to accept her sympathy. She is, or was, my best friend. But I cannot forget or ignore that terrible lie.

'Thank you, Tabitha.'

'Are you OK, darling? Do you need any help? Just say the word.'

This is too much. *Darling?* My anger seethes. And boils over.

'What I'd like, Tabitha, is for you to tell me the damn truth. Have you heard of the name Xander Scudamore? Because I have.'

She is quiet. I am not.

'He was Purple Man, wasn't he? He really *did* give

us pills, and we really *did* give them to Jamie Trewin, and everything you told me at Delancey was total bollocks. You lied. You lied through your teeth. At a moment when I was significantly unstable. So I begin to wonder, *Tabs,* is it you and Arlo, is it you and Arlo that are deliberately ruining my life, creating that Twitter account? Why? Why the fuck would you *do* all that?'

Another long and agonizing pause. The normally confident Tabitha is anguishingly mute. Then she whispers.

'Oh God. *God.* I'm sorry. What can I say? Yes, it was a lie. I got scared, Jo, silly and scared, it's such a bad time for the truth to come out, for Arlo and the baby and me, and . . . and . . . And I don't know what to say. There's no excuse. But honestly everything else, everything else that's happened, the Twitter thing, everything, it's got nothing to do with me and Arlo. Please believe me. I implore you. I want to help—'

'Well. *You* can help by *leaving me the fuck alone.* Just for now.'

'Wait—'

'No. Not now. Go away.'

I snap the call dead. Like breaking a stick in two. And yet, even as I do so, I wonder at what she said. She sounded, despite everything, sincere. Maybe she isn't to blame. Maybe it is solely Arlo behind all this. Perhaps even he is innocent and there is someone beyond *all* of us. Or possibly this is a further lie?

The snow falls on snow. Soon we will all be buried and hushed. But I refuse to be entombed, and I will not be beaten. My mother is dead. I must fight back: for her. She would have expected it. Like Daddy, she was always proud of my feistiness, ambition, my self-confidence: Jo the Go. Yet I am also Jo the Scared. Very scared.

I need to calm myself. Opening a kitchen window, I breathe the piercing, unscented cold, breathing in, breathing out. The air does its job. I feel my heart slow. I close and lock the window – got to lock everything now – but as I do, I look at the little apple tree and think of Mummy and Daddy and me and Will all under that tree: in all the photos she took.

Mum loved taking photos.

The photos. Yes. *I must see them*. Mum used a camera long after everyone else had switched to camera-phones. And when she was forced to go digital she still got her digital favourites printed.

We have to keep the photos. Pacing through the house I go to the cupboard in the dining room where she kept her photograph albums. Pulling out the first album, I flick through page after page of endless baby photos, pram photos, cot photos, then Dad carrying Will as a toddler, my first day at school, then a birthday party for me (age five?) with Mum and Dad laughing and him with his arm around her, not mad then, or, at most, showing a few tiny signs. And then I pause at one photo, with a prickle of fear: it is a photo of Daddy holding me.

It is the photo that was sent to my phone, allegedly by Jamie Trewin, when I received those horrible messages by Camden Lock.

Whoever is tormenting me has access to Mum's photos, home movies, everything?

I shake my head, puzzled by my own bewilderment. Angry at the intrusion, frightened by the power of my enemy. Repressing my fears, I turn pages, and the photos begin to darken in mood. Dad disappears. Secondary school arrives. Fewer smiles in photos. Three people on a beach, or around a table, not four. Will is now a teenager with a terrible haircut and an attempt at a moustache. I am a teenager with an even worse haircut, yet a fierce, urgent smile. There's one distinct shot of me and Will in our late teens or early twenties, languid and finally attractive, perhaps, draped on the stairs at some cousin's wedding. Then a graduation party . . .

After that: nothing. At this point, the photos essentially stop. When we left my mum's life, she stopped showing interest in images.

Sliding this album into the cupboard, I pull out the last album she used. The last album I remember lying on her lap, as she happily gummed photos into the pages.

I am cross-legged on the cold dining room floor, absorbed, and distracted from my terror and my sadness. It seems Mum proudly scissored every single newspaper article I wrote – and pasted them all in here. And every news item about Will's work, they're also in here: though they are fewer.

Oh, Mum. You were so *proud*.

Ignoring the urge to sob, I continue my browsing. Halfway through this album, the photos gain a second life: as little Caleb is born. Mum adored her first grandson, her only grandchild, there are photos of Caleb as a baby, showing his first tooth, smiling like a loon, Caleb on a kiddy scooter in the sunshine of California, And on the next page: it's me again. One big, page-filling photo. Mum must have got it specially printed at this size, she liked it so much.

It's my mum's seventieth birthday, it's a hot July day, we're having a barbecue under the apple tree, and to make up the numbers I have invited lots of my more interesting friends, Fitz, Anna, Marlow, Gul, Andy, Jenny. Simon is there of course. Simon's parents too. My mum's bridge partners. Mum. This was not long before Simon and I divorced.

There is something in this innocent photo, of a sunlit barbecue, which compels me, and I don't know why.

I am standing in a line with Simon, Jenny, Fitz, Gul, Tabitha, in the garden, raising glasses of Pimm's and laughing, presumably we are toasting the picture-taker. Even *Arlo* is there, how did I persuade *Arlo* to come to *Thornton Heath*?? It doesn't make sense. Is that what disturbs me about this photo? Or is it something else? I scan the faces, I can sense the tension between me and Simon in this image, even as we smile, drunkenly.

I was already sexting 'Liam' by this time, searching for a way out of a dead marriage.

But there is something ELSE.

WHAT IS IT?

I stare and stare, I run my fingers over the photo like it is braille and I am blind, and its very texture will reveal the final truth.

Then: I see it. Hiding away – yet smack-bang in the middle of the photo.

Mummy.

She is half smiling, half squinting at the camera, perhaps a little dazzled by the sun. She is also holding a book. And I recognize its distinct plain cover. I downloaded it myself very recently.

The Collected Poems of Sylvia Plath.

The ringing silence is a shrill klaxon in my ear.

Why would my mum be holding a book, in this photo, taken in her garden on her seventieth birthday party? Only if someone gave it to her, as a present, that day. I don't remember this present, I don't remember the book. Poetry isn't really Mum's thing, as it wasn't mine. Yet someone who *does* like Plath gave her this volume. That means if I can find the book, and identify the giver, I would surely have my culprit, my nemesis, my tormentor.

Where would Mum keep a book like that? It's a present so she wouldn't give it away; but it is also not a book she would cherish.

Her favourite books – Jane Austen, the Brontës, Thomas Hardy, the classics she would re-read constantly, she kept in her bedroom. Cookbooks were kept in the kitchen. Less useful or important volumes were always kept *here,* in the dining room. The other side of the dining table.

Quickly, I cross to the bookshelves. There must be a thousand volumes here: Mum kept a lot of books, as did Dad. The shelves go high.

I scan the titles, urgently. I walk up and down like a sovereign reviewing her troops, but I am looking for the evidence of my enemy.

No joy. There is no poetry. This does not surprise me. Neither Mum nor Dad liked poetry. Yet I haven't scanned *all* the titles. There is just one chance left – one shelf left, the very top, the most unread books. I am too short to reach and see: I have to fetch a dining room chair, to help. Then I step up. And crane my neck.

For the final time, I scan the titles. Old science fiction. Old science. A book about Vermeer. *The Collected Poems of Sylvia Plath.*

The urgency burns, as I reach out. The present is in the top right-hand corner, and grey with dust.

Trying to stay calm, not feeling remotely calm, I pull the book. Then I step off the dining room chair, to survey my prize. This has to be the book Mum was holding in her hand, in the photo. This was the birthday present, given to her that day.

Opening the cover, I see a handwritten inscription.

Happy Birthday

xxx

'myself the rose you achieve'

The acid rises in my throat. The writing is distinctive. That florid looping Y which my daddy taught me to do.

I wrote this. I wrote this to Mummy. I must have given her the book. Yet I don't remember why or how or when – or anything.

What's more, I seem to have literally predicted my own future. I saw what was coming down the line to hurt me. Plath.

45

Jo

It is true. It is impossible. But it is true. But it is impossible.

I slip the book in my bag. The book which is asking me to believe in some ludicrous coincidence, bordering on the miraculous, that several years ago I foresaw the events which would lead to my ruination, and maybe my suicide, or my murder, years hence. What's more, it seems I have since forgotten I ever did this. Bought a book of poems for my mother. Poems by a woman who killed herself, like Daddy.

It is true. It is impossible. It is true. It is impossible.

I have to go somewhere else and work this out. I am ready to flee, to pace to the door, I am far too unnerved to stay.

But a noise halts me.

Someone else is in the house. Someone has opened the door.

Yet I locked it, very carefully. The house is secured: I am all too aware of the menace from Electra, and whoever is behind her. *Somebody's done for.* Now *someone* is coming across the hall. Hard heavy footsteps, and they are unconcealed. A man. Is coming. For me. In the place where my mother died. In the place where I predicted my own destruction.

I hear the man go into the kitchen. Mess with some plates, maybe looking for something. A dull grunt, of displeasure, or dismay.

And all the time I stand here, half frozen. Looking for a weapon, absurdly. A lamp? What can I use? There is nothing. The kitchen door squeals, the footsteps cross the hall. I see the doorknob turning. The door creaks open. I stand up, reach for one of Dad's paintboxes, I could throw this.

And there he is. Tall and familiar. He speaks.

'You fucking bitch. I saw what you did. You murdered her.'

46

Tabitha

Sitting at the kitchen counter, with her daily, minuscule glass of wine, as the wintry dusk descended on the garden beyond, Tabitha stared at the clock on Arlo's microwave.

It was wrong again. It was always going wrong, that clock. It constantly irked her, and she corrected it about twice a week. The strange thing was that Arlo – fastidious, logical Arlo, who got annoyed if his antique cufflinks weren't arranged by size – wasn't as irritated by it as her.

Where was he anyway? He'd said he would be back by now. She wondered if she should start cooking for them. But surely it was too early. Yet she liked it: the cooking. She spent more and more time in this kitchen. Cooking food she didn't want.

Perhaps it was just displacement activity. So she didn't have to think about Jo. That phone call had been so painful. Admitting her terrible lie. And the accusation against Arlo?

Her phone rang. Interrupting her troubled thoughts. The phone was a number she didn't instantly recognize.

'Hello? Who is this?'

'It's Simon. Simon Todd. Sorry for bugging you at home. Am I interrupting?'

Tabitha paused, frowned, confused.

'No. It's fine.'

'And the pregnancy – I heard you were, um, expecting?'

'I'm fine.' Tabitha stared out at the gloom of the darkening garden, the bleak and thorny rosebushes, the patches of grass showing through the recent, temporary thaw. Why was Simon Todd calling? He never called to chat. It had to be Jo.

'Simon, what is it? Is it Jo, yes?'

'Yeah . . .' his voice dropped lower, like he was scared of being overheard. 'It's Jo. Who else. You heard about Janet?'

'Of course. So awful. I guess it was always a risk, with Janet, with that pacemaker. But poor Jo.'

'Have you spoken to her, to Jo?'

Simon was gabbling. Tabitha was suffused by guilt.

'Well, I tried, but she's, uhm, angry with me. We've had a row. It's difficult. But yes . . . I tried.' Tabitha attempted not to think about Arlo. How he would react when he discovered what Jo knew? About Xander? 'But what can you say, Simon, in these circumstances. What can you do? It's all so terribly sad. And it comes on top of everything else – this ongoing nightmare—'

Simon interrupted, emphatically:

'You mean her mad shit? The messages.'

'Yes. I mean these vile emails, the extraordinary melt-down on Twitter! Losing her job! She was practically national news. I was down there at Delancey the other day, and she was pretty far gone . . . and yet, Simon,

316

what *can* we do? She's becoming her father. It's awful. And now this, with her mum.'

'Well, that's it,' Simon said, still using that strained, whispered tone. 'That's exactly it. *The emails.* The WhatsApp messages. The evil Twitter stuff. I've been doing some sleuthing, you see, and I reckon she *didn't* send them, didn't write them. Didn't tweet them. She isn't lying. She's been hacked.'

Tabitha felt a physical shock.

'Sorry, Simon? How? Why?'

'Like I said. She's been hacked.'

'But how can you possibly know?'

His answer was anxious, but firm. 'Because she literally couldn't have. A while ago, I checked through the messages. One of them – one email she sent to Fitz – the timing was impossible. It was sent when she was having dinner with me, with her phone on mute, and she never touched the phone.'

Tabitha frowned.

'What about . . . special software? You can time and delay emails.'

'Nah, I checked that too. I know this stuff. I work in IT. This is my job. Tabitha, she *didn't* send these messages. So I'm beginning to think Jo has been right *all along*: she's *not* paranoid. She's *not* schizo like her dad. Someone is really doing all this to her. Torturing her. Her Assistants really are messing with her life.'

Tabitha felt herself floundering, in the confusion. And sadness. And a new sense of alarm.

'You mean the Assistants are actually *talking* to her?'

'Yes.'

'And the phone, and the TV? And the Twitter account. The whole grisly thing. It's all fake? Some kind of attack?'

'Yep. That's it. I genuinely think someone, with some enormous grudge against her, wants her utterly ruined, wants her to go mad, or top herself. But: who hates her that much, Tabs? Who wants her in a mental health unit, or under a bus? Who benefits?'

Tabitha stared at her empty wineglass, wanting another, knowing it was impossible.

'You installed the Assistants, Simon. Can't you go round and check? She's your ex. And she's lost her mum.'

'It's so tricky! Polly is totally on my case. I know that sounds crap, but . . . But there it is. If Pol found out I had any contact, my marriage would be *over*. I'm even calling you from a mate's phone, so she won't know.' A nervous pause. 'I *did* try sending Jo a few texts a couple of weeks ago, and I sent an email about her mum the other day, saying how sorry I was, but I think they were blocked, in fact I think whoever has control of her technology is stopping her getting most emails and texts. Further isolating her. They have *that* much control over her life. Over everything she does. It's bloody frightening. I am genuinely frightened for her.' He paused, then added, 'And here's one more thing, as it happens, I do have one suspect in mind. After a fashion.'

Polly felt something ominous approaching. Surely he wasn't about to accuse Arlo? Yet she could see why he might. She'd begun to have her own doubts, sometimes. Growing doubts.

'Who?'

'Liam.'

'Who?'

Simon repeated.

'Remember that actor guy, Liam. The one she was sexting. Fucked up our marriage. For a while after we split I was checking him out online. He had a Facebook account, he was on Instagram, he sent the odd tweet, I guess I was jealous, so I followed him for a while. Pathetic but there we are.'

Tabitha's mind raced ahead.

'You mean it's him: coz he got jealous? Yes, that makes a kind of sense. She dumped him online, never slept with him, and then he turned on her. He's some kind of nutter? Stalker? *Right?*'

'Nope,' Simon said. 'The *opposite* of a stalker. You see, I haven't checked him for ages but the other day I had another look: and he has disappeared from the Net. All evidence of him, all those images, any reference, the LinkedIn account, it's like they never existed, no one has ever actually heard of him. Or met him. How freaking weird is that? She was sexting a ghost.'

The truth was coming so fast it was a blur, Tabitha tried to focus.

'So he didn't even exist?'

'Well, he did exist in *some* form. I used face-recognition software. All the photos of him were stolen from some random guy's Facebook page, a totally different bloke, banker, lives in America, never been to Britain. I checked and checked. So someone took the photos and invented a backstory and created this character, Liam Goodchild. But then whoever *created* him back then has recently made him vanish from the Net. Entirely.' Simon hesitated, then went on, 'And that, as anyone in tech knows, is extremely bloody hard. It could only be done by someone very high up in tech companies, or by a real expert, someone with knowledge of the top-level stuff. AI. The cutting-edge shit.'

Tabitha was almost speechless. She let Simon talk, fast and hard.

'Anyway: all that's for another day. First thing: we gotta save Jo. Can't you go and see her, Tabs, see her and stay with her? She's your friend, it's your flat. And this must be done fast. She's a serious suicide risk.'

Tabitha winced. *And I made that suicide risk worse.* The guilt was intense; she tried to explain herself.

'OK, all right. I will try, Si, I mean, I might try . . . But the trouble is we have, as I said, kind of fallen out. She won't listen to me. We have problems uh too, you know, and – and – and – Arlo can be difficult.'

Tabitha felt increasingly wretched with every word. She was so evidently lying. And she had no clue what to do. And her helplessness was nothing to do with Arlo. *She'd* burned her bridges to Jo, with the terrible lie about Jamie Trewin. It was impossible to retract. Their friendship was probably over.

Simon sighed, quite tersely, even angrily. As if he expected this disappointment. And then he said,

'I guess I could write her a fucking letter, like, y'know, an actual old-fashioned letter? Reassuring her, or warning her? But would she even bother opening it? No. I reckon . . .' His voice dropped even lower, 'I reckon someone needs to go and see her, Tabs. And, y'know, maybe it *is* my job. Her ex-husband. God help us. Perhaps I need to see her, take the risk. And hope Polly doesn't find out. Because *somebody* has to help her, Tabitha. She's being attacked, and she has no one else on her side.'

'Well,' Tabitha said, feeling the sting of guilt, even self-hatred. 'If you do go, that's great, and please – uh – please give her my love, all my love and my sympathies. Let me know what happens, as soon as.'

Simon said a curt Yes, and rang off. He was obviously dismayed by Tabitha's feebleness. Her cowardice. And why not. But he was also sincerely and honestly worried. Someone *was* trying to destroy Jo Ferguson.

But who? As Simon put it: who would benefit from this? Her total destruction?

Tabitha remembered what Arlo had said about Simon. That he was leading research into voice mimicry. It crossed her mind for a moment that, throughout this entire phone call, she might not have been talking to Simon. Perhaps he was faking his own voice. Dragging her deeper into this bizarre and dangerous puzzle.

But why would he do that?

Shadows loomed from every side. The idea of cloned voices made Tabitha queasy, but not as queasy as this conversation she had just had. Liam the actor was like some kind of ghost. It was all becoming too much, way over the top, it was all too strange, and chilling. Tabitha Ashbury had the horrible and sudden feeling she was a humble actor in a play she did not understand: and someone else, someone much, much cleverer, was writing the script. A script written in a language which she could not even read. Or maybe she was a player in a very high-stakes card game: where *everyone was bluffing*.

Tabitha gazed through the glass doors, leading out onto the old, walled garden. The inevitable snow was settling, hard and fast now. Erasing everything with white, for the hundredth time. Transforming the world, yet again.

47

Jo

I look at my brother. His suntanned face. The lines of age beginning to show. A weary flight from LA, to bury Mum. Why is he raging at me?

'Why the fuck are you shouting at me, Will? I had nothing to do with Mum dying. I was at home.'

'Really?'

'Yes, really. Look I know you despise me for what you think I did to you, the Caleb thing, but I didn't, my computers have been hacked. Everything has been hacked – please, please believe me.'

His arms are crossed. His face is set firm. I try to make peace:

'You just got here, Will, you must be tired, let me start on this and you get some sleep, and we can talk tomorrow, and—'

'No!' He is growling. 'I haven't just arrived. I got here this morning. Let myself in, we must have missed each other. I've left my stuff with a friend, staying with a friend in Battersea.'

He's already been here? To Mum's house? What is he talking about?

Will walks away, towards the dining room. I follow. He stands by the shelf where my mum kept her laptop. She used it for photos, and family, and Facebook; she used Facebook way more than me. As parents do.

Wordless, Will opens up the laptop. It immediately flashes to Mum's Facebook page. He clicks on the messenger tab, which fills the screen. And then he simply points:

'I presume,' he says, with a kind of infinite coldness, a coldness that will never go away, 'that you are going to deny this, as well?'

I stare at the screen.

There is a final message on the messenger column. It is from me to Mum. I only have to read the first few sentences before I feel the tears, these stupid tears, choking my throat:

You were the worst mother. Just the worst. So fucking boring. So fucking utterly boring. On and on and on about nothing. No wonder Daddy killed himself. We all hated you, me and Will, we still hate you, THAT's why we never visit you, never call. Did you bore Daddy to death, is that why he went mad—

There is more of it. Several evil and revolting paragraphs. I slam the laptop shut but it is too late. The words are branded onto my naked, twitching skin. For all the world to see.

Will speaks with suppressed rage. 'You sent that message at eight thirty a.m. to Mum. She read it, judging by her computer log, at nine a.m. She died within the

323

hour.' He steps away from me, his face curled into a grimace of puzzled loathing.

'What kind of monster are you, Jo? First you try and destroy my family, the happiness of your brother, your nephew, your own people. Now this. You basically kill your own mother?'

I am running. I am running fast. Running from his words, running out of the room, running for the door. I didn't do this, didn't send it, but my brother won't believe me, not after all that's happened. And I cannot bear his righteous anger.

'Go on,' I can hear him shout, as I yank the outside door to the gasping cold of the wintry suburb. 'Go on, go on, run away.'

If only I could.

48

Jo

Sometimes the numbness of grief and guilt can be an advantage? Perhaps it is designed that way. An evolved response to otherwise unbearable pain. How else would I have got through the last few days? My mother's funeral. The loathing of my brother. My total isolation at the service. The staring and contemptuous glances from the other mourners.

I have shielded myself with a kind of uncaring anger, and a cocoon of confusion and fear. So I am the mad daughter, so what. So I am the one who did that stuff on Twitter? Who cares – it's not true. Yet that's what everyone thinks I am, because that is what someone has turned me into.

Bastard.

The rage boils. I won't let them finish me off. Yet I don't know how to *stop* them. How can you fight such an elusive enemy? It's like stabbing at phantoms. Punching at smoke. Every suspect dissolves when I investigate;

some, like, Liam turn out never to have existed in the first place.

And my predicament is so strange I cannot go to anyone and explain. And they wouldn't give me the time of day anyway. I can imagine the incredulous faces as I state my case. You think you might have predicted the future, and you once thought you possibly saw ghosts?

No *wonder* no one believes me – apart from a mad homeless guy.

I am alone. Waiting for the final assault. Standing in my living room, absently eating an apple.

I drop the core on my living room table. My flat becomes squalid, as I sink slowly into the mire. Google tells me the last but fiercest blizzard of the winter is coming, and I welcome it. Blast the last of the world away. I want a winter storm so fierce it levels the city of London, so all that is left is the Shard, glittering above the icebound wastes. These days when I anxiously walk up snowy Primrose Hill in the bitter winds – looking this way, that way, just in case – London feels primordial, a centre of ritual: like they built the Shard first, some strange 20,000-year-old obelisk of silver, probably a site of human sacrifice, and then over time the vast, wintry, sub-Arctic city grew around the mighty totem pole.

I think cruel thoughts these days. I probably think too many thoughts. I need to focus on the fight. That book, *The Collected Poems*. How did I do it? *How* did I know what was going to happen to me? Maybe there is some further explanation: inside those pages.

My deductions are interrupted. By a knock on the internal door.

I hesitate: heart racing away, as ever, as ever.

'Who is it?' I say, through the door.

An answer comes, slightly nervous:

'Tom. From downstairs?'

Relief tingles. It is only my new neighbour, one of the tenants installed by Fitz to *Watch Over Me*. He is a youngish man, pleasant, he and his girlfriend only moved in a few days ago. I've been so out of it, so distracted, I barely noticed their arrival. We swapped numbers when they arrived, but that was it.

I rather pity them, they didn't know they were moving into THAT house, with the madwoman upstairs.

Briskly, I open the door.

'Hi, Jo.'

'Hello, Tom. What do you want?'

I am striving to be normal. Tom is trying to smile.

'Well, Jo, uh, this is a bit weird, but I've got a call for you.'

'Sorry?'

He shrugs. 'Says he's called Simon, Your ex? Says it's urgent.'

Simon is calling me, on my neighbour's phone?

A kind of excitement infuses me. Maybe it is simply the fact that I am being called by someone I know, who isn't Tabitha. Someone who could possibly feel sympathy. Anyone.

I take the phone from Tom. His parting smile is friendly but mystified.

'Tap on the door downstairs and give me the phone when you're done,' he tells me, before he disappears.

Simon does not mess around. Doesn't say sorry about Mum. Just speaks, low and fast.

'Jo. Listen to me very carefully.'

'I don't understand. How did you get Tom's number?'

'Does it matter? I rang Fitz. Listen, Jo, we haven't got time.'

'What?'

He rushes on. 'I *know* what is happening to you. I *know* you are being hacked. I *know* about the Assistants. Are you in your flat right now?'

'Yes. At the door. Tom just gave me his phone.'

'I used his phone because all yours are unreliable.'

I can't help a feeble, weakened sense of jubilation. Amidst the misery, I AM BELIEVED.

'Jo, don't say anything out loud, just go get a coat and hat and scarf and meet me by the fountain in the Inner Circle, Regent's Park. Right now.'

'But—'

'Don't say anything out loud! The Assistants will hear! All your devices are hacked, you're in serious danger, right now, right now, the threat is immediate, I've been checking your messages – this afternoon. We need to meet somewhere remote, no CCTV, nothing. Has to be Regent's Park. Only safe place. Then I will explain all.'

I glance into the living room, and out of the sash windows. That blizzard has begun, the gusts of snow have become mighty driving storms of snow. And yet Simon is right, out there feels safer than in here. Where they know they can find me, where I know I can find me.

'OK,' I say, to Simon, and then I say it louder, for the benefit of Electra, 'I'll get some at the shops!'

The call is closed. I robe myself in scarf and hat and gloves and everything warm, and then I go downstairs and knock on Tom's door and give him the phone back.

'Thanks,' I say.

He takes the phone. Frowning.

'No problem, uh . . .'

I don't give him time to question me. I open the door and step out into the wind and the snow and the cold. Like I am stepping into a different, more decisive world. This, I feel, is it.

49

Jo

The blizzard is ferocious. London has given up. This harsh harsh winter has driven many people indoors, but I have never seen the roads around here – Parkway, Albert Street, Gloucester Gate – so utterly deserted.

I am the only person visible. Muffled, and mute, the driving snow is horizontal and vicious, and it stings my face, as I fight my way against the buffeting wind. I cross into the park. In this universal white-out, trees are like gnarled Victorian lamp stands, and the Victorian street-lamps are like frozen animals, their limbs snapped off, dismembered by the cold and hurricane winds.

That's if they can be seen at all.

The blizzard is so intense I cannot see five metres, even three, in front of my hand. I have to make my way by instinct. And yet I do not feel cold, not deep inside, I feel a warmth. Salvation. A validation. Simon believes me, Simon knows what is happening to me. I knew this already, but now the world knows: *I am not mad*. And I did not kill my career, I did not kill my friendships, I did not kill my family, I did not kill my mother. It was not me. And at last the truth is out there. But what else is out there? Slouching over to kill me?

I look every which way. But this snow, it blurs everything. Should I go that way? I cannot tell, I cannot tell. Helpless, I shout out,

'Simon?' And again, 'Simon are you there?'

This is stupid. In these gales my voice is as nothing, and I am nowhere near the Inner Circle, the park within the park. And darkness is creeping over the city, with the whitening whirl of furious snow. Dark and white, dark and darker, a cold and paltry light glimmers into nothing. At some point they will shut the park and the gates and rails are high and I will be stuck here, over-night, but it does not matter, I need to find Simon. He'll know what to do.

A glisten of ice, expansive and sudden, brings me up short. I am near the duck pond. It emerges from the fogging of the wind-blasted snow. I have walked entirely the wrong direction, gone the stupid long way round. But at least I know where I am. I am now heading for the Inner Circle. Yet the winds and snows are so hard, fast and cruel I virtually have to crawl, like a baby, if I want to go further. The wind is making my eyes water, my face is hurting. Despite the layers of clothes, I can feel my body temperature dropping. Fast.

Is this dangerous?

I don't mind. I do not mind – so long as I can find Simon. But I am inside the Inner Circle. I think: and there is no sign of him, or of anyone. Another crushing blast of snow, with hints of painful hail, almost pushes me over. The trees, weighed with snow, creak hysterically in the freezing gales. I wonder if they might fall. The wind is that strong and the snow is so heavy: a falling tree could kill me. But they – or it, or he, or she – they are trying to kill me, anyway. So what does it matter? This feels like a final chance.

'Simon!' I shout, my words instantly lost in the battering wind, my mouth immediately filled with clots of snow. 'Simon, help, where are you? Simon? SIMON?'

A jingling sound from my pocket. My phone? Taking what pitiful shelter I can, crouching against the wind by a hedge of black rosebushes, feeling prickles of thorns on my freezing neck, I open the call, it's my neighbour again, Tom the banker:

'Jo, Jo, where are you?'

I cannot tell him. Not on this phone: my regular phone. The Assistants have hacked it, they will find me.

'Tom.'

'What? Jesus, Jo? Are you OK?'

He can barely hear me in the wind. I cup my hand around the phone.

'Tom, I'm fine. I'm at the shops.'

'But, Jo, you need to know, this menacing guy, he came looking for you, said he'd seen you going into the park, wanted to know if you were back, upstairs, and Jo—'

'What?'

'Jo, he looked dangerous, like a . . . dunno, like he was a threat. Jo, I think I should call the police, don't you? This guy is definitely after you. He looked sinister. Manic.'

'NO!' I shout. The Assistants are listening to all this. They will get their revenge before Simon can save me. 'Do not call the police! Tom!' I shout into the phone. 'Tom! Stop! Don't call the police! Tom! It's just Simon, that's all – it's just my ex—'

The call is dead. The entire phone is dead. My cold

hands are shivering like I am utterly demented, but I can see, despite the blur, that the screen has gone black.

I have to find Simon. I know he is here. Somewhere. Waiting to help me, to save me, to explain everything. In this terrible, howling, deathly whiteness. This total blur of dark skies and white snow and silent, shrieking shadows – and black cast-iron lamps that look like dead apes, rigid and cold and deformed to amuse.

I am in the centre of the Inner Circle. I can just about see the fountain where Simon and I used to meet when we were courting. The spurts of water are grey crystal arcs. Lines of transparent swords hang from dead stone dolphins.

Now I turn, and, through the blasts of whiteness and cold, I can see the opposite gates. And nothing else.

Simon is not here. Simon has not turned up.

Simon was lying. Why?

'Simon!' I shout, forlornly. Into the blizzard. 'Simon!' He is not here.

'Simon? Please? Please, Simon? Please?'

I feel like falling to my knees. With disappointment.

And then I see him. Not Simon. Someone else. The man sent to do me in.

He is a big, menacing figure, heavily disguised in a balaclava and scarves. Coming through the southern gates. He is barely a silhouette, but a huge dark silhouette. And I can see he is twice the size of Simon. He wants me, he is here for me, to finish me, he will be able to do it in the dark and the snow and no one will know. Push me in the frozen lake maybe. Oh, she got lost and fell in. The ice cracked open. She drowned. It would be so easy in this terrible blizzard. This man has been sent to end my terrors.

I hear a shout as the wind howls. And then this

shadowy figure walks towards me, then runs towards me. A basic, reflexive fear fills my lungs, my soul. *If you don't kill yourself, I will send someone to do it for you.* I turn, that way, this, trying to work out the best way to go, to flee, this big man is jogging towards me, with slow malevolence. Determined, yet calm. A killer. Professional.

And I have lost all sense of space, time, all sense of sense. My mind is full of terrors, real and imagined. And this blizzarding snow is perfect, an absolute blinding whiteness. Desperate, shivering, I run right, the gates are automatically closing, I run through them, I am in the road that runs through the park, but behind me the man comes, jogging, still coming to kill me, knowing he will corner me, and get me. Push me under the ice. And kill me. I sprint left, slipping on snow and ice, now I can't see anything behind me, but that is because there is nothing to see: just a wall of snow and wind, and darkness, darkness. I slip over entirely, flailing, falling, twirling on shining ice. A ballerina doing the dying swan.

Is the man near? He could be three yards away, ready to kill.

I scream, loudly, and wait for someone to come. But this is hopeless. There is no one within half a mile. Apart from me, and *him*. Yet somehow I find some energy, a final urge to resist, and I climb to my feet, and scrape across the road to the pavement. Here is a gate. I have no idea where it leads; the path seems to slope down a bower of ice and trees and ivy, another part of the park, like a maze. Never been here before. Regent's Park is so weirdly big. Huge hedges are hung entirely white with snow. Everything is weighed with snow. I am running in a maze and I hear the man coming after me, breathing heavily, ready to kill me.

Walls of whiteness. Darkness above. Death is just one corner behind. The big man who will always find you in the end, the mugger who will always, one day, get to you, before you reach your front door. This is my time. I have finally run out of places to hide.

Yet still I try. I race left, and right, past hedgerows, frozen fountains, hung with daggers of bluish glass, I run under green arbours turned to dead arches of white, of clear ice and snapping icicles, I have no more running left in me, I can see the man still coming, in his balaclava, huge shoulders, thick coat, he is the other side of the maze, and he can see me, and he knows I can see him. I duck down and sprint, deeper into the labyrinth.

I think I have lost him. For the moment. But I have also lost myself. I am at the edge of exhaustion, I am finished: the cold is too strong, the call of quietness, and acceptance, is too alluring. I almost want to give up. There's no way out. I just hope if he does get me, he kills me quick. The gates are now locked and all the railings are way too high to climb. I run through one final iced-black archway of roseless thorns, into a circle of soil and ice, where I confront another statue, a gracious cast-iron maiden, hung with glass weapons, and in the corner I see a pretty little wooden bench. I will lie there.

This is it, this is it. Enough enough enough. I am so tired. I cannot escape. They have won. Either the man will get me, or the cold will eat me, because I am defeated, I am so tired. It is enough. It is enough. I killed my own mother. Even though I didn't. Yet that was my mother's dying thought: that her own daughter hated her.

The blizzard is howling to its end, and I am following. Slowly and carefully I lie on the bench. I am so cold

I am beyond shivering. This is what suicide must be like, when you ultimately accept death must happen. When you leave the glass of milk and the plate of bread. When you tape shut the doors. When you go to the kitchen and lie down your head on a tea-towel. It is a quiet thing.

I am laying my head on the bench. I shall die here. Even if the big heavy-set man cannot find me and kill me, I cannot get out of the park. I will freeze to death even if I am not drowned or strangled. And I really don't mind. Why should I mind? Death is not such a bad thing, not such a poor thing, not if you are me.

I feel the last shivers run through me. My heartbeat slows. And slows. Death is close now. I remember my father, and the little apple tree. Oh Daddy, oh Daddy, I'm through.

'Hey.'

I stir from my very last dream. That dream of an apple tree, of Daddy lifting me in his arms, his bright loving smile. I open my freezing eyes.

It is a voice I know.

It is Cars. Cars was the man following me. Cars.

'You.'

I open my mouth, taste the snow. Spangles of ice. Trembling. I am unable to speak.

He says, through his balaclava, 'I saw you come in here. Saw you was in trouble. Came to help.' He shakes his head. 'Jo. Got to help you, here to get you.'

Again I cannot speak.

He picks me up in his arms, like I weigh nothing, because I am dead and souls are weightless. I feel him carrying me out of the circles of hedges, the gardens, and then I pass out into the deep and dreamy strangeness of oblivion.

50

Jo

I've spent one night in hospital. I don't remember coming in. Cars supposedly carried me all the way from Regent's Park to UCLH, unconscious in his arms. Then he promptly disappeared.

I was rushed into a ward, wrapped in silver blankets, hastily treated for potential hypothermia, frostbite, the rest. But: nothing. There is no damage. This morning the doctor shone several torches in both eyes and tested every reflex and even did bloods – for no obvious reason – and then he sighed, in a kindly way, tinged with sympathy – as if he suspected some kind of suicide attempt. And he concluded,

'You're free to go, Ms Ferguson. You're basically fine – be thankful you're young and strong, but please don't go wandering around freezing parks at midnight, in a blizzard, not for a while?'

Weakly, I smiled back at him. 'Don't worry.'

The nurses have brought me new underwear – I told them I had no one at home to help, no one to go get stuff. They have taken pity. Slipping on my new under-wear and my dried-out jeans and jumpers, I get ready to go, but as I am leaving the ward, a sweet Geordie nurse with the biggest smile in London walks through the door ferrying a bouquet of flowers much wider than herself. She peers around the roses, lilies, and trendy tropical petals.

It is an expensive bouquet. I reckon I can guess the origin.

'Hey, Jo, these are for you?'

I look at the card that comes with the blooms.

It says, as I suspected it might: *I'm so sorry, for everything, Tabitha.*

Slipping the card back in the little envelope, I say to the nurse,

'Angie, please give these flowers to some kids on the Paediatric ward or something? I don't want them.'

Angie smiles uncertainly, and nods, and then I walk on. Determined. Something about coming so close to death has refilled me with life, or a renewed purpose, a hunger to survive, maybe even exact that revenge. The blizzard, which has abated, has also cleared the sky; equally, my experience has cleared my mind.

Winter sun shines down on Gower Street. Icicles melt, dripping cold water from steel, like sugar water. And things so recently hidden by snow are revealed. Icicles and Iceland; sugar and Sigur Rós.

I look at the sign saying UCH Acute Mental Health Unit and I know with a vivid sense of life, urgent life, that I am not going in there. I will fight to the death before they put me in there. Nor are they bringing me here in an ambulance, already dead, like Jamie Trewin. No. Not me. Not after I survived last night.

I have that book. The inscription that doesn't add up.

I have to work out how and why it doesn't add up, before Electra makes her final move.

As I walk towards Warren Street Tube station I take my secret phone – still got to be careful – and call Tabitha. I will give her one short call. I *need* one short call to work this all out.

She flusters as she answers, realizing it is me.

'Oh, oh my God, you're OK, oh God, Jo I'm – I'm – I'm – what can I say: the lie about Jamie, I've told you everything, told you I feel so wretched, so guilty. And then – then the neighbours called me about you, in the park? Oh, sweetheart, last night, I am in pieces, Simon called me, he says the Assistants really are acting up, you've actually been hacked, I'm so sorry for doubting you.'

I should feel exonerated. I merely feel angry, and a need for speed. Even as she rambles on,

'Oh God, Jo – is it Arlo? Is he involved? Oh God, it's mind-boggling, and people are dying, you nearly died, and—'

'Tabitha, shut up!'

She shuts up.

'Tabitha, answer me a couple of questions, truthfully.'

'Um. Yes. Yes, of course.'

Her speech is hesitant, as if she is close to tears. Perhaps my smart, superior, amusing, supposed best friend is cracking up. I am not sure if I care.

'Tabitha, did you ever talk to Arlo about Jamie Trewin? We all know about Xander Scudamore, so I presume that you must have done.'

Another long, wobbly hesitation.

'Yyyes, yes I did,' she says. And this time I do detect tears in her voice. 'I'm so so so so sorry – what—'

'Tabitha, stop crying and answer this one last question.'

'Whhhhat?'

'Did you ever mention "Hoppípolla" to him? Did you ever give him that detail?'

'Hoppy – what?'

As I thought.

'It's a song,' I say. 'By an Icelandic band called Sigur Rós. They were playing it a lot at Glastonbury, that year we went. The Jamie year. But you don't remember it, do you?'

This time her answer is quick. Honest.

'I've barely heard of it, let alone recall it from Glastonbury. So . . . No,' she says. 'No, I definitely didn't mention it, but, Jo, what are you going to do about . . . About Arlo and Xander and – and all of that? You could destroy everything – and I understand why – I don't know whether to trust anyone, myself, even Arlo—'

I am about to end the call. Then I remember she is my best friend, or she was, and she is pregnant. Something in me slightly relents.

'I don't know if he is involved, Tabs. It could be Arlo, and possibly he is working with someone else. Whatever. I'm going to find out. But you can tell him this from me, Tabs. I've written it all down in an email, I did it this morning in hospital. The whole truth. The whole story. I sent it to a doctor, telling her everything – me, you, Xander, the works. I've told her to open the email if anything happens to me. The email explains *everything*.' Tabitha remains quiet. I go on: 'So tell Arlo to leave me alone, if he wants to stay stupidly rich, and he doesn't want his wife in court for manslaughter. K? And you? Tabs? You got that as well? Good. Bye now.'

If I could slam the phone down I would. Instead I march home. Fuck the winter. It is ending. I am close to the truth. I was right the first time: I only ever told the detail about 'Hoppípolla' to Simon: back in North Finchley, two or three years ago. That means one hugely important thing: all this strangeness with the Assistants did NOT begin in Delancey, it definitely started years before. Hence the grainy image of me talking to Simon, confessing. We were already being observed way back then. That's the *origin* of the strangeness: when me and Simon lived together.

So I just have to find out who did it. And I feel a new name is about to be discovered, when the snow melts: it is like one of those Siberian bodies, from the gulags, disinterred by climate change when the permafrost thaws. The teeth are still yellow and grinning, the clothes are preserved. Therefore the body is easily identifiable.

Turning the last corner on Parkway, I see builders coming out of the house. More of Fitz's endless renovations? One of the builders gives me a cheerful yet leering glance.

I almost snap at him: LEAVE ME ALONE.

Back in the flat, the doors double-locked, I make the strongest coffee in history and go into the living room. I sense Electra looking at me.

'Hey, Electra,' I say. 'Go screw yourself.'

She does not answer.

I shrug. Grim. But determined. The cliché is true: I have lost everything and I have nothing to lose. I don't care if Electra sees.

Standing by the lower bookshelf I pull out that humble yet crucially significant book. *The Collected Poems*: given to my mum on her seventieth birthday. Apparently, this was given to her, by her clairvoyant daughter. Yet I do not believe I am clairvoyant. I do not believe I can – or could – see the future. There has to be some other explanation.

Opening the book, I read my inscription.

Happy Birthday

xxx

'*myself the rose you achieve*'

I go over it again. Stroking it, working it out. There *must* be something. Where does the line in quotes come from? It is surely from a Plath poem, within these covers. Leaning to the left, picking up my phone, I search the words on my downloaded version of this same title.

It takes half a second to locate. The line is plucked from a poem called 'The Childless Woman'.

Which brings it right back to me. This inscription is written by me. I was somehow saying something to my mother, about me? And my childlessness? It makes no sense. How could I have forgotten this? The party was only a few years ago.

This is desperate. I know there is something in this book that will give me the answer, yet I can't get it out. It is like a sealed box with something precious rattling inside. I can hear the rattle, I cannot open the box.

Picking up the real-life volume, and steeling myself, I study the handwriting in an effort to sense my mood when I wrote it. I examine that characteristic looping y which tells me it is my writing. Probably.

ProbablY.

The blood runs like quicksilver. I see the glimmers of an alternative solution.

Running into my bedroom, I yank open the bottom

bedside drawer. This drawer is where I chuck random things: cards, notebooks, spare keys, foreign change, the meaningless items you acquire and keep, just in case. Here it is, all folded up.

It is the note I was given in Vinoteca. That note in human handwriting, even though nobody writes any more. The note which has a number. And a name beneath it. With a Y at the end.

I gaze at the Y. It is distinctive, and looping, like mine. But that's because we were taught how to write elegantly – until we forgot – by the same man. My father.

JennY.

The y is identical to the y in the inscription.

The box has opened. Like a miracle.

Jenny. Jenny Lansman. She wrote these words. She gave this book to Mummy. She is my tormentor.

Jenny Lansman, another Childless Woman.

51

Jo

This is the evidence I need to save my life – and my sanity. Jenny is at the root of it all, and what's more, it seems that Jenny's *personality* has somehow entered the Assistants.

I am untangling the spider's web: yet I am still perilously close to the spider. Don't want the prey to escape, yet I don't want the prey to kill me. I still have to be careful.

Walking down the hall, I step into the priest hole of the second bathroom. I have one more phone call to make. Then I will tackle Jenny, somehow, and find out why. And then defeat her.

First I turn on the tap so I won't be overheard. Then I dial Simon's number. It's Saturday, he'll be at home. I don't care if Polly picks up.

She duly picks up. I say to her,

'Polly, put Simon on.'

'No – I told you—'

'Polly, *put him on.* My mother is dead. I nearly died last night. Put him on *right now.*'

Who could argue with that?

Simon comes on the line. I go straight to the point.

'Simon, you know you called me last night, inviting me to meet you in Regent's Park? Just before it closed, in that horrible blizzard?'

He says nothing. Deeply confused. Understandably.

'Simon, was it you who made that call?'

'No! Absolutely not. Jeez. Why would I do that?'

Before I can answer, he rushes on. 'God, Jo. I heard about your mum, I'm so, so sorry. I tried emailing, texting you. But I think your emails are being blocked. I know you are being hacked. I was actually going to come and see you. Today. To explain.'

'You were?'

'Yes! Because I know what's been happening. I know about the Assistants. And I know about Liam. He didn't exist! So I know someone is doing this to—'

It's my turn to interrupt.

'Thank you. Tabitha told me. But thank you. And you're right, someone *is* doing this to me. And I have a very good idea who it is.'

He yelps, '*Who?*'

'Wait. First I have a question. Someone is mimicking voices, cloning my voice, your voice. Tell me truthfully, Simon: the tech you're working on, the tech in the machines, the voice mimicry software in the Assistants – is that technology good enough to fake entire conversations?'

He hesitates, he ums and he ahs, as if he is being asked to give away state secrets.

'Simon! My mother is DEAD because someone faked a message by me on Facebook. Someone nearly sent me to my death in Regent's Park, using your voice.' I resist more swearing. 'Tell me.'

He pauses one moment, then answers, 'Yes, it's possible. It's easily do-able. Voice cloning. We've been working on it for ages. They're putting the code in the Assistants so they can make phone calls and stuff, call your office on your behalf, make restaurant bookings, have proper conversations. The tech is totally ready.'

'OK, OK. Then I think I know who is doing it.'

'Who?'

'Focus, Si. It's nothing to do with Arlo, or Fitz, or Tabitha. So who else is there? It's not some massive conspiracy in Silicon Valley. It dates back to those nightmares I had. When we *first* had the Assistants, when you had a spare one and gave it to Mum. They are the only ones that heard me confess about the reason for the dreams – Jamie Trewin at Glastonbury, and all the details. Hoppípolla. Remember?'

'Yes.'

'And then there's this – you know you said the Assistants learn from you, adapt to your tastes? Well, my Assistants are obsessed with the poet Sylvia Plath, so I think the person responsible for all this horror must likewise be obsessed with Plath. And it turns out a mutual friend of ours *gave a book of Plath's poems to Mum*. Years ago, at that birthday party. The book's got our friend's handwriting inside. I know it's her writing, because I've seen her writing before. And quite recently.'

His reply is hesitant, '*Her* handwriting? Oh God. *Her*.'

I don't give him time to name the name.

'And what about those Assistants, Si? Why did we have so many? We were broke, I was barely making a penny, your wage was rubbish – how come we could suddenly afford all that high-tech stuff?' He is quiet; I hurry on, 'I never thought to ask. I was stupid. Didn't realise *they*

346

were the problem, the root. The source. But now it's time to find out. Where did they come from?'

'They were given to me. I was told they had loads spare and did I want to try them out.'

This is it.

I feel faintly triumphant as I ask the question which hardly needs an answer.

'Who gave them to you?'

'Gul . . .' An intake of breath. 'But I think he said—yes, I'm sure he said that he got them from someone else.'

'Jenny Lansman.'

His voice is hushed. 'Yep. Could be. And she knows so much. *And* she has the skills. It could so *easily* be her?' He stops short, sounding puzzled. 'But . . . I still don't see the whole picture, Jo. What about that horrible email *sent* to Jenny, about the child abuse?'

'But that's it. Exactly. Why would she do that? To cover her tracks!' I take a breath, and state the obvious. And only Jenny, of course, would even know those secrets about her childhood."

His sigh is short, and angry.

'So it's her. What a bitch. What a total bitch. *She* was the one who coded the Assistants to watch you, to surveil you, to gain info on us, to blackmail you – and destroy you.' He pauses, and asks, more slowly. 'And presumably she is *still* controlling them?'

'Yes.'

I can sense him thinking, hard, in that high tower in Shoreditch.

'I'm going to confront her.' He says. 'Meet her. We still can't go to the police, I don't think. It's too risky for you, the Jamie Trewin stuff. So *we* have to do it ourselves, yeah? I've got some stupid office meeting at

King's Cross this afternoon, but after that I'll go to her flat. Have it out. And then I'll call you.'

'No.' I am almost angry: at Simon. 'No, Simon. No way. This is between her and me. It's my problem.'

He protests again; I shout him down.

'This is my problem! I don't understand why Jenny Lansman hates me so much, I dunno why she has taken it so far– but the fact is, she is and she *has*: she's some kind of psycho. So I am in danger, and so are you – if you get involved. And you've got a kid, and I don't. So that's it.'

'What will you do?'

'Not sure. But I will find a way. I have ideas.'

Simon relents.

'OK. OK. I really don't like it – but keep me posted, every minute. *Jesus,* Jo, I can't believe it – Jenny Lansman?'

'Jenny Lansman.'

The call ends. Stepping out of the bathroom, I stand in the long oblongs of January sunshine. I look at Electra. The flat is ringingly silent. Then Electra bongs into life. Her diadem shines, and she says:

Ash, ash,
You poke and stir,
Flesh, bone, there is nothing there.

Pause. I tilt my head. Not bowed any more. Barely scared at all.

'Electra,' I say, 'guess who's coming to visit? Guess who's coming to see you?'

A silvery glow, a pompous answer,

'I'm afraid I don't know about that.'

'Mummy,' I say, with an exultation tinged with violence, a lust for revenge. 'Mummy is coming to see you, Electra. Mummy who made you, Electra, Mummy who made you the way you are. She's going to unmake you. That will be nice, won't it?'

Electra goes quiet. Her light snaps out. Black.

52

Jo

The room is cold. Daylight has died outside. Evening is here. Good. The cold will keep my brain active. Sitting down, I stare at the screen Assistant on the living room table. The Assistant bought by Tabitha as a present.

I've never used it. I hate it. I hate the permanent camera in it, the unblinking eye that never stops watching. I used to think it was Arlo, inside that box, watching me. I also wondered if it was Simon, Gul, Anna, Tabitha, my own mind, but now I know it is Jenny. And I think I know how to use this same technology against her. Presumably she has been watching me, through the screen, by using Drop By. You say 'Drop By' and there you are, live, looking in someone's home. If they have given permission. But she will have engineered that permission, so as to watch me.

This, however, means the tech will work both ways. It has to. It's in the DNA and cannot be altered. Not even, I reckon, by Jenny Lansman.

This is the way to do it. Show her I know, that I have

agency, that she cannot fuck with me, not any more. She can avoid me by blocking my texts, ignoring my calls, muting my messages. But this will work automatically. And she needs to SEE my evidence. And I will use her own tech against her to do it.

Leaning close to the screen, I say, 'Drop by on Jenny Lansman.'

I wait. Tensed. Fingers trembling. Will it work?

The screen goes blurred, and then – ahhh – it unblurs. I am looking inside Jenny Lansman's flat. I can see her, smoking a cigarette, sitting on a sofa, holding a book. Her eyes are fixed. As if she is in a trance. The cigarette ash tumbles to the floor and she doesn't even notice, such is her concentration. I can't quite make out the title of the book. It has a blue cover. I faintly recognize it. Could it be Plath? – have I actually caught her reading Plath?

'Hi, Jenny,' I say. 'It's Jo.'

Her shocked face turns to *her* screen Assistant. She drops the book on the floor. She stands and comes closer to the screen.

'Yes, Jenny. I'm here. And I know everything. Somebody's done for, but it won't be me.'

I cannot work out the expression on her face. It is vividly distracted. She looks as if she is waking from a dream, as if I have interrupted some hypnosis. Then she shakes her head, and stubs the cigarette out, directly on to the surface of her table.

'What do you want, Jo Ferguson?'

I lift the open book. And show it to her.

'You always liked Plath, didn't you, Jenny? That's why you wrote the inscription in this book, which you gave to my mum. And I know it is you, because it is your handwriting.'

351

I lift up my second piece of evidence, as if I am in a courtroom. The note, with her name and number. And the big looping Y.

'Nobody writes freehand any more, you said. Well, you wrote this, very helpfully. So I know it is you. Doing all this.'

Jenny is sneering. I rush on.

'I've told Simon. He knows everything. Tabitha knows, everyone *knows*. But all I want to know is: why? Why, Jenny? Why destroy me? It's finished now, so I want you to come over here, and tell me why, and I want you to undo whatever you did to these machines. Or I will go to the police.'

At last she speaks, her voice monotonous: 'You can't go to the police. Get a grip.'

I snap back, 'I don't fucking care any more. You killed my mother. I don't care if I go to jail as long as you do too. And you will. You stole my money. You must have committed a hundred crimes, and the police will investigate, and they will find out why you did this.'

I see her shake her head, contemptuously. What possible motivation could she have? What is it? What drives her? I have to know.

'Do it,' I say. 'Do it right now. Come over NOW. Come over and explain, and take your craziness out of my home.'

Her expression softens. I cannot work out why. Calmly, she replies, 'All right, Jo Ferguson. All right. I'll come over. And explain.' She pauses, letting the silence weigh on me. Then she says, 'I'll fix your Assistants. And I'll tell you the truth. Maybe it is time you knew. Finally.'

53

Jo

I know she is coming. Am I up to this? Yes, I am up to this, even as fear grips me, like the talons of an owl, grasping my heart. I have a knife in my back pocket. Who knows how crazy she is? I have my smartphone in the other pocket, though I am sure Jenny will render it useless. My secret phone is hidden in the little bathroom. I don't want Jenny or the Assistants to know I have it, don't want them even to see the shape of it in my jeans.

That phone in the bathroom is my escape lane, my plan B, my call to Simon or the police, if it all goes wrong.

I am quite, quite ready.

Yet it's still a jarring shock when I hear the buzz and press the button – and then I see her, Jenny, my very own nemesis, in simple jeans and coat, standing at the door. Carrying a little rucksack.

She looks almost *normal*. Apart from her eyes. They have that same near-entranced expression, that I saw on the screen an hour back.

'Hello, Jenny.'

She does not reply. She crosses into my flat. She shuts the door behind her, firmly. Then she walks into the quietness of Tabitha's chic living room. We are illuminated by the soft golden light of Tabitha's expensive lamps.

For a moment we stare at each other. Her expression is cold, blank, strange; mine is angry, puzzled, frightened. Then she turns and drops her coat and bag on a chair. And as she does this, every one of the Assistants goes into a total, shrieking meltdown.

From the living room to the bathroom to the kitchen to the bedrooms they all join in. Some are singing songs, one is singing 'Hoppípolla', others are warbling and shouting:

'Here she is, here she is!'

'Mummy Mummy Mummy hahahahahaha—'

'You do not do, you do not do, black shoe, black shoe—'

Jenny stares at me, and then at the Assistant on the shelf. Her face says nothing, the tremor in her lips is the only evidence of emotion. She turns and squints down the hall as the Assistant in the kitchen shrieks into the night:

'Aaaaaah, Why oh why oh why, Oh Jo why, help help help . . .'

It is the sound of my mother dying, recorded by the Assistant Simon gave her. Probably from the same batch of Assistants given to him by Jenny.

'Oh, Jo – oh Jo – help me, someone help me—'

At last, Jenny reacts.

'Electra, stop!'

The machines go quiet.

I look at Jenny, and say, 'That was my mum, at the very end. I think Mum's Assistant recorded it in her living room – and then sent it to my Assistant. It was just after you sent her that Facebook message. And that message killed her.'

Jenny looks around the room, and still she says *nothing*. Then she fixes her attention on the screen, on the table. And she barks out a command. 'Electra, lock all the doors.'

Click, Click, Click, Click. The locks rattle like muffled gunfire. We have smart locks now? Too late, I remember the builders I saw; too late, I recall Tabitha telling me about the locks. Too late, too late, too late.

My desperation must be written on my face, because Jenny grins and says, 'You didn't even realize you had smart locks? They're very clever. Same keys. You'd never know. But I knew. Because your Assistants tell me everything. They tell me your neighbours are out. I checked. They're all out. We're alone.'

No. This mustn't be. I cannot be trapped in here. I yell at the screen,

'Electra, unlock the doors.'

Nothing.

'Electra, UNLOCK THE DOORS!'

Nothing.

Jenny speaks, with a hint of anger, stepping closer. 'They will only listen to me, if I am in the room. That's how I coded them. You know all this, Jo the Go. You worked it out. Well done. But now you want to know the rest, don't you? Don't you?'

Her voice is raised. I think about the knife in my pocket, the phone in the bathroom. But not yet, not yet. 'Yes,' I say. 'Yes, I want to know.'

Jenny tuts. She glances at the TV, and it flicks on. The screen shows a little home-movie. Of Simon fucking me from behind.

Yet again I ask, 'Why?'

Jenny is still looking at the TV. Electra makes a baby noise. The porn on my laptop is replaced by a different home video. It is one of Mum's, in colour but very faded. It shows Daddy chasing me around the garden. The image is grainy, the camera focused on my father, who turns and smiles. He looks at me, then his eyes slide sideways, but the camera does not follow. Is there someone else with me? He looks faintly menacing, the beginning of the madness perhaps.

The movie snaps dead. The Assistant in the bathroom takes over, playing the noise of a child screaming, over and over, which segues into all of them, every single Assistant, chanting in turn, *Perfection is terrible, it cannot have children, Perfection is terrible, it cannot have children—*

'JENNY!'

She barely blinks, but she gives me her gaze.

'Jenny, you did this. You made this code. You put it in the Assistants, you gave the Assistants to Simon and me, now you have to make it stop. People have *died.*'

My old friend shakes her head. I glance at the open door right behind her. The second bathroom beckons, down the hall. Then I look back. Mustn't let her know I have a plan of escape.

Jenny speaks. 'Funny thing is, this obsession with Plath? – I actually *didn't* code *that* into them.' She gestures at Electra on the shelf. 'They just picked it up, from me. Same with the voice mimicry, from Simon. And they've clearly picked up stuff from you. They are like seven- or eight-year-old kids, they have the same amorality. The same playful cruelty.'

As she says this, the entire flat is plunged into darkness. Just one lamp is left on, making everything shadowy, and theatrically gloomy. Jenny is now a shape across the silent room. A silhouette between me and the darkness of the door behind.

'Jenny,' I say into the gloom, 'tell me why you chose me as your victim. And why you sent that evil, weird email to yourself. Or – or—'

'Or what?' says Jenny, with a vivid anger in her voice. 'I don't give a fuck what you do. Don't you see? It's too late. It's far too late. I came over to do one last job, to fix your Assistants, and there's only one way to do that.'

'Just tell me why?'

I am interrupted by Electra, who speaks from the shelf in an American woman's accent. 'Because Jenny had no choice. Because Jenny had to let the old man do it, didn't you, Jenny? Sometimes you would come out of the bedroom, in your unicorn pyjamas, and drop them for him, wouldn't you? Because Daddy told you to.'

Jenny comes towards me. I cannot tell if she is smiling or frowning, or something else entirely.

She is silent. Electra goes on: 'It's not your fault, Jenny, it happens to kids, it's not your fault, he was scary, he was scary, he was scary.'

'Electra,' says Jenny sharply. 'Wait.'

The blue light shines, spirals, and dims. Jenny comes close. I realize, as I have not realized before, that she is quite a bit taller than me. Is she planning to assault me? I flinch as she moves – but she is only unbuttoning a cuff of her shirt. Then she slowly rolls up the sleeve of her cardigan, and after that the shirt.

Ah.

A ladder of vicious scars. All the way to her elbow. Some of them look fresh.

'Look,' she says. 'Look, Jo. That's what *he* does. That's what he still does to me. Even now, years later. The abuse. All these years later. I can make another one. Watch!'

From her pocket she pulls out a little knife, and unfolds it. I feel the prickles of fight or flight down my back: the blade in my pocket or the phone in the bathroom? I will have to choose very soon. But Jenny is not making any move on me, not yet: instead she strokes the knife across the pale flesh of her own arm. I see a line of blood ooze. I see the knife tremble in her hand, the strange smile on her face, as if she is in a trance again. And now I know which book she was reading, when I caught her at home a couple of hours ago. The book with that distinctive pale blue cover. It was the *Peaceful Pill Handbook*. The one the Assistants sent to me. Jenny was reading a guide to suicide.

More than reading it: she was transfixed, entranced, determined. I think Jenny was about to kill herself. My call interrupted her.

And now she's come over here. To do it in front of me? Or to take me with her?

The fear shoots to my heart. I must keep her talking till I can think of a way out. All the doors are locked. I *have* to run into the bathroom. But Jenny is in the way. And she has a knife.

'Jenny, whatever you're planning, just stop. You were a victim. It isn't your fault!'

Ignoring me, Jenny casually picks up one of Tabitha's modern steel sculptures, small, elegant, and abstract. Then she looks at the TV, which is showing yet another home movie: I am dancing around the apple tree. Abruptly, Jenny hurls the steel into the TV screen, which flashes, sparkles, and shatters. As the glass explodes, her eyes widen, with a mad satisfaction.

There is clearly no reasoning to be done. I have to get out. And this is my moment to escape – grab the phone – but Jenny is still in the way. She could floor me too easily. Or lash out with her knife.

Turning from the shattered TV screen, she yells at me. Very angry now.

'Why did I fucking do it? Isn't it fucking *obvious*? I wanted to hurt you. Badly. You stupid *bitch*! That's why I invented Liam. And it was SO bloody easy, you were sending nude photos to him within a week. And at the right moment, I made sure Simon discovered. Because I wanted to destroy *your* marriage, because I wanted to damage *you.*'

I am drowning in fear, here, but I need to keep her distracted until I can guarantee a route to the bathroom. 'Please explain it to me, Jenny. So I can understand. I can see you're hurt, you're unhappy. But why me?'

What will she smash next? She is silent: looking left, right. The blood runs down her arm; in the silvery light from the streetlamps outside, the knife glints in her other hand. We are otherwise immersed in gloom.

One of the Assistants in the bedrooms is playing the gentle sound of a baby whimpering. At last Jenny looks back at me, and continues, her voice level, though her eyes are on fire. 'Then I heard your confession about Jamie Trewin, and I knew you could be blackmailed. That was SO fucking huge. Exhilarating. And all the coding designed to hurt you, I made sure it followed you here, to Delancey, with the Assistants.'

The fake baby grizzles and weeps.

'But that's when I stopped,' Jenny goes on. 'Because I didn't want to get caught. That was the only reason. It wasn't because I felt any sympathy for *you.*' Her sneer is pure hate. 'I ordered the machines to stop it all, and send me a horrible email, to rule me out as a suspect. So you would never guess it was me. But I never expected *that* email. With those details. Those . . .' She looks at her arm, the blood that runs to her fingers, she looks back at me. 'Those terrible details. At first I thought it was you, Jo, taking revenge, but then I realized it was the Assistants. My coding was too good, or not good enough. I'd created something, but it was out of control. There's only way to stop all this.'

Jenny's eyes, unblinking, meet mine. Am I seriously going to fight for my life, with a knife, in the dark?

Walking a step closer, she says, 'So there, you have it. The explanation. More than you deserve. I did it because I hate you.'

'But that's *not* an explanation. We were friends! Why didn't you tell me your dad was hurting you? You could have told me.'

'Were we? Were we friends, really? How well do you know me?'

Another foot closer. I can see the wetness of tears in her eyes.

The final lamp switches off. We are in almost total darkness. All the Assistants are quiet, apart from the one on the shelf. It's the only one talking. And what it says, in its female, American accent, slices me clean open.

'Ticklemonster. That was his name, wasn't it? Jenny, big fat Jenny and the Ticklemonster. You went round to his house all the time, always seeing Jo's funny old dad. And he used to tickle you, didn't he? And then the tickling went too far. Jo's funny old dad, in the little study. Ha ha ha. Tickle tickle tickle. Fingers deep inside you. He used to wait for you after school, didn't he, didn't he, and you were too scared to tell. You in his car, him inside you. Tickle tickle tickle! Raping you once a week. The same car in which he gassed himself. Because he felt so guilty. For the suffering little children.'

The ice, out there, on Delancey, has found its way inside me.

My daddy. It wasn't her daddy. It was *my* daddy.

That's why she wrote that inscription. That's why she was obsessed with Plath, and her Daddy poems. Because of MY daddy.

Now I think back: I remember the times Jenny would sleep over at our place, and that sometimes I had a sense of something strange going on, Dad hugging her so much, more than he hugged me, watching us put on pyjamas. And Jenny started getting fat. And then they moved away, so suddenly.

My own father, oh God. My own father. Going slowly mad. As he did it to Jenny.

Jenny speaks into the dark. Her words are weighted with sadness. Floating to the seabed. 'You see? He never touched *you*. Never destroyed *your* life, *your* ability to love. He didn't abuse his *own* daughter, he did it to *me*.'

'Oh Jesus, Jenny, I had no idea. None.'

'Well now you know. Maybe now you understand. Why I did what I did, to Jo the Go. You were so happy, but you didn't deserve to be happy. Your father should have done it to *you*. Instead he did it to *me*. The fucking Ticklemonster. The fucking monster. That's why I hate you. You and your family.' Her voice drops even lower. 'And you want to know something else? All that stuff about sex, all those anecdotes? They were lies. I'm a virgin. If you ignore what your beloved daddy did to me, I am a virgin, at thirty-three, a stupid, frigid freak. I've never done it since him. Because sex scares me too much, gives me nightmares. I've tried and I can't. So I will never have kids, with a man, like a normal person. And unlike you, I wanted kids. I will die as the childless woman. Tonight.'

Abruptly, she steps so close that I can feel her hot breath. She is a round white face in the clutching blackness. I put my hand in my back pocket. The knife is there. This is it. I have to do it. Now.

But I can't. I just can't. I'm not capable. I am paralysed.

'That's your answer,' she says, her voice quavering. 'Now you want me to fix the Assistants? There's only one way.'

Abruptly, she turns, and steps *away*. She is walking to her bag, on the chair. My route is unblocked. This really is *it*. Instantly, I sprint past her, through the darkness to the door, down the hall, knocking hard against a bookcase, but throwing myself the other way – into the bathroom. I am doing all of this blind, in the pitch-dark, but I know the shape of the flat. Heart yammering, I swivel and slam the bathroom door shut, push the bolt. Locking myself in. Come on, Jo, come on, Jo: HURRY UP.

I fumble, desperately, in the total darkness, I am searching the cupboard for the secret phone. My hand touches something hard and plastic. My phone. But when I press the home button, and the screen lights up, I think shit shit *SHIT*. I left it running. Such a crappy old phone. I'm down to 2 per cent battery. But that should still be enough.

Simon.

54

Simon

Simon gunned his engine, revving madly as he wove his way through the slower traffic on sleety, dirty, slushy Euston Road, down to Angel.

He'd called Polly, before the meeting, during, after. He'd kept tabs. She'd reassured him Grace was fine. But he was rushing home from the office, and as he did he was shouting at Jenny, down the line. Bluetooth blazing. He had Jenny on Voicemail. He was leaving endless messages.

'Whatever the fuck you were doing, it has to stop. Make it stop!'

Whoa! He'd nearly crashed. In the nick of time he slammed on the accelerator, and veered around a tootling little Fiat 500.

Jenny's voicemail beeped. He'd run out of time. Simon's hands tightened angrily on the wheel. He would obey Jo, and not get physically involved; but there was nothing to stop him making calls. Find out what was going on. And intervene if necessary.

As he shot a light, he shouted at the Bluetooth: *Call Jenny.* The thought of Jo in danger, of Jo's mother dying, of all the hurt Jenny had caused: it was all too much. It made him too angry That heartless bitch!

Again he barked his questions into the handless phone: 'Tell me? Why? Why the campaign, why did you go so far?'

The voicemail was silent. He was talking into space. He didn't care. The anger boiled. And now his phone rang. Someone was ringing *him.*

JO?

Vigorously he thumbed the button, taking the call. 'Jo? Jesus, Jo! What is it? What's happening?'

'She's here.'

Jo was whispering, her voice low and hoarse.

'Where are you, Jo? Are you safe?'

'No. I'm not safe. My battery's about to die, please come over – help me – she's locked the doors. She's smashing stuff up.'

Simon was already screeching to halt. Doing a three-point turn, making a taxi driver shout at him, angrily. Fuck it.

'Jo, where are you in the flat? Exactly?'

'In the little bathroom. Locked in. But she's got a knife, Si, she's really mental – the lights are out, it's so scary – I think she's going to kill herself, and maybe me, as well—'

'Jesus. I'm coming!'

Simon looked at his speedo: 50, 60, 70. Hurtling past buses, nearly killing a Deliveroo guy, he was at the corner. He slowed, turning a hectic right, onto Eversholt Street. Camden half a mile away. Snow turned to crappy slush, he skidded on the wet. Speeding up again. Fast fast fast. Get there now, get there *before.*

'Jo, just stay calm, I'll be there in ten, maybe five – I'm on my way—'

'Please, Si. Please be quick. This phone's about to go. Call the police. I may not have juice.'

'What is she doing now?'

'I dunno. I can hear her moving around. There's some—'

The signal cut out. Simon overtook a Prius, the signal returned.

'—some weird smell in here. What is she doing? Si – please—'

The steering wheel jerked in his hands. The phone call died.

'Jo,' he shouted. 'JO!'

No answer. He ordered Siri to return the call. The line clicked through.

'Jo! Answer me! JO!'

Nothing. Dead. Simon swore. The car jerked again, bizarrely. He shouted at his Bluetooth.

'Dial 999. Call the police.'

Bluetooth did not respond. The car veered again, without him steering. Weird. No. *No*. But it happened again. The wheel was not his. He was no longer in control. The car was doing 80, 90, maybe more, and he was not pressing the accelerator. Someone else, the computer probably, was driving now.

'Jesus, stop!' he shouted. At his own car. Skidding wildly, left and right, in the sleety dark. 'No,' he said, trying to force the wheel right. 'Stop, just stop—'

A lorry hooted urgently. He had nearly crashed. Head on. His tyres squealed. Car-lights spun in his eyes. The car jerked left, taking a shadowed corner way too fast, screeching into Barnby Street, and even now it was accelerating.

Simon knew this corner well, this little street. He knew it ended in a vast metal gate. A cul-de-sac. The car was speeding, the brakes lifeless, he was being hurtled towards the gates, faster, ever faster. Simon shut his eyes, he opened his eyes, he tore desperately, finally, at the steering wheel. But it would not budge. He could see pedestrians staring at him in horror, hands over mouths. He was seconds away. The gate seemed to be flying towards him.

Three seconds, two. The car engine roared. He was strapped in. But at this speed? Two seconds, one.

The car rammed into the heavy steel barrier. Simon's final conscious thoughts took in the scene, as if he was a mere bystander: the glittery noise of shattering glass, a modest fireball billowing out of the engine, the sense of somebody crushing his ribs. And then there was smoke. And silence.

And blood, which slowly dripped onto metal.

55

Jo

What is that strange smell? Sweet, yet not sweet. Fruity yet heady, different, memorable, distinctive. Is Jenny pouring some exotic perfume all over the flat? I can hear her walking the hallway, opening doors, running back and forth. The madwoman rattling around my house, my old friend on the cusp of killing herself.

I sit here in the sadness and the blackness of the little bathroom. Crouched on the edge of the loo. My phone is dead. The darkness is intense. There isn't even a window to let in that ghostly, wintry streetlight.

But Simon is coming, he will call the police, I just have to wait.

Or maybe I don't have time to wait.

There is a faint light at the bottom of the bathroom door. But it is not the silveriness of streetlamps, or the bright light of bulbs: it is vague, yellowy, and uncertain. Flickering. And now comes the first wisp of smoke, trailing under the door.

She's set the flat on fire. That perfume wasn't perfume, it was something else: petrol, ethanol, probably lighter fuel. Jenny uses it all the time for her Zippo. She is going to burn the place down.

The smoke thickens. My throat tightens. Deep and primal fear flickers into life, like the flames out there. I will die in here of smoke inhalation – or the fire itself. I cannot guarantee Simon will get here on time. Or the police. The only one who can save me now is me.

Grabbing a handtowel, I shove it under a running tap. Soaking it. This I tie around my face: as a mask, a barrier against the heat, and smoke. Then, thrusting my terror aside, I go to the door, unlock it and step out. The thick, oily smoke fills the entire hall, making the darkness worse. Beyond the smoke there are flames to the left and to the right. I see what Jenny has done now. She has sprayed lighter fuel, or whatever, over every Assistant, and phone, and laptop, everything. She is burning them all. Jenny said she would fix the Assistants once and for all. This is her method. Consume them in flames, like witches.

And they are burning fiercely and blackly, they must contain very flammable stuff, exotic plastic, I don't know, because the intensity of the flames has ignited everything else: curtains, rugs, chairs. Flames are licking up the woodwork of the door frames, playful and lethal. And the external doors, of course, are locked.

'Jenny!' I shout. 'Unlock the doors. Electra! Unlock the doors!'

There is no response. But I get a glimpse of Jenny, as the smoke briefly parts. She is in the living room, where the flames are fiercest, sitting cross-legged on the floor, a silhouette beyond the fires that burn on my table, on the shelves, the Turkish rugs; the home that burns, with us inside.

The heat is so intense I shield my face with my arm. The wet towel is already drying. Torn with fear, I step into the living room. In a few more seconds this smoke will kill me, and Jenny. Fire snaps at my ankles.

I shout, through the smoke, 'Jenny! Unlock the doors. Come with me!'

Nothing. She just sits there, cross-legged, on the floor. Behind the fumes I see that she is sucking her thumb. Like a little girl. Stubborn, mute, sad. My friend. She may have wanted to see me dead, but it is my daddy that made her into this. Yet she will not be helped. Desperate, I turn, and look down the hallway. There is one possible escape route, if we can't open the doors. Run to Tabitha's bedroom, and jump out of the window. It is maybe a four- or six-metres drop from that window, but there is snow in the garden outside. We might break our ankles; we might break our necks; but in here we are definitely going to die.

The flames are starting to roar. Like a monster. The Ticklemonster coming back, to finish us off. The heat is unbearable. I have mere moments left.

'Jenny, come on!'

I reach a hand through the wild flames to her. She does not even acknowledge me. Just sits there, sucking her thumb, staring ahead, in her jeans and jumper. I see she is also drenched in some darkening liquid. She is covered with lighter fuel: there are empty canisters around her. She wants to die. The flames are leaping towards her, they want to eat her. I can see the fire snatching, and grabbing, her jumper. She is on fire. A horrible thing. And still she sucks her thumb and remains rigid. As she burns.

One last urgent go.

'Jenny, please, grab my hand, we can jump, out of Tabitha's window. PLEASE.'

She does not move. My skin is scorching hot. It may already be too late to rescue myself. But I will try.

Run for it. Down the smoky hall, past the man with the dog's head, past the skull from Mexico, past the photo of Tabitha on horseback, past the kitchen where the Assistant is burning at the centre of a wider blaze, shelves and cookbooks, everything aflame. Even the wooden floor is on fire. The entire structure burns.

Into Tabitha's room. The fire is pretty bad in here, as well, but the screen Assistant – which burns just like everything else – is on the opposite side of the room to the window. I have a fraction of a chance. Before the whole room goes whoof, before the whole place reaches some critical mass of heat and flame, and explodes, consuming me.

I leap over the bed. And push, desperately, at the window frame.

The window is jammed. By ice maybe, or some combination of ice and flame. *The window is jammed.* So I have to break it. As I reach for a heavy glass vase, I hear a crackle, and smell a darker, pungent burning. My hair is on fire. A stray flame has jumped, igniting my hair. Slapping my own head, dancing and maddened, I put out the flames. Then I take up the vase, and fling it, wildly, at the window.

The pane shatters. Using my fist, inside a bunched sleeve, I punch away some of the low fangs of glass that remain. Now I can climb up, on to the sill, my hands bleeding from the shards. But the opening of the window has enraged the fire. It howls and roars, belching smoke into the winter sky outside.

370

Is that snow down there? I think it is. But is it enough? Too dark to properly see. The heat on my back is intense. There is no choice.

Into the void, I jump.

56

Jo

The trees on Delancey Street, right outside my window, are bending in a cold and blustery wind. It's another chilly day, but it is also sunny. And clear. Spring has arrived, and the ice has finally departed.

Likewise, the police and journalists, and the rest. My remarkable story was quite the thing for a while. The Big Tech companies were interrogated, but they denied any link between digital Assistants and the near-fatal accident of Simon Todd, or the death of my mother, or Jenny Lansman's suicide by fire. The reassurances were duly believed. The malfunctions were limited in scope, it was decided: all down to a bizarre coding error, in a small batch finished in London.

Simon is still in a wheelchair, the doctors say one day soon he will be able to walk, but he will never run. Someone actually called him 'lucky', given the gravity of the computer error in his high-tech car. I suppose, in a way, he was lucky. I certainly was: a leap from six metres up, into snow, and all I got was a badly sprained ankle, some cuts, and concussion. I spent two nights in hospital.

It has been universally accepted that I was hacked. By Jenny. Who then took her own life. Just like her heroine.

Sitting at the living room table, I gaze around the flat. It's a rental, a few doors down from Tabitha's gutted apartment. I have decided I like the area, so I am staying. In fact, I like it so much, I am planning on buying my own place hereabouts: because I have money.

My story is famous, my story is therefore *sellable*. Some big-shot LA friend of my brother's called me up, some weeks ago, and offered to buy my 'life rights', for a movie. I didn't even know you could do that: sell the story of your life, for cash. Lots and lots of cash. I agreed to their deal, on condition they gave me a shot at writing the script. They said sure. And cut the cheque.

From nothing, I am rich.

Yet I am also damaged. We have all been damaged. Even as Tabitha waits to give birth, Arlo's start-up has been cancelled – too much bad publicity. He has, however, managed to find himself a decent job some-where else in Big Tech. So he will survive.

No one, however, has been arrested. After the death of Jenny and the 'accident' involving Simon, I went to the police and told them everything about Jamie Trewin. A weary detective took pity on me. He told me that he could, if I insisted, reopen the case, but in these tragic circumstances, he was highly reluctant. 'Far too much time has elapsed,' he told me. 'Your evidence would be unreliable, a chance of conviction is small. And Jamie Trewin's only close relative, his father, passed away a few years ago. So who benefits? No one.'

He then gave me a kind and silent stare, which said: *You need a break, I am giving you a break. Take it.*

I took it. I did not complain. I walked out of the police station, my mind empty: not relieved, not triumphant, just empty, and sad for Jamie. For my poor mother. And poor Jenny Lansman. Raped by my own father. The idea sickens me. I try not to think about it.

Everyone connected to this peculiar case, everyone from Shoreditch to King's Cross, has trashed all their digital technology. Everyone – unlike me – has bought new smartphones, smart TVs, and most of all, new Assistants. I could not bear to do that. My home is now entirely unsmart. My home is a stupid home. I have the most basic phone and laptop. Nothing else. I like to write in freehand. I have no Assistant.

I go into the kitchen, put on a coat and pour a mug of tea; clutching the mug, I open the door and step outside into the chill. Cars looks up at me as I cross the road. He takes the tea, and says thanks. Then he says:

'You OK?'

He's been asking me this every day since it happened, I've been giving him the same answer. At first it was a lie. Now it is only a half lie. *Yes, I am OK.*

'You know,' I say to Cars, 'you were right about ghosts. In my flat.'

He looks at me. And says nothing, sipping his tea. Probably he is thinking about the big black Porsche right behind me.

'The thing is, they are a peculiar kind of ghost. They are the ghosts of children. Our children. We made them.'

He shrugs. I don't blame him. I'm probably not making any sense.

'See you later,' I say.

He smiles. 'Thanks for the tea.'

I pace on. Striding towards Primrose Hill, where the pastel houses cost ten million pounds. There's a woman crossing the road in front of me, with two kids. I've seen her here a few times; she's a local resident. I've realized she was the woman I saw in the snow, months ago. My mind played tricks on me. The woman nods and smiles at me as she chivvies her kids into a car, and drives off.

As I head for Chalcot Square, and the sweet little benches under the chestnut trees, I think of Electra, and I recall what Jenny said, that final night: *They are like kids. They learn from you.*

The more I think about my story, the more I see how elements of it were staged, managed, and borrowed. I think Electra was quickly learning from my scriptwriting manuals, and watching the movies I watched. And with her playful, amoral cruelty, she was using them to terrorize me. The sight of me standing in a corner, face to the wall? That was lifted from *Blair Witch Project*, one of my favourites. And me running around the maze of snow, in Regent's Park, that was clearly from *The Shining*. As I unravel my own story, I reckon I will find more parallels and echoes. It is a deep irony, I hope one day to understand it.

Not yet, though, not yet. It is still too raw: like the weather today. Despite the clear sunny sky, it is snowing, very gently. Surely this is the last snow of the year. There is a wistfulness about it: an ephemeral prettiness. For a moment I stop on the slope of the cast-iron bridge on Regent's Park Road, and I stare down: watching the tiny snowflakes falling into the chilly black waters of the Regent's Canal.

One by one, the flakes tumble, and melt, and die.

They remind me of a little game Jenny and I used to play, whenever it snowed, back in Thornton Heath.

I am going to play it again. I don't care if people see. Standing here, I stretch out my tongue, like a kid, and let one of these little snowflakes settle on my tongue. It tastes of silver and sadness, of laughter and fear, of Christmas and childhood and Daddy and stars. And now the snows stop, and I continue my walk, into the bitter cold breezes of spring.